LOVE 'EM OR LEAVE 'EM DEAD

LOVE 'EM OR LEAVE 'EM DEAD

Midge Bubany

*To my dear friend
Joanie —*

Midge Bubany

NORTH STAR PRESS OF ST. CLOUD, INC.
St. Cloud, Minnesota

Copyright © 2016 Midge Bubany
Cover image © Adobe Stock
Author photo © Stacy Dunlap

ISBN 978-1-68201-066-2

First Edition: May 2017

Printed in the United States of America.

Published by
North Star Press of St. Cloud, Inc
19485 Estes Road
Clearwater, MN 55320
www.northstarpress.com

Dedication

To Tim Bubany and Anne Jansen for their continued encouragement, love, and support—and for helping me sell my books!

And to all those who have battled breast cancer including (but not limited to): Amanda, Amy, Angie, Anita, Ann, Anne, Annette, Ardell, Ardy, Audrey, Bailey, Barb, Barbara, Becky, Beth, Betty, Bettye, Bonita, Bonnie, Bonny, Brenda, Candy, Carol, Carolyn, Char, Charlene, Cheryl, Cindy, Chris, Connie, Corrie, Crystal, Deb, Diane, Dorothy, Dottie, Elaine, Elann, Eldean, Elsie, Evelyn, Gloria, Gretchen, Helen, Jack, Jan, Jane, Jane Marie, Janet, Janice, Jeannie, Jennifer, Jo, JoAnn, Jo Ann, Joanne, Judy, Julie, Karen, Karrie, Kathe, Kathy, Katya, Kay, Kelly, Kim, Kimie, Kristy, LaVonne, Leanne, Linda, Lisa, Lois, Lynn, Madalyn, Marci, Mary, Mary Ann, Mary Doris, Mary Jane, Mary Lou, Marion, Marsha, Melissa, Miriam, Molly, Nancy, Nena, Nina, Pat, Paula, Pip, Ricki, Rita, Sandy, Sara, Sarah, Shari, Sherry, Sherri, Sue, Suzi, Suzy, Teresa, Toni, Tricia, Vi, and Wendy.

1

Friday, December 12, 2014

THE FIRST AND ONLY TIME I saw Sonya Donovan alive was at the Birch County Sheriff's Department Christmas party a week ago. She attended as a guest of my boss, Sheriff Patrice Clinton. She'd been introduced as "The Radio Queen" and given the microphone after Patrice welcomed everyone. Evidently, it was Sonya's job to kick off Patrice's reelection bid. The celebrity was witty and articulate, tall and slim, attractive, alive. Today I stood above her dead body.

"I'm so glad you were able to come out, Cal. I wanted you to handle this case."

Case? Although her position in her bed struck me as odd, I hardly thought it was a suspicious death. She was lying stick-straight, and her arms lay at her sides outside the plush blanket. On a cold winter's night, most people snuggled under the covers. I walked around the bed and leaned in for a closer look. Her skin was tinged blue, eyes closed, mouth gaped open—obviously dead—but to follow procedure, I pulled on latex gloves and felt for a pulse. There was none, as expected. I lifted her left eyelid to find the eye already clouded.

I moved her arms to lift the blanket. She was wearing a sheer black negligee, revealing her slim hips and large breasts. Did women really wear this stuff when they slept alone? The flesh along the lower side of her hips was discolored. Blood begins to collect in the lowest parts of the body minutes to hours after death. I pressed the purple flesh, and because the spot didn't blanch, I knew livor mortis was at its peak—eight to twelve hours after death. I raised her arm to find complete stiffening, or rigor mortis. Patrice hadn't discovered her until late afternoon, so she'd died in her sleep sometime in the night. I glanced up at Patrice. She hadn't moved from the foot of the bed, watching and frowning as I went through the motions.

"My guess is she's been gone for at least twelve hours, but Doc Swank can tell us for sure. You have called him, right?"

"Yes. He should be here any minute," Patrice said.

Patrice narrowed her eyes as she stared at Sonya. "Her hair looks weird. It's too straight."

I shrugged. "Did she normally style her hair before going to bed?"

"You don't understand. She was always fluffing her hair."

"For crying out loud, Patrice . . . she's dead."

She closed her eyes.

"I'm sorry. That was insensitive. How old was she?"

"She turned sixty-four last month."

"She looks ten years younger. Did she have plastic surgery?"

"A wee bit, but she's always taken excellent care of herself. When she had a physical recently, her doctor told her she was more fit than most forty-year-olds, so I doubt she had a stroke or heart attack."

Her fitness didn't mean she didn't have a hidden medical condition, but I didn't argue. At the Prairie Days 10K, a thirty-two-year-old marathon runner had dropped dead ten yards beyond the finish line. He had a hidden congenital heart defect.

"There are no noticeable wounds or signs of trauma," I said.

Muscles slacken upon death, resulting in a release of feces and urine, but I couldn't see or smell the evidence of either. Could she have been moved?

I put the blanket back over the body and replaced the arms.

As I checked Sonya's bedside table drawer, I asked, "When was the last time you heard from her?"

"Last night around seven."

The only items in the drawer were her iPhone and a bottle of Advil. I bagged her phone to look at later, then glanced around the room. The shiny, gold comforter was neatly folded and placed on a trunk at the end of her bed. Not a single article of clothing was draped anywhere—just how I'd like my place if I weren't living with twenty-one-month-old twin tsunamis.

A glass of water sat on a coaster next to a *Cosmopolitan* magazine, on which a television remote control lay. Still gloved, I picked up one of two photos off the bureau. Sonya was near the bow on a yacht, holding onto a straw hat and smiling at the camera.

"Sonya was a handsome woman."

Patrice had come up behind me. "Yes, and she had panache. That picture was taken by her cousin a few years ago on Lake Minnetonka."

"What's the cousin's name?"

"Gary Williams. They seldom get together, even though he lives in Wayzata."

I wrote his name in my notebook.

"Dating?"

"No."

I pointed to the large photo on the wall above the bureau. It was of Sonya and a little girl with curly, dark hair in a pink sundress. Sonya was holding the child above her head, their faces lit with laughter.

"I adore that picture of Sonya and Zabrina," Patrice said.

"Her granddaughter?"

"Yes."

Patrice picked up the other photo on the bureau. "This is Sonya with her daughter, Justine, and Zabrina. Justine's been my best friend since grade school."

"I take it you've notified them?"

"Yes, Justine's on her way."

"Is she married?"

"Divorced for several years."

"Tell me about Justine's ex."

"He lives in Oregon. Makes an appearance every couple years and takes Zabrina up to Grand Rapids to visit his parents."

"What kind of work does he do?"

"He was a banker in Minneapolis, but last I heard he owned and operated a bed and breakfast."

I walked over to the bank of rear windows overlooking a pool.

"I've heard about this pool. I didn't expect a view of it through her bedroom window."

Patrice came up next to me. "It's indoor/outdoor. Part of the roof retracts."

"That must have cost a fortune."

She gave me a wry smile. "Money was no object to the Donovans."

I moved to the windows on the east wall. I could see lights on next door. "Did you know my mother and Bobby Lopez live next door?" I asked.

"That's who moved in?"

"He put in an offer on Sonya's house, which, of course, was refused because it wasn't even for sale."

"I didn't realize he had that kind of money."

"He sold his house in California." At least that's what he claims. I ambled into the closet. "This is practically the size of my bedroom."

She stood in the doorway. "Every woman's dream."

I fingered through her clothing: casual but classic—expensive. I might not know brand names, but I knew quality when I saw it.

"Looks like she planned to stay a while."

"She kept items of clothing up here, so she wouldn't have to haul much back and forth."

"How long was she going to stay?"

"She planned to leave on Monday. Then the three of them—Sonya, Justine, and Zabrina—planned on coming back for Christmas and New Year's."

I lifted the lid of a clothes hamper toward the back of the closet. It was half-full.

"She has a cleaning lady who does her laundry."

"Okay."

I moved to the ensuite bathroom. Two towels and a single washcloth hung on the bar near the large whirlpool tub. Three thick, partially burned candles sat upon the ledge of the tub.

I checked the drawers of the vanity cabinet. A purple Fitbit watch lay in the top drawer next to a couple bottles of OTC painkillers. I tapped the display of my own black Fitbit. It was nearly four o'clock, so if I was correct on the death being at least twelve hours ago, she'd passed away early this morning.

As I looked in the other drawers for prescription drugs, I glanced up at the mirror to find Patrice watching me. "To your knowledge, did she use any sedatives, drugs, or alcohol?" I asked.

"She drank wine and had an occasional martini—certainly not a lush—and she was proud of her lack of need for prescription drugs. Why? You think she overdosed?"

"Just asking questions."

She let out a big sigh. "She didn't use drugs."

I said, "There was no sign of forced entry or a struggle that I could see, so it'd appear she died from natural causes."

Patrice nodded. "She was a healthy woman. That's why her sudden death is so hard for me to fathom."

I followed as Patrice gave a tour of the additional two bedrooms on the second story. They were sizable and decorated in slightly different earth tones, each with its own bath. The closets and bureaus contained a small amount of women's clothes belonging to the daughter and granddaughter. I followed Patrice down the spectacular curved glass-and-steel staircase. What made the staircase spectacular were the colorful, geometric stained-glass panels inset every few feet.

The front half of the residence had high cathedral ceilings over the great room, library, kitchen, and dining area, whereas the rear was two-storied. The décor and furnishings were ultra modern—cream leather couches and chairs were accented with splashy, colorful pillows. Those same vibrant tones were picked up in three large area rugs placed in the dining area and in the seating areas on the cream marble flooring.

While we waited for Doc Swank, Patrice insisted on giving me a tour of the house. First, we walked behind the kitchen, glancing into the laundry room. Two laundry baskets contained used sheets and towels. We peeked in the small office, then crossed to the opposite side of the house. We turned just past the staircase, where there was another bedroom and a workout room. A crumpled tissue lay on the floor just inside the room. As an afterthought, I picked it up and placed it in a small paper evidence bag.

Patrice looked at me questioningly.

"Just in case," I said.

Down the hall, through a heavy door, was the entrance to the pool complex. By the time she'd pointed out the jacuzzi pool and changing areas beyond the Olympic-sized pool, I felt like a house hunter being given a tour by a realtor.

"Do the Pool Guys service her pool?"

"I would imagine; they installed it. Now come see what's downstairs."

The door to the basement stairway was next to the library corner and adjacent to the grand staircase. We made our way across the unfinished basement to a wine cellar.

Patrice's eyes flashed with excitement as she showed me racks filled with bottles of reds. A ladder on a track allowed access to the top levels. I looked at a few labels.

"No Three-Buck Chuck?"

She laughed. "Many of these wines aren't expensive. She buys what she likes."

They sounded expensive to me: French or Italian, nothing I was familiar with.

Straight ahead was a glass walk-in cooler. She opened the door, flipped on the light switch. "She also has at least fifty bottles of white."

I said, "And several bottles of craft beer. Yes, Patrice, your friend's possessions are impressive."

Patrice's cheeks grew rosy. She avoided eye contact as she selected two bottles of white. As a second thought, she grabbed and handed me a four-pack of Surly Furious. She flipped off the light and followed me back up to the main floor. She proceeded to the kitchen to set the wine and beer in the refrigerator.

A brown-and-black checked purse sat in the corner on the counter.

"Whose purse?"

"Sonya's. I can't afford a Louis Vuitton."

I shrugged. Opening the purse, I pulled out a matching wallet and found her driver's license. She used a Minneapolis address.

"Let's copy her license."

We walked back to the small office behind the kitchen. Patrice used the copy machine to copy Sonya's license. Still wearing my gloves, I tried to open the desk drawers, but they were locked. Nothing in this room or in the entire house appeared to be disturbed.

"When did Sonya arrive in Dexter?"

"Last weekend. That's why I invited her to our department Christmas party."

"So, she's been here a week."

"She is . . . was a wonderful speaker, wasn't she?"

"Yes," I said, as I turned my back to her and moved back to the kitchen, where I looked through the cupboards, wastebasket, and recycling bin. Empty deli food containers had been discarded in the wastebasket, and three wine bottles sat in recycling. Three bottles in seven days would average a half bottle a day. I opened the dishwasher to find it half full.

"For natural causes, you sure are giving the place a going over."

"Did you see her at all this week?"

"No, she said she had work to do."

Patrice pulled an opened wine bottle from the fridge and poured herself a glass.

"Want one?" she asked.

I raised a brow. "I'm on duty."

She smiled faintly. "I'm not."

"I'll make some coffee," I said, pointing to the Keurig coffee machine on the counter.

I found the box of K-cups in the cabinet above and brewed myself a cup of Starbucks. Then we sat at the counter and drank our beverages while we waited for Doc Swank.

Patrice rubbed the lip of the glass. "David says it was a mistake to make my reelection announcement at the Christmas party. He claims my deputies left the party early because of it."

"Hmm."

David was right. Who could have missed the mood change of the group after Sonya's so-called impromptu talk? Deputy Matt Hauser, who planned to run against her, and a number of his best buddies left right after Sonya proclaimed how her longtime friend, Patrice, was a wonderful leader and how we should all stand beside her in her reelection bid. Dallas and I waited to depart until after dessert, as did several others, then joined Matt at Buzzo's Bar and Grill in Prairie Falls.

"Is David right?"

"Yes."

Her back straightened as a stricken look crossed her face. "Oh . . . I wasn't expecting you to say that."

"You asked."

"I know. All right, how do I fix it? I don't want to alienate the troops."

I wasn't sure she could fix it. She was never part of the "we."

"Maybe you should start by apologizing for using our annual holiday party as a political rally," I said. "You do realize there are a fair number of deputies behind Matt."

"Is he running for sure? He hasn't filed yet."

"He is."

"How many deputies are behind him? More than half?"

"I haven't taken a poll."

"I thought I had a good working relationship with my deputies. What am I doing wrong?"

"Okay, right there, you said 'my deputies.'"

"What are you talking about?"

"Aren't we the county's deputies? Most of us were hired by Jack Whitman or Ralph Martinson."

"That's petty stuff, Cal."

"Look, if you want to find out how things are going for your deputies, you should meet with the union reps."

"I have. I gave them the white summer shirts."

"That was wise. The black was unbearable for summer, especially working outdoor crime scenes. The major complaint was the expense of buying new black uniforms because you didn't want to wear tan. They were happy with the traditional color."

"That's old news. What else?"

"Did Sonya marry well, or was she independently wealthy?"

"You're changing the subject."

"I am."

"All right." She took a sip of wine. "Well, her husband died a rich man, but she made her own fortune. She had a newspaper column years ago, went into radio, wrote a few best-sellers." She smiled. "She's strong and quite a lovely person—generous, funny, and unpredictable."

I noticed the constant vacillation between present and past tense—hard for people to let in the loss so quickly.

"What type of radio show does she have?" I asked.

"Relationship advice. Sirius picked it up a few years ago. It's called *Love 'Em or Leave 'Em*. She has one or two guest experts, sometimes celebrities in town for some other event. People call in giving the particulars of their relationship problems and are then given advice as to whether they should stay or leave."

"Making life decisions for people based on a single call? That sounds shaky."

"To be honest, I've had the same thought myself, but the show's very popular."

"Controversial is always popular. Did she have the credentials to give out this kind of life-changing advice?"

"A master's degree in counseling. She got her start in a clinic setting, but disliked it and quit. Her husband landed her a job with a small city newspaper doing the lovelorn column. The word spread and some bigger papers picked it up."

"Like 'Dear Abby'?"

"Exactly, only it was called 'Sonya Says.' And because of the popularity of the column, she did a few local guest radio and TV spots, which worked into her own show."

"How long has she had this house?"

"Twelve years. Donald and Sonya built it as a vacation/retirement home."

During Sonya's alleged impromptu speech at the Christmas party, she remarked it had been ten years since her husband died, and it was after this death she became close to Patrice.

"How often does she come up here?"

"A number of times each year. Cal, she was in her prime. What if it wasn't natural causes? Maybe she was poisoned."

"An autopsy and a toxicology screen will determine that. Tell me more about her husband."

"Donald owned an ad agency in Minneapolis. Handsome, charismatic. She joked about being his trophy wife. By the way, her stepchildren hated her. She has enemies, Cal."

"Don't we all?"

2

I WENT OUT TO HELP Doc Swank with the transport cot.

"Supposed to snow tomorrow," he said.

"Heard that."

Patrice met us at the door. "As I told Cal, Sonya was a healthy woman. She just had a physical and came out with flying colors. She could have been suffocated or poisoned."

"Well, hello to you, too."

"Oh . . . sorry. Hi, Doc."

"Hello, Sheriff Clinton. Anyway, an autopsy will tell us for sure. We'll transport the remains to Bemidji."

I followed Doc upstairs. He repeated the steps I had taken, plus a few others, including taking Ms. Donovan's body temperature, making notes on a form clipped inside a leather folder. He also did more lividity tests.

When he was finished he looked at me and said, "Looks like at least twelve to fourteen hours. There's foam in her mouth, so we'll do a thorough blood work up."

"What? Overdose?"

Patrice and her friend's appearance at the door halted our conversation.

"Can Justine see her mother before you take her, Doc?" Patrice asked.

"Certainly."

"Justine, this fine-looking gent is Doc Swank, our county coroner, and the big fellow is my ace detective, Cal Sheehan. He'll handle your mom's case."

Seriously? Ace detective? I shook hands with Justine. "I'm sorry for your loss."

Doc pulled off his glove to hold Justine's hand. "I'm so very sorry to meet you in these circumstances. You have my sympathy."

Justine was short and wide-hipped. She had a high forehead, a button nose, and small chin. Her eyes diverted from Doc to the bed, and as her eyes focused on her mother's body, she let out a small gasp.

Doc said, "An autopsy is wise to determine if there was a hidden medical condition."

"Patrice says you want to be sure her death wasn't something other than medical."

"Standard practice in an otherwise healthy person."

Doc and I stepped back and gave Justine time with her mother. She stood at the side of the bed, her hand over her mouth, as she and Patrice silently shed tears together. Patrice pulled tissues from her pocket and handed one to Justine. After a few minutes, Justine turned and walked out. Patrice followed. Doc finished his work, and I helped him take the body out to his van.

After Doc left, I told Patrice I was going next door to see my mom for a few minutes, then I'd stop back. As I walked out the door, I heard Patrice ask Justine if she wanted a glass of wine.

BOBBY LOPEZ'S CONTEMPORARY-STYLE home was by most people's standards large, but compared to the Donovan's ostentatious structure, it was modest. I rang the bell and waited a full half minute before I pushed the button again. The heavy wood door opened, and Bobby said, "Calvin, what a surprise. Your mother's not home yet."

"That's okay. I have a few questions for you."

"Oh? Well, come in and get out of the cold."

The spicy aroma of Mexican cooking filled the air. I moved in past this giant of a man, who clocked in at six-foot-five and 250 pounds. His size, rugged face, plus facial scars and a patch on one eye, caused many a stranger to stare. And it was this man my mother chose to love and trust, a secretive newcomer who had surveillance equipment in his house, couldn't tell us what he did for a living, and left for unknown places for days at a time.

He wanted me to believe he worked for the government, but I wasn't at all convinced. All I knew was the man had skills—and connections and access to information even the average law enforcement officer didn't. I wouldn't want him for an enemy, so I played the role of his girlfriend's son where I could keep him in my crosshairs.

His long, dark ponytail hung down the back of his blue plaid flannel shirt. Jeans and cowboy boots rounded out his winter outfit. In the summer he switched to either white T-shirts or Charlie Harper–type shirts.

Mom found a renter for her condo, and she and Bobby moved into the lake house early last month. Because the home had been vacant for many months, he talked the owner into letting him rent. They were using his furniture, which was Spanish style, dark and heavy, upholstered in a red-and-olive-green print. I tried to spot my mother's eclectic hippie taste in the furnishings, but it seemed to be absent. I followed Bobby into the kitchen, where he turned down the flame under two pots.

"Smells good," I said. "Are you cooking?"

"Rosarita is. She hides whenever the doorbell rings—which doesn't happen very often. We don't get much company."

It was my understanding they didn't want company. Rosarita was his brother's mother-in-law and an illegal. He said if we notified Homeland Security, she'd be deported and killed by the cartel. Her husband once had been the chief of police in a Mexican border town. Rosarita and her family fled when her husband's head was found on a pole placed along the main avenue.

He went into the hallway and shouted out, "Rosarita, it's just Calvin."

A minute later, Rosarita flitted into the kitchen, her skirt swishing with her rapid movements. I'd never seen her wear anything but a dress or skirt, and like today, she usually wore an apron. After she stirred the pots, she turned and gave me a quick smile. She spoke a few words to Bobby in Spanish.

He looked to me. "She wants to know if you'll be joining us for dinner."

"No, I can't. Thanks for asking, Rosarita."

Another quick smile and she attended to her pots. Bobby gestured at an opened Corona on the counter.

"Join me?" he asked.

"No, I'm on duty ... investigating a case next door. I just stopped by to see if you had any information about the homeowner, Sonya Donovan."

His eyes narrowed to slits. "Only that she refused my offer to buy her house."

"Never mind it wasn't for sale." Although it could be soon, which I didn't mention. "Did you see anything suspicious or anybody hanging around the area recently?"

"The only person I see around both properties is that beanpole by the name of Moore—the man who plows our driveways. What are you investigating? A burglary?"

I looked him square in the eye and watched his expression as I said, "Ms. Donovan was found dead this afternoon. Thought I'd check to see if you knew anything about it."

He cocked his head and said, "My, my. No, I certainly don't. Never met the woman. She didn't come a-knocking on my door with a welcome basket, if you know what I mean. But I imagine a celebrity like her wants privacy."

"But you met her when you tried to buy her house?"

"No, I made the offer through my attorney."

"Well, all right then. Say hello to my mother. You know how to get in touch with me if either of you should remember something." I turned to leave. He followed me to the door.

"Your mother will be disappointed she missed you. Calvin, are the circumstances of Mrs. Donovan's death suspicious?"

"I doubt it."

He nodded a few times. "Yeah, that's why you're here questioning me."

"No, really. I shouldn't have bothered you."

"You're never a bother, Calvin." He slapped me on the back.

WHEN I RETURNED to the Donovan house, Patrice and Justine were slurping down wine and sitting on the sofa facing the blazing fire in the massive fieldstone fireplace. Patrice asked me to have a seat.

She said, "I was telling Justine your mother lived next door with a big Mexican fella. Did they see anything suspicious?"

"No." I turned to Justine. "If you're up to it, I'd like to hear about your mother."

"Sure. Well, she was born and raised in Minneapolis by a single mother. Her dream was to sing and act on Broadway, but the closest she came was landing a gig as a lounge singer at the downtown Minneapolis Radisson—that's where she met my dad. He was twenty years her senior and married at the time. Six months later, he was divorced, and they flew to Las Vegas, where Mom became the second Mrs. Donovan. By the time she was twenty-two, she had James and me. When we were both in elementary school, she went to college to get a degree in psychology."

"Where's James living?"

"He was killed in a car crash at age eighteen."

The old familiar ache of grief squeezed my chest. "Sorry to hear that. I know how hard it is."

"It was truly awful."

Patrice shifted in her seat. "I remember the time so clearly. We were juniors in high school."

"Do you remember how my mother took to her bed?" Justine asked. "I remember thinking she was going to die, too. Dad said she was trying to sleep away the hole James's death left in her heart. He forced her into counseling, and after a few months, it was like she flipped a switch. That's when she decided to get a master's degree in counseling."

"Any recent bouts of depression?"

"No. She was on top of the world and enjoying her life."

"Patrice said your father had children by the previous marriage?"

"Kent and Natalie were teenagers when James and I were born. There are photos of the four of us kids, but I don't recall much about that time. I do remember sensing they couldn't wait to leave when they'd visit for the holidays. I thought it was because they didn't like me. After Dad died, there was no contact."

"Where are they now?"

"I wouldn't know."

"What about his first wife?"

"Ruth? She remarried and moved to San Antonio decades ago."

Patrice refilled Justine's wine glass, emptying the bottle. She went for another. From across the room she said, "I take it you still don't want a glass?"

"Correct."

I turned to Justine. "I understand your mother had quite a successful career."

"She did. Patrice, did Mother tell you we were working a deal with Bravo for a TV version of the radio show?"

"No."

"She didn't want anyone to know until the contract was finalized."

"What about your mother's cousin?" I asked.

"Gary?"

"Yes."

"We don't see much of him, even though he's her only one. He lives in Wayzata, single. His stores sell, as Mother put it, expensive junk from third-world countries."

"Can you tell me more about the radio show?" I asked.

"She was on air weekday mornings from nine to eleven. They repeated the broadcast afternoons from four to six."

"How did it work?"

"Her guest hosts would give a short talk about relationships, either why good ones worked or why bad ones failed. Then they'd accept callers for the rest of the show."

"Who were the guest hosts?"

"Usually experts in the field: professors, social workers, authors, psychologists. Sometimes I was able to book celebrities in town for other events. Those were my favorite shows."

"And the callers would ask for personal advice?"

"Usually, yes. Some just wanted to comment about what a previous caller or the guest host had said, but that was kept at a minimum. The screeners tried to pick callers who had the most dramatic issues or questions that would illicit the strongest reaction from our listeners. It boosted ratings."

"Where is the radio studio?"

"Above the garage. Which reminds me, I have to call Thomas."

"Thomas?" I asked.

"Our producer and business manager." Justine shook her head and sighed. "Gosh, I can't believe she's gone."

"When was the last time you spoke to your mother, Justine?"

"Yesterday around noon. I called to tell her I was waiting until today to leave."

"Why?"

"I had work to get done. Maybe if I'd come as planned, she'd—"

Patrice raised a hand. "Do not do that to yourself, Justine."

"When was the last time you spoke to her, Patrice?" Justine asked.

"Wednesday evening. We were going to touch base this morning to settle on a time to meet. I called but she didn't answer. When I still couldn't get hold of her by four o'clock, I drove out."

"Was the door locked?" I asked.

"Yes."

"How did you get in?" I asked.

"I have a key and know the code. Sometimes she has me check on things."

I stayed quiet. Sometimes people would say more if I was patient.

Patrice tilted her head and smiled at me, then put a hand on my arm. "Don't I have handsome deputies?" she said, turning to Justine.

"Yes, you do."

Heat rushed to my face. I scratched the sudden itch on my chin.

"Cal, you're blushing. Did I embarrass you?" Patrice said.

Justine set her glass down. "Ah, it's an inside joke. David makes constant remarks about her being surrounded by handsome young men."

Joke or not, my boss had way too much vino.

"So, Justine, back to your mother. Did she have employees?"

"Several." She ticked off on her fingers as she recounted. "Beside me, and I'm her executive secretary and publicist, she has a cook, a housekeeper, and a groundskeeper. Then, connected with the studio, there's the business manager/producer, a sound guy, and two screeners."

Patrice said, "They live in Kenwood, a beautiful area in Minneapolis with wonderful old homes."

"I know about Kenwood, Patrice."

She cocked her head and said with a snarky smile, "Oh, I wasn't certain . . . you being a country boy."

I gave her a long, hard look. About now, this *country boy* wanted to tell his boss to shove it. "How about this place? I noticed it's spotless."

Justine answered, "She's anal about tidiness. Up here, she does her own cooking, but her cleaning lady also does her laundry and stocks food. Her husband is the groundskeeper—does the mowing, plowing, some gardening and maintenance."

"Moore?"

"Yes, that's right."

"Why don't you try to find a phone number for the Moores?"

"Sure."

When she returned, she handed me a Post-it note. "How long will the autopsy take?"

"Depends," I said. "A couple days, but the toxicology screens will take more time. And I should head out."

"Do you want to stay for dinner?" Patrice asked.

"No, thanks." I couldn't wait to get the hell out of there.

ONCE IN THE EXPLORER, I took three deep breaths. What was that crazy shit about? Patrice had purposefully embarrassed me in front of her friend. Country boy, my ass. And the ace detective, handsome deputy bit? She would hear about this the next time I got her alone.

I put in my Chris Botti CD and tried to decompress while I drove the forty-five minutes home.

Bullet, my yellow lab, met me at the backdoor. It'd been too long since he'd been let out. He rushed through the door and did his business, then was begging to come in. His supper was late, and he lived for food.

As he scarfed down his chow, I foraged for mine. Clara Bradley, my housekeeper and nanny, was kind enough to store leftovers in the freezer for such occasions. I pulled out a glass container labeled "lasagna" and threw it in the microwave for eight minutes, per instructions on the lid.

I ate in the silence of my empty house. There were times I welcomed the quiet—but not tonight. The twins' sweet innocence, the sounds of their voices and laughter helped me escape the ugly side of my occupation. With the fifty-fifty split custody, Clara traveled back and forth between the houses along with the kids every other week. When they were gone, I missed them greatly. When it was my week and I had time, I'd come home and eat lunch with the Twinks, my pet tame for them, because Twinkies also come in packages of two.

I cleaned up my dishes, then went up to bed early. I turned on an old John Wayne western, but the image of Sonya Donovan's dead body kept popping into my thoughts. I'd never seen a corpse lying so straight, unless they were on the medical examiner's table. Perhaps Patrice was right, and the toxicology would come back with evidence she was poisoned. But who would want her dead? Her daughter? A secret lover? Bobby Lopez? He could have killed her in order to get her house. He knew stuff—like poisons that wouldn't show up in a routine tox screening. *Oh, man, just erase this bizarre shit from your mind, Cal.*

3

BECAUSE IT WAS FREAKING COLD outside, Bullet got only a short walk before I headed into work. The department gym was crowded for a Saturday morning. I spent thirty minutes on the treadmill, thirty minutes on the machines, briefly chatted with some guys, showered, then went up to the investigations office to start the paperwork on last night's call.

Around ten o'clock, I got a call from Dr. Butch Novak from the Beltrami County Medical Examiner's Office in Bemidji. He was beginning the Donovan autopsy at one o'clock, and my name was indicated as a witness. I hadn't attended many of them, and it wasn't my favorite pastime.

I spent the rest of the day with Dr. Butch, as he called himself, and his assistant, Beth, as they dissected Sonya Donovan. I tried not to focus on the smells and sounds and concentrated on the jazz music Dr. Butch had playing. He said Charles Mingus and John Coletrane were his favorites.

After he weighed the lungs, he brought one back down to the table, where he slowly sliced it open. "Thought so. Fluid in her lungs."

"What does that mean? Pneumonia?"

"We'll do some testing."

After the procedure wrapped up, I called my girlfriend, Dallas, and asked her to meet me at my house, where we'd order a pizza.

"How was the autopsy?" she asked.

"Lovely," I said. "The last thing I want to eat is meat, so how about I order a vegetable pizza?"

She laughed.

"Not funny. It's brutal."

"I'm a veterinarian. I get it."

Sunday, December 14

NOON ON SUNDAYS WAS our trade-the-twins time. Dallas and I had spent a leisurely morning reading the Sunday paper and eating bacon, scrambled eggs, and cinnamon rolls from the Sportsman. She made sure she was gone before the twins were dropped off because she didn't want to interact with Shannon, my ex-wife. Just as well.

During the transfer of the babies, Shannon was exceptionally quiet.

"What's wrong?" I asked.

"What makes you think something's wrong?"

"Because you look pissed off. Did I do something?"

"Probably, although I haven't heard about it yet."

I laughed. "Well, if you don't know about it, I ain't confessing." That got the tiny smile I was going for. "How's Luke?"

She took a deep breath and said, "His grades are improving. I cut back on his electronics time like his teacher suggested."

I'd suggested it when he and Shannon still lived with me, but in those days, both she and Luke resented my parenting attempts.

"Good idea," I said.

She cocked her head and paused. Perhaps she heard the intended sarcasm in my voice. I uncurled my lip. Not helpful.

Shannon took two deep breaths and said, "Lucy's had an ear infection for five days. Her medicine's in the bag. She's better, but just make sure you remember to give her the medication this time."

This time. "Why didn't you let me know she was sick?"

"I didn't see you."

Shannon was the artful dodger at work. I wasn't sure why she was avoiding me lately, other than I'm her ex, and she was usually mad at me for something I did or didn't do.

"That's something I should know. What if I had kept that kind of information from you?"

She twisted her lips while choosing her words. "From now on, I'll let you know every time one of the twins is sick."

She then turned her back and headed toward the door. I followed. Just before she placed her hand on the knob, she hesitated and looked back at me. On impulse, I leaned over and kissed her on the cheek. Her mouth dropped, and her eyes got big and teary.

"Bye," she said, and promptly left without another word. I shouldn't have kissed her, but I'd done it to shock her—and apparently, it worked.

The receiving parent was to feed the twins lunch, so I had prepared macaroni and cheese chiefly because it was their favorite, and I wanted them to like being at my place as much as their mom's. After lunch and before their naps, we had playtime. I lay on the floor making stupid noises to make them giggle, and they treated me like a jungle gym. Then, in an attempt to calm them down, I read them ten baby books before I got a yawn. They went down surprisingly well. I crawled on my own bed to catch a few winks when my phone rang. Shannon. These days, the first thing that came to my mind with an unexpected phone call was, *What did I do now?*

I had a sneaking suspicion it was the kiss, so I apologized.

"What? No, that's not what I want to talk to you about."

"Oh." Other possibilities fired through my brain. She wanted full custody. She needed money. She'd found someone new.

But it was nothing like that. What she told me tore a hole in my heart.

"Are you there?" she asked.

"Did you just say you have a malignant breast tumor?"

"It's two-point-eight centimeters."

I used my thumb and index finger to approximate its size. To me that seemed large—over an inch. My throat constricted, my heart pounded.

"And it's cancerous?"

"Yes, but they still have to do more tests."

"When did you find this out?"

"Last Monday. I found a lump, and I'd just read an article about younger women like me getting cancer even though the recommended age for the first mammogram is forty. Anyway, Dr. Locher ordered a mammogram, and I was called back in because the radiologist in St. Cloud wanted additional pictures and an ultrasound. Then last Friday, Dr. Locher called me back, telling me the ultrasound showed it was likely cancer. So I have more tests tomorrow."

"Why didn't you tell me sooner, Shannon?"

"Because I wanted to wait until I knew for sure."

"Okay . . . so after the tests, what happens?"

"I'll know more when the results are in."

"Who all knows?" I asked.

"My family . . . Clara."

"We need to make sure you have the best medical care. Do you want to go to the Mayo Clinic for a second opinion or treatment?"

"No, Rochester's too inconvenient."

I heard her sniffing. "You're gonna be okay, Shannon."

"I know," she said through tears. "It's just when I heard the word cancer, I started planning my funeral."

"Shannon, cancer's not a death sentence anymore. We know tons of people who've survived cancer."

"Well, I'm scared despite everyone's rosy predictions."

"We'll handle this together."

"I have to go." She hung up.

I GOT UP, WENT DOWNSTAIRS, paced the family room, cleaned the counters, emptied the dishwasher, then cleaned and straightened the silverware drawer. By the time Clara arrived fifteen minutes early, I had settled down, cracked a beer and had the Vikings game on.

"Who won?" she asked.

"Is it over?"

She gave me a curious look and stood in front of the television to read the screen. "The Vikings beat the Jets in overtime."

"Okay, good."

I took the grocery bag from her, set it on the counter, then went out to her car to get the other two bags. As I helped her put the food away, she said, "Why didn't you know the final score? You were sitting right in front of the television."

"I've been a bit distracted since Shannon told me she has breast cancer."

"Oh . . . I'm so relieved she finally told you. Personally, I think we should wait to see what tomorrow's tests show. A friend of mine went through all the tests, and when she had the biopsy, it was negative."

"Thanks for telling me that."

"Well, it's the truth." She had her back to me when she announced, "Vince called Dallas this afternoon."

"Why?"

"He wants her back."

"What did she tell him?"

"She said no, of course. He's been to treatment and sober for six months, as if that would make a difference."

"Are you sure it won't?"

"I told her if a man smacks a woman in the face once, he'll do it again. People don't change their basic personalities with treatment."

"I'm concerned."

"Look, she seems so much happier since she's been with you." She pointed at me with a package of hamburger. "But maybe you better reassure her."

"What are you saying? She's insecure about us?"

"Seems like it."

"What do I do to make women insecure?"

"I'm not sure, but she's heard Shannon remark how women fall all over you."

"Well, that's an exaggeration. I'm one of a few single men in town—"

"And women today are way more aggressive than they were in my day. I'm making chicken noodle soup for dinner. It'll be good for Lucy's cold."

As if on cue, Lucy cried out. I loped up the stairs to find her standing in her crib. Her little cheeks were bright pink and streaked with tears, and her nose was running. She put up her arms, and I picked her up, then sat in the rocker. I put her on my lap so I could wipe her nose and face, and she repositioned herself to face me and snuggled in. I held her close and rocked her. My throat tightened as I thought about how much my little girl and boy needed their mother. I kissed her silky hair and rested my cheek lightly on the top of her head.

She must have dozed off because she lay still against my chest for ten minutes before she stirred again. I changed her, then brought her downstairs. Henry walked into the room. He'd crawled out of his crib for the first time. Shit.

BEFORE I WENT TO SLEEP, I called Dallas, as I usually did.

"Hey, babe, did you get my flowers?"

"Oh, thank God, *you* sent them. There was no card."

"It must have gotten misplaced. I bet you thought it was Vince."

A pause. "Mother told you."

"Yes, but why didn't you?"

"I was going to mention it tomorrow night when we went out for dinner."

"You can tell me that kind of thing by phone."

"I suppose. Anyway, I love the flowers now that I know you sent them."

"You know how I feel about you. Right?"

"Do I?"

We'd not used the "love" word yet, and I believe it was expected about now.

"I love you, Dallas Grace Bradley." There, I said it.

"Did you feel coerced into saying it?"

"Not at all."

I expected her to say it back, but she didn't. We talked for an additional twenty minutes, then said goodnight. She could have said it then, but she didn't. What the hell?

LUCY WOKE UP CRYING TWICE during the night. The first time I went in to tend to her, Bullet followed me. When I picked her up, she reached down for him. I squatted, put her on my knee, and she put her hand on his head and said, "Bowee." That's what she called Bullet. He turned to give her a big lick across the mouth. She giggled. I stood and kissed the top of her head. When she brought up her chubby fingers to touch my bottom lip, I kissed them and buzzed them with my lips. She giggled again. I repeated the motion several times just to fill my soul with the sound of her laughter. She yawned. I sat in the rocker and within minutes she was sleeping, and I was able to put her back into her crib.

The second time she woke, I gave her drops to make her more comfortable and then rocked her. I must have fallen asleep because when I woke, I was still sitting in the chair with her up sleeping on my chest. Dang. That was not good. I gingerly put her in the crib. When I was nearly to my bed, Henry cried out. Clara met me in his room.

"It's my turn. You've been up enough tonight. It's four thirty. Go get some sleep."

I nodded in appreciation and shuffled to my bedroom. What a day. What a night.

4

Monday, December 15

THE ALARM ON MY RADIO went off at 7:00 a.m. I rarely need it, but it's always set as a precaution. I lay there listening to the weather report: heavy snow expected for the region today into tomorrow. I showered, dressed, and went downstairs.

"Thanks for letting me sleep, Clara."

"I always let Shannon sleep in when she can. There's no reason I shouldn't let you."

I WAS ONLY AT MY DESK a few minutes when Tamika Frank called. She was the only African American in the department and one of a handful in the conservative central Minnesota county. Tamika was six-foot, big boned, and tougher than most deputies in the department. She was on medical leave after a hysterectomy.

"Miss me?" she asked.

"Of course. How are you feeling?"

"Great. My doctor should sign the return-to-work order this afternoon. Then I'll be back."

"Terrific."

"So what's been happening?"

"A friend of Patrice's died Friday—looks like natural causes."

"Who?"

"Sonya Donovan."

"Oh, my God. I listen to her radio show all the time. She's real famous."

"She was at our Christmas party."

"No way."

"Well, using the party to kick off Patrice's campaign didn't go over with all the deputies. The staunch Matt Hauser supporters wanted to send her a bill for their dinners."

24

"Why didn't you tell me this juicy gossip?"

"I am now. Anyway, we're trying to keep her death quiet as long as we can. Hopefully, we can send the body down to the Cities before the media storm descends upon us."

"My God, I missed my only chance to meet her. Oh, my call waiting is beeping. I should go. It's probably Anton."

"Later, gator."

I phoned Louie Magliano, the chief of police for the city of Dexter Lake, as a courtesy. His jurisdiction ended at the city limits.

"Well, Cal, what a coincidence. I'm having breakfast with the man who's practically your step-father."

"Say what?"

"Bobby Lopez."

"You're having breakfast with Bobby?"

"Yeah, sure. We do so frequently since he moved into the area."

"Why?"

He laughed. I wasn't trying to be funny.

"He's been telling me his neighbor passed away," Louie said.

"That's what I was calling you about."

"I suspect it was an aneurism, maybe a stroke or heart attack."

"It'll be a few days before the autopsy reports come back."

"Yeah, takes time."

"I'll let you know."

I then dialed my mother.

"Oh, Cal, I'm so glad you called. I'm so sorry I missed you last night. I have something to ask you."

"Why's Bobby chummy with Louie Magliano, having breakfast with him?" I asked before she could get a word in.

"Louie asked him."

"How did he meet him?"

"Bobby met with the mayor to ask the city what they needed. It just so happened the chief of police was with him."

"I thought he was trying to stay on the down-low."

"Why would he do that?"

"Oh, come on. He's supposed to be hiding from his papa and the big bad cartel he's involved with. That's the story he gave me."

"How would the cartel know Bobby gave a city in Minnesota a donation for the community center?"

"My question is why he's ingratiating himself with the local cops."

"Do you think everything a person does has a sinister motive?"

"Pretty much, yeah—at least a selfish one. Think. Why does Bobby want the local police to like him?"

"You tell me, Mr. Detective."

"So they'll overlook what he's up to."

"Oh, for Pete's sake. Now, I'm changing the subject. What do you say we have Christmas dinner here? You, the kids, the grandmas. Bobby and Rosarita will make a genuine Mexican tamale dinner. It'll be great."

We always had prime rib for Christmas dinner, not tamales. My first impulse was to refuse outright, but instead, I said, "I'll have to check with Shannon. We haven't discussed who has the twins."

"Shannon had them for Thanksgiving. You need to stand up for your rights."

"I'll see what I can do. Are you okay out there in the boonies without family and friends close by?"

"It's nice and quiet. I can write my book without interruption."

I smiled. "Book?"

"I'm writing my memoir."

"You mean like a journal?"

"No, like my life story, and I think I have an interesting one. I hope to get it published."

"Well, no shit, you have an interesting life story, but no." I was incredulous she'd even consider putting our lives out there for the world to read.

"What do you mean, no?"

"No, I don't want you to publish your memoir because our sordid family business is private."

"I wasn't asking your permission, Cal. I have a right to write about my life."

"Well, delete everything about me and my children."

"How can I do that?"

"There's a key just for deleting. Are you putting Bobby in your book?"

"Sure, but I'm changing his name."

"Change mine, too. And set it in a different location. How about Iowa or Wisconsin? I better go."

"See you on Christmas."

ACCORDING TO MY MOTHER, she had a wild and crazy young-adult life, which I was absolutely positive was factual and would be in her book. After graduating with a degree in social work, she worked as a Hennepin County social worker for six months. She gave up her idea to save the world when one of her clients threw an ice cream bucket of human feces at her. He'd been saving it to prove he was being poisoned by the drug companies. She moved back home and started working at Grandma Dee's gift shop in Nisswa. Chances of getting shit bombed selling souvenirs to tourists was pretty low.

Then she married my father, Patrick, and he shit bombed her by getting her sister, Grace, pregnant. She didn't know Patrick had been having an affair with Grace, and when Grace decided a baby was too much for her, Hope—who I call Mom—wanted to adopt me, and Grace agreed. But Grace and Patrick continued their secret affair for four more years, and when they were exposed, they took off for California in disgrace. I wasn't told the complete truth until four years ago.

After the divorce, Mom dated several men. A few could even have been good step-fathers, but most not so much. And now she claimed Bobby, whom she met during a California vacation when she was twenty-two and recently reconnected with, was the one. I just had to shake my head.

I considered how to approach Shannon about having the twins for Christmas dinner. A woman planning her funeral would feel a need to be with her babies. I Googled "breast cancer" and read several articles, but it wasn't especially helpful since I didn't know what kind of cancer Shannon had.

Spanky entered the room and sat at his desk with a thud. "I must be living right. I didn't have a single call this weekend. Thanks for taking the Dexter Lake call."

"I didn't have a choice."

Before I could expound, Doctor Butch phoned. "Cal, I have a cause of death for Sonya Donovan. She drowned."

It took a second for his words to register. "What?"

"The fluid in her lungs was chlorinated water. You remember I pointed out the foam in her mouth? I thought it could be an overdose. Foam's most indicative of drowning, but since she was in bed, it wasn't my first thought."

"She didn't crawl from her pool up to bed herself, did she?" I said. "Now we have a murder."

5

BECAUSE WE'D NEED the state lab's forensic help, I called the Bemidji Regional Office (BRO) of the Bureau of Criminal Apprehension (BCA). Leslie Rouch and her techs were to meet me out at the Donovan property. The scene had already been compromised with Patrice and Justine there—and more so, if they had continued to stay at the home the last seventy-two hours.

I called Patrice, who didn't answer until the sixth ring. I almost had hung up.

"Where are you?" I asked.

"At Sonya's. Why?"

"Because it's a crime scene. Doctor Butch just called. I'm afraid you were right. Sonya didn't die from natural causes. She had chlorinated water in her lungs. She drowned, and someone moved her up to her bed in an attempt to make us think it was natural causes. I'm meeting Leslie Rouch's crew there as soon as they can get a team together. Tell me you didn't go in the pool area."

"We didn't."

"Her bedroom?"

"No."

"You should get out of there until they've completed their work. A storm is coming in, so you and Justine should leave now."

"Her hair didn't look right."

"For me it was the position of the body. So who benefits most from her death?"

There was a few seconds delay before she said, "You're not thinking it's Justine?"

"I just asked a question."

"She's not a killer."

"You need to let me do my job."

A pause, then, "Of course."

I COULD JUST HEAR a defense attorney saying, "You mean to tell me, Detective Sheehan, that you didn't seal off the crime scene? You let the victim's daughter and her friend stay in the home, further contaminating the scene?"

I called Dallas and cancelled our dinner date and told her why.

"Dang. I was looking forward to pizza and beer at Buzzo's."

"And I was looking forward to the pie a la mode at your place afterward."

"Well, if you get done early enough, come by for that pie."

It was our code for a roll in the hay, which meant we would be alone—no Clara, no kids.

I said, "Sometime, I'd also like to have real pie—any kind except raisin."

"I love you because you hate raisins, too."

"There . . . you said it."

"Oh, shoot. I was going to hold out for at least a week."

"Are we playing games?"

"Nope. I'm just being stubborn. Good luck tonight."

I smiled and continued to do so for the first few seconds while I began to fill out the paperwork for the extensive search warrants for Sonya Donovan's two residences, business, phones and computer records, credit card accounts, and financials. I stopped off at the courthouse and waited thirty minutes until Judge Olann was free to sign the documents.

"Strange situation you have there," he said as he signed the documents. "Good luck."

"Thanks."

But I wasn't sure I needed it. Justine was looking good for this murder. But a small woman couldn't move a body from the pool upstairs to the bed; she had to have an accomplice.

THE SNOW HAD PICKED UP in the last hour and because my own four-wheel-drive, red Ford F-150 extended cab truck was better in deep snow than a department Explorer, I drove it to Dexter Lake. For a portion of the time, I was behind a plow and a sanding truck, which had advantages and disadvantages. It made for safer but slower driving. The county vehicles worked in tandem to clear the roads. The larger plow was in front, and the smaller rear plow cleared the edge and shoulder of the roadway at the same time it distributed sand and salt from the back of the truck. I kept a distance to prevent my truck from being pelted with the mixture spewing onto the road surface.

IT WAS AFTER FOUR O'CLOCK when I pulled up to the Donovan home. Two cars were in the driveway: a red Mazda Miata and Patrice's Audi. Both cars were covered in a canopy of snow, and because I fancied myself as a nice guy—and to expedite their departure—I cleaned both cars off with my brush. I retrieved my equipment bag and briefcase and made my way to the door, where Patrice was waiting for me.

After pulling off my boots, I placed them on the rug just inside the door. Justine freed her arm from the shoulders of the young woman seated next to her on the couch and walked toward me to shake my hand. Dark circles underscored Justine's and Patrice's puffy eyes.

"I was sorry to hear your mother's death was ruled a homicide. It certainly doesn't make your loss any easier."

"Thank you for saying that. Detective, my mother didn't swim, and not many people knew."

"She was afraid of the water?"

"I'm not sure how to answer that. She loved boats, and she'd sit in the shallow end and wade in the lake. Dad suggested she take swimming lessons, but she unfortunately refused."

I nodded and then faced Patrice. "I thought you'd have taken my advice and would be gone by the time I got here."

"I had to let you in, didn't I?"

"Point taken. Before I forget, I should know the security code so we can lock up when we leave. You should change it after this is over."

Justine nodded. "It's 3993."

I recorded it in my pocket notebook.

Patrice said, "Come meet Zabrina."

We made our way to the seating area in front of the massive fireplace. Flames licked upward from the large logs, creating an atmosphere akin to a ski lodge.

"Cal, this is Zabrina. Deputy Sheehan is investigating your nana's death."

Zabrina was small boned and slim. She resembled her grandmother except for her mane of dark curly hair. As I approached, she curled her long legs up under herself, then dabbed her red and puffy eyes with a tissue from the pile in her lap.

"I'm sorry for your loss, Zabrina. This must be very difficult for you."

She glanced up, nodded, then her young, pretty face twisted into a grimace, and she began wailing, the high volume of which took me aback. Justine rushed to sit at her daughter's side and engulf her in her arms. Zabrina buried her face in her mother's bosom.

Patrice turned away from the two women and leaned toward me. "She's taking this pretty hard."

"Of course. As long as they're still here, I'd like to get fingerprints and DNA samples."

"To eliminate theirs from the killers."

I narrowed my eyes and said, "Yes."

It took only a few minutes to run Justine and Zabrina's prints on our portable print scanner.

"Are you ready to go?" I asked.

"Yes."

"The plow just went through, so you'll be okay if you follow my tracks."

Patrice said, "Okay, ladies, let's head out."

"Justine, would it be convenient for you and Zabrina to come into the department before you travel back to Minneapolis?" I asked. "We can wait until after the storm because I don't want you driving on these roads. I have search warrants, and unfortunately, we'll have to be a bit intrusive during our investigation."

I pulled the paperwork out of my briefcase, and Justine waved them away.

"Patrice has filled me in on what to expect. You need to find out who murdered my mom." Tears filled her eyes and Patrice and Zabrina surrounded her with hugs.

"I'll be in touch to arrange a time that's convenient for you," I said.

"When will her body be released?" Justine said.

"It shouldn't be more than a few days," I said. "Patrice, to expedite our investigation, would you please help Justine make a list of the employees, friends, coworkers, and associates' phone numbers and addresses? Include Sonya's husband's ex-wife and her step-children."

"Great idea. Cal, may I speak with you privately?" she said.

"Sure."

I followed her into the library. "Shannon shared with me she has breast cancer. Since you two are officially divorced, you can't legally take family illness time off for her medical issues, but I'll turn a blind eye to any days you feel are necessary—to support her—within reason."

"I appreciate it."

"Did they catch it early?"

I shrugged. "I hope so, but we'll know more next week."

"You understand this case is our priority, but testifying at Michael Hawkinson's trial coming up will take a day or two from the investigation."

We were both witnesses for the prosecution. I'd put his upcoming trial out of my mind. Michael, Mike, Hawk, depending on who you were talking to, was my ex-buddy who'd been charged with the murder of his brother. He'd confessed to me, and I was the one who brought him to the jail.

Patrice pulled a set of keys off the end table. "One of these is a house key, and another should fit the desk. You can return them later."

"Thanks. Please put out the fire before you leave."

"Sure."

"And I know you added to the garbage, but did you take anything to the laundry room?"

"No," Justine said.

After the three women left, and I was alone, I donned my gloves and footies and went up to the master bedroom. All linens would be taken by the BCA. Hopefully, the killer left a little something for us—hair, a drop of sweat, fingerprints.

Death wasn't glamorous. When people died, their muscles relaxed and urine and fecal matter were excreted. Because Sonya was moved, it was possible the water or filter in the pool would contain traces of feces. Whoever killed her had dried her hair. I would specifically request a DNA sample from her hair dryer. I pulled her Fitbit watch from the drawer and bagged it. I'd check later to see if it was synchronized with her phone.

When I checked out her linen closet, it struck me how the sheets and towels, all a wheat color, were stacked in perfect, even rows. I checked the tag: Ralph Lauren.

The bedrooms upstairs had their own baths. The sheets and towels in each room matched, but each room had a different color scheme, and the used towels and washcloths were still hanging on racks.

I went downstairs and looked in the laundry room for linens that the killer—or killers—might have used to clean up or dry off the victim. There were two sets of the same wheat towels in the laundry basket. I'd let BRO bag them.

6

MY FIRST SUSPECT WAS JUSTINE, but Sonya's death could have been an accident and someone else covered it up. Maybe she was having hot sex in the pool with a secret lover, accidentally died, and he or she panicked because they didn't want the scandal. Or she was swimming laps, then *bam!* Someone caught her off guard, held her head under until she was dead. End of the radio queen. But there were no bruises, which would be likely if she fought for her life. Plus, she didn't swim.

I glanced out the front window. The snow was really coming down, and if the roads were impassable, I could always go next door and stay with my mom and Bobby Lopez . . . but it would have to be one honking blizzard before I resorted to that.

DARKNESS HAD FALLEN by the time Leslie's BCA crew arrived.

"How are the roads?" I asked her.

"Not good. The forecast was bumped up to a foot of snow by morning. We're going to try and work as expediently as possible."

"Wonderful. If you need my help, let me know."

I STOOD ON THE SIDELINES as the technicians did their thing in and around the pool: taking water samples, vacuuming the entire tile floor and the changing room, removing the pool filters, taking DNA swabs from various surfaces. After they finished with the changing room, I took the opportunity to examine it myself. I hadn't considered it part of a crime scene earlier, so I hadn't given it a glance—yet another lesson for me.

The room was ten by twelve. Along the left, shorter wall was a set of storage cubes holding sage-green towels. Two of the cubes had six towels each, but one held a skewed pile of four. I took a photo and checked the brand: Ralph Lauren. They were larger than bath towels but smaller than a beach towel.

The other cubes held various supplies: lotion, deodorant, hairspray, tissue, toilet paper, and extra swimsuits. There were two small hand towels on the rack by the sink in the small bathroom.

I didn't know if the uneven stacks were significant, but they struck me as odd for Sonya's persnickety housekeeping ways, so I went upstairs to the master bath and photographed her perfectly stacked wheat towels. I looked up and saw Leslie standing in the doorway.

"Did you do any swabbing around the cubicles in the changing room?" I asked.

"Yes, we noticed the disarray. We pulled fingerprints, but we'll see. The culprits could have worn gloves."

"If the murder had been planned."

"Yes."

LESLIE AND CREW HAD MOVED up to the master bedroom to swab for DNA and take fingerprints, most of which would belong to the victim herself, her family, or the cleaning lady. Which reminded me, I needed to question her as well.

After I asked them to swab the hair dryer, I made my way down to the office off the kitchen. I found the correct key to the four-drawer desk on the set of keys Patrice gave me. The top left drawer held an unlocked metal box containing five-hundred-fifty dollars. The lower drawer held a plastic container of several CDs, labeled by months and years. The last one had been dated October of this year. The top drawer on the right contained a tablet filled with notes, but no other paper documents or bills. The bottom drawer was empty. My guess was she had mail sent to her Minneapolis address.

I then examined the contents of her purse. The only items worth entering into evidence were her cellphone, wallet, and address book. I slipped them into separate evidence bags. I would also bag the CDs. Maybe some nutjob connected with her radio show killed her. But that seemed unlikely with the staging—unless it was a clever psychopath.

I rechecked all the kitchen cabinets. The amount of trash had multiplied in the few days since Sonya's death; the recycling bin contained six empty wine bottles. Obviously, Patrice and Justine were drowning their sorrows. It was now all going to have to go to the lab.

BEFORE THE BRO TEAM pulled out just after ten o'clock, I made sure they had the bags containing the family's DNA swabs. I locked up the house, then walked through a half foot of snow to my truck. Because Dallas got up early, she went to bed promptly at ten. I sat in my truck and texted her, saying I was on my way home. I waited for her to text me back to tell me my pie was waiting, but she didn't.

I followed the tire tracks of the BCA vans out of the driveway. At Highway 10, the vans turned left and would head north up 371. I turned right. The plow hadn't been through lately, and I took my time on the slippery roadway. I put on Chris Botti's *Impressions* album.

I hadn't met a single car for ten miles when an orange Camaro zoomed past in the other direction, throwing snow into the wind. The fool would end up in the ditch. I glanced at the rearview mirror. Sure enough, the red taillights fishtailed, then sharply veered into the ditch. *Shit.*

By the time I turned around and parked on the shoulder, two individuals had exited and were at the rear of the vehicle, attempting to push it out. I put on my flashers, grabbed my Fenex flashlight, jumped out and, staying on the road, shined the beam down on the Camaro wedged in a snowdrift.

"Everyone okay?" I asked.

"Yeah, but we're stuck."

"Yeah, there's no way you're pushing that baby out," I said.

The driver rolled down his window. Smoke curled out. "Hey, buddy, do you have a chain?"

"Nope, and it doesn't surprise me you ended up in the ditch. You were driving way too fast for the conditions."

"Hey, asshole, if you ain't gonna help, move on."

"Hey, asshole, I'm Deputy Sheehan with the Birch County Sheriff's Department."

He lowered his head to the steering wheel.

As I called dispatch, the front seat occupants moved about in the vehicle, indicating they were trying to hide something. The passenger opened the window and chucked objects out, most likely beer cans. I told the two young people still attempting to get hernias by pushing a 3,500-pound vehicle to come up to the road. They trudged their way through the deep snow and came up beside me. As I suspected, they were kids, one a female. I pulled my badge, then asked, "Where are you headed?"

"Home," the young male said.

"Mind if I pat you down for my own safety?"

"Uh . . . okay," he said.

I asked them to put their hands on the front of my hood. While patting them down, I detected beer breath. I pulled the wallet from the boy's pocket and looked at his ID. Kirk Jackson, age twenty, Dexter Lake address. Since I had my own vehicle, I had no cuffs, no computer, or my citation book to make an arrest. Where was dispatch?

The girl's pockets held nothing but tissues, which she was going to need since tears were rolling down her cheeks.

"You have an ID?" I asked her.

"I . . . I don't have a driver's license."

"What's your name?"

"Morry."

"Last name?"

"Um . . . Jones."

Right.

Kirk's eyes shifted to Morry, verifying she'd just lied to me.

"How old are you, Morry Jones, and where do you live?"

"Eighteen. I live in Dexter Lake."

"Any weapons in the vehicle?"

"Are you kidding me?" the young male said.

"We don't kid about these things."

Darlene from dispatch finally answered. "Hey, Darlene, Cal Sheehan," I said. "I need a unit or two dispatched ten miles west of Dexter Lake and a tow. I was just coming from a scene when I came upon a car in the ditch. Passengers are chucking objects out the windows. You know what that means?"

Kirk and Morry gave each other "uh-oh" looks.

"Besides being dumb as dirt?" Darlene asked.

"Bingo, and underage."

"I can have a unit there in ten minutes and another shortly after."

"Perfect. They aren't going anywhere, but I'll sit tight until they arrive."

"Ten-four."

"How much have you had to drink?" I asked the kids, their faces filled with regret.

"Nothin'," Kirk lied.

Nothing or a couple of beers is the standard answer on DUI stops, even if the driver can hardly stand.

"Right . . . then why do you smell like beer?"

Miss "Jones" whimpered.

As I made my way down to the Camaro, the driver opened the door. I placed my hand on my Smith & Wesson M&P forty-caliber and yelled, "Stay in the vehicle. Stay in the vehicle."

You have to repeat yourself with drunks, especially the young, dumb ones.

"Driver, put your hands on the steering wheel. Passenger, put yours on the dash. Keep them there."

They complied.

I approached the open window from behind. The acrid odor of marijuana drifted out. I shined the flashlight into the car and onto the two young people.

"Driver, let's start with your driver's license and registration."

He pulled his wallet out and said the registration was in the glove box. I asked the girl in the passenger seat to find it. The driver was Adam Larson, twenty. He also had a Dexter Lake address. I had Larson exit so I could pat him down, then even though he wasn't wearing boots, I directed him to stand with his hands on his trunk.

I asked the girl for her ID. Her name was Rochelle Farber, eighteen, also from Dexter Lake. The girl had to crawl out the driver's side, because the passenger door was wedged up against the snow bank. I patted her down.

"The fact I smell weed and beer gives me probable cause to search you, your passengers, and your vehicle," I told Larson.

I searched under the seats and glove box.

"Where's the weed and beer I smell?"

"Don't have any," Larson said.

I shined the light through the car windows. "No, you tossed it all out into the snow. See the cans sticking up?"

"Are you arresting us?" Larson asked.

"I don't have my *arresting stuff* with me, so that will be up to the deputies who'll arrive here shortly. Because of the weather conditions and the fact you aren't going anywhere, I'll let you all wait in the car. Adam, clean the snow away from your tailpipe, so you don't asphyxiate your passengers."

As I made my way up to my truck, Larson gunned the engine.

"You're just burying yourself deeper," I shouted back.

His tires whirred as he gave it another try.

"You spin your tires one more time, and we'll add attempting to flee."

I sat in the warmth of my cab, keeping a steady eye on the four in the Camaro, lest they plot to overtake me and steal my shiny, red truck.

Eight minutes later, I heard a siren. Within seconds the red and blue lights flashed through the veil of snow. Veteran Deputy Greg Woods pulled up in front of me. He turned the spotlight on the Camaro. We both exited our vehicles and walked toward each other.

"They're in there pretty good," he said.

"That they are. You're on nights now?"

"Dan Blackwell slipped on the sidewalk in front of the department, hurt his back, so I volunteered to cover for him tonight. Jenny Deitz is on her way."

"That's not good for Dan. Okay, here's what we have . . ."

I stayed until Jenny arrived. She was new enough for the eagerness to show in her eyes. Nights could be long and lonely for patrol. It was nice to get the drunks off the road and have a good arrest to help pass time.

BULLET WAS WAITING BY the back door, furiously wagging his tail, so I let him out. Up to his haunches in snow, he stopped to sniff the air, then tromped through the drifts to find the perfect place to do his thing.

I'd missed dinner and was headed for the refrigerator when Clara walked in wearing her pajamas and robe.

"Did I wake you?" I asked.

"No. How were the roads?" she asked.

"Poor. I would have been home an hour ago, but some drunk kids going way too fast slipped in the ditch. Why are you up so late?" I said.

"Can't sleep. Did you find your plate in the fridge?"

"Haven't looked yet."

She pulled out a plate heaped with some sort of macaroni dish and put it in the microwave. She poured me a glass of milk, and herself a glass of water.

When the microwave beeped, she placed it in front of me. I took a bite.

"This is really good."

"It's just hamburger hot dish—the twins liked it, too." She stayed to watch me eat.

"What's on your mind, Clara?"

"I've been thinking. What if Shannon stayed here while she's recovering and going through treatment? Then I can help her and watch the kids at the same time. Shannon's folks are flying back from Florida before the surgery and Christmas. You get along great with them, so they shouldn't mind visiting her here."

"Whatever it takes to take care of our girl."

She nodded and smiled. "Good, then."

"Clara, I'm not sure how Dallas will feel about having Shannon here."

"She'll be okay with it."

"You make sure you tell her it was your idea."

"She's not the jealous type."

"Did she hear anymore from Vince?"

"He sent flowers today."

"*I* sent her flowers."

"There was no card, so she assumed they were from Vince."

I guess I didn't send them often enough. I hated that she assumed Vince sent them.

"Is there anyway she'd give him another chance?"

"No, but I hope he gives up soon."

"Me, too."

If not, we may have to have a face-to-face meeting.

7

Tuesday, December 16

WHEN MY EYES POPPED OPEN, I smelled Shannon's perfume. It took me a few seconds to realize I'd been dreaming and the fragrance was an olfactory illusion. In my dream Colby was still alive, and Shannon and I were back together—and happy. Must have been my brain trying out Clara's suggestion she stay here while she recovered. I doubted Shannon would agree anyway. And no matter what Clara thought, Dallas would not be pleased with the arrangement.

I glanced at the time: eight o'clock. I purposefully hadn't set my alarm but rarely slept this late. I rolled out of bed and stopped to glance out the window. The town was silenced by a thick blanket of snow, and there wasn't a car in sight.

Time for me to get up and clean off my driveway. I dressed in warm clothing, then headed downstairs. Bullet met me as I stepped off the bottom step. I knelt beside him and loved him up before I entered the kitchen, where Clara was feeding the "Twinks" oatmeal. I kissed the tops of their heads, avoiding their faces smeared with goo.

"They're having a late breakfast," I said.

"They slept in like their daddy," she said. "What would you like to eat?"

"I'm going to clean the driveway first."

Clara pointed to the couch. "It's a snow day, so Shannon dropped Luke off at 6:45. She had nowhere else to take him."

"Hi there, Luke," I said. "Glad to have you here."

Luke was Shannon's eleven-year-old son from her first marriage. I'd adopted him right after Shannon and I were married. Luke and I never fully bonded, and after the car crash that killed his younger brother, Colby, he withdrew from me completely. In his mind, I was to blame. His mother and I had a fight that morning, and she was distracted. She entered an intersection on a green light and didn't see the semi running the red light. Since last summer, Luke had "allowed" me to attend his soccer and basketball games, but still refused to stay at my house during my weeks with the twins. But with his grandparents now in Florida, he had no choice of where to go today.

He kept his attention on his iPad. My instinct was to get in his face and teach him some manners, but I had to pussyfoot around the kid because he was "sensitive." There was a lot of power in being miserable. People were always trying to make him happy. In my opinion, he knew it and worked it.

"Luke, before I go to work, I'm going outside to blow out the driveway. I'd appreciate if you'd shovel the front porch and steps."

He tapped his device screen, ignoring me.

I glanced at the indoor/outdoor thermometer on the kitchen counter near the sink. Thirty degrees. Nice winter day. I put on my parka and boots and opened the backdoor. Bullet pushed through and beat me outside. He leapt into the snow and his legs disappeared. We must have had at least ten or eleven inches.

As I did my preliminary shoveling on the back steps and in front of the garage, Bullet bounded and jumped through the snowdrifts like a puppy. He romped ahead of me as I slogged down the driveway and around to the front of the house to set the shovel on the front porch. I wasn't going to say another word to Luke. That was how both my grandpas handled me. They'd give me my jobs (raking, shoveling, stacking wood, or mowing the grass), and I always did what they asked without hesitation. We'd see about Luke.

The streets weren't plowed yet and void of traffic or human movement. I took in the beauty of nature's blast. The pine trees were veiled like nature's brides, their branches swooping from the weight of the snow. The deciduous tree limbs, bare yesterday, were now trimmed with thick slabs of white. The blinding white against the cerulean sky was breathtaking.

I glanced across the street to Eleanor Kohler's plowed driveway. I suspected her boyfriend, Deputy Matt Houser, got up in the wee hours to clean her driveway, so she could make it to her bakery. He was that kind of man. He would make a good sheriff.

The stillness was broken by the sound of a snowplow rumbling a block down on Fifth Street. A snowblower started up in the distance. My elderly neighbor lady across the street had come out with a shovel and began scooping snow. She has a grown lazy-ass son who lived with her, and yet she did all the outdoor work. I shouted across the street.

"Mrs. Anderson. I'll clean your driveway after I finish mine."

"Oh, how nice. I have a doctor's appointment this morning at ten."

"Okay, then I'll do yours first. But you should call to see if the doctor's office is even open before you venture out."

"I didn't even think of that."

This deep, wet snow was too much for most people to shovel. Every year 911 got medical calls because people didn't realize how dangerously out of shape they were. I fired up my snowblower, then made a path down the driveway and across the street. By the time I was finished with Mrs. Anderson's driveway, my next-door neighbor, Doug Nelson, had his machine going, an arc of snow cascading through the air as he cleaned the elderly couple's drive next door to him on the other side. We gave each other a friendly wave, and I continued to clean my own driveway and sidewalk. By the time I was finished, Luke still hadn't appeared. I whistled for Bullet.

I grabbed the dog's towel off the hook by the back door, then threw it over him before he could shake the wet snow clinging to his fur across the room. He smelled like what he was—a wet dog. He gave two good shakes, then skidded across the floor to find the kids. I heard squeals and giggles when he found them.

"Where's Luke?" I asked Clara. "He needs to clear the deck and steps before the mail carrier comes."

"He's playing with the twins in the living room. Go look. They made a zoo of the stuffed animals. I'll encourage him to do his chore after you leave. That might work better with him."

"I'd like to see if he does it on his own. Call it my little experiment."

She arched her brows like I was playing it all wrong.

LUKE HAD ARRANGED the dining room chairs to create spaces for the stuffed animals. He was sitting on the floor and talking for Henry's stuffed rabbit toy. The twins were trying to copy him.

Clara came up behind me. "Aren't they adorable?"

"Yes. Luke's good with them."

"When are you going to buy a Christmas tree?"

I groaned. "Does Shannon have hers up?"

"For a week now."

"Can't it wait until it's closer to Christmas, so the kids don't destroy it?"

"Where are your decorations?"

"I think Shannon took them."

"She says not."

I had little motivation to decorate for Christmas. Last year, the holiday spirit was nonexistent. It didn't feel right to celebrate without Colby, but we numbly forced ourselves through the motions. Shannon sent me out to buy a tree, she bought the kids presents, we plastered on happy faces and faked Christmas joy for the kids. This year the grief was somewhat diminished, but her cancer loomed like a storm warning—and a part of me wanted to take cover and hide.

Clara offered to make my breakfast while I got ready for work. Then as I ate scrambled eggs and sausage, I watched the news on TV. The storm that hit the Midwest was the big news of the day. The snow was to end by afternoon. Nothing about a celebrity dying in Birch County. Perhaps the storm had distracted the local reporters, or she wasn't that well known.

THE MAIN THOROUGHFARES THROUGH town were plowed, so I was able to drive to the Sportsman Cafe to pick up three dozen cinnamon rolls to celebrate Tamika's return. When I walked into the office, Greg Woods was sitting at the table having a cup of coffee. He eyed the boxes. I opened one and he dug in.

"Thanks, what's the occasion?"

I smiled. "Tamika's coming back today. How did it go last night with the drunk kids in the ditch?"

He chuckled. "They denied the beer cans they tossed in the ditch were theirs. Some were half full, and you could see a trail of beer from the car window. They attempted to bury a bag of weed right outside the front passenger window."

We laughed.

"We snapped good photos of it all. Anyway, Jenny got all four to admit they'd been drinking. She's got a way with kids that makes them feel like their world isn't going to crash down on them for one citation. We wrote up the passengers for underage consumption, gave them a break on the pot, and then Jenny drove the three of them home. I arrested the driver for a DUI and brought him in. He acted all pissy about his car being towed, but he was scared because when he called his parents to come and get him, his dad said he wasn't driving in that kind of weather and to sit in jail."

"Good choice. I'm curious about the girl who called herself Morry Jones?"

"Jenny said the girl insisted on getting out with Kirk. She had another call, so she couldn't follow her home."

"Why were they out in a storm?"

"Celebrating a sure snow day. The driver thought it would impress me if he said he was a friend of the sheriff's grandson."

"Patrice doesn't have grandkids, so he must mean Jack Whitman, and the friend is Zach."

"Exactly. Stupid kid obviously didn't even know Jack wasn't the sheriff anymore."

I chuckled at how the kid thought dropping Zach Whitman's name would help him out of a DUI. Zach always seemed to be on the fringe of trouble, and hanging out with the town druggies didn't help. One of these days he was going to get caught with drugs, and being the former sheriff's grandson was not going to help him. Although Granddaddy Jack was a current county commissioner, so maybe it would.

"Cal, speaking of sheriffs, are you supporting Matt Hauser or Sheriff Clinton? She's doing an okay job, but she acts like we don't know ours. You know what I mean?"

"Yeah, I do. It's a long way off yet. Well, I better get to my detecting."

"Any leads?"

"Too soon."

"Thanks for the roll."

"Have another."

He reached into the box.

Since neither Patrice nor her secretary were in yet, I went to my office.

TAMIKA AND I WERE IN the conference room across from our offices, nibbling on cinnamon rolls and plotting our strategy when Clara texted to tell me Luke had finished the shoveling. I texted back a happy face. Emojis were faster, even though I disliked how human communication had deteriorated to symbols.

Patrice entered holding a travel coffee mug. I held up the box of rolls, of which there were two left, but she waved them away.

"You're declining a Sportsman cinnamon roll?" Tamika asked.

Patrice patted her trim stomach, then studied the whiteboard where we'd written what little we knew of Sonya's death.

Tamika shrugged and grabbed another. She mouthed, "More for me."

"You okay?" I asked Patrice.

"Not really. How about you, Tamika?"

"Happy to get out of the house."

"Good you're back. We need all the help we can get on this investigation." She handed me a sheet of paper. "These are all the people Justine and I could come up with. We also wrote the connection to Sonya, but unfortunately, we don't have phone numbers or addresses for all of them."

"This will help a lot." I looked it over. "I see Justine and Sonya have the same address."

"Justine and Zabrina have the entire second floor of the Logan house. Why? Do you think that's weird?"

"No, my mom and grandmother lived together until just recently. So, how are Justine and Zabrina doing?" I asked.

Deep sigh. "Not good. We're all in total shock."

Tamika leaned back in her chair. "Absolutely understandable. How was the drive in?"

"Awful. If the roads are plowed, they're still icy."

I nodded. "There's nothing on the news. I'm surprised the local media didn't get wind of Sonya's death."

"It's a good thing. Maybe the weather kept them home."

"Plus, old people dying isn't exactly news," Tamika said.

Patrice shot Tamika a dirty look. "She wasn't that old. Cal, why don't you write something up for the media."

Oh, no. She's not passing that off on me. "Patrice, I understand you're grieving, but if you don't buck up and act like the sheriff, the public will perceive you as weak and emotional . . ."

Tamika pointed at her and said, "And they'll say it's because you're a woman and not suited for the job. And you don't want that with the election—"

Patrice slammed a fist down on the table. "Oh, for fuck's sake. Give me a piece of paper."

Tamika tossed her a writing tablet. Patrice grabbed it and stared at it. After an awkward delay, I handed her a Prairie Falls First National Bank pen. She yanked it out of my hand and wrote a few words, then scratched them out.

"Take yourself out of the equation, Patrice. You're a sheriff reporting the suspicious death of a woman who owns a vacation home in the county. Stick to the facts of the case and don't mention she's a celebrity. Most people don't know who Sonya Donovan is."

Tamika lifted her brows. "No, that's just you, Cal."

"No, Cal's right," Patrice said.

Tamika rolled her eyes at me.

"Do you know when her body will be released?" I asked.

"She's being cremated in Bemidji today or tomorrow."

"Okay. We're going to need a search warrant on Justine's accounts, too."

Patrice furrowed her brows. "Why?"

"You know why."

Tamika sat forward and pointed a finger. "Don't you want to clear your friend before the media accuses her?"

I nodded.

Patrice worked her jaw as if she was chewing pebbles.

"The killer has to be someone she knew and someone who benefits from her death in some way," I said.

"What makes you so sure about that?"

"They went to great lengths to make it look like natural causes. Tell me, does Sonya always arm the security system at night?"

"Yes."

"That's another thing. There was no sign of a break-in, so she either let the person in, or they knew the code."

"I see your point."

"Are you certain she doesn't have a lover?"

"Quite. Well, pretty sure."

"Does she entertain much at the Dexter house?" I asked.

"No. Just family and a few close friends."

"Are all those people on the list?"

"Yes. What I came up to tell you is that I got the autopsy report. Those damn things are Greek to me, but from what I can decipher, she was in excellent health. There was no evidence of her having had been assaulted. She did have a trace of alcohol in her system, but I expected that, seeing the wine bottles in the trash. The full toxicology report will take longer."

"She had no defense injuries, which is strange if someone was trying to drown her," I said. "She would have struggled. There were no wet swimsuits or other clothing, and obviously they dried her hair—"

Patrice pointed a finger at me. "That's why it looked so bad."

"Our perpetrator dressed her in a dry negligee before he placed her back in bed," I continued. "Plus, the pool towels were uneven."

Both women stared at me blankly.

"All the towels in the cabinets and shelves were stacked evenly, but those in the pool changing area were askew and uneven by two. I could understand one . . ."

Tamika said, "So our killer dried her with two towels and took them?"

"That's my thought."

"You need to know the brand and color," Patrice said.

"They were all Ralph Lauren, sage green."

"Send me a daily report of who you're interviewing and when," Patrice said.

"We'll head down to Minneapolis as soon as the roads are better to interview her employees and associates."

"Okay, and now I'm going down to my office to work on a frickin' press release," Patrice said as she stalked off.

When I heard the elevator doors close, I said, "Your comment about being a woman and perceived as not suitable hit a nerve."

"Think so?"

"Definitely. I don't want her passing off her responsibilities on me. That's why she gets the big bucks. Besides, she can delegate to her deputy chief she insisted she needed."

"What does Carole Knight do anyway?"

"Patrice's paperwork. And now I'm going to call the Moores."

"Who's that?"

"The Dexter Lake housekeeper and her husband. He does plowing and yard work."

"And we have to get Justine in—try and yank a confession out of her."

"'Yank' doesn't imply a smooth, calculated questioning technique," I said.

"How's 'squeeze'?"

"Better."

"How about you call Justine and arrange for her and Zabrina to come in this afternoon or tomorrow morning before they head home to Minneapolis," Tamika suggested. "They can wait until the roads are better."

"Got it."

Tamika put her half-eaten cinnamon roll between her teeth, picked up her belongings, and made her way across the hall to our office. I followed with the box holding the remaining roll, which I wasn't going to eat. The third gave me a sugar high.

First, I made a copy of the list of names for Tamika. Then I reserved two rooms at the La Quinta off 394 in Minnetonka for Wednesday and Thursday. When Tamika hung up the phone, she said, "You're not going to believe this. Patrice's husband said Justine and her daughter just left for Minneapolis."

"On these roads? Didn't Patrice tell them we needed their statements before they left?"

"He said Justine felt it important she tell the employees of her mother's death in person before it hit the news. He mentioned Patrice told them their interviews could be held in Minneapolis."

"Shit." I punched in Patrice's number on my cell phone.

"Yes, Cal," she said.

"Justine already left for Minneapolis."

"Did she? I advised her to stay until after the interview."

"But you mentioned it could be done in Minneapolis?"

"Well . . . yes."

"I wanted to tape her here, damn it."

"Oh, relax, Cal. It'll be fine."

I took a breath. "We're heading down tomorrow."

"Good. Keep me updated."

I hung up and shook my head.

Tamika had a pencil in her mouth. "You ever notice how Patrice discounts what I say? She never ever agrees with me like she does you."

"Nope, never noticed." Females have all sorts of stuff going on in their heads I couldn't begin to understand.

"Pay attention next time."

"Okay."

"Shannon stopped by yesterday to tell me the bad news. Cancer's such a bitch. Do you know what she said to me?"

"No."

"She said she was confident you could raise the kids as well as she could."

"Jesus. She's thinking she's going to die?"

"When I thought I had uterine cancer, I picked out the songs for my funeral."

"Well, she's not going to die."

"No, of course not."

Tamika diverted her eyes to the list of names and started taking notes. I took a deep breath and started making calls. The first was to Della Moore, Sonya's housekeeper.

"My husband doesn't want me to drive on these roads," she said.

"Is he home?"

"He's out plowing and will be all day."

"Okay. Would tomorrow morning be a convenient time for you both to come in?"

"If I can come in before work. Is seven okay?"

"Perfect. Ask for me at the front desk and have Marvin call to arrange a time. When was the last time you were in the Donovan house?"

"Friday, the fifth."

"Did you clean the entire house?"

"Most of it."

"The workout room?"

"I wiped down the equipment and floor."

"Thanks."

If she'd seen the tissue, she would have picked it up, but perhaps she's the one who dropped it.

WITHIN MINUTES. MARVIN MOORE called. I set the interview for the next day at 8:00 a.m. Then Tamika and I split the tasks and would spend the day gathering information about our victim. I had Tamika look into her finances, while I checked phone records.

After an hour, Tamika twirled around in her chair, her face pinched. She leaned back, crossed her arms across her stomach, and said, "Do you realize Sonya spends about as much money in a month from her personal account as I gross in a year? She's loaded."

"I assumed as much."

"Anything interesting on your end?"

"The week before she died, she received four calls from Patrice's landline, two from her cell. Six calls. Isn't that a lot?"

"Women communicate, Sheehan."

"But there was only one from her daughter."

"Maybe they didn't like each other much."

"Why would they plan to spend the weekend together if they didn't?"

"To throw us off. It's got to be Justine."

"Investigations are thousand-piece puzzles."

"But what if it's one of those baby puzzles with a few pieces, and we muck it up by making it too complicated?"

I shook my head. "Even if solving the murder is simple, the county attorney needs a shitload of evidence to prosecute. At this point we know nothing. We just dig and dig and then dig some more until something stands out."

"The interview stuff is my favorite part, and this storm is screwing it up."

I sighed. "It is."

TOWARD MID-AFTERNOON Tamika was folded over at her desk, her head on her arms.

"Why don't you go home and rest, pack for our trip to Minneapolis, if you think you're still up for it."

"I'm up for it," she said. And with lightning speed, she had her coat and boots on and was headed out the door.

As a courtesy, I contacted Minneapolis Police Department, notifying them we were investigating the death of one of their residents. After explaining the situation to whomever answered the phone, I was put on hold. After a few minutes I heard, "Homicide. Ryan."

I told Ryan the story. He said to let him know if there was anything he could do.

SINCE OUR DINNER DATE had been canceled the night before, I invited Dallas over for Buzzo's pizza. When it was the twins' bedtime, she said she was going home. Clara gave her a look I couldn't interpret. Dallas usually avoided coming over when I had the kids. She once told me she didn't want to confuse the children, that they didn't need another mother figure in their lives. When she did come over, she didn't give them as much attention as she gave Bullet. Made me wonder if she was cut out to be a mother.

As I walked her out to her car, she handed me her phone. On the screen was an email Vince had sent her. He said his family had booked a cruise for Christmas, and they'd paid for her passage. He said she owed him a second chance.

"You owe him nothing."

"I know."

"Is there any part of you that wants to go?"

"I can't believe you just asked me that. No. No. No."

"Okay, good." I would make a point to look him up when I was in Minneapolis.

8

Wednesday, December 17

M Y DEPARTMENT CELL PHONE'S ring cut through my sleepy fog. I glanced at my clock radio. 5:07 a.m.

"Detective Sheehan," I said, more asleep than awake.

"This is Will Ryan, homicide detective with the Minneapolis PD. We spoke yesterday. I hope I'm not calling too early, but I'm about ready to go home to catch a couple hours of shuteye."

"It's fine. What's up?"

"I thought you'd want to know Justine Donovan was shot and killed last night outside her residence."

I bolted to a sitting position.

"Her daughter, Zabrina, was also wounded—hit in the shoulder. She should be okay."

Holy shit. "Do you have any leads?"

"Appears to have been a drive-by. A neighbor out watering his dog in the park said a dark vehicle with a loud muffler drove by. A few seconds later he heard the shots. He couldn't identify the model or plate number."

"What time was that?"

"About eight o'clock. I would've called you earlier, but I left your number at my desk."

"Well, this changes things. Justine was my prime suspect for her mother's death."

"Stands to reason."

"Where did they take Zabrina?"

"Abbott Northwestern. Anyway, since we share some witnesses, you might want to interview in our department."

"Sure. We plan to be down later this afternoon. Hopefully the roads will be better by then."

"Yeah, hell of a storm passed through. How many inches did you get up there?"

"Close to a foot."

"Us too. I'll give you my phone number and email address. Let me know if you find out anything I need to know. I'll do the same."

"You bet."

We exchanged information and hung up.

"What the bloody hell?" I said to myself.

I turned on the news on the TV in the bedroom. The male anchor was reporting the shootings on Logan Street in Kenwood, but the police hadn't released names. Then a photo of a much younger Sonya Donovan appeared on the screen.

"Authorities in Birch County have confirmed the death of Minneapolis resident Sonya Donovan. Ms. Donovan was an accomplished author and columnist but may be best known as the host of the popular radio program *Love 'Em or Leave 'Em.* An official from the Birch County Sheriff's Department states the circumstances are suspicious and they are investigating. Her family is unavailable for comment."

"Unavailable? That's putting it mildly," I mumbled.

"After the first major storm of the year dumped up to twelve inches of snow across the metro and most of the state, this morning's commute continues to be a challenge for drivers. Let's go to Johnny Cross for current road conditions."

I called Tamika. "What time is it? It's dark out," she croaked.

"Justine Donovan was shot to death outside her home in Minneapolis last night. Her daughter was wounded."

An audible gasp, then, "Oh, my God in heaven, it's a conspiracy."

I told her what I knew and said I was going in early and would see her when she arrived.

AT 7:00 A.M., TAMIKA was sitting with her feet up on her desk. "What took ya?" she said.

"First, I had to walk Bullet, and when we got back, the twins were up, so I had breakfast with them. I feel guilty leaving them when it's my week."

"That's why you have the best nanny in town. Seriously, how much do you pay Clara? I'm going to offer her more and steal her from you."

I glared at her.

"Wow, don't look so lethal, Sheehan. I'm just kidding. So the MPD detective thinks it's a random drive-by?"

"Sounds like it. Why would someone want to wipe out the entire family?"

"Maybe because Sonya wrecked theirs."

I considered. "Possibly. She pretty much destroyed her husband's first family."

"Do her step-children live in the area?"

"I believe they live somewhere in the Cities. I should see if Patrice is in. See how she's handling this one."

I made my way to first floor. Her secretary, Georgia, wasn't at her desk, but Patrice was. She had her back to the door and faced the window.

"Patrice . . ."

She swiveled her chair around. I couldn't tell by her face if she knew about Justine or not.

I said, "Minneapolis Police Department called this morning."

"I meant to tell you I called them yesterday to give them a heads-up." Her eyebrows furrowed. "Why are you looking at me like that?"

"Patrice, Justine was shot and killed outside of her home last night. Zabrina was hit in the shoulder and is in the hospital, but she's going to be okay."

Patrice's face turned ashen. Her eyes rolled back, and she began sliding out of her chair. As I rushed around to grab her, I heard her head hit the floor with a thud. I used her desk phone to call 911.

I found her coat in the closet, folded it, and placed it under her head. I used two printer packs for her feet. Patrice's eyes fluttered open. She appeared disoriented as she lifted her head.

"Lie still. You've just fainted."

"I don't faint."

"Smile," I said.

"I don't feel like it," she said.

"I'm checking for stroke. Raise your arm."

"Oh, for Chrissake." She simultaneously lifted her arm, stuck out her tongue, and said, "There. Now help me up."

"No, lie still. I called 911," I said.

"What did you go and do that for?"

Within five minutes, the EMTs bustled in. They just happened to be nearby after finishing a call. Georgia walked into the office as Patrice was being rolled out on the ambulance cot.

"This is ridiculous. Georgia, I'll be right back. No siren," she shouted at the EMTs.

When they disappeared around the corner, Georgia asked, "What on earth happened?"

I told her, then asked for Patrice's husband's cell phone number.

He answered, "David Clinton."

"Hey, David, this is Cal Sheehan. I'm a deputy with Birch County."

"I know who you are."

"Look, Patrice fainted in her office, and they took her to the hospital. She's not very happy about it, but we thought she should be checked over."

"Absolutely. I've never known her to faint. It's all this business with Sonya. She hasn't been eating and sleeping properly."

"Well, I'd just delivered some startling news. Her friend Justine was shot and killed last night outside her home in Minneapolis."

"My God."

"Also, Justine's daughter was wounded and taken to Abbott Northwestern Hospital. Anyway, Patrice is probably fine, but I knew you'd want to know."

"Yes, thanks."

ON THE WAY BACK to the interview rooms, I pondered why David snapped at me when I told him who I was. When I returned to the office, Tamika was eating a Granny Smith apple. "After all those cinnamon rolls, I'm trying to eat healthier. So how did she take the news?"

"Not so well. She fainted and was taken to the hospital."

Her eyes widened. "Well, the steely sheriff of Birch County is human after all. Geez, I wondered what was taking you so long. So what do we do now?"

"We carry on. First, we interview the Moores, then we head to Minneapolis."

My cell phone rang. Patrice's number.

"Patrice?" I asked.

"I need you to do something for me."

"What?"

"Zabrina needs to be protected. I want someone stationed outside her hospital room twenty-four/seven. She's in danger."

"They think it's a random drive-by."

"That's bullshit and you know it. You need to guard her around the clock."

"Patrice, I have far too much to do to sit with Zabrina."

Big sigh. "All right. I'll handle it."

I heard talking in the background, the phone being muffled. Then Patrice came back on and said, "They're making way too much of a little fainting spell. They're making me have an MRI, for God's sake. What a waste of time and money."

"Just let them do what they need to."

"Damn it," she said and hung up.

I looked at Tamika and said, "She wanted me to guard Zabrina."

"I heard you. So who's going to do it?"

"She can hire someone."

"Do you think we'll be in Minneapolis for more than two days?"

"We'll be there as long as it takes to talk to everyone we need to talk to."

"I checked out the Moores. I expected with their old-fashioned names, they'd be old peeps, but the DMV records indicate they're only thirty-nine. They live in Dexter Lake, neither has a criminal history, not a single traffic violation between them."

"Weird, every time I turn around, someone from Dexter Lake is on the radar."

"Maybe it's because your mama lives there now, and she's stirring up the karma."

"Could well be."

I checked my emails. Leslie Rouch had sent one saying Sonya's time of death was somewhere between two and four in the morning. The water collected from the pool contained coli form, and the pool filter and skimmer contained traces of feces, suggesting she expired in the pool.

I signed out Sonya's phone and Fitbit from the evidence room. If Sonya had been wearing her Fitbit watch at the time, I may be able to pinpoint the time. I tried the same passcode as her security system, and it opened right up. People foolishly use the same passcode for everything. I opened her Fitbit application on her phone and tapped "How did you sleep?" Low and behold, the last information recorded was for December 11. She had slept from approximately 11:00 p.m. to 2:00 a.m., then nothing. The watch was either removed or hit the water at that time. The time of death just narrowed. Just then my phone rang. Della Moore, Sonya Donovan's cleaning woman, had arrived for the interview.

A DISMAL-LOOKING WOMAN stood in the lobby. She wore a long, gray, quilted coat, a brown knit hat pulled down low on her forehead, and a pair of old-fashioned brown moon boots, the likes of which I hadn't seen since I was a kid and had a similar pair.

Her pale-blue eyes met mine, then bounced to the floor.

"Mrs. Moore?"

"Yes."

"Cal Sheehan. Thanks for coming in this morning. How were the roads?"

"Slippery."

"Glad you made it safely."

We walked the rest of the way to interview room number three in silence. It was one of two rooms with recording capabilities. I radioed Tamika to make sure she was in the observation room ready to film.

Della looked about the room nervously. I helped her out of her coat, which I then placed over the back of her chair. When she pulled off her hat, a mane of long brown hair tumbled down to the small of her back. Two silver barrettes held the hair off her face, odd to see on a woman her age.

I wanted to inquire how she managed all that hair when she used the bathroom or slept, but such a question was neither appropriate nor my business. I moved on, recited the case number, and gathered the pertinent information from Della: her name, address, phone number.

"We don't have a home phone, only cell phones we use for business." She clutched one hand in the other, her fingers long and thin, the nails chewed to the quick. She swam in her beige sweater and blue jeans. Anorexia crossed my mind.

With a voice as timid as her body language, she said, "Could you please tell me why I'm here?"

"Oh, sorry. I assumed you'd heard the news that Sonya Donovan was found dead last Friday."

Her mouth gaped open, and her eyes widened. "No," she whispered. She swallowed in slow motion as if what I had said was something she had to physically ingest. "What happened?"

"The circumstances are suspicious."

She cocked her head as she waited for more. I let a couple seconds pass, then said, "Because you work for Mrs. Donovan, you may have information that could help us. I'm surprised you didn't hear anything on the radio or television about it."

Her back stiffened as she placed her hands in her lap. "We don't own a television." It was a statement filled with self-righteousness, rather than "poor us, we can't afford one."

"There's more. Her daughter and her granddaughter were shot outside their home in Minneapolis. Her daughter did not survive."

"Oh, my goodness, how terrible."

"Did you know the daughter and granddaughter?"

She shook her head in slow motion. "No, sir."

"Mrs. Moore, how long have you worked for Ms. Donovan?"

She placed her hands back on the table. "Three years come January."

"How did you get the job?"

Della rubbed her thumbs together. "One of my other clients had recommended me."

She'd look at me while I asked the questions, but when she answered them, her eyes diverted to her hands.

"What are your duties?"

"Before she arrives, I freshen up the house, stock the house with groceries and fresh flowers. Then after she's left, I clean and do the laundry and ironing."

"Do you see her on these visits."

"No, only the first couple times I cleaned, so she could show me how she wanted things done."

"So you never saw her guests?"

"No."

"And when did you know about her latest visit?"

"She called a few days before her arrival."

"What did she tell you?"

"She said she was coming up and to buy grocery list number three, but to add two T-bone steaks."

"She has different shopping lists?"

"Yes. If she's going to be alone, she wants list number one. It has fish and chicken, lots of vegetables, no red meat. List two has more snacks and frozen items, and list three has fancier items like artichokes and avocados. I have to drive to the Save-Rite in Prairie Falls to get those things."

"What if she needs additional items through the week?"

"Then she buys them herself."

"How do you pay for her groceries?"

"She gave us a credit card. Marvin uses it if he needs parts."

"I thought he just mowed and plowed."

"She's asked him to do some repairs on occasion."

"Does he take care of the pool?"

"No. The Pool Guys service it. I let them in."

"Do you clean around the pool area?"

"As needed. I make sure the bath supplies are stocked."

"Everything looked particularly neat and orderly in the house."

"Yes. I've never worked for anyone quite so picky."

"Tell me about that."

"Food items in the refrigerator and cupboards had their specific place."

"How about the towels?"

"They have to be folded in thirds and placed in even stacks of four."

"She's that particular?"

"Yes, sir."

"And the towels were evenly stacked in the pool area as well?"

"Yes, sir, in stacks of six."

"Did you check the pool towels the day you were there?"

"Yes, sir."

"Were they evenly stacked?"

"Yes, sir. Just how I left them after Thanksgiving."

"Where are the used pool towels placed?"

"Sometimes they'd be hung on hooks or placed in a hamper in the pool area."

"So you would know if someone used towels?"

"Yes."

"And how often did she stay at Dexter Lake?"

"It varied. More often in the summer and on holidays."

"Do you keep track of these visits on a calendar?"

"Yes. I recorded the grocery list for the visit so I wouldn't forget which to buy."

"Do you have the calendar with you?"

"Yes, in my purse in the car."

"May I copy it before you go today?"

"Okay."

"At any point since you've been working for Mrs. Donovan, have you noticed anything that gave you pause?"

"Not really, sir."

I remained purposefully quiet to see if she would come up with something. About a half minute passed before she asked, "How did she die?"

"I'm not at liberty to say. Tell me, did you like her?"

Della shrugged. "I guess so, but I didn't know her well."

Again, I waited her out.

"But she patronized me. She felt the need to teach me how to clean, as if I didn't know how."

I nodded. "I see. Have you given any more thought to whether you saw or heard anything unusual before that visit?"

"Not that I can think of." Her eyes betrayed her.

"Mrs. Moore. You have something to tell me, don't you?"

"Only that I shouldn't have said anything bad about her."

"You didn't."

"Because she was very generous to us."

I nodded. "Did you know Mrs. Donovan had a radio show?"

"Yes, sir."

"Have you listened to it?"

"We only listen to spiritual programs or the weather."

Explains some things. As I took a minute to look over my notes, she asked, "Why would anyone want to kill Mrs. Donovan?"

I gave her a small smile. "That's my job to find out. I'll be looking at every aspect of her life with a magnifying glass."

Her eyelids flickered. She didn't like what I'd just said.

"Is there anything you want to tell me?"

"No, sir."

I gave her a hard stare; she couldn't maintain eye contact. I waited a few seconds—the quiet can be intolerable for some folks. Many begin to fill it by repeating themselves or with detailed explanations and sometimes, if you're lucky, you'll hear an unexpected confession. But Della remained perfectly still, not that I expected her to have murdered her employer.

"Since the Donovan house is a crime scene, you shouldn't go back there unless contacted."

She nodded.

"Also, I'll need you to come with me to get fingerprinted and give a DNA sample to distinguish yours from others taken at the scene. First, let's grab that calendar."

Her forehead became furrowed with concern, but she showed me to her rusty Dodge van. Duct tape held the rear bumper in place. When she handed me the paper pocket calendar, her hand was shaking. Was she hiding something? Or was hearing of the murder of her employer upsetting her? It would be a loss of income, after all. Or was she by nature a nervous Nellie?

"May I have my fingerprints taken later? I need to catch up on my jobs from yesterday," she said.

"No, I need you to do it now."

I walked her through the tunnel to the jail. While her prints and DNA were taken, I used the jail's copy machine. By the time she was done, I handed her calendar back to her, and she wasted no time leaving.

Before Marvin Moore's interview, Tamika and I discussed Della's.

"Did you pick up how nervous she was?" I asked.

"Not really. Do you think Della and Marv killed Sonya?" Tamika asked.

"I don't know what their motive would be. The death means a loss of income for both. Anyway, I texted Crosby to tape Marvin's interview. Do you want to join me as I question him?"

She grinned. "You think you have to ask?"

"His wife will have filled him in."

"As any good wife would. We should have brought them in together and separated them, so they couldn't collaborate on their stories."

"If they're responsible, they've already done so."

She shrugged.

"We have time before he shows. I think I'll make a few calls, set up some appointments."

Sonya's cousin, Gary Williams, was first on my list. He said he'd heard about Sonya's death on the news. No one had notified him.

"They aren't giving many details. What happened?" he asked.

"I'm not at liberty to say at this point. I'd like to ask you a few questions. Would you be available this evening?"

"Where?"

"How about your home?"

"If it's after eight."

Tamika found addresses and phone numbers for Sonya's step-children, but Crosby called and said Marvin Moore was waiting in the interview room.

When introductions were made, Marvin made a point of looking me in the eye as he shook my hand a little too vigorously. He only nodded at Tamika, however. He was an odd-looking man with widely spaced eyes, concave cheeks, and a haircut right out of the fifties.

"Have a seat," I said.

He smiled widely. "You could've knocked me over with a feather when the wife told me Mrs. Donovan had passed and her death was suspicious." Smiling while talking about a suspicious death is, in my opinion, downright creepy. "It's ironic," he said.

"How so?"

"She had it all, ya know?"

"Yes, it would seem so."

I nodded at Tamika. She began to solicit his personal information for the recording. While his wife appeared shy and reticent to answer our questions, Marvin's eyes flashed with eagerness.

"How well did you know Mrs. Donovan?" Tamika asked.

He looked to me when he answered her question. "Just as well as I know my other customers. When I'd see her, I'd make conversation. She'd tell me if she'd want something trimmed or even ask me about her plants at her Minneapolis place. She said I could take care of that place, too. I was even tempted to take her up on it, but that's a lot of miles. She never told me how much she'd pay me. It could have been worth it if the price was right." He winked. It made me want to cuff him and put a hood over his head.

Tamika didn't react to his lack of eye contact with her as she forged on with the interview questions. "How long have you worked for Mrs. Donovan?"

He stopped grinning and put a finger to his temple. Must be his thinking pose.

"Hmm. Della got a job cleaning for her first, then when Mrs. Donovan found out I did plowing, she hired me on. That was three winters ago, I believe. The next spring she asked me to do her yard work, too. She gave us more money than what we asked for and gave us a Christmas bonus every year . . . I s'pose this year that ain't gonna happen, unless the daughter carries on the tradition."

"The daughter was shot and killed early this morning."

Marvin's mouth stretched into a grimace. "No! Somebody kilt her, too? The devil is at work in this country. Good luck fightin' him."

"What was Mrs. Donovan like?" I asked, attempting to push the devil from the interview.

"She was real good to us. She was a fussy one, though—she wanted a showplace. She was the only customer who had me mow twice a week."

I nodded.

"Did you ever witness any confrontations with anyone?" Tamika asked, re-taking the interview.

"Can't say as I did, but I just did my job and didn't pay much attention to her or her company."

"Did she have a lot of company when you were around?" she asked.

"More in the summer. Mainly her daughter and granddaughter.

"When was the last time you were on the property?"

"I plowed this morning. I s'pose I won't get paid for it."

Tamika crossed her eyes at me, so I said, "I'm sure they'll settle her debts through the estate."

"Any men visitors?" Tamika asked.

"Not that I saw. But I was only there twice a week and in the daytime."

"How were you paid?"

"We sent a monthly invoice to Minneapolis and were sent a check within a few days."

"Did you have any issues with her?" Tamika asked.

"Nope, she was more 'an fair with us."

"Detective Sheehan, do you have any questions for Mr. Moore?"

"Not at this time."

Tamika pulled out her business card and said, "Well, thanks for coming in, Mr. Moore. If you think of something you believe would be helpful in the investigation, please give one of us a call."

I put a finger up. "Mr. Moore, one more thing. Have you gone inside the Donovan house within the last few months?"

He lowered his head as he thought. "I don't remember. Why?"

"If you have, we'll need to get your fingerprints and DNA," Tamika said.

With the goofy grin plastered on his face, he said, "Well, better safe than sorry, I always say."

Tamika stood, walked around, then asked him to open his mouth. He complied. She scraped the inside of his cheek with more vigor than necessary.

"Deputy Frank will take you down to the area where they'll fingerprint you," I said.

Before he left, he turned and said, "You do your own mowing and plowing?"

"Yes."

"Yeah, you look the type. Well, if you ever need my services, give me a call. And I'm real sad to hear about Mrs. Donovan and her daughter. It's just terrible."

"Yes."

He lost the smile as he said, "I'll pray for their souls."

9

WHEN TAMIKA RETURNED she said, "Is Marv a racist or sexist?"
"Probably both. Since you've already done some work on Della and Marvin, why don't you check into their financials? I'll take Gary Williams, Sonya's cousin."

We worked silently and diligently at our computers for fifteen minutes before Tamika said, "Sheehan, the Moores' property taxes and water bills are in arrears."

"Not surprising."

"What if Sonya named them in the will?"

"Highly unlikely, but we'll know soon enough."

"What did you find out about cousin Gary?"

"He's in the import business and has three stores in the Midwest called Sojourns. The closest is in the Mall of America; others are located in Chicago and St. Louis. According to his driver's license, he's fifty-three. As far as I can tell, he has no siblings. I'm about to check the database for a criminal record."

"Does Marvin Moore look deranged to you?" Tamika asked. "Man, I wanted to slap that ridiculous grin off his face."

"Did you see him wink at me?"

"Yeah, you're definitely his type."

I threw an eraser at her. She chuckled. It was good to have her and her sense of humor back.

I made us each a mug of coffee on the Keurig we'd purchased together. As I set the cup on her desk, she asked, "Are you going to support Matt or Patrice for sheriff?"

"Why is everyone talking about this already? It's a year and a half away."

"Because the candidates have to begin to get their campaigns together. Remember how Troy's campaign failed because he started too late?"

"Also, he's a prick."

She gave out a little giggle. "Okay . . . the real reason I brought it up is that Patrice asked if I'd work on her campaign. I didn't know what to say."

"What did you?"

"I said yes, damn it. I haven't had my review yet."

"That's not a good reason."

She made a face. "Oh, yeah? You aren't brave enough to say who you'll back."

"You're right. Now back to work. What did you find out about the Moores?"

"Google netted zero hits on them—it's like they don't exist. Wanna bet they belong to a cult?"

"Is there one operating in Dexter Lake?"

"I'll ask around."

"Gary Williams doesn't have a criminal record, either. Okay, let's split the list Patrice gave me."

We worked for another ninety minutes, then shared what we'd learned. No one on our lists had a criminal record, and their presence on the social media sites showed them to be ordinary people with normal lives. But I wasn't naïve—appearances could be deceiving.

I signed out a department vehicle for our trip, and I went home to pack. Bullet greeted me at the door.

"He's just been out," Clara said, looking up from her knitting. She was sitting in the great room watching a soap opera on television, her fingers expertly dipping and swirling the needles around the red yarn.

I said, "I really don't know how long I'll be gone. I've made reservations for two nights, but I'm hoping we can wrap things up earlier."

Her fingers grew still. "Patrice is very upset about Sonya and Justine."

"I know."

"You do what you have to do to solve the case."

Much to my dismay, my boss and Clara had become friends after they met at a party I threw. I didn't like the idea they'd discuss my personal business, but I was sure they did.

"She and David are not getting along lately, then this business is—"

I raised a hand. "I don't want to know anything about it."

She shrugged and resumed knitting.

MY CLOTHES HAD BEEN LAUNDERED and put away. I didn't know how Clara did all of what she did or what I would do without her.

I made the decision not to pack uniforms. Shortly after Patrice took office, she decided we investigators were to wear them instead of plain clothes, like most detectives in most jurisdictions. I packed for three days, just to be safe, changed into jeans and a white shirt, holstered my Smith & Wesson M&P, put on my tan suede sport coat, grabbed my badge, and went downstairs with my carry-on.

"I bagged some Christmas cookies for you," Clara said. "While you're gone, I'll mix up another batch of those peanut blossoms you like."

"Thank you. You are marvelous." I threw her a kiss.

"Oh, pish. Did you have lunch? I can whip up something for you."

"No, thanks. We'll grab something on the way."

I PICKED TAMIKA UP FROM her house and drove to Highway 10 heading toward the Twin Cities. Tamika chattered about her family until she stopped mid-conversation when we went by a small ramshackle church all by itself in the country.

Tamika said, "I don't know how that little church survives. I called my friend Franny and asked her about cults in the Dexter Lake area. She's the wife of the minister of the First Lutheran Church. She teaches at the high school and says she thinks the Moores are members of the Church of the Everyday Apostles. It's conservative evangelical, not associated with any traditional denomination. They have really strict rules about what the kids can do in school—they have to leave the classroom for certain subjects and if a teacher shows a movie or plays music.

"Did you ask her if she knew any of the Moore children?"

"She says she's had three of them, and they're all good students, well behaved."

Then she jumped back to talking about her own. I tuned out and started thinking about Zabrina. I hoped she could give something to MPD, so they could find the shooter.

"Sheehan?"

"Yeah?"

"I just said I told Anton we were sharing a room."

"Say what?"

"He said I should go for it."

"Jesus Christ."

"He said he didn't think you could handle this much woman, anyway." She burst out laughing. "Oh, get that scared look off your face. He knows I was kidding."

"He'd better."

She pointed to the bag of cookies in between us. "Can I have a cookie?"

"Give me one, too."

She took a bite. "Mm-mm. These are tasty," she said.

I grabbed two more.

"Are you gonna see Adriana while we're down here?"

I threw her a crusty look. "Why would I?"

"Why not? Are you afraid to see her?"

"I'm not *afraid.* I just don't want to."

She gave me a sly smile. "I'm not sure I believe you."

"Don't care. I'm with Dallas."

"And you're a one-woman man."

"I am."

I hadn't seen or heard from Adriana Valero in months, which was fine by me. Way back when we were still together, she took a job at a Minneapolis high-powered law firm without telling me she'd applied. She assumed I'd just pack up and go with her, but I didn't really want to live in Minneapolis, plus, at the time there were no openings in law enforcement anywhere. She said she made enough for the both of us—and with that completely emasculating notion, our relationship amicably ended. A scant five months later she married an old rich dude she'd previously dated. Within months they separated and she was back in Prairie Falls hoping to rekindle our relationship, but by then I was already engaged to Shannon.

Adriana then took up with my partner, Troy, who was totally wrong for her. She got pregnant and delivered their son soon after the Twinks were born. Adriana talked Troy into applying for positions in Minneapolis. He got a job with the Hennepin County Sheriff's Office, and off they went to the big city. When they broke up, Troy blamed me. Last time I saw him, he came at me fist first. We rolled around on the ground beating the crap out of each other until my neighbor called 911. But he was justified—Adriana and

I had just spent the night together. That was when she proposed the idiotic idea we meet periodically to have casual sex. She never called, but I would have turned her down.

NEAR ST. CLOUD, I TOOK the turn toward Waite Park to get to I-94 with its seventy-mile-per-hour speed limit. Once in Maple Grove, I turned south on 494, than east on 394 until we reached County 73. I took the north frontage road to the La Quinta. We checked in, then made our way to Abbott Northwestern Hospital on Twenty-eighth and Chicago in Minneapolis.

I had to drive around the ramp for a while before we found a spot to park. We walked briskly through the frigid air to the front door and into the lobby. Tamika pointed to the sign reading "PATIENT INFORMATION." Two women who appeared to be octogenarians were seated behind the desk: an orange-haired woman of advanced years and a gray-haired lady with a ponytail. They continued their conversation for a minute before they noticed or acknowledged our presence.

Tamika clicked her long nails on the counter. Orange-hair looked up. "May I help you?"

"Yes. If you would be so kind as to tell us what room Zabrina Bennett is in, please," I said, tossing her a big smile.

She turned to the computer in front of her, did some typing and then, gazing up at me with a concerned look, said, "There's a no visitors notation here."

I pulled out my badge. Tamika followed suit. "Detective Cal Sheehan and my partner, Detective Tamika Frank. We're here on official police business."

"Well, let me do some checking."

She spent the next ten minutes on the phone and finally got an okay from someone, somewhere, to give out the room number.

Flashing another smile, I said, "Zabrina's safety is our primary concern at this point, so thank you for being cautious."

She smiled back and handed us a slip of paper with the room number, then instructed us on how to find it. We found an elevator and Tamika pressed the button for our floor.

"Thanks for promoting me to detective."

"Trying to keep things simple for the girls."

As we exited the elevator, we followed the signs and turned down a hallway, where an officer sat on a chair at the end of the corridor.

"I'd bet your life savings our pal there is guarding Miss Zabrina," Tamika said.

"You're all about easy money, aren't you?"

The uniformed Minneapolis PD officer stood as we approached. He was short and looked twelve. I flipped open my badge case and said, "Birch County Detective Cal Sheehan, and this is my partner—"

"Detective Tamika Frank," she said.

"Detective Ryan said to expect you," he said.

"Good."

"I'm Officer James Kimmel," he said.

We shook hands.

"For real? Like in Jimmy Kimmel?" Tamika said.

He nodded. "I go by James, but yeah, that's my name."

"You should use Jimmy to get restaurant reservations," Tamika said.

"No, because they're always so doggone disappointed to see me as it is."

They shared a chuckle.

"Has Ms. Bennett had any visitors?" I asked.

"Just the detectives on the case."

"Okay if we go in?"

"Sure. Sign in first."

He picked up a clipboard propped up beside the chair and handed me a black Bic pen. We signed in, then went in the darkened room. A dim lamp above the sink in the open bathroom cast enough light to show an empty bed; the curtain was pulled around the bed closest to the window. I sent Tamika around the curtain to make sure Zabrina was presentable. She waved me in.

Zabrina was sound asleep and hooked up to a monitor and an IV. Her left shoulder was bandaged. We took the two chairs at the foot of the bed and waited. We spoke quietly, going over our interviews for tonight and tomorrow, thinking she'd hear our voices and wake up. But she didn't flutter an eyelash. Twenty minutes passed before a nurse came in to check on Zabrina. When she saw us, she scowled.

"Who are you?" she asked.

"Detectives Cal Sheehan and Tamika Frank," I said. "We're here to ask Zabrina a few questions."

"I'm afraid you're wasting your time. We've given her something to help her sleep."

I glanced at Zabrina. Her eyes had popped open. I stood and moved to her side. "Hi, do you remember me?"

She nodded. Tears began to roll down her cheeks. She looked so grief-stricken that it got to me, and I was afraid I'd have to blink back my own tears.

"Patrice asked us to check on you. She'll be here as soon as she can," I said.

"I need her here with me now," Zabrina said through her sobs. "She's the only family I have left."

"She's family?" Tamika asked.

"She's my godmother."

I said, "We think there could be a connection between your grandmother's death and your mother's."

"They tried to kill me, too," she said, and let out a shuddering sob. "I'm really scared."

"There's a guard posted outside your door," I said.

"Can't this wait a day?" the nurse asked sternly. She pointed to the monitor as if we could interpret its beeps.

"Sure," I said. "We'll come back tomorrow."

"Grand idea," the nurse said sternly.

As we started to move out of the room I heard the nurse say, "Zabrina, I'm Gretchen. I'll be taking care of you this evening."

As we walked out, Kimmel looked up from his book. He probably pulled this duty because he's on the bottom of the seniority list. This kind of duty was filled with long, boring days . . . unless something big happened. Then it was critical to be on your toes. Was this baby-faced kid up to the task?

"We'll be back tomorrow," I said.

"Okay."

"How long is your shift?"

"Twelve hours."

"What about breaks?"

"I notify the desk when I take them."

"There's a breach in security then?"

He shrugged. "My sergeant said we were doing this as a courtesy to your sheriff. That it was overkill."

"Overkill? Her grandmother and mother were both murdered, and she was seriously wounded."

"Right. Look, I don't know about that. I just do as ordered."

"Well, just be vigilant. If something happens to this girl, it's on your head, and that ain't good for your department . . . or your career."

"I see your point."

"Good."

As we walked away from young James, I muttered, "Maybe we should take turns guarding Officer Kimmel guarding her."

"She looks so frightened and fragile. Why the hell would someone want all three of them dead?"

"Our only job is to find out who killed Sonya. It's Minneapolis PD's job to figure out the rest of it and to protect their only witness. I'll call Patrice and tell her the situation. Then she can do what she wants."

10

O N THE WAY BACK to our vehicle, Tamika said, "It's five o'clock and all I've had to eat today is cookies. I need real food." She typed something in her phone, her phone dinged, she typed again. "We're going to Broders." She looked up at me brightly.

"Where's that?"

"Fiftieth and Penn. I'll put it on the GPS."

"We could go to Wayzata, where we have to be for tonight's interview."

"You'll love this place."

We spoke little as we made our way in heavy traffic to the restaurant. Fifteen minutes later, we parked on the street a block away. Tamika practically skipped to the door.

"What's your hurry?"

"We're late."

"For what?"

"Dinner with Adriana."

I stopped in my tracks. "Damn it. When did you set this up?"

"This afternoon."

"Did you not hear what I said earlier about not wanting to see her?"

"Oh, chill. I haven't seen her for an age."

"You should have consulted me."

"Do you want me to cancel?"

"Tamika, we're here. Man, you must drive Anton up a goddamn wall."

She shrugged. "That's my job."

"You owe me big time."

"Fine, I apologize."

Waving madly, Tamika scurried off toward the back of the room. My muscles tensed as I followed. I abhorred being manipulated like this. Adriana stood to give Tamika a hug, then wrapped her arms around me. I took a deep breath in an attempt to calm myself.

73

When the waiter, who introduced himself as Jamie, showed up with waters and menus, Adriana ordered a bottle of wine.

"Um, I don't think you should do that," I said. "We have an interview tonight, and we won't be drinking."

"Speak for yourself," she said, and ordered one anyway—she was never one to be told what to do. Jamie hustled off before she changed her mind.

"You look great," Adriana said to me. "Have you lost weight?"

"A little. I like the short haircut," I said.

She pulled on her bangs. "It's easy."

Then I had nothing more. She had nothing more. Tamika leapt in to fill the awkward silence. She pummeled Adriana with questions about her son, Marcus, just a few weeks younger than my twins, then moved on to quiz her on her job and mother.

She loved her job, she said. She was promised a partnership within five years. Yes, she was still living with her mother, Magna, a bitch with a capital B. My words, not hers. Troy Kern had moved out a while ago; I don't know how he lasted as long as he had. It would have been my worst nightmare.

After a while, perhaps as much as fifteen to twenty minutes of me not contributing a solitary word, Adriana turned to me. "Tell me about your new homicide."

Tamika leaned in close to her. "This isn't public info, but she was drowned in her pool, moved, and staged in her bed. Chances are the killer thought we'd think she died of natural causes and not do an autopsy."

"Which frequently happens because many families don't want the expense," Adriana said and looked to me to add to the conversation, which I didn't.

Tamika continued to speak softly. "Yeah, you know the Kenwood shooting? It was our victim's daughter."

Adriana's eyes grew large. "What?"

Tamika nodded.

Jamie brought the wine, uncorked it, and began pouring. I gave Tamika the eye. Jamie filled her wineglass.

"I'm just going to have a tiny bit." she said, wiggling her arms in excitement.

Right. She downed it like water and refilled it. The more Tamika drank the more talkative she became, and that night was no exception. She talk-talk-talked through dinner. I just wanted her to shut up. When Adriana had eaten half her meal, she got up and said, "Excuse me, I have to use the restroom."

After she was out of earshot I said, "Tamika, cool it on the wine. You're running at the mouth—and you can't go to an interview inebriated."

She shot me a dirty look, then stood. "I have to use the ladies, too."

They were gone long enough that I considered leaving. When the women returned, Tamika, tossing me a defiant look, poured herself another glass of wine. Adriana was still nursing her first. The tension was palpable as we finished our dinner in complete silence. Adriana, not one to enjoy conflict, turned and questioned me about the twins. I answered succinctly.

Tamika topped Adriana's wineglass, then finished off the bottle when refilling her own. There was no way I could take her along on the interview, and I didn't want an argument or have to physically remove her from the car at the hotel—mainly because it would be difficult and embarrassing.

I looked at my watch. "We have an interview in Wayzata at eight. We should be getting on our way."

"I have to use the ladies first." She walked off in the wrong direction, looked around in a confused state, then turned around.

"They must have moved the restroom," I said as she sashayed by.

"Humph," she said.

Adriana looked at me. "She's tipsy. She can't go on an interview like that."

"I told you not to order a bottle."

"I'm sorry. I should have known better. Why don't you go, and I'll drop her off at the hotel."

I thought about that for all of a split second and said, "Thanks. That solves my problem."

I handed her more than enough cash to pay for the three dinners. She threw forty dollars back at me, and I left hoping Tamika wouldn't come screaming down the sidewalk after me.

I plugged in Gary Williams's address and followed the GPS instructions via Penn, to Highway 62, to 494, then Highway 12 to Wayzata. I was routed through the quaint city itself, bustling with traffic at 7:00 p.m., down Lake Street where there were several restaurants, any of which we could have chosen for our meal and saved the bloody disaster that dinner became.

Although I was over an hour early for the appointment, I continued on. The GPS led me down Ferndale, a street of multi-million dollar estates, and around a curve where the voice announced my destination had been reached. I turned onto the first road, which branched into three driveways. I decided to double back to Wayzata to kill time.

I parked in a free ramp then walked on down to Lake Street, which was lively with pedestrians. Christmas decorations hung on all the lampposts along the street, creating a festive atmosphere. I stopped at Talbots and bought a soft, yellow sweater for Shannon for Christmas from the Twinks, then I meandered down the sidewalk until I spotted a Caribou Coffee. I bought a cup and found a window table.

A couple with three-year-old triplet girls walked into the shop. They were dressed to the nines in little wool coats and matching hats. I immediately phoned Clara to check in.

"Things are just fine, Cal."

"Who's crying?"

"Henry. He's just tired. We spent a good amount of time outdoors today. I took them on a sled ride, and we built a snowman and a little fort."

"Clara, you're the best."

"They had fun. Now they're tired and crabby."

"Sorry I'm not there to help."

"That's why you're paying me."

AT 7:55 P.M., I WAS at the GPS dumping point. I phoned Williams, and he directed me to take the middle drive.

The large, light-green house had two wings off from the central two-story structure. I muted my phone, grabbed my briefcase, then walked between the evergreen shrubs lining the sidewalk up to the house. When I pressed the doorbell, a gong sounded and a dog began yipping. A man with fading good looks and a paunch opened the door holding a little white mop of a dog who continued barking. Frankly, I found it amusing to see big men with tiny dogs.

"No, Corky," he said, shoving his index finger in the dog's face. The dog looked up at his owner and growled.

"Mr. Williams? Detective Cal Sheehan." I showed him my badge to prove I could ask him invasive questions.

The man nodded. "Gary Williams. Come in." He held the dog tightly with his left hand while he extended his right. "He won't hurt you."

"Just sounds mean, huh? What breed is he?"

"Maltese. Do you have a dog?"

"A yellow lab."

"Figures," he said.

I didn't ask what he meant because I didn't care.

An island of long, dark, sparse hair topped Gary's large head. His tanned, broad face made his dark eyes look even smaller. Dog hair clung to his black slacks and the cashmere V-neck sweater he wore without an undershirt.

I followed him through a foyer directly into a living room filled with exotic, large, chunky art pieces. Like a scene in a bad movie, a bearskin rug lay before the large brick fireplace.

"Hello," said an attractive woman sitting on the sofa. "I'm Charity."

"Hello, Charity," I said and smiled.

"Drink?" he asked as he made his way to a portable bar.

"Just water, thanks."

He filled a glass with ice and poured water from a pitcher. He handed it to me, then took another glass and poured three fingers of an amber liquid, then a bit more.

I took a seat in a chair across from Charity, who wore a long white dress with a plunging neckline and slit up one side of the skirt revealing a long, shapely leg. She looked to be in her late twenties or early thirties, which was considerably younger than Gary's fifty-three years. But money was an aphrodisiac to some, and I guessed that was why she was with an aging fat man with minimal hair.

Gary, standing by the sofa, caught me admiring Charity. "Isn't she lovely?" he said. He sat next to her and gave her a kiss.

"Yes."

"Are you sure I can't get you something stronger? Charity, get him a glass of champagne, will you, love?"

She started to rise.

I put a hand up in protest. "No, thanks. Water's fine."

She sat back down.

"I'm assuming the detective would like to speak to me privately. Am I right, Detective?" Williams asked.

"It's up to you, sir."

He leaned over to whisper in Charity's ear loud enough for me to hear: "Be a good girl and go watch dirty movies and get yourself nice and wet for me."

Classy guy. Charity's eyes met mine, and her face turned scarlet. She grabbed a wine glass and an open bottle of red sitting on the small silver cart. "It was nice meeting you, Detective Sheehan," she said sweetly.

"On second thought, stay."

She returned. I pulled out my iPad, propped it on the marble coffee table top, turned it on, then adjusted the location so I had a good angle on the couple.

"You're recording this?"

"Yes, sir."

Gary took the Maltese off his lap and placed it next to him, brushed off dog hair, then ran his fingers through his wisps of hair.

"If you're ready, I'll press play."

He brought his arms around and folded his hands on his lap, then nodded. I had pressed the red button minutes ago and recorded all the preening. I gave the case number, date, place, and stated who I was interviewing, where, and why.

"Mr. Williams, I understand Sonya Donovan is your cousin?"

"Yes, our mothers were sisters."

"How often did you see her?"

"Not very often. I believe the last time was two years ago at my Aunt Violet's funeral. That's Sonya's mother."

"Did you have any contact with her after that?"

"There wasn't much interest on either of our parts. I didn't see the point."

"Did you know of any conflicts or problems she had with anyone?"

"Sonya had a conflict with everyone she met."

"Oh?"

"She had a tendency to make people feel they were disappointing her."

"You as well?"

"I didn't let her get to me, but my mother did. Okay, I lied earlier. I saw her once, about three months after Aunt Violet's funeral. My mother wanted me to arrange a lunch with Sonya. So I agreed. Well, it was a disaster. Mother came away so upset I told her she never had to see her again."

"What happened?"

"Sonya told my mother she hadn't helped Aunt Violet enough. You see, Violet got herself knocked up right out of high school, then expected my folks to support her. Mom said it was like a bottomless pit. She was constantly coming to them for money. They finally cut her off. Sonya said they had to go on welfare. Well, my parents never knew that, and it wouldn't have made a difference if they had. People make choices. Hers was to get pregnant and not get married."

"What about Sonya's father?"

"Mother said she doubted Violet knew his name. She was running wild in those days. Sonya was a product of a one-night stand."

"Where were you last Thursday and Friday, December eleventh and twelfth?"

A look of concern spread across his face. "Here. Why?"

"Alone?"

"No. Charity was with me." His eyes narrowed, then looked at Charity.

"We were home," she said.

"Should I call my attorney?" Gary asked.

I shrugged. "If you feel it necessary."

"Well, if you're insinuating I killed Sonya, you're wrong. Why would I?"

"She's a wealthy woman. You may have believed you're in line to inherit."

"Look at me." He made large swooping gestures with his arms. "I don't need—or want—her money."

"Charity, what is your full name?"

"Charity Ann Vosika."

"You work for Mr. Williams?"

She giggled. "No, I'm his girlfriend. I live here."

He patted her knee. She smiled at him.

"For how long?" I asked.

"Almost a year."

"Where were you last Thursday and Friday?"

"I was home, except for the two hours I went shopping at Ridgedale on Friday afternoon."

"What about Gary?"

"He went to work during the day, but we were home together both evenings."

"Had you met Sonya Donovan?"

"No."

"Do you have any information that could lead me to Sonya Donovan's killer?"

She shook her head. "No, sir."

"Okay, that's all I have for you both now, but Minneapolis Detectives Ryan and Gill may have questions for you later."

The sleeping Maltese didn't stir from the couch as Gary Williams led me to the door.

"Detective, I didn't particularly like Sonya, but I respected what she'd accomplished. Good luck finding her killer."

11

I HAD FIVE PHONE MESSAGES. None were from Tamika.
Adriana sent me one: "I got Tamika back to the hotel safely. She didn't
seem upset you'd left without her. It was good seeing you, Cal, although
Tamika mentioned you weren't thrilled to see me. I get it. Maybe it's better
that way."

I knew Tamika was sloshed, but it pissed me off she said something to Adriana. Then again, they were close friends—what did I expect? An unexpected wave of relief passed over me when I realized I didn't have to worry about Adriana calling and screwing things up with Dallas like she did with Shannon.

One message was from Detective William Ryan. He said, "I'm interviewing witnesses in the Kenwood case, and you're welcome to come down this evening and sit in."

I left a message telling him I'd be down ASAP.

Patrice had left three messages, each one increasing in curtness. I called back, and she answered on the first ring.

"Hey, Patrice, sorry I couldn't get back to you sooner. I was interviewing."

"Did you see Zabrina?"

"Yes. She was too sleepy to talk, so we're going back tomorrow morning."

"Did MPD post a guard outside her door?"

"Yes, and we had to show our ID to even get her room number."

"Good. I'm coming down tomorrow. I'm executor of Sonya and Justine's wills, and they're being read at the same meeting."

"The doctor said it was okay?"

"I'm fine. I just fainted, no concussion. Where are you and Tamika staying?"

"At the La Quinta on 394, but I'm hoping we'll be finished up here by tomorrow. I'm going down to MPD right now to co-interview witnesses."

"Pulling an all-nighter?"

"If that's what it takes."

"Isn't Tamika with you?"

"Oh . . . she's not feeling well."

"Flu? It's going around."

"I'm not sure what she has."

"Call me tomorrow morning. I'll be up early."

I would make it very clear to Tamika that I covered for her for the first and last time.

The traffic was lighter this time of night as I made my way on 394 to the downtown Minneapolis Police Department on South Fifth Street. I showed my badge and asked for Ryan. The officer at the desk said Ryan was expecting me. He had me sign in, gave me a visitor's pass, then had me wait for someone to come and fetch me.

It wasn't long before a woman somewhere in her forties approached me. She was wearing tan wool pants, a white button-down shirt and a navy blazer; her badge hung from a lanyard.

"Cal Sheehan?" she asked.

"Yes," I said, extending my hand.

"Martha Gill. I'm Will Ryan's partner."

"Thanks for including me in the interviews."

"Sure."

As we walked down a long hallway, she said, "Right now Will's talking to Thomas Falcon, the business manager for Donovan Enterprises. You can observe. Then when Will's done, feel free to step into the room to ask questions."

We went through a security point, then down a long hall through a large common room, and into an observation room. Gill directed me to a folding chair, then sat next to me. Ryan's back was to the camera.

Thomas Falcon was younger than I expected. His curly, dark hair framed his round face. He was saying Justine was Sonya's executive secretary and publicist. "I only know what she told me. I think the guy's last name was Fischer. In any event, he harassed Sonya with threatening emails and tweets. Justine blocked him."

"What was the context of his communication?"

"He called her vulgar names. The mildest insult was she was a piranha feeding her bank account on other people's pain. He made it clear she ruined his life."

"Did he say why?"

"Sonya and her guest had told his wife to leave him because he was abusive. It's what they did. Judge a relationship. The show was called *Love 'Em or Leave 'Em*."

"Did Justine ever personally interact with Fischer?"

"No. She reported him to the police, and they suggested she contact her Internet provider and have his emails blocked, which, as I said, she did."

"Okay. Hang here a minute," Ryan said. He walked out of the room and came around into the observation room.

He said to Martha Gill, "Have Cyrus Fischer picked up."

Then he turned to me and extended his hand. "You must be Cal Sheehan."

"Yes, nice to meet you, and thank you for inviting me in."

"No problem. I'm done with the business manager if you want to interview him. His name is Thomas Falcon."

"He's the money-handler?"

"Yes."

Falcon's overly applied aftershave did little to mask the stale odor of the room. I introduced myself as the investigator on Ms. Donovan's murder case, not only for Falcon, but for the record.

He nodded.

"I understand you're Sonya Donovan's business manager."

"Yes."

"For the Dexter Lake household as well?"

"Yes."

"Any expenditures out of the ordinary lately?"

"No."

"No blackmail payments or such?"

He smiled. "No."

"You paid Della and Marvin Moore for their services at the Dexter Lake household?"

"Yes, but there's something you should know about them."

"What's that?"

"They were using her debit card for their own purposes."

Whoa. "Did Sonya know?"

"Yes. All the extra charges were made at Save-Rite in Prairie Falls, and she said as long as it was spent on groceries to let it go because they were using it to feed their family. It was her charity case."

"How long was this going on?"

"About six months after they started working for her I noticed the debits were larger."

"How would you have known?"

"Because Sonya was an organized person. She had grocery lists prepared, and we knew about how much each list should cost. They got increasingly bold—charging groceries for a time she wasn't even there, buying things at the hardware store she wouldn't have needed. They probably thought I'd never figure it out."

"When I interviewed them, they expressed concern about not being paid for the services they performed recently."

"Ha! That's rich. I'll pay them off, but I'm also going to inform them she knew they were stealing from her."

"Good for you. You mentioned the stalker to Detective Ryan. Are the shows archived?"

"We have audio recordings. She had me make copies of most contentious broadcasts for her next book. Fischer's wife's call was one."

"Do you remember the date she called in?"

"Maybe early June, and I believe the emails started shortly after."

"Were his the only negative emails she received?"

"No, but his were threatening."

"Did Sonya use social media? Facebook? Twitter? Instagram?"

"Abbie Brotherton handled all social media accounts. Most posts from listeners were positive. Of course, there are always the Internet trolls who make it their job to post hateful comments to incite other haters to post. Abbie would block those ASAP."

"What was your relationship with Sonya?"

"We got along very well. Of course, I always did what she wanted me to." His brow lifted as he tossed me a half smile.

"I'd like to speak to the studio crew."

"They're coming in tomorrow before noon to pick up their final checks before we close up the studio. That might be a good time."

"Okay, thanks. Do you know of anything else that might help me in finding her killers?"

"Killers? As in more than one?"

"We don't know who all is involved."

"I wish I could help, but I can't imagine who would do this."

I thanked him and handed him my card.

When I returned to the observation room, Ryan said, "Time for a break." Gill and I followed him to their office. He brought over an extra chair and poured a cup of coffee in a Styrofoam cup and handed it to me. I took a sip and had to suppress a shudder. I'd become a coffee snob.

When we were seated around a table, he asked, "Do you have anything to share with us?"

"I've interviewed four people: Della and Marvin Moore, her employees at the Dexter Lake house of whom Thomas Falcon spoke; and Gary Williams, Ms. Donovan's only cousin, and his live-in girlfriend, Charity Ann Vosika, from Wayzata."

"What are your thoughts?"

"Mrs. Moore was nervous, and her husband is odd. He was trying too hard. Did you hear Thomas Falcon say they were using Sonya's debit card for their personal use?"

"Yes."

"They're having financial difficulties and are in arrears on their property taxes and water bill."

Gill pinched her face. "From what I heard, Ms. Donovan was kind of a tough cookie, so it's surprising she let them get by with the theft."

"I guess she had a softer side."

"What was the cousin like?"

"Do you want to see the interview? It's not that long." I pulled the iPad from my backpack and turned on the video.

As it was playing, Gill interjected, "He's a bit of a prick."

I nodded. When the recording was completed, Ryan said, "Do you think he's responsible for Sonya's death?"

I shrugged. "Charity Vosika gave him an alibi."

"We also need to speak to Sabrina Bennett."

"It's Zabrina with a 'Z.' I'm not sure you know Sheriff Clinton is a personal friend of the family—the girl's godmother. I think she'll want to be present when you speak with her."

"That explains her strong request to station a guard outside her door."

"She'll be down tomorrow. She's executor, and there's a lot for her to do."

"I'm sure. The sheriff expressed her belief that she feared for Zabrina's life— that someone could be trying to execute the whole family. What's your take?"

"I think the deaths are connected," I said.

Gill cocked her head. "Would the cousin have motive? If he takes out the whole family, is he in line to inherit?"

"Not necessarily. Sonya had estranged step-children who were teenagers when their father left the family for twenty-year-old Sonya."

Ryan screwed up his nose. "Forty years later they seek revenge?"

"When you put it that way, it does sound wacky," I said.

"But you never know. They should be questioned, Will," Gill said.

Ryan tapped the eraser end of the pencil on the table top. "Okay."

"What about the stalker that Falcon talked about?" I said.

"Cyrus Fischer," Ryan said. "It's a good lead."

I copied the name down in my notebook. They then shared the recordings of the earlier interviews with the Logan household employees: John and Erica Anderson and Sarah Crosby. John Anderson served as the live-in groundskeeper; his wife was the housekeeper. She also served meals. The Andersons lived in the basement suite of the mansion. Other than hearing the shots and calling 911, they knew little, or so they said.

Sarah Crosby, the household chef, was off duty and not present at the residence at the time of Justine's shooting. She had not expected Justine and Zabrina to return until the next day. She lived in an apartment in Uptown and arrived by six o'clock each morning and stayed until after the dinner dishes were washed and put away. She also claimed she knew nothing.

Ryan lifted a hand to his temple. "I doubt any of their Minneapolis employees are responsible." He yawned, setting us all off.

"I agree," I said.

"Are we picking up Fischer tonight?" Martha asked.

"First thing tomorrow morning. My pillow is calling," Ryan said.

"Coming back tomorrow?" Martha asked me.

"If I may."

"Of course," Martha said, with a lingering smile.

12

Thursday, December 18

I WAS SHOWERED AND DRESSED and searching for coffee in the lobby at 6:30 a.m. Tamika sat at a table reading the *Star Tribune*. I poured a cup and took a seat directly across from her, waiting for the shit storm.

She handed me the front page. "The Logan shootings are in the paper." I skimmed the brief article. They didn't have many details, including names.

"We're meeting Patrice at the hospital this morning," she said.

"When did you talk to her?"

"An hour ago. She woke *me* up because she couldn't get hold of *you*."

I pulled out my phone to check for recent calls. "She called at 5:45 a.m. I must have been in the shower."

"It takes you almost an hour to get ready?"

"I watched *Dog the Bounty Hunter* in between."

She scowled as she pretended to read the paper. "So what did you tell Patrice last night?"

"Nothing. Why?"

She slapped the paper on the table and looked at me with her mean-girl face. "Because," she sputtered, "she asked me how I was *feeling*." She leaned back in her chair, crossed a leg, and glared at me. "I repeat. What did you tell her?"

"I said you weren't feeling well."

"Why would you say that?"

"Because you weren't with me at Minneapolis PD last night."

"Well, shit!" she said too loudly, capturing the attention of the family nearest us, their faces registering disgust at such language. "How did she know I wasn't with you?"

I sat forward and spoke softly. "Because I inadvertently told her 'I' was interviewing. Don't worry, I didn't tell her you got drunk before the interview."

"I wasn't *drunk*."

I shook my head. "You were tipsy. You drank four-fifths of a bottle of wine by yourself."

"I was fine."

I leaned in. "Don't be an ass about this, Tamika. Just admit you screwed up, and we'll be done with it."

Her eyes narrowed. "You just left me at the restaurant without discussing it with me. That was rude."

"Adriana was the one who said you couldn't go on the interview. She volunteered to drive you to the hotel. Does that give you a clue as to your sobriety?"

"She said *you* asked *her* to take me back to the hotel."

"That's not how it went down. Whatever, I just need you to know I won't cover for your drinking again. If you have a problem, you need to address it."

"I don't *have* a problem. Look, I was stuck at home for six whole weeks, and I was celebrating getting out. You know what? You're a self-righteous asshole like Shannon says. Why Adriana thinks you're perfect is beyond me."

The parents of the family gave us dirty looks and left.

"Adriana thinks I'm perfect?"

"Oh, that's what you heard? Not the biggest self-righteous asshole part?"

"Tamika, stop trying to make me the bad guy."

She sighed deeply. "Okay. So shoot me. I was having a good time with a friend. Okay, okay, I admit I should have stopped after one drink. Feel better?"

"Yes, but *none* would have been better. And don't you fucking set me up like that again. I didn't appreciate it."

"Sorry. My bad. But honestly, I thought you'd thank me for arranging to have dinner with Adriana."

I shook my head in disbelief. "I'm with Dallas, and you don't seem to get that Adriana and I are over. I have no desire to see her again."

She nodded. "Yeah, she didn't have fun, either."

Grimacing, I said, "I'm hungry. Want to eat here?"

"The guy at the desk said there's a good breakfast place not far from here called the Good Day Café. It's on the way to the hospital."

"Adriana's not showing up, is she?"

"No." Only she pronounced it "No-ah"—like the word had two syllables.

AFTER WE BOTH ORDERED IGGY'S fried egg sandwiches, and I had a half a cup of good coffee in me, I said, "Shannon thinks I'm a self-righteous asshole?"

"Okay, I added the 'asshole' part. And to clarify, Adriana said you'd be perfect if you were a city boy, which you're definitely not."

I could only shake my head and smile. Tamika's too honest sometimes.

Before our food arrived, I was able to reach Kent Donovan, Sonya's "stepson." We were to meet him in his office in the Medical Arts Building on Nicollet Mall and Ninth Street at eleven o'clock. He said he'd ask his sister, Natalie, to join us.

ABOUT 8:00 A.M., WE WERE walking down the hospital corridor to Zabrina's room.

"Uh-oh. Why's the guard gone?" Tamika said.

I had a bad feeling about this. When I pushed through the door and found the room empty, I immediately called Patrice.

"Zabrina's not in her room."

"No, they released her. She's here at the Logan house."

"A phone call would have been nice. We drove all the way to Abbott."

"I expected you to check in with me this morning."

"You spoke with Tamika. Why wasn't that enough?"

"I wanted to talk to you, but you didn't answer your phone."

"I was in the shower. Anyway, we're on the way."

When I hung up, Tamika patted me on the back. "Sheehan, I'm proud of you for standing up to her. Reverse the situation and we'd have hell to pave."

"It's hell to *pay*."

"Don't be silly—it's pave. Hell would be hot to pave. Get it?"

"You're getting it confused with 'the road to hell is paved with good intentions.'"

Tamika remained silent for one whole block. "Sheehan, I shouldn't have told you what Adriana and Shannon told me in confidence. We women complain about our men even though we love them to death. It's a sisterhood thing."

"That's been abundantly clear to me since I was a small boy."

She patted me on the back again.

I said, "Love them to death. Does that mean *until* death? Or so much you'd like to kill us?"

"Mmm . . . maybe both. I'm going to buy you a book on idioms for your birthday."

"Hell to pay. Look it up."

She clicked on her phone for a minute, then put it away and gave me a dirty look. "You may be right this once."

I nodded. "Elvis has left the building."

She looked the phrase up on her phone. "'The event has ended.' What event?"

"This discussion."

I PULLED UP TO THE SPANISH MISSION–style home on Logan Avenue across from a park in Kenwood, an affluent Minneapolis neighborhood of beautiful old homes, and parked behind a dark sedan on the street. A few feet of crime scene tape lying by the driveway was all that remained as evidence of the shootings—no strangers sitting in parked vehicles watching the house, or cars with bad mufflers driving by.

When a woman opened the front door, I recognized her as Erica Anderson from the interview film. "You must be Sheriff Clinton's deputies," she said. "Follow me."

Tamika muttered, "Sheriff Clinton's deputies?"

I shrugged and followed the housekeeper through the expansive foyer, past a formal living room, and up the grand staircase. We moved by a living room, a small kitchen, a den, and two spacious bedrooms. The second floor was set up as an apartment.

Zabrina's room was at the end of the hallway. She was propped up in bed, her left arm in a sling resting on a pillow. Patrice, in full uniform, sat on an armchair to her right. Gill and Ryan stood on opposite sides of the bed. They nodded a greeting as Tamika and I moved in. I introduced Tamika.

Patrice said, "To recap what Zabrina told the detectives this morning— she heard the car's muffler approach, but can't identify the vehicle or the shooter."

"Zabrina, which direction was the vehicle moving? North or south?" Ryan asked.

"I don't know."

"North toward Mount Curve or south toward Franklin?" he asked.

"Franklin."

"Then the driver or a backseat passenger could have taken the shots," I said.

"Yes," Ryan said.

Zabrina started sniffling, which quickly turned into a full wail. Tamika blinked, her cheek muscles tightened; obviously she was trying not to laugh. Gill and Ryan were eyeing each other, scratching cheeks, clearing their throats, running hands through their hair. Patrice patted Zabrina's hand, and said, "She's exhausted. She didn't get much sleep in the hospital."

Zabrina sniffed and wound it down fairly quickly.

"Are you up for some questions?" I asked.

She nodded, sniffed again.

"Do you live here full time, Zabrina?"

"I live on campus."

"I'll summarize what she's already told the detectives," Patrice said. "She goes to Hamline, where she's been living on campus since August and, on average, comes home a weekend a month. She usually brings friends."

"Were you aware of any problems your mom and grandmother had with anyone?"

"She's already answered that, also," Patrice said. "And no, she wasn't."

There were a few moments of uncomfortable silence before Gill said, "Well, we're going to let you rest, Zabrina. We'll leave our cards in case you remember something later."

They both pulled the cards and placed them on the bedside table. As Martha passed by me, she rolled her eyes. I followed the detectives down the stairs.

In the foyer, Ryan said, "We're hoping ballistics will help us out. Too bad she didn't see the shooter."

"It's unfortunate," I said.

Gill crossed her arms and leaned in. "Boy, your boss is something. You might try to interview the girl when she's not around."

"Do you think she knows more?" I asked.

"Not necessarily, but wow. How is she to work for?"

"Good, although she sometimes micromanages a bit."

"A bit?" Martha said.

Ryan said, "Ms. Donovan's cousin and his girlfriend are coming in at nine thirty. You're welcome to join the party."

"Thanks. What about Fischer?"

"We're still trying to locate him," Martha said. "We should have picked him up last night."

"Wouldn't have made a difference," Ryan said.

Martha rolled her eyes.

I went back upstairs. Tamika and Patrice were sitting in the living room.

"We're letting her rest," Patrice said.

"How long are you staying in Minneapolis?" I asked.

"I'm not sure. The wills are both being read tomorrow morning. I'm executor, but the attorney will do most of it. David thinks we ought to put both houses on the market as soon as possible, put the proceeds in a trust, and when Zabrina's older she can buy a condo or whatever she wants."

"She'll be without a home?" Tamika said.

"My home will be hers now. I think she should take spring semester off and come and stay with me."

"That's a lot of change for her," Tamika said. "She's grieving. Maybe going to class and keeping busy would do her good."

Made sense to me.

Heavy, quick steps up the staircase had all of us sitting up straighter. A figure wearing a black jacket with the hood up strode past us.

Patrice stood. "Stop!" All our hands shot to our holsters.

The individual stopped and walked backwards, glancing into the living room. He pulled off his hood, then smiled. He was a tall, slim kid, light hair down to his shoulders.

"Oh, it's you, Grady."

"Hi, Mrs. Clinton. Zabrina's waiting for me."

"First, come meet my deputies, Cal Sheehan and Tamika Frank. This is Zabrina's boyfriend, Grady LaMere."

"Nice meeting you," he said as he extended his hand. Firm handshake. Nice looking kid.

"They're investigating Zabrina's grandmother's death," Patrice said.

"Oh, that whole deal was freaking weird." He pointed toward Zabrina's bedroom and started to edge his way out. "Well, she's waiting for me."

"She's sleeping," Patrice said.

"She just texted me saying to come straight up."

"Oh, well . . . go on, but keep it short, dear. She needs to rest."

The kid smiled, nodded, and slipped back into the hallway.

"Nice boy. Justine liked him a lot."

"How long have they been dating?" Tamika asked.

"Since last summer. He goes to the U. He's studying to be a veterinarian . . . like your girlfriend." She nodded in my direction.

She got up and headed toward Zabrina's bedroom.

Tamika leaned in and said, "Patrice needs to chill out. That girl needs her boyfriend right now."

"This afternoon I'd like to talk to him and her friends. The murders have to be connected, so anything to do with the Logan case has to do with ours."

"That's how we justify questioning them."

"You got it."

Grady came back down the hall, waved as he passed by, and then headed down the stairs. I jumped up to follow him. Tamika was at my heels.

"Hey, Grady, do you have a minute?"

"I have class. I needed to stop and see for myself she was okay."

"I only need a minute."

He looked at his watch. "Yeah, okay."

Tamika said, "Do you really have class, or did Sheriff Clinton kick you out?"

He snuffled a laugh. "Well, both, but's it's all cool. She said I should come back later."

"You know Zabrina better than we do. How do you think she's doing?" Tamika asked.

"She took the bullet in the arm, but I guess she should have full use of it when it heals. It could have been way worse"

"And emotionally?" I asked.

He twisted his face into a grimace. "She's having a hard time. Who wouldn't if your family is wiped out?"

"True," I said. "How did you and Zabrina meet?"

"At Lake Calhoun beach last summer. We talked all afternoon, had a date that night, and we've been together since."

"When did you realize she was from a wealthy family?"

He blushed. "She hid it from me for a good month. We always met somewhere else. Then when she asked me to come to dinner here to meet her mom and grandmother, I was blown away. I had no idea her grandmother was famous."

"Did she indicate to you any problems her family was having?"

"No man, things were cool until . . . *boom*. Man, it's too crazy."

"Who are her closet friends?"

"Her roommate and a couple other girls at school."

"What are their names?"

"Autumn is her roommate. She went to high school with her. Molly and Sophie live on her floor. I don't know their last names. I've met a few others, but I don't think they're that close."

"You wouldn't have their phone numbers?"

"No, but I can get them from Zabrina."

"That'd be terrific."

He started to text and seconds later he looked up at me and said, "She asked why I wanted to know."

"So you can report to them how she's doing," I said.

He nodded, texted, and then began reciting phone numbers. I copied them in my notebook.

"Thanks. And your address and phone number for our records?"

He gave us his information, and then I asked, "So what's your hometown?"

"Minneapolis."

"Were you with Zabrina when she found out about her grandmother's death?"

"Um, yeah. We were at my place when her mom called."

"When was this?"

"Friday evening. I'm not sure of the exact time. Zabrina wanted to drive up to be with her mom but . . . well . . . we'd been drinking, so I talked her into waiting until the next day. Look, I should go. I don't want to be late for my final."

"Sure, go ahead," I said.

After he left, Tamika said, "He seems like a sweetie."

"Yeah, nice kid."

13

GARY WILLIAMS BROUGHT his attorney with him to the interview. Ryan and Gill interviewed Charity Vosika and Williams separately. The night of the Minneapolis shootings, they had entertained a party of twenty from seven o'clock to midnight—an alibi easily checked, therefore, I doubted they'd lie about it. He was off the hook for Justine's murder, unless he'd ordered a hit. But my gut told me he didn't kill his cousin or her daughter for their money. As he himself pointed out, he was a wealthy man.

After the interviews concluded, Tamika and I were chatting with Martha in her office when I brought up our conversation with Grady LaMere.

"I'd like to speak to him, as well," she said.

"We have some of Zabrina's friends' phone numbers, too." I took out my notebook and shared the information.

Gill leaned back in her chair and said, "How about I arrange a meeting with the friends for this afternoon after your interviews with Sonya's estranged stepchildren. If I can get something set up, I'll text you."

"Sounds like a plan."

AT 10:30 A.M., TAMIKA AND I PARKED in a ten-buck parking lot three blocks from Dr. Donovan's office building. According to the board in the lobby, his office was on the third floor, one he shared with other dentists.

We entered the reception area and approached the counter decorated with a plastic wreath. An instrumental version of "Deck the Halls" filled the room. A sparsely decorated artificial tree had been placed in the far corner.

The receptionist, Granny Clampett's doppelgänger, greeted us. "Can I help you?" she asked, her smile revealing perfect, white teeth too large for her mouth—implants or dentures.

"Detectives Cal Sheehan and Tamika Frank to see Kent Donovan," I said.

She looked at her watch. "*Doctor* Donovan is with a patient. Have a seat." She pointed to the waiting area. Her smile faded; the friendliness vanished.

I gave her my sweetest smile and said, "Thank you so kindly." She pointed again. As we moved away from the counter, I raised my eyebrows at Tamika, and she let out a tiny giggle.

Four adults and two children took up the seating in the corner where the tree had been placed, so Tamika and I sat on vacant chairs under the large window. I soon realized why no one chose those seats. Cold seeped through the windows like an open door.

Tamika zipped up her jacket farther, then blew into the air.

"What are you doing?"

"Checking to see if I can see my breath."

"Guess not," I said.

She hiked her shoulders, then picked up a *People* magazine and started flipping through pages. I stared at the ugly tree. *I suppose I should get one on the way home,* I thought.

Tamika shoved the magazine in front of my face, showing me unflattering photos of celebrities in bathing suits. She found this way too amusing. She giggled as she kept flashing me pictures. I don't know why—maybe it was a combination of Tamika's enjoyment of the photos and the icy greeting we received at reception—but I started laughing. When we got looks from the other patients and Granny Clampett, whose head was barely visible behind the counter, I whispered to Tamika, "Stop showing me that shit."

I grabbed a *Business Weekly* to get my mind focused on something else, but I wasn't interested in the articles and our giggles kept bobbing to the surface.

As patients were called, more entered to take their places.

Tamika nudged me. "It's now quarter past eleven. Want me to give the gray-hair some grief?"

"Granny Clampett?"

She giggled. "I was trying to think who she reminded me of."

"She probably isn't controlling the situation, but if it makes you feel better, go ahead and ask."

Tamika stood, strutted over to the desk, leaned on the counter, and said, "How long is Doctor Donovan going to keep the police waiting? We have important things to attend to."

"He had an emergency, and I also believe he is waiting for his attorney to arrive, so I would advise you to be patient."

"And I'd advise you to—"

"Tamika," I said.

She turned to give me a dirty look, then turned back to the woman to say, "We don't have all day. Hurry him up."

I didn't hear the woman's response.

Tamika returned in a huff.

"What did she say?"

"She said she understood, or something similar."

"What did she *really* say?"

"Nothing. She pointed to our window."

"I don't think you push Granny around."

"Geez, she really looks like her."

"Shh. Here's another *People* magazine for you to look at."

At 11:20, a woman wearing a long, sable fur coat rushed in and stopped at the desk, then disappeared down the hallway. Shortly after, a man wearing a black wool coat and carrying a black leather briefcase did the same. We waited another ten more minutes before Granny stood and said in an exaggerated manner, "The doctor will see you now."

Tamika glanced at me, her mouth turned up into a grin.

"Don't," I said. "And if you laugh in there, I will shoot you in the foot. I mean it this time."

She said, "Sure, Sheehan. You're a real badass, shooting people's feet off all the time. Don't worry. I'll think of diarrhea poop in toilets."

"Oh. My. God." I shook my head in disgust.

We followed Granny to the end of the hallway and into a conference room where three people were seated at a table: a man with a deep tan dressed in a white dentist's coat, the woman in the fur, and the man in the black coat, who looked a tad like George Clooney.

The men stood to shake hands with us. Clooney said, "I'm James Sinclair, Dr. Donovan and Mrs. Freeman's attorney." He pointed to his clients as if we wouldn't spot them without his help. Justine was clearly from the same bloodline as the Donovans, with their pinched, pointy noses, small chins, and high foreheads.

"Detective Cal Sheehan, and this is my partner—"

"Detective Tamika Frank." She blinked at me. I'd upped her status at the hospital, so why not now?

We took chairs side by side across from Dr. Donovan and his sister. Sinclair sat to our right. Sinclair had "successful attorney" written all over him: expensive suit and tie, dark hair graying at the temples, styled perfectly, confidence. He was sitting sideways in his chair, so he could cross a leg and face us.

He said, "We are extremely curious why you called this meeting."

"We're investigating the murder of Sonya Donovan." Gesturing to the Donovan siblings, I added, "Dr. Donovan and Mrs. Freeman's step-mother."

"What does her death have to do with either of my clients? They haven't seen her in thirty years."

"No contact at all?" I asked.

"None," the attorney said.

"Do you mind if they answer for themselves?" I asked.

The three exchanged glances, Sinclair lifting a brow, which I interpreted as a warning.

"I can speak for myself," Dr. Donovan said.

Mrs. Freeman nodded. "Me too, Jim."

Sinclair lifted his hands in resignation. I pulled out my iPad and set it on the table, then Tamika and I got out notebooks ready to take notes. I gave the date, time, case number, and who was present in the room. While glaring at us suspiciously, they supplied the information I asked for: full names, home addresses, and phone numbers.

"You want to find Sonya's killer? I'd start by finding out whose home she wrecked recently," Dr. Donovan said.

The attorney frowned and lifted a hand in disapproval.

"Do you hold her responsible for your parents' break-up?" I asked.

"Of course," he said.

Natalie Freeman sat back and crossed her arms across her chest. "Seriously, Kent? My God, Sonya was Katie's age when she married him. Do you think if she fell for an older man she would be at fault? No, you'd say she was seduced."

Donovan sighed. "Nat, don't be ridiculous." He then scowled at me like I was responsible for his sister's opinion. "What do you need from us?"

"Your whereabouts on December eleventh and twelfth."

"Both of us? Or just Kent's?" Natalie said.

Kent gave out a groan of irritation.

"Both," I said.

"Must I, Jim?" Dr. Donovan asked his attorney.

"Like I said, it will eliminate you immediately, and this will end. If you don't cooperate, they can get a warrant and dig into your personal life."

Dr. Donovan's face contorted into a full grimace. "I was in Hawaii."

"At a *convention*," Natalie added, smirking.

"Where did you stay?"

"The Royal Hawaiian in Oahu."

Natalie cleared her throat. "Except there was no convention. He was with a—"

"Elizabeth Wells," Kent said, flashing a look of contempt toward his sister.

"A convention of two," Natalie said. "He's cheating on his wife. Just a chip off the old block."

Kent grunted and looked to Jim Sinclair, who chastised Natalie by touching her arm.

"Natalie, where were you on those two days?"

Her eyes danced with self-satisfaction. "I had a full calendar of meetings and lunches. I can supply phone numbers of people I was with." She took a white leather datebook out of her purse, turned some pages and pushed it across the table toward us. "The numbers are in the back. Feel free to make a copy."

Tamika took the small book and disappeared.

"You seem to harbor antagonism for Sonya, Dr. Donovan," I said.

"He's had years of therapy to get over our father's betrayal," Natalie said. "Worked swell, didn't it?"

"Screw you," Kent said to his sister. She pointed a finger back at him.

"Were you aware of Tuesday's shootings on Logan?" I asked.

"Yes," Sinclair said.

"The woman killed was your step-sister, Justine Donovan. Her daughter was also wounded."

Natalie's mouth dropped open. "Oh, my God."

Dr. Donovan shook his head. "I had nothing to do with any of it. I haven't seen Justine since she was a child."

"You didn't attend your father's funeral?"

"I went," Natalie said, "but left immediately after the service."

"I chose not to attend," Donovan said. "Sonya wanted us out of their lives, and I obliged the bitch."

My, my.

Everyone stared at him. I'd say he was pleased she was dead.

His attorney leaned forward. "Kent, just answer the questions without the commentary." Dealing with a client like Kent Donovan wouldn't be a picnic.

Natalie folded her hands and said, "Kent, you're being unfair. Sonya tried— too hard, I think."

Donovan rolled his eyes.

Tamika returned with the datebook and a few pages of printer copies. She slid the book back to Mrs. Freeman, who picked it up without taking her eyes off her brother.

"Where were you on the evening of Tuesday, the seventeenth?" I asked.

Donovan held his philandering chin up high. "At home with my wife."

"And you, Mrs. Freeman?" I asked.

She paged through the datebook. "My husband and I were at the Ordway."

"I copied that page, too," Tamika said.

Dr. Donovan stood. "Well, enough of this bullshit. I need to get back to my patients. Jim, thanks for rearranging your busy schedule." He shot me a look like I should appreciate his attorney attending the interview.

Sinclair also rose. "No problem . . . and that's what this should be for you— no problem." He turned his gaze on Tamika and me. Donovan left the room.

"Minneapolis PD may also want to question your clients. Separate investigations, you understand," I said to Sinclair.

Sinclair gathered his coat from a rack in the room and said, "I hope you'll pass the information along so we can minimize the process." He also exited, but Natalie remained in her chair.

"Were you through with us?" she asked.

"For now. You and your brother seemed to be at odds," I said.

"Always have been. Kent's always been about Kent. His current wife, Carrie, is aware of his dalliances, by the way. I sometimes wonder if Mom hadn't kicked Daddy out, if Sonya would have just been a brief interlude like Kent's women."

"How many times has he been married?"

"Three, but I'm speaking about his women on the side."

"How do you even know about them?" Tamika asked.

"Carrie confides in me. She has a private investigator practically on payroll. I like her more than my brother, so I've encouraged her to divorce him, but her lifestyle would change too much."

"Why does she bother with a PI if she doesn't do anything about it?" Tamika asked.

"Oh, there's power in the knowing." She turned her head sideways and lifted a brow.

"Do you work outside the home?" Tamika asked.

She smiled. "I volunteer my time to a number of charities."

"What does your husband do?" Tamika asked.

"He's in pharmaceuticals."

"Sells or partakes?" I said.

Natalie cocked her head, studying me. I smiled.

"Oh, you're teasing," she said, breaking into a smile. "He's in sales."

"His name?" I asked.

"Julius Freeman."

"Did you stay in contact with your father while he was living?"

"Somewhat. He managed a visit once or twice a year and phoned every now and then."

"Was Sonya included in those visits?"

"No."

"Did you inherit anything when he died?"

"We each received two million—small potatoes compared to what Daddy was worth."

"Where's your mother now?"

"San Antonio. She has an advanced case of Parkinson's."

"Was she mentioned in his will?"

"No, but she received a generous divorce settlement and invested wisely, so financially she's set. My father had been cheating on her for a long while. I believe once the shock of being dumped had worn off, she was relieved to be out of the marriage."

"Did you ever listen to Sonya's radio show?" Tamika asked.

"No."

"Not even once for curiosity's sake?" Tamika asked.

"No. Look, I don't blame Sonya for my parents' divorce like Kent does, but I disconnected from her when I was young because I never felt her approval."

"Who's Katie, who you referred to earlier?" I asked.

"Kent's daughter—she's nineteen."

"Does Kent have any others?" Tamika asked.

"Just Katie. Carrie didn't have her until she was thirty-nine."

"Do you have children?" Tamika asked.

"No. I never wanted any."

"Thanks for staying . . . and being candid with us," I said.

"I should be on my way to my luncheon."

"Okay, thanks for meeting with us," I said.

As she was about to exit the room, she turned and said, "I've been unfair to my brother. He's actually a good man in most respects, and he certainly wouldn't kill anyone."

TAMIKA AND I PARKED outside of the Logan house and walked to the garage. Thomas Falcon met us wearing a sheepskin vest, a black turtleneck, jeans, and cowboy boots. He showed us up the stairs along the outside of the garage and into the studio. There were four desks just inside the door. A room with a set of double doors was straight ahead with an "ON AIR" light flashing green. Two young ladies, somewhere in their mid-twenties, were sitting together at a table eating doughnuts and drinking coffee. One was petite and brunette, the other had a sturdy frame. Her brown hair was pulled into a top-knot, with spiky strands trying to escape bondage.

Thomas pointed to the girls and said, "Abbie Brotherton and Jordan Larson. We call them the Courageous Crew of Two. Their tasks are many: screeners, social media, research, etc. And Sam is our sound man."

Sam was a lanky kid with a man bun and dark-framed eyeglasses. "Was," he said.

"Yes, sorry . . . *was* our sound man. Detectives, help yourselves to the coffee and doughnuts." He pointed to a small rectangular table up against the wall.

"Not all cops like doughnuts," I said.

"Yes, we do," Tamika said, grabbing one.

"Well, if you insist," I said.

"What's happening with the show?" Tamika asked.

"We're finishing the week by rebroadcasting the best shows as a tribute to Sonya."

"How long were the broadcasts?" I asked.

Thomas leaned against a desk, his legs crossed at the ankles. "Two hours, but a two-hour show extended to five or six hours with the pre-show meeting, rehearsal, the actual broadcast, and then a post-meeting to discuss the next day's show."

"Was her show local or national?"

"National on Sirius XM."

"So Sonya broadcast from right in that room?" Tamika asked, her expression incredulous.

"Yep. Monday through Friday," Thomas said.

"Did Justine work here as well?" I asked.

"She preferred to work in the house. The rest of us worked here in the studio."

Thomas handed me a packet with the guest schedules for the past six months—Justine scheduled the guests at least four to six weeks in advance, he mentioned—and names and phone numbers of every caller who had been aired for the last month, which was as long as they held on to them.

"I found copies of Sonya's radio shows at her home in Dexter," I said. "Any insight for me?"

"Those were the copies of the most contentious shows. She was writing a book."

"Was Cyrus Fischer's wife's call in this batch?"

"Definitely. It should be in June of this year."

I handed Thomas my business card. "Let us know if you think of anything that would help us."

"Sure will."

JUST AS WE FINISHED QUESTIONING Sonya's employees, Martha Gill called. She'd arranged a 2:30 meeting with Zabrina's friends on campus. She said if I picked her up we could grab some lunch before we met the girls at Hamline University.

When she hopped in the car, she said, "If you're up for Turkish food, may I suggest the Black Sea? It's a short distance from Hamline and has fabulous food."

"I'll eat anything," Tamika said.

"Sure, I like to try new foods," I said.

I found a spot in the lot reserved for customers. The restaurant was a little hole in the wall and nothing fancy. The menu was displayed on the wall, and their prices were reasonable. The women ordered kebabs and I selected a gyro. While we ate our lunch—which was delicious, by the way—we drafted a set of questions for Zabrina's friends.

On the way back to the car, Martha said, "Thanks for picking up the check, Cal. You didn't have to do that."

"No problem. Good choice of restaurants, Martha."

I picked up the check because the server put the bill in front of me. I wrongly assumed everyone would chip in. Okay, I admit I'm cheap, but we aren't business tycoons on expense accounts.

We were to meet Zabrina's friends at Starbucks in Anderson Center on the Hamline campus, located a short distance up Snelling. The center was a modern building with a dramatic glass front.

When we walked into the coffee shop, Martha touched my arm and said, "I'll check those two out." She walked toward two girls sitting together.

The aroma of coffee was calling my name. I worked my way through the crowd and stood in line. Tamika came up behind me and said, "Will you get me a tall salted caramel mocha?"

I put out my hand. "Am I the money train?"

She gave me a look but she reached into her fanny pack, pulled out a five and slapped it in my hand.

Martha moved up beside me. "It's them."

I asked if she wanted anything. "Just a black coffee—tall."

I joined the four women at the table with a tray of coffees.

"Looks like dessert, Tamika," I said. She giggled.

"Try it," she said, thrusting the cup mounded with whipped cream in my face. "No . . . thanks."

Martha said, "Can I pay you for the coffee?"

Yes. "No, I got it."

After she introduced us all to the girls, Martha said, "We want to talk to you about Zabrina. First, could you please state your full names, where you're from, and how long you've known her?"

The round-faced girl with blond hair and blue eyes said, "Sure. I'm Autumn Jane Spencer from Minneapolis. I've known Zabrina since we were BFFs in high school."

I looked to the other girl, who was rolling her short, dark hair around her fingers. Her T-shirt said, "Don't bother, I'm not drunk yet."

"Interesting saying on your shirt," I said.

"Oh." She pulled her jacket closed.

"Your turn," I said to the dark-haired girl, whose face had turned the color of cotton candy.

She let out a nervous giggle. "I'm Molly Estes from Stillwater. I met Zabrina the first day we moved into Schilling."

"Molly lives on our floor," Autumn said.

Martha asked, "Was Zabrina having any problems with anyone? Boyfriends? Girlfriends?"

"No."

"No stalkers?"

"Uh-uh."

"What about her family?"

"Her mom was real nice," Autumn said, looking to Molly, who nodded in agreement.

"She got along well with her mom?" I asked.

"Yeah."

"What about her grandmother?"

"Well . . . she could be crabby. You had to be real careful around her. One night we were having a sleepover at Zabrina's and were making popcorn. I guess it was toward midnight. Anyway, her grandmother came up and yelled at us to go to bed. After that we only went there when her grandmother was gone."

"Zabrina didn't get along with her grandmother?"

"I'm not saying that, but Zabrina worried about what she thought. Her grandmother had a lot of influence in big things like where she went to college, what she was going to major in, that kind of thing."

"She tried to please her grandmother?"

"Oh, yeah. Her grandmother wanted her to attend an Ivy League college—like Harvard or Yale. Zabrina applied to several but didn't get in. Her backups were Hamline and UCLA, which is where she really wanted to go. She ended up at Hamline because her grandmother refused to pay for UCLA, which made me happy."

"Did her mom have any say?"

"She said it was Zabrina's decision, but it really wasn't."

"I liked her mom," Molly said. "She was nice."

"She was always happy to have us over, and they have a maid and a cook who made us anything we wanted," Autumn said.

"Like a hotel?" Martha asked.

The girls giggled. "Yeah, sorta," Molly said.

"So how often did you visit her home?" Martha asked.

"Maybe one weekend every six weeks," Autumn said.

"Who else does Zabrina hang out with, other than you two?"

"Her boyfriend, Grady."

"Did Zabrina date a lot in high school?" I asked Autumn.

"Not really. She was with boys, though."

"Hooked up?" Martha asked.

Autumn nodded. "They didn't mean anything until Grady. He liked her, not just for . . . you know."

"Sex," I said.

She nodded.

"Were you with her last Thursday and Friday?" I asked.

"Not Thursday night, but Friday night she invited us to Grady's."

"Which is where?" Martha asked.

"By the U on Seventh Street. He lives in a house with some guys."

"Did you see her at all on Thursday?" she asked.

"Yeah. Early. We ordered a pizza in the dorm before she left and drove over to Grady's," Autumn said. Molly nodded.

"What about Friday during the day?" I asked.

"Yep. After lunch I went back to our room to get my books for my afternoon classes. That's when she asked us if we wanted to go to a party at Grady's that night."

"So tell us about Friday night," I said.

Molly said, "We had just gotten to the party when her mom called to tell her about her grandma. Everything was pretty quiet after that."

"What time was the call?"

Autumn pinched up her nose. "Seven, maybe eight. Zabrina was hysterical. She wanted to drive right up to the lake to be with her mom. We had to take her keys because she already had too much beer."

"Does she get drunk often?" Tamika asked.

"Just beer on weekends. None of us do drugs or anything," Autumn said.

"Did she go back to Hamline with you that night?" I asked.

"No, she stayed with Grady," Autumn said.

"Does she sleep over at Grady's often?" I asked.

Nods from both girls.

"Do you like him for her?" I asked.

"Uh-huh, he's an awesome boyfriend," Autumn said. Molly nodded her agreement.

The interview may have been a waste of time, but we gave the girls our cards in case they thought of anything, then headed back to MPD. Martha got a text from Ryan.

"Fischer's in custody," she told us.

14

RYAN HAD BEEN INTERROGATING Fischer for an hour when he left him in the interview room to come out and brief us. His eyes flashed with excitement as he told us Fischer had had Thursday and Friday off and didn't have an alibi for the times of the murders.

"What does he do?" I asked.

"He's in IT for a cable company. We have a warrant, but he gave us permission to examine his laptop."

"Which means there's nothing incriminating on it," I said.

"We're also checking phone and email records to try to retrieve the harassing emails Fischer sent. Anyway, he's waived his rights, so have a go at him."

As I walked into the warm room, the sharp stench of perspiration hit me. Slouched in his chair, Fischer raised his eyes to meet mine as I took the chair across from him. He jutted out his lower lip and crossed his arms over his large belly. I didn't expect this defiant excuse for a human to cooperate, but it happened more often than not.

"Mr. Fischer, I'm Detective Sheehan from Birch County. Do you know where that is?"

His eyelids fluttered. A facial tic manifested below his left eye. "Ah, sure . . . north of St. Cloud, west of Brainerd?"

"That's right. Have you ever been there?"

He gave me one nod. "Yep."

"When?"

"Oh . . . ah . . . last year, I guess. Me and my dad went fishing."

"Where did you stay?"

"At a resort on Rodgers Lake."

"I know the one. It closed two years ago."

"Oh. Then maybe it was the year before that, because that's where we stayed."

I nodded. "Mr. Fischer, I'm in Minneapolis investigating the murder of Sonya Donovan."

He screwed up his nose. "Who?"

"You called her radio show and left harassing messages and emails. So let's skip the silly I-don't-know-what-you're-talking-about bullshit."

He slouched even farther into his chair. I leaned forward and folded my hands on the table and spoke my next words softly, as if telling him a secret. "I know you know she was murdered."

He leaned in and whispered back, "Just between you and me, the bitch got what she deserved. I hope they cut her fucking head off."

My gut reaction was to jerk back away from this foul-melling piece of shit, but I stayed put, looked him square in the eye and nodded. "Why so hostile?"

"Why? Because she wrecked my life."

"How so?"

"Are we pretending you don't know?"

"I don't."

He took a deep breath and leaned back. "I gave the story to the other cop."

"I haven't heard it, so oblige me."

"Is that one of your tactics to trip a guy up?"

"Sometimes, but not today. I just got here."

He drummed his fingers on the table. "Okay, it started when my wife called the radio show and told fucking lies about me, and bingo bango bongo, she tells her, 'Throw the bum out.'"

"Were you listening to the broadcast?"

"No, my ma does, and she recognized Lilly's voice. Called herself Susan, but Ma said it was definitely Lilly."

"Doesn't seem fair not to get both sides. What lies did she tell?" I asked.

His face softened. He leaned in like I was suddenly his pal.

"Things like I don't help around the house, how all I do is watch sports and expect her to wait on me. Crap like that."

"Even if it were true, sounds like a typical guy thing to me, eh?"

He nodded. "Exactly."

"She must have said something else."

"Okay, she said I slapped her, but she didn't tell the broad she hit me in the face with a pork chop first."

"So you hit her back."

"The bone fucking cut my face." He pointed to his check bone. I couldn't see a damn thing but greasy skin. "Ah, I just tapped her on the head a little. So this bitch tells my wife to dump me—right on the air, see? So Lilly hangs up the phone and texts me at work saying we're through. I tried texting and calling her back all day. I can't just leave work to fight with my wife, you know, or I'd never get any time in. Anyways, by the time I gets home, she had the locks changed and set my things in paper bags on the goddamn step—not even the suitcases . . . which I paid for, by the way."

"So you blamed Sonya?"

"Shit yeah, I blamed her. Lilly'd never of left me if she hadn't been told to."

"What did you do then?"

"I went to my parents."

"Where's that?"

"Nordeast, on Pierce and Thirty-third."

"Is that when your mother told you about the radio show?"

"Yeah."

"So what did you do next?"

"I got an efficiency apartment because that's all I could afford."

"And how did you make contact with Sonya?"

"I looked up her website."

"And?"

"I sent her an email."

"One?"

"A few."

"How many days did that go on?"

"Until she filed a restraining order. Well, what about my first amendment rights, huh? Freedom of speech and all that?"

"Harassment doesn't count as freedom of speech, Mr. Fischer."

His jaw muscles flexed.

"You're still angry with her," I said.

"Damn right. And now just cuz I sent a few emails that cop thinks I was the one who killed those women. Don't he?"

I scratched my neck. "I gotta be honest with you, Mr. Fischer, the thought crossed a few minds. So tell me about your job."

He cocked his head. I had changed gears. "I do tech help for Central Com."

"In this job, you can open accounts, see how people's computers are working, that kind of thing."

"Yeah."

"You have access to customer information?"

"Yeah, I guess."

"If Sonya Donovan was one of your customers, you'd be able to access her address?"

"*If* she was one of our customers. I don't know that she is. But you remember I said I didn't know her last name?"

"Yes, I recall you said that. Where were you last Thursday and Friday, December eleventh and twelfth?"

"I was off those two days, so like I told the other cop, I pretty much just stayed home and played games."

"All day and all night? If you went out, someone may have seen you and would be able to verify your whereabouts."

"Okay, yeah, I got some beer and some snacks at the corner liquor store, then I went home."

"Anyone come over? Any neighbors who could verify you were home? Maybe they saw you pick up your mail, for example."

He pointed a finger at me. "Hey, that's right. I saw one of the people in my building when I threw my garbage out."

"Name?"

"Dunno."

"What time was that?"

"About three o'clock."

"On Friday afternoon?"

"Yes. Look, I didn't kill nobody. I didn't even know that Justine person."

"Well, we'll see what the evidence shows. Won't we?"

He shrugged.

When I walked out into the hallway I inhaled, trying to clear my nose of the stench.

"Whew. He's a ripe-smelling fella," I said to a grinning Martha.

"No alibi for either killing," she said.

"We got the bastard," Ryan said. "In October he applied for a gun permit."

"We're still checking to see if he actually purchased one," Martha said.

"What was used in the Logan shootings?" I asked.

"A thirty-eight caliber."

"We have motive," Tamika said. She gave Martha Gill a high five.

The celebrating was a bit premature because if the creep was confident we'd find nothing, we probably wouldn't. And if he had a handgun, why wouldn't he have shot Sonya Donovan at her home here in Minneapolis? Why on earth would he stage her death in Dexter Lake to look like natural causes? No, I didn't like him for Sonya's murder.

15

TAMIKA AND I WERE GOING to tag along to Fischer's in the off chance I was wrong about his being responsible for Sonya's death. After we put our coats on, Martha handed me copies of Sonya's appointment calendar.

"Thanks."

As we were taking the elevator down, Patrice called and said, "You need to come back to the Logan house right now." She promptly hung up before I could ask what was going on. Obviously, something big.

"We have to bow out," I said. "Will you do me a favor and look for large-sized sage-green Ralph Lauren towels at Fischer's?"

"Towels?" Martha asked.

"There were some missing from Mrs. Donovan's pool area. They would tie him to the crime scene."

"Sure, okay. I'll bag them if I find them." She winked.

ONCE BACK IN OUR VEHICLE, Tamika said, "I think Martha has a little crushy-poo on Deputy Cal."

"Don't be ridiculous."

"You don't see all that smiling and drooling?"

"Nope."

"You big, fat liar."

Okay. She was right. How could I not notice?

The traffic downtown was thick, but it was a simple route to Kenwood via Hennepin.

"Patrice didn't give you a clue as to what was wrong?" Tamika asked.

"Nope."

"Well, I hope no one else is dead."

We didn't talk much during the drive. I considered using lights and siren, but decided against it. Once there, I rang the doorbell. When the door was pulled open, I wasn't expecting to see a smile. Patrice took our coats and showed us to the living room with brocade wallpaper.

"So, what's the big emergency?" I asked

"Whatever gave you the idea there was an emergency?"

"Because we were to stop what we were doing, however important, and race over here."

"I didn't want you to be late for the special dinner Sarah prepared for us."

Whaaat?

"Have a seat and relax."

"Wait a minute. We were on our way to a suspect's apartment."

"In your opinion, was this suspect responsible for Sonya's death?"

Tamika nodded and I said, "I have my doubts. He's too cooperative."

"Well, then, enjoy this dining experience."

By the smile on Tamika's face, I'd say she had no complaints. She immediately chose one of the two green-and-cream striped fabric chairs. I stayed standing and looked about the room. My eyes were drawn to the large Christmas tree in the corner decorated completely in elegant gold trimmings. I'd get one half that size.

I glanced around the room and focused on the large oil painting of Sonya and Donald Donovan. He was sitting in one of the green-and-cream chairs, Sonya posed at his side with her hand on his shoulder. The artist captured an air of sophistication in the couple, Sonya's beauty, and Donald's pointy chin and high forehead.

Sarah appeared with a wine bottle and glasses on a tray. She poured us each a glass of a chilled white. I sat on the edge of the couch next to Patrice and watched Tamika lift an eyebrow as she took her first sip, her pinky finger high in the air. Then she pursed her lips, lifted her chin, and batted her eyes at me. I wrinkled my nose at her silliness.

Seconds later, Sarah came back with a tray of hors d'oeuvres: spinach balls, crab puffs, bacon-wrapped something or other. I chose one of those. As I chewed, I speculated as to what the center was—perhaps a date.

Then Patrice asked for a summary of our day's activities. I told her about the interviews, neglecting to mention the Hamline girls. As Tamika grabbed for a spinach ball, she said, "Cal was a star this afternoon questioning Cyrus Fischer, the number-one suspect in the drive-by."

Star?

"Did MPD arrest Fischer?" Patrice asked.

"Yes, they're searching his place now, which is where we were headed when you called."

"Tamika, you think this Fischer character is a good suspect?" Patrice asked.

"Totally. He has motive, he harassed Sonya, and he looks like a pervert." She reached over to grab a couple appetizers from the plate.

"You don't agree, Cal?"

"I'm not sure he's the type to go to all that trouble of drowning Sonya, placing her in her bed, meticulously executing every detail. He's a slob," I said.

"But he's creepy enough," Tamika said.

"Well, we'll see what they get on him," Patrice said.

"He applied for a gun permit. They're checking to see if he actually bought one. What about Zabrina's father?" I said.

"Honestly, I don't think he cared about either one of them anymore, but it wouldn't hurt to look into him."

Zabrina appeared in the archway, and the room went still. She lifted the phone in her hand. "Daddy wants to know when the funeral is going to be."

Patrice said, "Oh, hi, darling. Soon. I'll arrange everything. That is, unless you'd like to help."

"No, you can do it," she said.

She spoke into her phone, then hung up.

"Come sit by me," Patrice said, patting the empty space beside her on the couch.

Zabrina was clad in Hamline Pipers logo wear: black pants, a white T-shirt, and a red zippered sweatshirt with only one arm in the sleeve, the other side of the garment draped over her wounded arm. She shuffled across the room in over-sized frog slippers and sat next to Patrice, who pulled Zabrina in close to her.

"Did you call your dad, or did he call you?" Patrice asked.

"I called him. He's flying here to be with me."

"Hmm," Patrice said.

Zabrina sat up and looked at Patrice. "Why are you reacting like that?"

"I just didn't think he'd come," Patrice said.

"Why not? He loves me."

Patrice pulled her in closer. "Oh, of course he does."

"I overheard you say he didn't care about us."

"I meant your grandmother and mother."

Zabrina turned to stare at me. "Why are you talking to my friends instead of finding my mom and grandma's killer?"

Patrice narrowed her eyes. "Why on earth would you need to interview Zabrina's friends while investigating *Sonya's* death?"

I cleared my throat. "I'm pretty sure the murders are connected. Zabrina's friends could have picked up on something Zabrina didn't."

"And?"

"And we got nothing."

"Humph. What a surprise."

"I have to try every angle."

"Some are a waste of time—like that."

"We interview many people in investigations. Sometimes people acquainted with family members can deliver great clues," I said.

"And did my friends deliver great clues?" Zabrina asked.

I smiled. "No."

Both she and Patrice delivered smug looks, then Tamika said, "They're anxious to see you, Zabrina."

"They're coming over after dinner," she said.

"Are you up for company?" Patrice said. "I think you need to rest."

She pulled away to glare at Patrice. "I *need* my friends."

Tamika was nodding like a bobble-head doll. I don't think she understood the whole keep-your-opinions-to-yourself concept—especially when none of it was her business, and her boss was involved.

"What's for dinner?" Zabrina asked.

Patrice said, "Your favorite—crab legs."

Zabrina's pushed out her lower lip into a pout. "How am I going to manage crab legs with one arm?"

"I'll crack them for you," Patrice said.

"This sucks so bad," Zabrina whined.

I understood the frustration. The girl's entire family was dead, and she was in emotional and physical pain. But even so, I couldn't help thinking she acted like an immature brat.

A man I recognized from the MPD video interviews entered wearing a flippin' tuxedo. "Dinner is served," he said.

I stood and offered my hand as I introduced myself. I was fully aware I was committing a faux pas, but he politely shook my hand and said, "John Anderson. Nice to meet you, sir."

"You serve as a groundskeeper and a butler?" I asked.

"My duties are wide and varied," he said. "Please follow me."

He escorted us across the hall into the formal dining room where the large mahogany table was set in Martha Stewart style. The elaborate crystal chandelier illuminated the room with a soft glow; the stemware and china sparkled. The elegance of the setting was completed with purple and pink flowers and pale pink candles, magazine perfect for an ordinary weeknight meal.

John rushed over to pull out Zabrina's chair, then pulled Patrice's at the head of the table.

"Miss, this is your chair," he said to Tamika, as he pulled out a chair across from Zabrina. An enormous grin grew on Tamika's face as she touched the pink linen napkin folded into a flower. John pointed to the seat next to Tamika's, indicating my place. A stringed-instrumental piece played softly in surround sound. *People actually live like this?*

Erica carried in a soup tureen on a tray, which she placed on a side table. She wore a maid's uniform: a black dress with a white collar. We watched silently as she ladled and served a bowl of creamy soup to Patrice, then Zabrina, then she approached me.

I pointed to Tamika and said, "Please serve Tamika first."

Tamika rolled her eyes at me. She remarked to me once that she chose to let racist slights roll off her back, and I wasn't to concern myself. But it pissed me off, and when I thought it appropriate, I said something. Erica blushed and did as I asked.

"Lobster bisque," Patrice announced, as she sipped the first spoonful. "Mmm, delicious."

Tamika made a funny face at me, which made me feel like we were playing roles in a comedic movie scene where the country bumpkins screw up at a high-society dinner, spilling beverages, dripping soup on the pale pink linen placemats. Patrice, on the other hand, seemed comfortable with the formality. It was like she had taken over the role of matriarch of the house—and enjoyed every minute.

The Andersons served the dinner in courses: the bisque was followed by a butter lettuce salad, then the main course of crab legs, risotto, and roasted

Brussels sprouts with bacon and shallots. The meat from Zabrina's crab legs had already been removed and cut into bite-size pieces. I had never eaten crab legs before and waited to attack them until I observed how Patrice used the tools provided. Seemed like a lot of work for a tiny bit of food. Sarah Crosby came out while we were eating to ask how we were enjoying our meal.

"It's like a gourmet meal in a five-star restaurant," I said.

She smiled. "Thank you."

"It's absolutely delicious, as usual," Patrice said.

Tamika lifted her pinky finger as she took a sip of wine. "It's fabulous, darling. Am I in *Downton Abbey*?"

Everyone chuckled except for Zabrina, who asked what dessert was.

"Mixed berry cobbler, your favorite," Sarah answered.

"I'll take mine upstairs."

"Sure, I'll have Erica take it up."

"How do you manage to eat dorm food after this?" I asked.

"I mostly eat out."

How would it be to grow up with such privilege? Even though her life had been controlled by a grandmother with the purse strings, the girl had opportunities afforded few. She had yet to experience all the reverberations from the murders. She would never again celebrate another holiday or birthday with her family. Sure, Patrice would try to be fill their shoes, but it would never be the same. Okay, I did feel sorry for the girl.

AFTER DESSERT, I SUGGESTED to Tamika we should leave and get some work done.

"What work?" Tamika asked.

"I need to examine Sonya's social calendar, the list of radio program guests, and listen to the CDs we found in Dexter."

Patrice lifted a finger. "Oh, and I need someone to be here tomorrow morning by seven thirty while I meet with the attorney. I want Zabrina protected."

"I don't have time, and I'm planning to go home tomorrow afternoon."

"I'll do it," Tamika said.

"Great. I'll see you before you take off, Cal?"

"No doubt."

"Have you heard anything about Michael Hawkinson's trial?" Patrice asked. "Has jury selection been completed?"

"I don't know."

Tamika smiled and said, "I could ride back up with you, Patrice, if you need me to stay to guard Zabrina."

"Excellent idea."

That "excellent idea" fueled the slow burn I was feeling about how Patrice and Tamika were treating this investigation.

I stood to take my leave. "Thank you for inviting us to dinner, Patrice," I said.

"Well, now your meal won't have to show up on your expense report."

Ah, we're trying to conserve money here. The woman is a walking contradiction.

"I'll drop Tamika off in the morning."

WHEN WE GOT TO THE CAR, I pulled out one of Sonya's CDs and put it in the player. She was giving a lecture on the art of listening. As we were pulling away from the curb, Grady LaMere pulled up, followed by three girls in an old Chevy Impala.

"I wonder how long ol' Dragon Lady will allow them to stay this time," Tamika said. We didn't get a block before Tamika turned down the sound.

"You can give these to Crosby and Spanky to listen to. They're happy to do the grunt work."

"It's our job."

"You sound pissed. What did I do?"

"You're treating this trip like a junket."

"What are you talking about?"

"Remember, we're down here on a murder investigation, not fancy dinners."

Her head whipped toward me. A few seconds passed before she spoke. "This is about Adriana, isn't it?"

"No." I turned the sound back up.

Tamika remained silent until we got back to our hotel. As I parked the Explorer, she said, "I've overdone it after my surgery. I need to lie down."

"Be ready by 7:15 a.m."

We walked into the hotel and to our rooms in frosty silence. Her door was next to mine. She slammed it when she went in. Good grief.

First thing I did was call Dallas. After I unloaded about my frustrating trip, I finally asked how she was.

"I'm good. Went snowshoeing yesterday with the gang in South Park."

"Fun. We'll go again maybe next weekend."

"Perfect. I miss you, Cal."

"I miss you, too. Anything more from Vince?"

"He called again. I told him to stop."

"File a restraining order."

"For what? He hasn't threatened me or anything."

"If he does, do not hesitate. Promise me?"

"I will. I promise."

"Unless something unforeseeable happens, I'll be home tomorrow."

"Okay."

I PULLED OUT THE NOTEBOOK where I had written Vince Palmer's address. I grabbed my keys and left.

Palmer lived in a condo near Lake Calhoun, the lake where Zabrina met Grady LaMere. The building was secured, so I held back until I saw a couple exit the elevator and when they came out of the front door, the man held it open for me. I took the elevator to the ninth floor and followed the signs to apartment number 913.

I rang the bell. I'd never met Vince or saw a photo of him, so it surprised me how short and out of shape he was. I had to give him one thing: he was good looking in a chiseled sort of way. Yeah, I was tempted to pop him in his perfect Roman nose.

"You have to be Cal," he said.

"That'd be me."

"Let me guess. You want me to leave Dallas alone. Well, she's my wife, and you really have no right to make such a request."

"Ex-wife."

"No . . . *wife*. She hasn't sent in the divorce papers."

Stunned, I was at a loss for a snappy comeback.

He smiled. "You didn't know that, did you?"

"Why don't you invite me in so your neighbors don't have to hear what I have to say?"

"Oh, I want them to hear your threats." He pulled out his phone and tapped on it and pointed it at me.

"No threats, Vince. But I am going to tell you she doesn't want to hear from you or see your face again."

"That's what she tells you, Deputy Cal." He smirked.

The only other person who called me Deputy Cal was Zach Whitman, and I didn't like him, either. I made a fist. He slammed the door in my face before I could break his nose with it.

16

AS I RODE DOWN in the elevator, I ruminated why Dallas never sent the divorce paperwork in. What the hell? I got all the way to the front door, and decided the jerk was lying. I took the elevator back up, knocked on Vince's door. He opened it with a cell phone in his hand. He handed it to me.

"Cal?"

"Dallas?"

"What in the hell do you think you're doing?"

"Talking to Vince."

"This is not your business. Leave now. We'll talk when you get home."

I glared at Vince and handed him back the phone. "If you ever lay a hand on her again, I will come for you."

"You and whose army?"

"What are you? In fifth grade?"

It was his smirk that did it. Like a kid in a school yard, I picked him up under the armpits and held him inches off the floor and up against the wall. His mouth dropped open, and his eyes signaled fear.

"No, just me." I dropped him and backed out of the door.

I WAITED TO CALL DALLAS until I was back in my room. I paced back and forth because I was too agitated to sit.

"Is it true?" I asked in response to her "hello."

"Is what true?"

"That you never signed the divorce papers?"

I could hear her sigh. "Our attorneys are still working on the settlement, so no."

"I thought you were legally divorced. Your mom thinks you are."

"You *assumed* I was, and I don't tell Mom everything."

"Or me, obviously."

"Because she thinks I should just let him have everything. He only wants me back so he doesn't have to pay me the two hundred thousand for my share of condo."

"Tell me something. Did Vince call you tonight, or did you call him?"

"He called to tell me you showed up at his door, which upsets me greatly."

"I can imagine. Your lies are now exposed."

Another audible sigh. "I didn't lie."

"I gotta go," I said.

I watched the phone for five minutes. She didn't call back. It was strange how being hurt could deliver such intense physical reactions. I ached from my stomach to my throat. Why wouldn't she tell me she was waiting for money? Because she knew I would say the same thing Clara did. She left him over a year ago. How long did these settlements go on?

I SAT ON MY BED LISTENING to the sounds of the television coming from next door. I got up, paced a few times, then decided to text Dallas: "So let a judge decide."

Nothing back. *She's mad at me? I didn't have time for this.* I turned on my own television for company, then opened Sonya's social calendar. It wasn't giving me much. She wasn't as busy as I'd presumed a person of her position would be. She attended very few social events and only went on one business trip to New York in November to do an interview on *The View*.

Dallas kept creeping into my thoughts, so I shut off the TV and pulled out my portable CD player and put in earbuds. Maybe the sound going directly to my ears would be less distracting. I selected the disc labeled "June." Sonya was letting the first caller have it for talking over her. She called her a horrible listener. She was right. The woman wouldn't shut up.

I had a bit of luck when the third caller was named "Susan," the alias Cyrus Fischer said his wife used. The guest host on that particular broadcast was Edward King, a divorce attorney. Sonya spoke for a few minutes, giving three justifications for divorce: addiction, abuse, and serial betrayal. King concurred and repeated what Sonya said, adding, "One affair should not have to result in a divorce." What would Sonya have said to Dallas? Her marriage had two out of the three criteria. Shannon and I had zero. What about marrying the wrong person?

Lilly, a.k.a. Susan, explained she'd known Cyrus for seven months before they married. He'd swept her off her feet, giving her flowers, taking her out for dinners, and opening doors. He called her several times a day to say he was thinking of her. She'd never been treated so well. I couldn't imagine that piece of shit appealing to anyone—ever.

"Let me guess," Sonya said. "After the wedding, things changed."

"Well, it was more like six months."

"Then he stopped with the flowers, dinners, or opening doors?"

"Exactly."

"And you tried to keep the romance going?"

"Yes, but I eventually gave up."

"How old are you?"

"Twenty-five."

"And your husband?"

"Twenty-seven."

King jumped in, asking, "How long have you been married?"

"It'll be three years next month."

"First marriage for both of you?" he asked.

"Yes."

"Do you have children?"

"No."

Sonya took the reins again. "Tell me his redeeming qualities and what he contributes to the relationship."

"Nothing, anymore. He's obnoxious. He does nothing around the apartment but mess it. He eats in front of the television and gets food stains on the carpet. All he watches is sports and fishing shows."

"Have you tried talking to him about your issues?"

"All the time. He's not interested in changing."

"Sounds like you married the wrong man. Are you attracted to him sexually?"

"Not anymore. He was a little chubby when we met, but he's put on fifty pounds since."

"And you?"

"I take pride in how I look. I may be ten pounds overweight, but that's it."

"We're all ten pounds overweight, honey," Sonya said. "So what made you call today? Did something happen?"

"He hit me."

"He hit you?"

"Yes, last night." Lilly started to cry.

King spoke again. "You should report this to the police immediately and get a restraining order, then get out. Go to your mom's or a shelter."

Sonya said, "Edward's right. But if she wants the house, she can't vacate it. File the restraining order, change the locks, pack up all his personal belongings. Text him that it's over and set his things on the step. Just get out of that situation for the immediate time until things are handled legally."

"Okay, I will." Sniffing.

"Okay, darling, we're giving you a leave 'em! Throw the bum out!" Sonya laughed. "Thank you for the call, and take care."

After she'd disconnected with Lilly, Sonya said to King, "Why do women think they know a man well enough to marry in seven months? Wait three years, minimum, people! I think there should be a law that no one can marry before age thirty. Jordan, who's our next caller?"

Martha Gill texted me saying Fischer had purchased a Ruger LCRX 38.

"Hot diggity!" I texted back.

Martha: "We took his computer and phone into evidence. Place was disgusting. Surprised he let us in."

Me: "Why would he?"

Martha: "He wants the credit."

Me: "Any sage-green towels?"

Martha: "No."

Me: "Keep me informed.'

Martha: "C U 2morrow?"

Me: "Yes."

Martha sent me a smiley face emoji, and I replied with a thumbs-up.

The ballistics tests would confirm whether the gun used in the drive-by shootings was Fischer's thirty-eight caliber. MPD had motive and opportunity, but it didn't exactly help me, and Russell Bennett may have also had motive to kill his ex-wife and her mother.

The amount of information available on the Internet is astounding. Bennett was born in Grand Rapids, Minnesota, and now lived in Salem, Oregon. No criminal record. He obtained a bachelor's degree from the University of Minnesota in business. He went on to obtain a master's degree in finance and was employed by Norwest Banks in Minneapolis from 1994 to 2006.

Justine and Russell were married in 1993, and Zabrina was born in 1995. The couple divorced in 2006.

Divorce. Was Dallas hanging on just for the money? I understood two hundred thousand dollars was a lot to give up, but it was a matter of principle rather than her needing it to live.

17

Friday, December 19

A FTER I CHECKED OUT Friday morning, I made my way to the parking lot where Tamika was waiting, sipping coffee from a hotel paper cup, her luggage by her side. I planned to tread lightly. Maybe she was doing too much too soon after surgery, and I was taking my frustration out on her.

"Good morning," I said as I loaded the vehicle.

"Morning."

"You feeling okay? Not too tired."

She narrowed her eyes.

I said, "I'm not being sarcastic. Maybe you should be part time for a while."

We got in the vehicle. Tamika said, "I am more tired than I thought I'd be. I'm sorry I crapped out on you last night—actually, I'm sorry for a lot of things, like I shouldn't have invited Adriana without asking you."

"No harm done."

"I was thinking last night."

"Now that's dangerous."

"Maybe you should run for sheriff. You're a hero in Birch County."

"Oh, please."

"I'm serious. You'd be great."

"Not interested."

"Did you get to the calendar?"

"Yeah, not much there. I listened to a few discs—the one of Fischer's wife. He was accurate in his account of the call his wife made. Oh, but the big news is Martha said they found a thirty-eight in his bedside table."

"Holy crap," she said. "Do you think he killed Sonya, too?"

"I'm not even convinced he shot Justine and Zabrina. If he was the drive-by shooter, why would he hang onto the murder weapon?"

"Maybe he's one of those sick puppies who wants credit."

"That's what Martha said. I did some checking on Zabrina's father, Russell Bennett. I hope to speak with him before I drive home today."

"You miss your babies?"

"Of course. And Dallas."

"Hey, how is she?"

"Why?"

She cocked her head and knitted her brows. There could have been an edge to my voice.

"Just asking. Why so defensive?"

"Because you rarely ask about her."

"Really? Well, I think you two are good together."

"That's why you tried to get Adriana and me back together."

"Yeah, but she's dating someone else now."

"Good."

"Aren't you going to ask who it is?"

"Nope."

"Hunter Hughes," Tamika said. "He's a famous underwear model. You'd probably recognize him from magazine ads."

I screwed up my nose.

"He's hot."

"Won't last."

"Why?"

"'Cause he's probably as pretty as she is."

"You're a pretty boy . . . in a rugged sort of way. You could make a heck of a lot more money doing underwear ads."

I screwed up my nose and turned up the volume on the radio.

THE AROMA OF HOMEMADE bread greeted us when we walked into the door of the Logan house. Patrice immediately put her coat on over her gray pantsuit. "Sarah is making your breakfast, now I have to run," she said.

When the door closed behind Patrice, Sarah appeared. She was wearing black slacks and a shirt with a white professional chef's apron.

"I'm making omelets. Any special requests?"

"Thanks, but I'm not staying," I said. "I need to be on my way."

"Please, let me earn my keep for the time I have left."

"Were you given notice?" I asked.

"Patrice is closing up the house within two weeks, which means I'm out of a job now, doesn't it?"

"You should be able to find work," Tamika said.

"Yes, but this was the ideal situation for me. I made a great salary and had all holidays and many weekends off, especially in the summer."

"You'll find something," I said.

There were many victims in murder cases, and in this one you could include all Sonya's employees.

"So what kind of omelets would you two like?" she said.

"Surprise me," I said.

"I'm not a fussy eater, as you can tell by my petite figure," Tamika said.

I heard footsteps coming down the stairs and was surprised to see Grady making his way down.

"Hey," he said.

"Did Patrice let you stay overnight?" Tamika asked.

"Zabrina didn't want to be alone."

"And Patrice was okay with that?" Tamika asked.

"Shh!" he said, holding a finger to his lips. "She didn't know. Zabrina begged me to stay until she fell asleep . . . then so did I."

"How long did the girls stay?" she asked.

"Mrs. Clinton kicked them out after an hour."

"I'm making omelets, Grady," Sarah said.

"Thanks, but I gotta run. I have a final."

WITHIN FIFTEEN MINUTES, Sarah was serving us crab omelets with toasted homemade bread and strawberry jam. The table was set with multicolor striped ceramic plates and coffee mugs.

Sarah came back with a coffee carafe and filled the cups.

"Mind if I join you?" she asked, sitting at the third place I assumed was for Zabrina.

"Please do," I said.

"Where are Erica and John this morning?" Tamika asked.

"They took the day off to meet with their agency about new employment."

"Does Erica serve breakfast and lunches?" she asked.

"No, everyone eats at different times, so I serve. Then Erica is free to do the cleaning uninterrupted."

"Seems like Sonya ran a pretty formal household," I said.

"In this bracket, it's expected."

"I suppose."

The doorbell rang and Sarah got up to answer. Tamika and I followed, lest some undesirable was on the other side.

A slight man in a long, black wool coat stood on the stoop. His dark hair and beard were neatly trimmed. His eyes went to my hand resting on my firearm.

"Can I help you?" Sarah asked.

"I'm Russell Bennett, Zabrina's dad. She's expecting me."

Sarah's shoulders noticeably lowered an inch.

"Oh, sure," Sarah said. "Come in." After the door closed behind him, she added, "She's still sleeping, and I think we should let her get as much rest as possible."

"I agree," he said.

"Did you fly in this morning?" I asked.

"My flight arrived at eight o'clock last night, but I thought it was too late to drop by. I went directly to my sister's in Blaine."

"Have you had breakfast, Mr. Bennett?" Sarah said.

"Yes, and call me Russell."

"Would you then join us in the dining room for a cup of coffee or tea while we finish ours?"

"Oh, sorry to have interrupted your meal."

"No, it's fine."

We all followed Sarah back into the dining room. She said, "Coffee or hot tea, Mr. Bennett?"

"Coffee would be wonderful."

As I took my place at the table, Tamika followed Sarah into the kitchen. I could hear her say, "From now on, Sarah, let me answer the door. That's my job today."

Dish noises drowned out Sarah's response.

"And who are you?" Bennett asked.

I explained, then Tamika returned, followed by Sarah with another mug of coffee, which she set before Bennett.

"When did you first know about the deaths?" I asked.

"Zee called me last Saturday morning to tell me about Sonya, then again the night she was shot. Poor thing was so distraught I caught an earlier flight. Is she correct in that her grandmother drowned?"

"Yes," I said.

"Do you know who's responsible?"

"We're still investigating."

"I know Zee's suffering emotionally, but how is she doing physically?"

Sarah said, "She was lucky. The bullet passed through her upper arm, missing the artery and bone. She's wearing a sling and taking antibiotics and pain meds that make her sleepy. But you're right—emotionally, this is super tough on her."

Bennett nodded, his face displaying concern. "I can imagine."

"How often do you see Zabrina?" I asked.

"Unfortunately, not as much as I'd like. With the bed and breakfast, I can't get away very often. This is only the third trip back since I moved to Oregon."

"Are you the owner?" I asked

"Simon and I run it together. He's my business partner and husband. When Justine and I split up, I came out. Justine didn't want me to tell Zee, so I haven't. But I think it's time."

"Maybe you should wait until after the funeral," Sarah said. I found it odd for her to voice an opinion on the matter.

"When's that?" he asked.

"Patrice is arranging it today," Sarah said.

Zabrina entered the room, with bed hair, in the same outfit she wore yesterday. "Daddy," she moaned.

Bennett rose to hug his daughter gingerly. When she began to whimper, he said, "Let's go upstairs." He took her right hand, and they walked out of sight.

After a few moments of silence, Tamika said, "I don't think Russell's our killer."

"Would you please interview him further and then verify he was in Oregon for the past six days?"

She nodded. "Of course. Anything else?" She seemed to have had an attitude adjustment.

"Try and get hold of Edward King, the attorney who guest hosted the day Fischer's wife called in to the radio show. I have his information in a file."

SINCE I WAS ANXIOUS to find out how the ballistics test turned out on Fischer's Ruger, right after breakfast I texted Martha Gill.

She immediately returned a text, telling me ballistics weren't a match and Fischer had been released.

"What now?" I texted.

Martha asked if I'd meet her at Starbucks, and gave me directions for a store a block from the government center.

AS I WALKED INTO STARBUCKS, I took in the fragrance of freshly brewed coffee. I caught sight of Martha sitting alone at a table for two.

I bought a coffee and sat across from her.

"No luck with the Ruger, eh?"

"We were so sure it was him," she said, "and we have no other leads at this point."

"I know the feeling. Zabrina's father arrived from Oregon."

"Did you interview him?"

"We're giving him some time with his daughter first. I know we can't rely on gut instinct, but I don't think he's responsible. Tamika is checking out his whereabouts for our case. He runs a bed and breakfast, so it'll be easy enough to check out. His guests would be witnesses."

"I don't get why anyone would want to kill the girl. Do you?"

"No, I sure don't."

"We've looked through Justine's financials and cell phone records," Martha continued. "I don't think she had much of a social life."

"Neither did her mother."

"The few calls on her cell phone were mostly to or from her mother and daughter. Looks like all the business calls were made from the home phone. When are you going back home?"

"This afternoon."

"Dang. I wanted you to come to my place for dinner tonight . . . to pay you back for the lunch you bought me. Can't I change your mind?"

Uh-oh. "No, sorry. I have to get back."

"Okay." She looked disappointed. "Lunch, then? I could pick something up."

"Martha, I have someone. And I've always been a one-woman-guy."

"Lucky woman. Well, can't blame a gal for trying."

My phone rang. Patrice. "Cal? Where are you?"

"Downtown."

"Damn it. I can't get hold of anyone at the house. Have you talked to Tamika recently?"

"No, but she was going to be making some calls. Zabrina's dad showed up, so she's probably with him."

"But why isn't anyone, including Sarah, answering their phones?"

"I don't know, but I can be at Logan in ten minutes if need be."

"Good, go."

"Are you finished with your meeting with the attorney?"

"Soon. I'll be there ASAP."

And given an excuse to get out of there, I took it. That entire conversation with Martha could have been handled by phone. Besides, Patrice had succeeded in amping my level of concern. Why wasn't anyone answering their phones? Shit.

18

I MADE IT BACK TO THE DONOVAN residence before Patrice did. Bennett's rental car was not in the driveway, and no one answered the doorbell. With a gloved hand, I turned the knob of the door to find it unlocked. I entered cautiously. All was quiet.

Finding no one on the first floor, I made my way upstairs, checking rooms as I approached Zabrina's. The girl's bedroom was unoccupied, the bed unmade. I glanced into the bathroom, spotting Tamika lying in a heap by the claw-foot tub.

I rushed in and knelt down. I looked her over. No wounds or blood. I felt for a pulse. Found it. I touched her shoulder. "Tamika? Are you okay?"

She opened her eyes and said, "The devil isn't red. She's green."

"What?"

Patrice rushed in the room. "Where's Zabrina?" she shouted. "What's Tamika doing on the floor?"

"I found her like this. She's not making sense."

Patrice knelt beside her. "Tamika, where's Zabrina?"

Tamika tried sitting. Her hand flew to the back of her head. "Woo. My head hurts."

"Let me see." She turned her head to reveal a gash and a goose egg the size of, well, a goose egg.

"And Zabrina's gone. Damn it all to hell." Patrice called 911 and requested an Amber Alert for Zabrina. She answered a series of questions, then hung up. "The dispatcher said she's too old for an Amber Alert, but they'd send someone over."

I couldn't believe Patrice ignored Tamika's need for medical aid. I picked up my phone and dialed 911 again to tell them we had a deputy who had been knocked unconscious and needed an ambulance. Patrice let out a puff of air, her face registering recognition that she'd screwed up. She closed the toilet lid and sat down.

"Where's Sarah?" I asked.

"How the hell would I know? I just got here."

"Russell was here when I left. The Taurus he rented was gone when I got back, so he and Zabrina must be together."

"If that's true, why won't she answer her phone? And if you thought that, why did you just let me call 911?"

I pointed to Tamika.

"Oh, what was I thinking?" She tapped her head. "Why were you downtown?"

"I met with Detective Gill. She wanted to tell me Cyrus Fischer was released—there was no ballistics match."

"Son of a bitch." She abruptly left the room.

"What's your name?" I asked Tamika.

"Tamika Frank."

"Good. Who's the president?"

"Obama."

"What year is it?"

"2010." She was a few years off. Not so good.

Patrice came back in full uniform. She gave me a look. "And why aren't you in uniform, by the way?" she asked.

"I didn't bring any."

She shook her head and stood over Tamika. "You should have stayed here, too. Neither one of you seems to understand the seriousness of the situation."

Rather than argue, I said, "I'm going down for some ice for Tamika's head."

When I returned upstairs, Patrice had at least covered Tamika with a blanket. However, instead of attending her, she was looking on a white iPhone.

"Zabrina wouldn't leave without her cell phone," she said.

"Is that hers?"

Her finger swiped the display surface several times. "Yes. These kids constantly text."

"What are her recent calls?"

"Nothing this morning."

By the time the MPD squad arrived and the ambulance had come and gone, Sarah had returned. I met her in the kitchen. I took the two Lunds and Byerly's grocery bags from her and put them on the counter.

"Why are there patrol cars in the driveway?" she said with a look of concern.

"Zabrina's gone, and my partner was just taken to the hospital with a giant goose egg on the back of her head. I found her unconscious in Zabrina's bathroom."

"Oh, golly. What do you think happened?"

"I don't know, and Tamika's talking gobbledygook."

"That sounds serious."

I nodded. "Do you have Russell's number?"

"I can locate it."

"Thanks. I better call Tamika's husband."

RUSSELL WASN'T ANSWERING his phone, and because it appeared Tamika had been attacked, Patrice was pressuring the Minneapolis PD sergeant on scene to put out a BOLO for Russell's car since Zabrina was too old for an Amber Alert. Patrice shot me a dirty look when I suggested they call Bennett's sister in Blaine first.

A few minutes later, I started dialing Gill, thought better of it, then called Ryan to apprise him of the situation.

"I just heard your partner was knocked out and the kid's gone? Oh, wait . . . They just located Russell Bennett at his sister's in Blaine."

"Was Zabrina with him?"

"No. He said she's probably with her boyfriend."

19

I WANTED TO GO TO THE HOSPITAL, but Patrice insisted we first drive downtown, where Russell Bennett had been taken for questioning.

"How did your meeting with the attorney go?" I asked.

"What? Oh, Zabrina's inheritance goes into a trust fund, of which she has no control until she's thirty. I'll manage it and transfer funds for her expenses as needed—college and what not."

"What's the kid worth?"

"Millions. All Sonya's assets went to Justine and because she's deceased, everything now goes to Zabrina."

"So she owns both homes."

"Yes, but at her age, she can't be expected to maintain either one. We'll sell them."

"Out of curiosity, was anyone else named in the will?"

"I was in Justine's."

I stared at her, but she avoided eye contact.

"When Zabrina was a baby, Justine asked me if I would be Zabrina's guardian in the event something should happen to her. I was to get a salary for taking on the responsibility of raising another child through college age, but I wasn't aware of the sizable sum."

"Mind if I ask how much?"

"Yes, I do mind."

"That's fine," I said. It must be quite substantial if she wouldn't tell me. "So Russell Bennett gets nothing?"

"Not a thing. Why should he?"

"Did you know he was gay?"

"Of course. That's why they got the divorce. He told Justine he wanted a three-way, and she finally agreed, thinking they needed something to spark up their sex life. Russell brought a man home, and Justine said when she realized they were really into each other, she got out of bed, and they didn't seem to notice. She questioned him that night. He admitted he thought he was gay, and that's when she asked for the divorce."

"He seems like a loving father."

"He may love Zabrina, but he seldom makes the effort to see her. So what does that tell you?"

"Do you feel he's back to seek out Zabrina's affection for her money?"

"Well, like that's going to happen. I'll make sure he doesn't get one damn cent. Trust me on that one."

PATRICE AND I WALKED into the interview room where Russell Bennett had been placed.

"Patrice," he said, standing and moving toward her with his arms outstretched.

Patrice froze. Then she crossed her arms. "Right now, I don't know whether to smack or hug you."

"What did I do?"

"Where the hell is Zabrina?"

"I don't know. She said she had an appointment to get ready for and to come back for dinner tonight."

"What kind of appointment?"

"I assumed a doctor's."

"It's not until tomorrow. Where was Deputy Frank when you left?"

"She was at the dining room table making calls."

"Did you have plans for Zabrina?"

"What do you mean?"

"Like taking-her-to-Oregon plans?"

He looked confused. "No, why? Did she say that?"

"No." Patrice addressed me. "Cal, give Grady a call. See if he came to get her. And if not, call her girlfriends."

"And one of the kids knocked out Tamika?"

She grimaced. "Damn it."

A look of concern washed across Bennett's face. "The big deputy was knocked out?"

I nodded.

"Well, what the hell happened to my daughter? Did someone abduct her?"

THE POLICE QUESTIONED not only Russell Bennett, but his sister and her husband, and asked the Grand Rapids Police Department to question Bennett's family. The reports came back the same: Russell had planned to spend a week with his sister in Blaine, so he could spend time with Zabrina in Minneapolis, then he'd drive to Grand Rapids, with or without his daughter, to see his parents. Russell said it never occurred to him to have Zabrina come and live with him in Oregon because her life was here, and Patrice would do a good job with her, that she was like a second mother to his daughter. He sounded convincing, and much like someone who didn't want the responsibility of a young-adult child.

Zabrina's friends were eventually tracked down. No one had heard from her since last evening, which was odd to me, but her phone activity proved it.

Bennett was released, and Patrice and I drove to the hospital to see Tamika. She was sitting up in bed drinking cranberry juice when we walked into her private room.

"Hey, girl, how are you doing?" I asked.

She gave us a bizarre smile. "Goooood. Where am I?"

"You're at Hennepin County Medical Center."

"They're real nice here. I like these drugs they're giving me."

"What do you remember?"

"Everything." She blinked a few times.

"Did you fall?" I asked.

"Or did someone hit you?" Patrice asked.

"Huh?"

A nurse came in to check her vitals. "How is she doing?" Patrice asked.

"She's much better than when she first came in. She has a CAT scan scheduled in a half hour."

"How long will she be here?" I asked.

"Depends. A day or two for observation, for sure."

"She's having trouble with her memory. When will it come back?" Patrice asked.

"That all varies so much with head traumas. It's a very good sign she's so alert now. Has her husband been contacted?" she asked.

"Yes, he's on his way from Prairie Falls," I said.

"What's for dinner?" Tamika asked.

"I don't know," the nurse said, smiling. "I'll be right back."

"Tamika, where did Zabrina go?" Patrice asked.

"Zabrina?"

"Was someone else at the house?" I asked.

"I don't know."

Her nurse returned and said, "Here's your menu, honey. This is one funny lady. She must be a riot to work with."

"Yeah, a real riot," I said.

When the nurse left, I said, "Shit, Patrice, I don't remember seeing Tamika's firearm on her in the bathroom."

"Oh, crap. Where're her things?"

She went to the tiny closet in the room. She pulled a plastic bag out. Tamika's ID, cell phone, clothing, and holster belt were accounted for.

"Why didn't we notice back at the house if her firearm was missing?"

Just then Tamika said, "I don't feel so—" and vomited over the bed railing.

Patrice put her hand to her mouth and made a speedy retreat. I grabbed the call button to report. When the nurse entered, she took a look and called for housekeeping. She handed Tamika a receptacle and wrote on her chart.

Patrice poked her head in the room and said, "Cal, let's go."

I touched Tamika's arm and said, "I'll come back later to see how you're doing."

Tamika didn't look like she cared a rat's ass what I did.

Patrice was waiting in the hall. As we walked down to the elevator she said, "I don't do well with vomit. Did you see the color of that stuff? Was it blood?"

"I suspect it was cranberry juice. Patrice, was Zabrina's car in the garage?"

"Good God, I don't even know. What's wrong with us? Why didn't we look?"

"Call Sarah."

Patrice made the phone call asking Sarah to look in the garage for the car. After waiting a minute, she said, "Well, let's hope so. We'll see you later." She hung up and turned to me. "The Miata's gone. Sarah thinks she drove over to campus and doesn't even know we're worried."

"You don't think Zabrina knows Tamika was hit in the head in her bathroom?"

"We don't know for sure she was actually hit. And with what? Maybe she slipped and fell."

"But her weapon's missing."

"Maybe it's in her suitcase."

"She was wearing it when I brought her to the house this morning."

WE DROVE ALL AROUND the Hamline campus, but no red Miata, and Zabrina wasn't in her dorm room.

"Drive over to Grady's," Patrice barked.

I handed her my notebook to locate the address. She read it off, then I had her put it into the GPS system. It directed me to 94, which was currently a parking lot, and we sat in traffic. I was directed to North 280 to University, then down University, separating off to Fourth Street when University became a one-way.

I found a parking spot down the street from Grady LaMere's house, which was typical college housing, complete with a soggy sofa on the front porch. We looked up and down the block and around the back for Grady's burgundy Mazda and Zabrina's red Miata, but neither was in sight. I knocked on the front door. Patrice was behind me.

A big redheaded kid with pale skin and freckles answered the door with a Miller in hand. His beer belly muffin-topped over his waistband. We both flipped our badges open and simultaneously announced our names and positions. The kid stepped back and said, "Whoa, man. What's up?"

"May we come in?" Patrice asked.

"Uh, what's this about?"

"Zabrina Bennett," she said.

He stepped to the side and swept an arm inward. We followed him to a living room smelling of marijuana, stale beer, and Doritos. Old pizza boxes, empty Miller beer cans, and chip bags were strewn everywhere.

"You guys trying to attract vermin?" I asked.

The kid laughed nervously.

Two young men, with their backs to us, were on the couch facing the television and playing video games. Neither one bothered to look up until the freckled Dough Boy shouted, "Hey! Shut that off. The cops are here."

Both boys looked over their shoulders and their mouths dropped open. I was surprised to see who one of them was.

"Well, Zach Whitman, as I live and breathe," I said.

He stood, a grin crossing his face. "Well, Deputy Cal. Whatcha doing down here in the big city?"

"Cop stuff. Hey, I was thinking about you last week."

"Oh, yeah? Why?"

"Came across some friends of yours—drunk underaged kids from Dexter Lake. They were out in the worst storm of the season—so far, anyway—and ended up in the ditch. And guess what? They mentioned your name."

"A lot of kids want to say they're my friend. So, who's yours?"

He made a distinct point of checking Patrice out.

"Sheriff Clinton, this smartass is Jack Whitman's grandson."

"I see," she said as she stared at him for a few seconds. "We're looking for your roommate Grady LaMere and his girlfriend, Zabrina Bennett. Have you seen them?" Patrice asked.

"No, ma'am. Not since last night," Zach said. "How 'bout you guys?" He looked to his roommates.

They shook their heads.

"May I have your names?" I asked.

I recorded their names and phone numbers in my notebook. Silas Hill was the redhead, and Mark Nelson was the athletic kid playing video games with Zach. With a couple of questions, we found out Zach, Silas, and Mark had lived together for two years, and with Grady since last June. Mark said he met him in a math class, and when one of their roommates flunked out and went back to Fargo, Mark called Grady because he knew he was looking for a place to live.

"Is he in class or working today?" I asked.

Silas had his hands in his pockets of his baggy jeans. He made a face. "I think he only works at night."

"Where?" Patrice asked.

"Beats me," Zach said.

"He works at some vet clinic," Mark said.

"What else do you know about him?" I asked.

"He's neat. His bed's always made," Mark said.

Zach snorted, like it was a bad thing.

"Don't you youngsters *talk* to each other?" I asked.

The young men eyed each other, then shrugged in unison.

"May we check his room? Perhaps he's asleep," Patrice said.

"Sure, go ahead." Silas said.

"Is this about the shootings?" Zach asked.

"We need to talk to him about something else, so if you know how to get hold of him, I'd do it now. Tell him to contact me ASAP," she said.

Silas showed us to second floor. At first glance, the brown carpeted runner up the center of the wood stairs appeared to be multicolored, but it was just loaded with lint. The same brown carpet ran down the hallway, and hadn't seen a vacuum in years. The doors to three of the bedrooms were open, and the rooms were as trashed as the living room. The door to the fourth room was closed. Silas pointed to it. "That's Grady's."

Patrice knocked then turned the knob slowly. She stepped in, and I stood in the doorway. The room was orderly—not a single item of clothing or a wet towel lay on the floor. It could have been mine. I'd always been neat like that.

"Do you need me?" Silas asked.

"No," Patrice said.

He turned around and descended the stairs.

The room held a full-size bed, desk, and dresser, on the top on which was a five-by-seven framed photo of Zabrina standing next to a tree—looked like a senior picture. I meandered over to his desk, where only a University of Minnesota coffee mug held a few pencils and black Bic pens. A backpack lay between the desk and the bed. I unzipped the pack, used a finger to spread it open. Textbooks and notebooks. Patrice opened the closet door. Dark-blue towels neatly stacked alongside a few sweaters on the top shelf of his closet.

Patrice said, "Holy cow, this kid is unusually tidy. He doesn't have many clothes, does he?"

"No."

The longer we were in the room, the more uneasy I became. This illegal search could get us in big trouble.

"Let's get out of here," I said.

But instead of moving out, she pulled out her phone and punched in a number and asked for Detective Ryan.

"William, this is Patrice Clinton. We checked out Zabrina's boyfriend's place. Neither are here. I suggest a BOLO on their vehicles."

She disconnected, then said, "He's going to hold off. Let's find his parents' place."

Just then music came from a desk drawer. I moved in and pulled the drawer open to find last year's iPhone playing Pink's "Don't Leave Me."

"Answer it," she said.

"Hey," I said into the phone.

"Hey, man, this is Silas. Glad I got hold of you. The cops are here looking for you."

"Yeah?"

"Yeah. What do you want me to tell them?"

"That I left my phone in my room."

There was pause, followed by a click.

I put the phone back in the drawer because it would have been illegal to take a look at it. Besides, it had a coded lock.

"One of his roommates," I said.

"Why did they leave their phones home?" she asked.

"They obviously didn't want to be tracked."

"Let's go," Patrice said.

As we descended the stairs, Silas looked up and said, "That was you, wasn't it?"

I nodded. "Have you ever known him to leave his phone behind?"

He shrugged and said, "I don't know, man."

"If you see or hear from him, call me immediately. Here's my card."

He took the card, examined it, flicked it between his fingers for a second, nodded once, then put it in his wallet. I threw a couple more on the table. I'd had very few people actually call me after I'd given them my card, but you never knew. As I exited the room, I glanced back to see Zach pull out his phone. Who was he calling?

I let Patrice drive, so I could use my iPad to find Grady's parents' address. I quickly found one for a Lloyd LaMere on the 4700 block of Blaisdell. I put it in the GPS. It directed us across the Hennepin Avenue Bridge and south to Lake Street.

I was able to reach Zabrina's roommate. "Autumn, this is Deputy Sheehan."

"Oh, hi. Have you found Zabrina yet?"

"No, but if you speak with her, would you please tell her to call Patrice?"

"Okay."

When I hung up, Patrice said, "It almost sounds like you think she went willingly."

"We don't know she didn't."

Patrice shot me a dirty look. "Don't forget your partner was clubbed over the noggin and her S & W is missing."

My cell phone rang. Shannon.

"Hi, how are you," I asked.

"I'm fine. I called to ask if I should pick up the twins since you're still out of town."

Zing! "I'm coming home later today, but I'm fine if you want to drop by to see them."

"As long as you're on your way, I won't. How're things going?"

"Not well. Tamika's in the hospital. We found her unconscious on the floor with a goose egg on the back of her head, and Zabrina, who she was supposed to be guarding, is missing, and so is Tamika's firearm."

"Oh, wow. Is Tamika going to be okay?"

"I think so, but she was talking crazy when I found her. Told me the devil didn't wear red, she wore green."

Shannon giggled, then said, "That's not really funny, is it?"

"No. She can't remember anything and puked over the bed railing."

"Not a good sign with a head injury. Are you with her now?"

"No, we're looking for Zabrina. Have you heard anything about your biopsy?"

"Not yet. I'll call you when I know something. And if you end up staying down in Minneapolis, call me and I'll get the kids."

"I'm coming home."

20

I SUGGESTED TO PATRICE we stop at the Logan residence before we headed over to Grady's parents' home to make sure the kids hadn't returned in our absence or that there hadn't been a burglary before or after Tamika was clobbered. When deaths were announced in the obituaries, families might become a target of burglars who watch and wait for the opportunity to break into the grieving family's house.

Patrice conducted a hurried search of places where she knew valuables were kept and rapidly came to the conclusion that nothing had been stolen or disturbed. When I asked if she was sure, she placed her hands on her hips and delivered me a look that would make small children pee their pants.

"Just trying to do my job, Patrice."

"Let's go," she said.

Minutes later, Patrice and I stood on the icy front steps of Lloyd LaMere's small two-story home located in the middle of the block. As soon as Patrice hit the doorbell, it set off the yipping of small dogs, which grew louder as they moved closer.

"I hate small dogs," Patrice said.

"Someone's home. I see the television flickering. Wonder if they can hear the doorbell over the TV blasting."

The LaMeres had a storm door with the screen still in it. Through a translucent curtain on the inside door, I saw movement. The door opened, and a small elderly woman with silver ringlets and kind eyes stared at us. Patrice flashed her badge and said, "Mrs. LaMere?"

The woman placed a hand on the appliquéd poodle on her sweatshirt. With a sweet smile, she said, "Yes?"

"Hello. I'm Sheriff Patrice Clinton from Birch County. This is my detective, Cal Sheehan. Do you know Grady LaMere?"

"Yes, what's wrong?"

"May we come in to ask you a few questions?"

She hesitated but opened the door.

Two white toy poodles with crusty eyes ran circles around Mrs. LaMere, continuing to bark shrilly. Patrice and I removed our shoes just inside the door. The dogs ran ahead a few feet, turned to give us hell for intruding into their territory, then repeated the behavior.

An elderly gentleman wearing gray work pants and shirt, like my grandpa used to wear, was seated in a recliner with his back to us. He was watching *Duck Dynasty*. The volume was turned up so loud it would not be surprising if neighbors two houses down could hear Uncle Si's conversation with Phil.

The odor of urine overpowered the scented plug-ins I spotted in two different outlets. *The two dogs must pee in the house,* I thought with disgust.

Knickknacks, mostly religious statues, filled two antique glassed-in cases along the left wall. Wedged between the cases was a print of *Grace* taken by Eric Enstrom in Bovey, Minnesota, in 1918. My Grandma Sylvia had a copy in her dining room.

"Lloyd, we have company. It's the cops. Turn down the TV."

"Huh?"

She grabbed the remote from the edge of his chair and muted the television. "The cops are here." Her voice carried a tone of frustration for having to repeat for the old man.

He turned to face us and scowled. "What's the problem now?"

Both dogs jumped on the sofa to continue their blustering protest. Lloyd swiped at the dogs and yelled in a gravelly voice, "Shuddup!" They didn't. Mrs. LeMere scooted them off the blue velveteen sofa, which faced the small boxy Sony TV. Suddenly the dogs jumped up onto Lloyd's lap and settled in, satisfied their work was done.

Patrice made introductions, and then I said, "We're looking for Grady. He gave us your residence as his home address," I said.

"Oh, uh-huh," she said. "He's our grandson. He's lived with us since he was a tot."

"When his folks got sent to the slammer," Lloyd said.

Aha.

"What's going on?" Lloyd asked.

"We want to question him in the disappearance of his girlfriend," Patrice said.

The LaMeres exchanged looks.

"Disappearance?" Lloyd asked.

"Girlfriend?" Mrs. LaMere asked.

"Zabrina Bennett," I said. "We can't seem to find her or your grandson. They're probably at a movie or something."

Patrice flashed me a sharp look. I wasn't convinced she'd been abducted—they could be anywhere having a good time and unaware we were frantically trying to locate them.

"Have you spoken to Grady today, Mrs. LaMere?" Patrice asked.

Lloyd scratched his chin. "When was he here last, Becky?"

Becky?

"A couple weeks ago, when he came to pick up his check."

"His check?" I asked.

"We give him a monthly allowance so he doesn't have to borrow money. He goes to the University of Minnesota and holds down two jobs and that's enough."

"Where does he work?" I asked.

"At the Rainbow on Lake Street and Hawley's Vet clinic in Robbinsdale," Lloyd said. "That's where we take these ankle biters." He stroked the poodles in unison. One grunted, the other made a sound like a wild turkey.

"Do you know his work schedule?" I asked Becky.

"No."

"What does he do at the vet clinic?" I asked.

Becky said, "He takes care of animals they house overnight, cleans cages, that kind of thing. He's wanted to be a vet since he was a little boy. He used to pretend Penny was his patient. Remember that, Lloyd?"

A nod from Lloyd.

"She was our sweet little apricot poodle. He'd bandage her all up. That dog was unusually patient with him." She smiled, immersed in the memories of the good old days.

Lloyd nodded.

"And what does he do at Rainbow?" Patrice asked.

Becky said, "He stocks shelves at night. Lloyd got him that job."

Lloyd said, "That's where I worked up until I retired. I worked for the Red Owl out on Highway Seven 'fore that."

"It's kind of you to take Grady in," I said.

Lloyd said, "Well, whatcha gonna do?"

"Why are his folks incarcerated?" I asked.

"They got involved with the wrong people," Becky said. She sighed and shook her head.

"Drugs," Lloyd growled.

Whoop, there it is. "When?" I asked.

Becky's hand lifted to her chin. "Well, Grady was only five, so I guess it must be fifteen years already. I suppose his mother should be released this summer, but our Orton had some trouble. Some inmates picked on him and, well, he fought back, and they increased his sentence. Does that seem right to you?"

"I don't know. I wasn't there," I said.

"Would you mind if we look at Grady's room?" Patrice asked.

"What do you think, Lloyd?" Becky said.

"I suppose it's all right."

WE FOLLOWED MRS. LAMERE up a steep, narrow staircase to the second story, which consisted of a large single bedroom and a bathroom.

She pointed to a photo on the wall of a young man in an army uniform. "That's Orton. This was his room before it was Grady's. I was told I could never have a child, but I got pregnant at forty-two. The doctor thought something would be wrong with him because I was of a certain age, but we prayed and prayed, and he was a perfect little boy." She chuckled. "We fooled the doctors."

"What a wonderful story," I said.

Patrice tossed me an amused look. I wanted to keep Becky talking.

"He joined the Army and was stationed at Fort Leonard Wood, Missouri. That's where he met Brenda. She was born in the Ozarks and was looking for a husband to get her out of Missouri. When he was discharged, she followed him back up here. She got herself pregnant, and lucky for her, we raised Orton to be a responsible man. He married her. The economy was bad at the time, and they had a hard go of it. Guess they turned to selling drugs to make ends meet."

Yeah, that's one option that'll get you three hots and a cot.

I surveyed the room. The furniture carried a layer of dust, but the place was orderly, like his current room at the house by the U. There was a poster of Kirby Puckett tacked on the wall, the edges frayed and curled. From the condition, I'd say it was most likely Orton's, not Grady's. But the books in the small bookshelf, including the entire Harry Potter and The Girl With the

Dragon Tattoo series, were his. An old Dell desktop computer sat on a small desk in the corner. The closet contained few items: a graduation gown, a couple of plaid shirts, a suit, and two pairs of dress pants. Boxes of Legos, an Atari game console, and a remote control car were stored on the upper shelf.

"He's always been as neat as a pin. You ever heard of a kid who put his toys away without being told?"

Yeah, I was like that. "When did he move out?"

"Two years ago, when he graduated."

"Who were his friends in high school?" Patrice asked.

"He never brought any around. I think he was ashamed his parents were in prison."

"You didn't find it unsettling not to know his friends?" Patrice asked, her voice full of self-righteousness.

Becky tightened her lips and didn't answer.

"Did he play sports?" I asked, trying to regain a thread of rapport.

"No, he wasn't interested."

Before Patrice could jump back in, I pointed to the computer. "He liked working on the computer?"

She nodded. "Oh, yes. He asked for one when he was a freshman in high school. Said it would be his Christmas and birthday presents for four years. Lloyd got a good deal on a used one, so we didn't hold him to the bargain."

"What kind of student was he?"

Becky's chin lifted as she glared at Patrice. "He was always on the A honor roll. He's a wonderful boy." Abruptly, she turned and headed back down the stairs, and we followed.

When back in the living room, I said, "Well, if he contacts you, could you give us a call? We want to make sure he and his girlfriend are all right."

"Well . . . now you've got me worried. When you find him, you tell him to call me."

I nodded.

Patrice winced as we stood in the entry putting on our shoes. "Oh, for Chrissake," she said. "One of those damn dogs peed on my boots." She took a tissue from her pocket and began wiping it dry.

I made a face, but was pleased they hadn't pissed on mine.

As Patrice stepped off the first step, her feet went out from under her. I caught her arm before she hit, but her foot turned at an odd angle. I kept hold as she took the next step. Her leg buckled.

"Damn, I think I sprained my ankle."

As I helped her to the Explorer, Ryan and Martha Gill approached us on the sidewalk.

"Saw you fall," Martha said. "Are you okay?"

"I'll be fine," Patrice said.

"So, you beat us here?" Ryan said.

"I'm responsible for the girl. I thought they might know where they were," she said.

"Did they?" Ryan asked.

"They claimed they didn't," Patrice said as she shrugged off my supporting hand and hobbled the few remaining steps to the Explorer. I used the remote to unlock the door.

Ryan said, "Why wouldn't she wait for us?"

"She's pretty worried."

"Where are you headed next?"

"Back to Logan."

"Zach Whitman said you searched Grady's room without a search warrant. I told him you were operating under ours."

"Thanks," I said.

"We can't screw this up. Not that I believe Grady would shoot his girlfriend and her mother."

"No, it's unlikely," I said.

Gill said, "Do you know his parents are serving fifteen years on a drug conviction? Their drug of choice was cocaine. Orton's father, Lloyd, on the other hand, has never had so much as a speeding ticket."

Ryan said, "We have some things to discuss. Stay put at Logan until we get there."

"You got it."

When I got back in the car, Patrice said, "My ankle really hurts."

"Want to find a clinic?"

"It's just a sprain. They can't do anything anyway. Let's go to Sonya's, so I can ice it." After a few blocks, she said, "I slipped because the bottom of my boot was wet from the dog pee."

"Probably."

She then said, "You're better with people than I am."

"If you want cooperation, folks have to feel respected."

She nodded. "I just get so disgusted with denial and ignorance. Grady didn't bring his friends over because he was ashamed of *them*, not his parents."

"You don't know that. By the way, Ryan's pissed we didn't wait for them."

"Too bad. My goddaughter's missing, and some psycho killer may have her. What if she's been kidnapped and a ransom's demanded? I don't know if I can get access to that kind of money easily. Maybe we should call the FBI."

"Calm it the hell down, Patrice."

She blinked at me and didn't say any more.

RUSSELL BENNETT'S RENTAL WAS sitting in the driveway of the Logan house. Patrice handed me the house key, and I acted as her human crutch as she hobbled up the steps and all the way to the living room, where Russell was sitting reading and sipping tea. I helped Patrice get situated on the sofa and propped her swollen foot onto a silk pillow. She grimaced in pain.

Sarah entered. "What happened to you?"

"I slipped. Is Zabrina back?"

"Unfortunately, no."

"Do you have an ice pack?" I asked.

Sarah hustled off.

"Have you heard anything at all?" Russell asked.

"We've just spoken to his grandparents, who raised him, and they don't know where he is either."

"They could be lying," Patrice said.

"I don't think so," I said.

"Whatever."

Sarah brought in a cold pack and placed it on Patrice's ankle. "Do you want something for the pain? I have some left from when I had my wisdom teeth pulled."

"That would be wonderful," Patrice said, managing a small smile.

I thought better of reminding her taking someone else's medication was illegal and stupid because she very well knew it. Sarah came back with a glass of water and two white pills. "I'll go find the crutches Justine used when she sprained her ankle last summer."

Patrice swallowed the pills down and asked me to fix her a drink.

"Alcohol with someone else's pain meds?" I asked.

"Oh, just do it."

Russell rushed to his feet. "I'll get it. What would you like, Patrice?"

"Scotch."

"You want something, deputy?" he asked.

"No, thanks. It's eleven o'clock, and I need to drive back to Prairie Falls this afternoon."

"How can you leave?" Patrice asked.

"This is my week with my kids."

"Wouldn't Shannon take them?"

"Patrice . . ."

"Fine."

Sarah came back with a pair of crutches. I adjusted them to fit Patrice.

"Will you be joining us for dinner, Deputy Sheehan?"

"No, but thanks."

"I'm making a rib roast."

"Sounds tempting, but I have to get back home."

This whole scene felt off to me. A girl was missing and her father and god-mother were sipping beverages and a grand meal was being prepared.

When I heard the front door open, I scrambled to the foyer. Zabrina and Grady brushed past me and headed for the stairs, Gap shopping bags in their hands.

"Stop. I think you better stop and say hello to your father and Patrice," I said. "No one knew where you were, and we couldn't contact you by phone because you weren't carrying yours."

Zabrina turned, looked at me, and rolled her eyes. Russell rushed to his daughter.

"Thank God you're okay," he said.

"I'm fine. Dad, this is my boyfriend, Grady."

When they entered the living room, Patrice hollered, "Where the hell have you been?"

Zabrina burst into tears. Russell wrapped his arms around his daughter. "It's okay, sweetheart. When you weren't here, we thought you had been abducted."

"Abducted?"

Patrice's face was beet red. "Yes, abducted!"

"Stop screaming at her. She's pregnant!" Grady yelled back.

Boom.

21

N O ONE SPOKE FOR SEVERAL SECONDS. Zabrina's face was locked in shock since Grady announced her uterine passenger. Embarrassed for everyone, I averted my attention to the fireplace, the popping and spitting of the burning logs and mesmerizing flames licking upward.

Patrice broke the spell. "You didn't have sex education in school? You weren't aware condoms would prevent pregnancy?"

Zabrina stepped away from Grady, as she whispered, "This was our secret, remember?"

As Grady pulled her in close, her body tightened. "Sorry, sweetheart, I didn't like you being yelled at."

One would expect him to look sheepish or scared like most kids in his predicament would be, but he was standing tall and proud. This was a story from which movies were made: Handsome, poor fella falls in love with and knocks up a pretty, rich girl.

Patrice lifted a hand. "Maybe you're just late with all the stress you're experiencing," she said.

Grady said, "She used one of those tests."

"Why didn't you tell me?" Patrice asked, her voice sharp, accusing.

"Why are you so mad at me?" Zabrina fired back.

"Because your mother can't be," Patrice said.

Whoa. Once again, the room fell silent.

Zabrina's face pinched up, and I prepared myself for the caterwauling. Russell found his way back to his chair, while Grady engulfed Zabrina in his arms as she bawled. When the wailing subsided, Grady said, "What made you think she'd been abducted?"

I said, "We found my partner knocked out cold on Zabrina's bathroom floor."

"What? How did that happen?" Zabrina said.

"We assumed it had something to do with the fact you were missing. You left your cell phone, which only substantiated our theory."

Zabrina scowled. "I just forgot it. God, Aunt Patrice, you need to chill out."

"Chill out? Did you hear what Cal said? We thought you'd been abducted. We almost had a damn BOLO put out on your cars."

"Explain how Deputy Frank got knocked out," I said.

"How would I know?" Zabrina said. "She was fine when we left."

"Where was she when you last saw her?"

"In my room. No one was here to help me take a bath, so she did. Then Grady showed up and we left."

"Is she okay?" Grady asked.

"Not really. She's in the hospital with a concussion," I said.

"She can't remember a thing, so we were hoping you knew what happened," Patrice said.

Oh, shit. Double shit. Telling them Tamika was suffering from amnesia was beyond stupid.

Grady said, "That's terrible."

"Sarah, may I speak with you?" I said as I pointed to the hallway. Once away from the others, I asked, "Where are Tamika's things?"

"Downstairs in the guest room."

I followed her to the lowest level, past a laundry room and a workout room. Tamika's purse and suitcase were on the floor near a small bureau. I searched through her things and found no firearm.

"What're you looking for?" she said.

"Tamika's firearm, a Smith & Wesson. Did you see it?"

"No."

As we exited the room, I pointed to a closed door at the end of the hall. "What's in there?"

"Erica and John's suite."

"Are they home yet?"

"No."

"You're sure."

"Positive. Their car isn't here."

She knocked on the door and shouted their names. When no one answered, she said, "Should I get the master key and open it?"

"No, I'm going upstairs to check Zabrina's room."

THE BED WAS MADE, the towels were picked up from the bathroom floor.

"Did you clean up in here?"

"Yes, I do light cleaning on Erica's days off," Sarah said.

"Where did you go this morning after I left?"

"I ran errands."

"Was Russell still here?"

"Yes, he and Zabrina were upstairs."

"And Tamika?"

"She was making calls at the dining room table. I'm sorry, I thought she had everything under control, so I took my time running errands. I even shopped for a new dress for the funeral. I didn't know all this was going on."

"How would you? Wonder what Sonya would think about Zabrina's pregnancy."

She gasped. "Zabrina's pregnant?"

"Yes."

She sunk to a kitchen chair, her hands at her temples. "What next?"

I sat across from her. "The girl has a large safety net."

She nodded. "Yes, but still, I worry. She's like a lost lamb without her family." She took a deep breath.

"What was Zabrina's relationship with Sonya and Justine like?"

She raised her brows. "Justine was a pushover as far as Zabrina was concerned. I get it; she was her only child, but Mrs. Donovan worried Zabrina was ill-equipped to enter the real world. She wanted her go to boarding school, but Justine nixed that idea. Then Mrs. Donovan pushed for her to get away from home and go to an eastern college, but that didn't pan out."

"Who told you all this?"

"No one. I overheard all of it." She gave me a sly smile. "We service employees are invisible, you know." She touched my arm. "I do wish you'd stay for dinner."

"Unfortunately, I must get home to my twenty-month-old twins."

Her hand retracted, and her eyes lost their part of the smile. "Oh." She rose and said, "I better start lunch."

"Sure, I'll get out of your hair."

I should have used the twins to fend off Martha Gill.

When Detectives Ryan and Gill arrived, I met them at the door to tell them the kids were back. They listened to what I had to say, then Ryan said, "Why doesn't this surprise me?"

"I can guess."

I showed them to the living room, then leaned against the wall to listen to Zabrina retell how Tamika helped her with her bath and how she was perfectly fine when she left.

I said, "See, I have a problem with your story, Zabrina. Deputy Frank's job was to guard you—she wouldn't have let you leave without her."

That got everyone's attention.

Patrice nodded. "I agree."

Zabrina jutted her chin out. "Could it be she trusted me? Which is more than I can say for you, Patrice."

Patrice leaned forward and jabbed a finger at Zabrina. "It's not about trusting you. Do you recall you were shot right outside your own house in your own driveway?" She redirected her jab toward the window.

"How could I forget?" Zabrina screamed. "My mother died in my arms!"

The room grew silent.

After an uncomfortable few seconds, I said, "Zabrina, we're concerned with why your grandmother was killed, why you and your mother were shot, and if the person or persons who did that will come back for you."

"You don't have to try and scare me anymore than I already am."

"Okay, but where have you been all this time?"

Grady said, "Zabrina needed a dress for the funeral."

Patrice jerked her head toward Zabrina. "I would have helped you buy a dress."

"I didn't want your help."

Patrice exhaled and looked away.

"You looked for a dress for hours? The stores probably weren't even open when you left," I said.

"We went out for breakfast at Five Watt Coffee on Nicollet before we went to the mall," Grady said.

"What's it to you guys anyway where we went?" Zabrina said.

Detective Ryan scratched his head and said, "Well, I think I've heard enough." Ryan and Gill stood. "Young lady, I suggest you keep Sheriff Clinton informed of your plans. You worried a lot of people."

Zabrina looked up at him with a pouty face. "I apologize, sir . . . to you too, Auntie Patrice. I shouldn't have assumed your deputy would tell you where we were."

Patrice's face softened. "Oh, come here."

I didn't get why everyone pandered to her. Grieving or not, she was a snot. I followed the detectives out to their unmarked Buick parked next to Zabrina's red Miata convertible.

Martha crossed her arms. "Did you not consider she went somewhere with her boyfriend before you pushed the panic button?"

"We had an officer down and Zabrina's cell phone had been left behind. Deputy Frank's firearm's still missing, by the way. Does your department know anything about that?"

"They would've indicated it in their report if they found it, but I'll check," Ryan said.

Gill walked to the passenger side, "The kids may be right. She could have slipped in the bathroom after they left."

"My boss mentioned to the kids Tamika has amnesia—they could say anything they wanted at that point."

"You think they assaulted your partner?" Gill asked.

"I don't know," I said.

"Well, we need to spend our time on real crimes," she hissed, and got in the car.

"Tamika wouldn't have let Zabrina go out without her," I said to Ryan.

"Do you think the kids hit her with something just because they wanted to go shopping by themselves?"

"Sounds far-fetched, I admit, but where's my partner's firearm?"

"Sheriff Clinton said the door was unlocked when you got back. Is that right?"

"Yes."

"Then perhaps the kids forgot to lock the door when they left, and someone came in and knocked her out and stole her gun."

"And how likely is that?"

He laughed. "Maybe one of the employees took it. I should think since your sheriff seems to be the current head of household she could authorize a thorough search."

"Yes."

"When are you going back home?"

"This afternoon."

He came to shake my hand. "We'll be in touch, Cal. Good working with you." He lowered his voice to say, "Don't mind Martha. I think she has a thing for you."

I shook my head. Yeah, Martha was a woman I wouldn't get involved with—too moody.

WHEN I REENTERED THE LIVING ROOM, the tension in the room was palpable.

"It's not your decision, Patrice," Russell said.

"Nor yours," she answered.

"What's going on?" I asked. I figured I was already far enough into the personal business of this family I could get away with asking.

"We want to get married. Patrice disagrees," Grady said.

"They're legal adults," Russell said.

"Teenage marriages are doomed for failure, Russell, and you know it."

I had other concerns. "Grady, where's your car?"

"In the repair shop. Zabrina followed me over, and we dropped it off before we went shopping."

"Bad muffler?" I asked.

"No, brakes."

"How could you drive with one hand?" Patrice asked Zabrina.

"Perfectly fine." The girl had worn a perpetual snarl since she returned.

"Seems strange neither of you had your phones," I said.

Grady said, "Oh . . .um . . . I didn't mean to leave mine. I guess I was in a hurry to pick up Zabrina."

"Does Zabrina know about your parents, Grady?" Patrice asked.

A deep rosy hue crept up his neck and on to his cheeks. He turned to Zabrina and took her hands in his. "Patrice wants you to know I was raised by my grandparents because my parents are in prison for selling drugs."

"So, you didn't know?" Patrice said.

Defiance set in Zabrina's face as she turned to Patrice. "I don't see why that's important. Grady's obviously not like his parents."

"Grady, might I have a private word?" I said.

Patrice tossed me a curious look. He followed me into the foyer and down the hallway. I ducked into the office opposite the kitchen.

"Am I in trouble?" he asked.

"Yes and no. Besides knocking up Zabrina, you took off with her without telling anyone."

"We just wanted to get away from Patrice. She butts in all of Zabrina's business."

The kid had a point, but I knew Tamika simply wouldn't let Zabrina go off without her.

"I need to know where you were on December eleventh and twelfth, the night when Zabrina's grandmother was killed."

He blinked his eyes in confusion. "Um, a lot of places—at school, my apartment, work."

"Write down where you were and who may have seen you, in chronological order—to the best of your ability."

"Seriously? Am I a suspect or something?"

"Not if you can prove to me why you couldn't have committed Sonya's murder."

The muscles around his eyes tightened. People don't like to be suspects. I walked over to the printer, pulled a piece of paper from the tray, grabbed a pen from a container on the desk, and handed them to him.

"Use the desk in here."

I went back to the living room to officially ask Patrice if I had her permission to search the house for Tamika's firearm.

"Of course."

Then I asked Zabrina if I could search her car.

"Why?" she asked. "And where's Grady?"

"He's doing something for me."

"What?" She started making her way out of the room.

Patrice put her hand up. "Nope. Stay here until Deputy Sheehan is done searching."

"Oh, for God's sake," she said, and plopped down on the love seat.

"Do I have your permission?"

Big attitudinal sigh. "Yeees." I was starting not to like this girl.

AFTER I CONDUCTED THE CAR search and didn't find Tamika's firearm, I glanced in on Grady, who was busy writing. Although he seemed like a nice kid, he was one of the few who had motive to kill Zabrina's mother and grandmother. His pregnant girlfriend was now one wealthy young woman. But he had no idea what he was in for if he married this girl.

AFTER I FINISHED my unsuccessful quest to find Tamika's Smith & Wesson, Grady found me. He handed me a chronological accounting by the hour of where he'd been and who may have seen him. I thanked him, then told Patrice I was stopping at the hospital before heading back home.

"Take Tamika's things with you."

"Okay."

"With Tamika down, I'm gonna need more hours from Spanky and Crosby," I said.

"Fine. Just find Sonya's killer." She enunciated each word like it was a sentence of its own.

"That's. The. Goal," I said.

She narrowed her eyes but let it pass.

Just before I opened the front door with Tamika's bag in tow, Sarah rushed over and handed me a white paper box and a manilla file folder.

"When I left, Tamika was working on these papers in this file."

"Thanks. What's in the box?"

"Chicken salad sandwiches and a slice of key lime pie—for your lunch."

"Thank you, how kind." It was an awkward moment.

Once in my vehicle, I called Clara to tell her I'd be home in time for dinner, then drove downtown. What a strange set of circumstances: Someone knocked out my partner, she had no memory, her firearm was missing, and I still had no idea who killed Sonya Donovan. My next step was to check on Grady's alibi. If it panned out, which I suspected it would, I had no idea what to try next.

22

AFTER CONSIDERING THE CHOICES in the hospital gift shop, I bought Tamika a modest vase of pink and white flowers the clerk called "lovely alstroemeria," then headed up to her room.

I hadn't expected to see Adriana Valero sitting next to Anton Frank. He got up from his chair to give me a man-hug: short duration, ending with pat on the back and a "Hey, man." The stress showed in his closely set, dark eyes. He rolled Tamika's luggage off to the side.

"Her purse is inside the luggage," I told him.

"Thanks. She asked for her phone."

I nodded and looked toward the empty bed. "Where's our patient?" I asked.

"She's getting a CT scan."

I pointed to Anton's newly grown facial hair. "Nice beard," I said.

The short boxed beard, the black-framed eyeglasses, and tweed sweater gave him the look of a distinguished professor, rather than a mechanic and gas station owner.

"Thanks," he said, touching his hairy chin. I turned my attention to Adriana. "We meet again," I said, clever devil that I am.

"Yes," she said, giving me a weak smile. She uncrossed her long legs to rise, but instead of coming to give me a hug, she took the vase from me, saying, "I'll put these on the window ledge."

She set the vase next to two massive bouquets: one of red and white roses and the other a colorful mixed floral arrangement like the one I'd rejected because it was forty bucks more.

Anton retrieved a chair from the other side of the room and motioned for me to have a seat. He sat between Adriana and me as if to shield us from one another. She must have said something to him.

"So tell me what happened," Anton said, crossing one arm over his abdomen, propping an elbow on his fist, placing his fingers on his chin as he waited for an explanation of how I let his beloved get clunked on the back of the head.

"I found her out cold on the bathroom floor."

"She doesn't remember anything."

"We don't really know whether she was hit or she fell."

"What about the girl she was guarding?" Anton pressed.

"She was gone for a few hours but came home after a shopping trip. She says Tamika allowed her to go shopping, which I highly doubt. She also said Tamika was fine when she left the house. Whatever the explanation, we can't ignore the implications of her missing firearm."

"Perhaps Tamika did trust her," Adriana said.

"She was supposed to be guarding Zabrina—you know she takes things like that seriously. I found the front door unlocked, so it's possible someone else came in."

"Was anything missing? Beside her firearm?" Adriana asked.

"Not to my knowledge."

"It may have been something not easily detected, like a document."

"You should be the detective."

She rolled her eyes and was about to comment when Tamika was wheeled in. We watched two technicians help her back into her bed.

"How'd it go, Puddin' Pop?" Anton said, moving to his wife's bedside.

"The stuff they gave me made me feel like I had to pee."

"So, look who's here," Anton said.

Tamika smiled and said, "Hi, when did you two drive down?"

We three shared "uh-oh" looks.

Anton patted her hand. "Oh, sweetie, you know Adriana is down in Minneapolis living with her mother."

Tamika batted her eyelashes. "I know that."

"How are you feeling?" I asked.

"My head hurts and I'm nauseated, but other than that I'm dandy as candy. Right, Anton?"

"Right." He kissed her hand. I should take lessons from Anton.

"Cal says the girl who disappeared came back home," Anton said.

"What girl?" she asked.

Anton lowered his face to meet hers and kissed her on the nose. "Are you hungry?"

She stuck her tongue out. "Bleh. No, but I'm so tired."

"Close your eyes and rest, my darling," he said.

The doctor came in to speak with Anton, so Adriana and I left and walked to the family lounge. We sat in chairs perpendicular to each other.

"This is not good. She can't even remember we're not together," Adriana said.

"She's just confused right now. Things will get better . . . I hope, anyway."

We sat in silence for a few seconds. We both started to speak at once.

"Go ahead," she said.

"I'm heading home in a few minutes."

"Okay." She stared at her hands, rather than me, and picked at a scrape in her bright red fingernail polish. I wanted to make a snarky comment about her underwear model, but refrained. A lengthy silence ensued. I finally stood and muttered that I should get going. I stuck my head in Tamika's room to see if the doctor was gone. He was.

"What's the deal?" I asked.

Anton's voice trembled as he said, "She has what he called moderate traumatic brain injury . . . because she was out for a longer time and is confused." He took a deep breath.

"What's the prognosis?"

"He says her memory should return, but he can't predict when because it varies greatly in patients. The good signs are she has no vision or hearing problems, her speech is good, and her limbs seem unaffected. They want to keep her here for at least a couple days. I could stay in her hotel room. Is the key in her purse?"

"We checked out this morning. She was going to stay to guard Zabrina and drive back up with Patrice."

Anton frowned. "She hadn't told me."

"It was a last-minute deal."

ONCE ON THE ROAD, I called to give Patrice an update on Tamika. "How's everything at Logan?"

"Russell and I are discussing what should happen next with Zabrina. We're going to ask her to postpone marriage until after the baby is born. I'm hoping she'll either end the pregnancy or the relationship."

"I have a feeling the more you push her, the more she'll move in the opposite direction," I said.

"I suppose so."

"Where's the happy couple now?" I asked.

"Upstairs. We're not worried about her getting pregnant . . . anymore." She snickered. "But he is not sleeping over."

"I thought his car was in the shop. How can he leave?"

"Well, he's *not* using the Miata," Patrice said.

"Well, good luck with all that."

"I'll be coming up as soon as I settle things here," Patrice said.

"When might that be?" I asked.

"Memorial service for both is next Tuesday, so I'm hoping Wednesday or Thursday."

"See you then," I said.

"If I don't see you before you testify in your friend's trial, good luck."

"Thanks."

The trial that I dreaded.

ON THE DRIVE, I RECEIVED a call from Leslie Rouch.

"The DNA results are back. I thought you'd want to know right away that someone else's DNA was on the sheets in the hamper and basically all over the house."

"Whose?"

"Waldo D. Clinton's."

"I don't know him."

"I believe you do. He's Sheriff Clinton's husband."

"Her husband's name is David."

"David is his middle name. He was in the system because of a DUI conviction in 2011."

"Jesus, this is not what I expected to hear."

AT FIVE O'CLOCK, Waldo David Clinton would either be at home or at Birch County Community College, where he worked in the business department. I tried reaching him at the college first and was told he'd already left, so I drove directly to the Clinton home on Island Lake.

The house lights were on when I rang the doorbell. David appeared at the door still dressed in a business suit.

"Cal? What's wrong? Is it Patrice?"

"She's fine. May I come in?"

"Of course. I'm having a cocktail. Join me?"

"No, thanks."

We sat in the great room, where he had a fire going and sixties music blasting.

He turned down the music and said, "So what's up?" He tossed me a big smile. His hand was shaking so much the ice rattled in the glass. He set it down on a coaster.

"You had to know I'd eventually come and talk to you."

"Why's that?"

"Because Waldo D. Clinton's DNA is all over Sonya's house."

His head dropped as he buried his face with his hands. "Shit."

"Yeah."

"Does Patrice know?" he asked.

"Not yet."

"Damn it. Okay, all right. I was at Sonya's."

"When?"

"Just the once."

"The date?"

"The day before Patrice found her. Oh, my God, this is bad."

"I'm going to need you to come in for questioning."

"You don't think I killed her, do you?"

"I don't think anything right now."

"Does Patrice have to find out?"

"Oh, yeah, and I suggest you tell her ASAP."

He shook his head. "How am I going to find the words?"

"You just do. Come to the department tomorrow morning at eight." I made my way to the door. "Have a nice night, Waldo."

WHEN I DROVE UP to my house, I noticed Christmas tree lights in the living room window. It was lucky I had forgotten to buy a tree. I pulled around Shannon's Pilot parked by the garage. Bullet met me at the door, and I gave him a good loving up. The kids came running for their hugs and kisses. They'd been confined to the family room as the gate had been put up in the doorway, most assuredly to keep them away from the tree.

"Who put up the tree?" I asked.

"I bought it and Shannon helped me trim it while the children napped," Clara said.

"Thanks, Shannon."

"How's Tamika?" Shannon asked. She leaned back on the sofa, a glass of wine in her hand.

Clara brought me a glass without asking, and I recounted what the doctor had said.

"Gosh, that's bum luck for Tamika. She's just off leave and now injured again. Who has the kids?"

"I don't even know."

"Maybe Tamika's parents came up."

"Where's Luke?" I asked.

"He's on a sleepover at Josh Waxler's."

"Josh on his soccer team?"

"Yes."

"That's a good thing."

"Yes. Um, I decided I would take you up on your offer of staying here while I recover from my surgery. If you're still offering."

"Yes, absolutely. Do you know when that will be?"

"No. I'm anxious to get it over with, so I'm taking the first available date."

Anxiety grabbed me by the throat, but I smiled and patted my ex-wife's hand.

"If you don't mind, I'll stay over tonight . . . in the guest room."

"Sure."

After dinner, Clara helped me with the dishes while Shannon was upstairs bathing the Twinks.

I went up and tucked them in, then told Shannon I had some work to do. She smiled and nodded and followed me downstairs. I stopped at the office at the front of the house, and she headed for the family room in the rear.

I wrote out notes for my interview with Waldo Clinton. Waldo—no wonder he went by David. I didn't believe his "it only happened once" claim. Then I began the paperwork for the Minneapolis trip. Close to ten, I stopped by to say goodnight to Shannon and Clara, who were watching *Keeping Up with the Kardashians*. Shannon was curled up under a blanket on the couch. I let Bullet out one more time, then sat down by Shannon's feet.

She said, "Since I'm having the twins for Christmas Eve, my folks wanted me to invite you to dinner and Christmas morning brunch."

It was her attempt at appeasing me for missing the best part of the holiday with the Twinks.

"We'll see."

When Shannon excused herself to go to the bathroom, Clara said, "You know you're invited to our house for the whole holiday. My boys are coming home, and Dallas and I'd like you to meet them."

"Thanks. I'll at least stop by."

Shannon returned. I said goodnight and headed up to bed. I heard the downstairs television playing late into the night. She must have been having trouble sleeping. Me too. I tossed and turned for several hours thinking how hard it was going to be for Patrice, who'd lost two friends, to learn her husband was screwing Sonya Donovan. Or did Patrice find out and do the deed herself? But she never would have been able to get Sonya back upstairs by herself. Perhaps a collusion between David and Patrice to gain control of the Donovan funds? Or was I just having crazy middle-of-the-night thoughts?

23

Saturday, December 20

WHEN I CAME DOWNSTAIRS, Shannon asked what I was giving Clara for Christmas.

"A gift certificate to a spa."

"Great idea. Put my name on it, too."

Get your own gift was on the tip of my tongue, then I remembered she had cancer, and I was thinking like an asshole.

"Sure."

She then asked if she could take the kids a day early. I had a feeling she wanted to spend as much time with them as possible, so I agreed. I kissed my babies, then I gave Shannon a hug. She clung to me as I patted her back.

"Everything is going to be fine, Shannon. Hear me?"

She pulled away and said, "Go to work." Her cheeks were streaked with tears. *Damn cancer.*

I HAD RESERVED THE INTERVIEW room and arranged for Crosby to film. When I met Waldo David Clinton in the lobby, his usual confident swagger was gone. Once seated across from him at the small table in the interview room, I began by giving the case number and documenting his personal information. He was forty-eight, sixteen years younger than Sonya. *Stupid shit.*

Waldo first met Sonya years ago at Justine and Russell's wedding. She came on to him when he and Patrice had dinner with her at the Dexter house the Friday after Thanksgiving. While Justine and Patrice went for a walk, she jacked him off. He said he and Patrice had been having a difficult go of it . . . yada yada yada.

"Do you want to revise the number of sexual encounters?"

"Huh?"

"Hand jobs count."

"Okay, then . . . three times. She gave me oral sex at the Christmas party."

"The sheriff department's party?"

"Yes, do you want details?" he said, lowering his head.

"No."

"I assume you're taping this. Is my wife going to see it?"

"Up to her."

He covered his face with his hands. Beads of sweat formed on his brow.

"Because you had been a guest at the Dexter house, any DNA of yours found there could have been innocent—except for your semen on her bedsheets. Not so innocent."

"I assumed she'd wash the sheets."

"She didn't do her own laundry. Besides, your DNA was taken from fingerprints all over her bedroom and bathroom. Did Patrice suspect you of having an affair?"

"I doubt it. She often worked late."

"I have a feeling you saw her more often than you've indicated."

"Maybe a couple more times," he admitted.

"Was she planning to tell your wife?"

"Absolutely not. Why would she?"

"To break you two up. Then she could have you all to herself."

He shook his head. "No, it was just sex."

"Did Sonya threaten to tell Patrice?"

"No."

"Did you kill her to shut her up?"

His face turned sour. "No, of course not."

Even though I hammered him with variations of the same questions, he maintained he'd been at home with Patrice all Thursday night. She could exonerate him, but he would likely pay a steep price.

I THEN CALLED HAWLEY's Veterinary Clinic in Robbinsdale to verify Grady's claim he was working all night Thursday. A woman named Bev said he normally worked the night shift on weekends, but sometimes the kids traded shifts. I could hear keys clicking. A few seconds later, she said, "He worked Thursday the eleventh from eleven to seven, but didn't work Friday or Saturday nights, and he didn't pick up any shifts that week."

"What about the sixteenth?"

"Just a second . . . no."

"Are you aware that his girlfriend's grandmother died on the eleventh, and his girlfriend's mother was shot to death on the sixteenth? His girlfriend was also wounded."

"The Kenwood shootings?"

"Yes."

"Oh, my word. No, I didn't know. Thank you for telling me."

"What do you know about Grady?"

"Not a lot—he's here when I'm not—but we hired him because he was a pleasant young man and is studying to be a veterinarian."

"Is he a good employee?"

"Yes, I have no complaints."

"Well, thank you for the information," I said.

Next, I called the manager at Rainbow to find out if he had worked on the twelfth or the sixteenth. He transferred me to the personnel director, who said Grady quit last September because of his heavy course load at the university.

"How long did he work for you?"

"Over two years."

"And was he a good employee?"

"He's a nice kid and did his job, stocked shelves. It's not exactly quantum physics."

Martha Gill called, and I almost let it go into messaging.

"Did Grady's grandparents tell you he wasn't in any activities or sports?" she asked.

"Yes."

"Well, I spoke with personnel from South High School, which he attended. He played high school soccer all four years. His coach said he was an A student and one of his better players, never missed a practice or game, but he never showed up for the awards banquet at the end of the season. He knew Grady's parents were incarcerated, but didn't think his classmates did."

"Could be."

"His coach said he was closest to Ben Smith and Tom Obermeyer. They both said they had limited contact since high school. Ben said Grady was a great guy but very private. He also mentioned Grady dated Bailey Caldwell his senior year, a young woman who went to Breck. So, I stopped by the

Caldwells' Edina home on Kellogg. It's one of those grand old brick mansions built in the thirties. Anyway, Mrs. Caldwell gave me Bailey's number, so I got hold of her in Boulder. He told her his grandparents raised him because his parents were killed in a car accident. She said she never met the grandparents because they didn't like him to bring friends home. She said he was possessive; he didn't like her having other friends that were boys. She only dated him about nine months because he was already talking marriage and having kids, and she wasn't ready for a serious relationship."

"So perhaps dating wealthy girls is a pattern. Did the mother have an opinion of Grady?"

"She was relieved when Bailey ended the relationship. She said he was a nice boy but was always at their home, which bugged her."

"Have you checked Russell Bennett's phone records?"

"Yes, with his permission. I don't see anything that implicates him in either of our murders and, because of the divorce, I don't see how these deaths profit him."

"I suppose he could try to obtain conservatorship of Zabrina's finances."

"That's true. Look, I'm late to a team meeting."

"I'll let you go. Thanks for calling."

"No worries."

I sat for a few minutes watching the clock as I thought about Tamika and her missing firearm. She hadn't slipped. Someone hit her and stole her gun. I looked at my watch and decided it wasn't too early to call Anton Frank.

"Cal, thanks for stopping by last night. I know how busy you are."

"No problem. How's Tamika?"

"Her symptoms aren't getting any worse, and they tell me that's a good sign."

"Is she remembering anything about what happened?"

"Not yet."

"Do you know when she'll be discharged?"

"Soon, I hope."

I ended the call because a text came in from Shannon.

"What's up?" I asked.

"My doctor just called. The biopsy confirmed I have invasive ductal carcinoma. I won't know the stage until after surgery. The MRI showed two more lesions so he did biopsies, but they were negative. I also had a bone scan yesterday, and if it's negative, he says a lumpectomy is a good option. Do you think that's what I should do?"

"I know nothing about this. Whatever you think."

"I guess I have to go with what the doctor says."

"I would."

"My surgery is scheduled for December 30."

"Then you'll be home for Christmas."

"I kind of wanted to get it over with. Get this cancer out of my body."

"I understand."

A wail in the background. "Uh-oh, I gotta go. Lucy's crying."

I then texted her saying if the kids were too much for her with all that's going on, she should let me know.

I WENT DOWN TO THE SQUAD ROOM to check my mail slot. There was a subpoena from Crow Wing County to testify on Tuesday in Hawk's trial. My childhood friend Michael Hawkinson had been kidnapped and held against his will for three weeks while his captors waited for a check to arrive after forcing him to cash out his investment accounts. When one of his captors got careless, Hawk took advantage and grabbed the gun and shot him. Unfortunately for his brother, Paul, when his involvement became clear to Hawk, he chased and gunned him down as well.

In the time Hawk was missing, I thought he was dead and was shocked when he showed up at my door. But he lied to me, saying his captor was sympathetic and had set him free—nothing about Paul's involvement. Later at a party I threw, he got drunk and passed out. When putting him to bed, he mumbled he'd killed his brother. When I questioned him about it the next day, he admitted what had occurred. I had to take him in, and Crow Wing County arrested him for second-degree murder but he was charged with voluntary manslaughter.

Although I did what I had to do, I was conflicted and not looking forward to testifying against a lifelong friend—or facing his parents, who blamed me for their son's legal problems. He hadn't made contact in the months he'd been out on bail, which I was grateful for. What a fricking mess—just like Waldo D. Clinton's affair with his wife's dead friend. Jesus Christ.

I walked across the hall and added Patrice and Waldo D. Clinton to the list of players in Sonya's life.

DALLAS TEXTED ME AND ASKED if she could bring Chinese take-out for dinner. Her pending divorce hovered between us like an overfilled balloon ready to burst. When she and her dog, Willie, a border collie/golden retriever mix she'd bought from the pound in Brainerd last summer, walked into the house, the dogs took off for parts unknown. I took the bag from her and put it on the counter. I turned, crossed my arms, leaned on the counter, and said, "We need to talk."

"About the divorce?" she said as she took off her coat and hung it on the hook.

"Yes, about the divorce. I understand your desire not to let Vince win. The law says you should get half the property, so stop pussyfooting around and get a court date. You should have done it a long time ago. He's an ass, Dallas."

"I called my attorney this morning. He's filed the case."

"Oh . . . well . . . good."

"I'm sorry I didn't tell you all about it. I won't keep things from you again."

"It's not good for a relationship."

"I know. And I'm starving. Can we eat?"

We filled plates, Dallas found a testosterone-filled Mark Wahlberg movie called *Pain & Gain*, and we ate in front of the television, which we rarely did. The dogs finally calmed down and lay together in front of the fireplace.

As I stabbed a broccoli spear with my fork, she touched my arm.

"You're quiet tonight. Are we good, or is there something else bothering you?"

"Work." I took a deep breath. I had to tell someone. "DNA tests proved David Clinton was boinking Sonya Donovan."

She gasped. "You're kidding."

"Unfortunately not."

She stared at me, the wheels turning as she realized the ramifications.

"And now he's a suspect in her murder."

"Yes."

"What does Patrice say?"

"I don't think she knows yet. A sinister part of me even wonders if she knew and killed Sonya herself, or if she and David were in cahoots. And I'm suspicious of Zabrina's boyfriend, Grady. She's pregnant and he's pushing to marry her."

"And if they marry, he'll be very rich." She pointed a chopstick at me.

I pointed my fork back at her. "But he was working the night of Sonya's murder. However, it is possible he could make the two-hour drive to Birch County, kill Sonya, and get back to his job before seven a.m. But he isn't a particularly muscular kid, so I doubt he could have carried her deadweight up those stairs by himself. He would have needed an accomplice, as would Patrice. But Waldo is a big guy."

"Waldo?"

"Patrice's husband's real name is Waldo David."

"I'd go by David, too."

"Maybe Sonya was threatening to expose their affair. Even if Patrice agrees he was home, he could have snuck out of the house while she was sleeping."

"Why would he shoot the daughter and granddaughter?"

"He wouldn't. Okay, I have to look at who profits from both killings. Only the boyfriend does—if he marries Zabrina."

"But he wouldn't shoot his girlfriend. I bet the murders aren't related. The Minneapolis shootings could be random, a gang initiation or something?"

"Shit. Why can't it be easy?"

"I know something that is."

"What?"

"Me. Let's finish our dinner and dabble in a little dessert."

I put down my fork. "I'm full."

She put down her chopsticks. "Me too."

I scooped her up in my arms and carried her up the stairs to my bed, where I set her down.

"You did not just test your theory to see if David Clinton could manage to carry Sonya all the way upstairs, did you?"

Yep. "No, of course not. I'm being romantic."

She raised a brow, smiled with her amazing aquamarine eyes, and kissed me, causing something of mine to raise down below.

24

Sunday, December 21

SUNDAY MORNING AFTER BREAKFAST, Dallas and Willie left for home, and I went directly to my office and worked on my reports. Patrice had sent me an email message at midnight.

"The memorial service is Tuesday at two o'clock," it said. "I'll be back Wednesday. I've talked Zabrina into staying with me in Prairie Falls until the start of the second semester.

Nothing about Waldo's infidelity or Zabrina's pregnancy dilemma, not that I cared one way or another what the girl did. I just found it interesting. I called David Clinton and left a message saying he should tell his wife today—or I would.

AT FOUR O'CLOCK, I WENT down to the gym, jogged on the treadmill for an hour, lifted weights, then on my way home, stopped and bought steaks. After dinner, Dallas and I took Bullet and Willie out for a short walk, then Dallas turned on some Lifetime movie oozing estrogen. I fell asleep, woke up when the movie was over, then we went upstairs to bed.

"How did the movie end? Did they get a divorce?"

"Yes."

She snuggled into me and after I kissed her, she said, "I originally didn't sign the divorce papers because I couldn't let Vince bully me into letting him have everything."

"I get it."

We kissed again, then I removed the T-shirt she was wearing. I kissed my way down to her nipples.

"He expected me to give in."

My fingers traced a line from her belly button downward.

"Ohh, that feels good," she said.

"Don't you dare say his name again tonight."

"Whose name?"

Monday, December 22

AT THREE O'CLOCK IN THE MORNING, I woke drenched in sweat. I dreamed Patrice and David had killed Sonya and Justine so they could gain control of the Donovan fortune. It seemed so realistic I lay there for several minutes trying to calm down. I eventually got up and went downstairs. Bullet and Willie followed, hoping to score an early breakfast. Both dogs lay by their respective bowls for a half hour. Willie gave up his food watch first and jumped up on the couch by my feet while I watched *Ferris Bueller's Day Off* on Netflix. Bullet eventually got jealous, came over and nudged my hand. As I ran my hand over his thick coat, I said, "Things were a lot simpler for us when we were single, Bullet, and I was still on patrol duty."

He looked at me, licked my hand, then jumped up next to Willie, even though there was no room. I moved my feet to the coffee table. Yeah, we both had friends we loved now, even if mine was not legally divorced.

At 5:00 a.m., I went to the department to work out in the department gym. As I ran on the treadmill, my dream about Patrice and David commanded my thoughts. I ran through the logic of a sheriff and her husband killing for Sonya's money.

"Nah," I said to myself, as I went to the weights.

If Grady married this girl, he'd be set for life—and he was a bit of a liar, and ashamed of his family, his station in life.

Feeling guilty for buying more cinnamon rolls from the Sportsman than Eleanor's, I stopped to buy a dozen from her bakery, then went home. Dallas had left a note on the counter saying, "I love you. My divorce will be finalized before we know it."

I showered and changed into my uniform, grabbed the rolls, and dropped them off at the squad room.

AT 8:00 A.M., I WAS at my desk when Patrice called.

"David drove down yesterday afternoon. He told me you brought him in for questioning and why."

"I'm sorry."

"Right now I'm so furious I can't see straight." She began to cry.

"Did you suspect anything?"

"Not a thing. That stupid, stupid son of a bitch." She sniffed. "This is going to go public, isn't it?"

"Are you sure he was home with you all Thursday night? Could he have snuck out in the middle of the night?"

"I'm a light sleeper. Every time he gets up to pee, I wake up."

"I'm sorry. I don't know what to say."

"Nothing you need to say. Anyway, Tamika's being released today, and she'll be out for at least two weeks."

"I have more information about Grady. He dated a wealthy girl named Bailey Caldwell a year ago, who he was talking marriage to. Unusual for a boy his age to be thinking that way—most just want to get laid."

"That would apply to males of any age, evidently."

"Okay . . . anyway, he never introduced her to his grandparents, either—and he told her his parents were dead. I think he never introduced her because his lies would have been exposed. Bailey also said he was possessive. Do you see any of that with him now?"

"I haven't noticed, but I'll surely watch now. Cal, he was at work in Minneapolis. How can you think he had something to do with this?"

"It's physically possibly for him to have left work, done the deed, and returned to Robbinsdale before the next shift."

"Wouldn't they have noticed if he hadn't done his work?"

"He could have hustled at the last minute. If he does marry Zabrina, he'll be instantly wealthy."

"What a mess. If she won't have an abortion, then I'm going to push for adoption—she's too young to raise a child or get married."

"On that we agree."

"How can she even know what she wants? Grady's her first boyfriend. Justine had worried about Zabrina going off to college and getting swept off her feet."

"She seems immature to me. Did Justine like Grady?"

"She adored him, but she was concerned about their different backgrounds."

"How will your kids like Zabrina living with you?"

"Gina and Zabrina are friends of a sort. They keep in touch through Facebook. Lane's twenty-one and has never liked her, so he'll ignore her as usual."

"How did they take the news that Waldo moved out?"

"You're getting a kick out of calling him Waldo, aren't you?"

"Yes."

"To answer your question, I haven't told them about 'Waldo' yet. I'm waiting until they get home on break."

"Seems like a good idea."

"Cal, if you're convinced Grady had something to do with the killings, why don't you drive down to Minneapolis today and see what you can dig up on him."

"I have to testify in Brainerd tomorrow, so it'd be a quick trip, but maybe I will. I need to check something out."

I then called Hawley's Veterinarian Clinic and told them I was investigating an incident in the area and asked if they had security cameras that might have caught any suspicious activity in their parking lot or street in front of their clinic between the hours of 11:00 p.m. and 6:30 a.m. on December eleventh and twelfth. The receptionist said I should speak to Ed Lindgren, the owner of the strip mall. Ed said he would check his video feed and get back to me.

Next call: Silas Hill, Grady's roommate. I could hear the explosive sounds of video games in the background. *Do these kids do anything else?* He remembered me. I suppose it's not every day a deputy and a sheriff show up at your door.

I asked Silas if he was certain Zabrina stayed all night the Thursday before Zabrina's grandmother was killed.

"Uhhh, yeah," he said. The game sounds continued.

"Would you mind pausing the game?"

The sound ceased.

"Did Grady and Zabrina go upstairs together that night?"

No answer. He could be playing with the sound muted.

"Silas, what time did they go upstairs?"

"About ten, I think."

"Did you see him go to work that evening?"

"Um, yeah, but I didn't talk to him again until about six o'clock on Friday night, when Zabrina and her friends came over. He was in his room all afternoon."

"Did Zabrina stay overnight on Friday?"

"Yep."

"Okay, man, thank you."

"Sir?"

"Yes."

"I don't know if this is important, but I heard Grady arguing with someone on the phone. I remembered it after you left that day. He sounded really mad. I've never heard him speak to anyone like that. He's usually so soft spoken."

"When was this?"

"I think it was around the time Zabrina got shot. I couldn't exactly hear what he said, though, so it's probably not helpful."

"Probably not, but that's the kind of the thing that could be important, so thanks."

I called Oliver Bakken, our county attorney, and told him my suspicions about Grady.

"I doubt you have enough to convince a judge to sign a search warrant. So I'd hold off until you have more."

Then I checked Facebook. Grady didn't have a page, but Zabrina did and she had no privacy screen, therefore, I could see the photos of herself with her friends and her constant companion, Budweiser.

AROUND TWO O'CLOCK, I drove by Grady's. The empty parking lot, the quiet streets, and no one answering the door indicated the students had finished finals and had gone home for winter break. I drove to Blasidell in the off chance Grady went to his grandparents' home. His burgundy Mazda was nowhere in sight, but I knocked on their door anyway. When Mrs. LaMere answered the door, I asked if she knew where he was.

"I haven't seem him since the first of the month."

"Will he come home for the holidays?"

"He usually does."

"Are you aware he quit his job at Rainbow?"

A look of confusion crossed her face. "He needed that job. He must have taken a different one, then."

"Do you still have my card?"

"Yes."

"If you hear from Grady, would you let me know? I have some questions for him."

I heard her say, "Oh, dear," through the closed door.

OUT OF CURIOSITY, I LOOKED up where Grady's parents were housed. Maybe he visited them. Orton LaMere was at Lino Lakes Correction Facility; his mother was in Shakopee. I phoned Lino Lakes—they said Grady LaMere wasn't on Orton's visitor's list. However, a corrections officer at Shakopee said Grady had regular weekly visits with his mother. I had nothing else to do, so I made arrangements to interview Brenda LaMere to gain more insight on her son. The CO suggested I speak with Fawn Donato, Brenda LaMere's cellmate, as well, because Fawn had asked for a new roommate and might be willing to talk.

FAWN APPEARED TO BE in her forties, thin, and of average height. She wore what Minnesota inmates wore: ill-fitting jeans and a gray sweatshirt. Her light-brown hair hung limply past her slumped shoulders. She wore some sort of makeshift eyeliner, probably from a regular pencil. If you saw Fawn on the street, you wouldn't peg her as an inmate. One bad decision, a moment of losing control, and people find themselves in jail, and possibly prison, like Fawn.

I introduced myself and told her I was investigating a homicide I was sure she had nothing to do with.

"How long have you bunked with Brenda LaMere?"

She rolled her eyes. "Only a few months, but it seems like decades."

"Sounds like you're not happy with the arrangement."

"She's tiresome . . . and delusional. She just talks and talks about stuff that's never going to happen."

"Like?"

"Like when she gets out she's gonna live in a mansion." She gave me a faint smile.

"Does she mention how that's going to happen?"

"Her son's marrying a rich girl."

"She talked about the details?"

"Brenda says the girl's pregnant and they're flying to Vegas. Would you believe she encouraged her son to get the girl pregnant? Who does that?"

"Sounds crazy, doesn't it?"

She raised her brows and nodded.

"I understand her son visits weekly."

"He has since I've known her."

"Does anyone else come to visit her?"

"Her boyfriend."

"What's his name?"

"Rob . . . Quinlan, I think."

I recorded the name in my notebook. "Is she still married to Orton?"

"Orton? I didn't know his name. She calls him The Big Mistake, and I don't know if they're officially divorced."

"Has she ever mentioned a woman named Sonya Donovan?"

"Yes, that's the girl's grandmother."

"I'm investigating her murder."

"She was murdered? Oh, my God."

"So she's never mentioned it?"

"No."

"I'll leave you my card. I'd appreciate your call if you hear something."

"Would I be a confidential informant?"

"Not officially, and maybe we should keep our little talk a secret from Brenda."

"We better. I don't want her slitting my throat in the night."

"No, we don't want that."

BRENDA LAMERE NARROWED her small, widely spaced eyes as she sat with a thud in the chair across from me. Her spider tattoos, one on her cheek, one on her neck, and on both wrists, and her dishwater-blonde hair braided in cornrows added to her tough-girl appearance. She leaned back, crossing her arms over her belly bulge. She toted an extra thirty pounds on her short frame—too much prison food and too little exercise.

She read the patch on my sleeve and said, "Birch County? Where's that?" Her voice was low and husky.

"Central Minnesota," I said.

"What's Birch County want with little ol' me?" she said, trying the flirty act.

"I'm investigating the homicide of Sonya Donovan."

"Who?"

"Your son's girlfriend's grandmother."

"Oh, her. I was busy in the prison kitchen at the time." She gave out a raucous laugh, which led to a coughing fit.

"What time was that?"

She looked around, then said, "You have a cigarette?"

"No, sorry. You're avoiding my question. You said you were busy at the time of the homicide. What time was that?"

"It was a joke. I work in the kitchen and am always there. Get it?"

I nodded. "But you've heard about the murder?"

"Yeah, sure. Grady told me his girlfriend's mom was also killed in a drive-by. That's so weird, right? Both of them?"

"Your son likes the rich girls?"

"Doesn't every guy?"

"Grady's rich girlfriend is a freshman in college and now pregnant. It was part of the plan. Right?"

"Why would he *plan* to knock up anyone at his age?"

"To be rich without working for it?"

"That's an asshole thing to say. You don't even know my son. He's a straight-A student and trying to do the right thing by marrying the little cunt. I think we're done here."

She got up and headed for the door.

"Who's Rob Quinlan?" I asked.

She swiveled her head and glowered at me. I stood and towered over her. A little size intimidation sometimes worked with people like her. She was five-foot-three at most, but she glared up at me and said, "My private life is none of your fucking business, asshole."

Yeah, size didn't intimidate this little pit bull. She stared at me for a few more seconds for added affect and kicked the door twice.

I gave her a puzzled look and said, "Gosh, I can't figure out what Grady does for money. He quit one of his jobs, cut hours on his part-time job. He continues to take his grandparents' money for tuition, even though it appears they don't have much to spare."

"How is this any of your business?" She pounded on the door. "Guard!"

"So when did Robert first start coming to visit you? Does Orton know about you two?"

She pounded on the door with both fists.

"Is Rob taking care of your son for you?"

The corrections officer stuck his head in and asked if I was done with her.

"For now," I said.

She pushed her way out and gave me the finger behind her back.

What a sweetheart.

It was late afternoon and I hadn't eaten since breakfast, so I stopped for an early dinner at the Arizona Lounge and Grill on Canterbury Road, recommended by one of the corrections officers.

I brought my laptop in with me to do research on Quinlan. He'd done time on burglary and drug convictions, but nothing in the last three years. I recorded his Burnsville address and the license plate number of his 2005 black Chevy Cavalier.

After dinner, I plugged his address in the GPS, then drove to an apartment building off Highway 13 and 35 W. The large complex did not have a security entrance, and the apartments were off interior hallways.

A short, round, gray-haired woman, somewhere north of sixty, opened the door to apartment 113. She pushed her eyeglasses up on her nose and looked up at me.

"Are you Lenny?"

My peacoat covered my uniform shirt, so I showed her my badge. "No, ma'am. I'm Deputy Cal Sheehan from Birch County."

She didn't seem surprised to see a deputy at her door, which was telling.

"Is Rob home?"

"Not at the moment."

"When might you expect him?" I smiled.

"I have no idea. He doesn't tell me where he's going."

"Maybe you can help me."

"How?"

"Do you know Grady and Brenda LaMere?"

She screwed up her nose. "No."

"They're friends of Rob's. Would you let him know I stopped by and would like to speak with him about Grady and Brenda?" I handed her my card. "He can reach me at this number."

She took the card and said, "Okay." She closed the door in my face. The chances of Rob Quinlan calling me were zero to zilch.

As I sat in my vehicle in the parking lot, I gave the Burnsville Police Department a call and had a chat with an Officer Michael Neuman. I let him know Quinlan was a person of interest in a homicide investigation in Birch County.

"Heard about that one," he said.

"Do you know Quinlan? I may need your help in rounding him up."

"Sure. He's been a frequent flyer, but he's always been pretty cooperative. How long are you in town?"

"I'm heading back tonight. I'll be back down at some point."

"Just a second."

I was placed on hold and when Neuman came back, he said, "Quinlan currently works at the airport on the cleaning crew. I can give you the number of his employer."

"Thanks, that'd help."

The call to the company immediately diverted to a recording giving their office hours as eight to five, Monday through Friday. I drove by Grady's apartment once more, then, concluding he wasn't home, I made the two-hour drive to Prairie Falls. I was psyched with the information I'd gained about Grady, his mother's plans, and the name of her boyfriend.

25

Tuesday, December 23

I T WAS STILL DARK when my eyes popped open. My upcoming court appearance weighed heavily on my mind, and I had woken up several times during the night. I dressed and took Bullet for a quick walk. In an attempt to ease the jimjams, I worked out at the department gym. Close to eight o'clock, showered and shaved and dressed in my uniform, I left for Brainerd. I checked in at the courthouse, then waited in a small room. About nine fifteen, a Crow Wing County bailiff came to fetch me.

"Cal, we're ready for you," he said.

I stood.

"How ya doing?" he asked.

"All right, I guess."

"You don't remember me, do you?"

I looked at him closely. "Ricky Kozar?"

"Yeah."

"You graduated a couple years after me."

"That's right. Hey . . . I know Mike's your good buddy, but he was always kind of a dick to Paul and me. Anyway, good luck in there."

"Thanks."

I avoided looking at the defense table and gallery where Hawk's parents were sure to be seated. My eyes were trained on the court clerk, who swore me in, then shifted to Lowell Pennock, the county prosecutor, who was shuffling papers.

Pennock had called a meeting with me shortly after they'd arrested Hawk to ask if I was up to the task of testifying against my friend. I said, as a sworn officer of the law, it was my duty to testify to the facts. A slow smile had grown. Just before I'd left the meeting, he suggested I would have been a good military officer. For a brief time, I'd considered joining the Air Force. My grandpa, a Vietnam vet, talked me out of it. Pennock himself was a retired JAG, hired as an assistant prosecutor with Crow Wing County, then four years later, ran against his boss and won. I did my research; I liked to know who was asking me questions.

Pennock straightened his broad shoulders. He ran a hand over his salt-and-pepper hair shorn in a buzz cut, then bid me a good morning in his rich, deep voice. He stayed seated and began by getting my long-term friendship with Michael Hawkinson on the table. Question by question my history with Hawk became part of the court record: how we had been childhood friends, had roomed together in college, and were the best men at each other's weddings.

During the questioning, I let my eyes inadvertently slip to the gallery to Hawk's parents, Tom and Barb Hawkinson. Their contemptuous glares made me divert my eyes to Sydney Dirkson, a private investigator and Hawk's cousin. She gave me a wink and a smile. We got to know each other when we were searching for him in Vegas. After Hawk's arrest, she called to tell me she and her husband knew I did what I had to do. Remembering that call and seeing her single gesture of support calmed me. I turned my attention back to where it belonged—to Pennock.

Most court cases moved at a snail's pace. By the time we had recessed for a two-hour lunch, we hadn't gotten to Hawk's confession, and I had managed to avoid eye contact with him.

I drove to McDonald's on Washington and ordered a Big Mac and fries, which I hadn't indulged in since I'd been with Dallas. She ate healthy, except she was addicted to cinnamon rolls, too.

While I savored my lunch, I took out my notebook and studied my jottings. I circled Ed Lindgren's name. He was the owner of the strip mall who was going to check the footage from the security cameras. My call was transferred to his secretary, Susan Knoll, who said Ed was on vacation in St. Thomas. I'd like to go to St. Thomas. Maybe when this case was over.

She listened politely to my request, then said, "I'll see what I can do. I know the electronics store next door to the vet's office had security cameras installed after they had a break-in a few months ago. I'll see what I can find. Give me the date."

I gave her the info she needed, then looked at my watch. I had an hour and a half before I was due back in court, so I drove to Westgate Mall and walked around. I decided I may as well buy Christmas gifts, even though I wasn't in the mood, because I never would be. I bought a remote helicopter for Luke, a chunky metal necklace and earring set for my mother, and a belt for Bobby Lopez. I was back at the courthouse by two o'clock.

Once seated in the witness chair, I was reminded I was still under oath. A sudden burst of curiosity caused me to look at Hawk. He narrowed his eyes and mouthed, "Fuck you." And with those kind words, my guilt was cured. As Ricky Kozar mentioned, Hawk could be a dick when he wanted to be. Maybe Paul's ability to screw over his brother came from a deep-seated resentment of Hawk's mistreatment of him when he was a kid.

I WAS WARNED HAWK'S LAWYER, Arlo Strong, would be intimidating. He stood before me with a straight back and a stern expression and proceeded to drill me for a couple of hours. He stabbed a finger at me as he hammered me with questions about why I hadn't taken Michael to the hospital the night he first came to me for help, and why I hadn't notified the sheriff until the next morning. I responded that I wanted Hawk to relax and rest before he was subjected to the media storm that would ensue but neglected to mention I wanted to question him first. The interview I'd conducted at my house after I fed him beers and pizza was never entered into evidence because I later discovered he was lying about what had occurred.

By four thirty that afternoon, I was excused. I stopped at Sally's Salon and Spa and bought a five-hundred-dollar gift card for Clara. I'd also add a bonus to her check. And since I was instructed by Shannon to buy the twins the Santa gifts, I stopped at Target and filled a shopping cart with toys. I hauled everything inside the house and looked at the pile of gifts.

"Aw, shit, now I've got to wrap them."

Dallas was going out for dinner with her office staff, so I ordered a pizza. About ten o'clock, I'd just finished wrapping everything when my home phone rang. Thinking it was Dallas saying goodnight, I picked up.

"Hey, you prick, proud of yourself?" Hawk said.

"You're drunk."

I hung up. He called back. I pulled the plug on the phone. And now I was too pissed to sleep. I waited for my cell phone to ring, but it didn't. I imagine his mobile was in evidence, and he didn't remember my cell number.

On the day I turned him in to Crow Wing County, Hawk told me if I had been betrayed and kept hostage for three weeks, I'd have taken the shot, too. I don't know, maybe, but the jury would decide Hawk's fate. It should have occurred to me earlier, but if he got a not-guilty verdict, my life might be in danger. I made sure I turned on the alarm system.

26

Wednesday, December 24

SHANNON WAS ALONE in the squad room when I checked in. "You look like shit," she said. "Not sleeping well?"

"Hawk called me about ten last night, stinking drunk."

"He must be scared."

"He mouthed 'Fuck you' during my testimony."

"You can't expect him to be thrilled with his life-long buddy testifying for the prosecution."

I grimaced. "Then he shouldn't have shot Paul in the back and told me about it."

She shrugged. "If I'd been held captive for three weeks and my brother had been part of it, I'd been pretty pissed off, too."

"Meaning?"

"I understand his rage."

"And you think he was justified to shoot Paul in the back? "

"No, of course not, but I get why he did it."

"I hope the jury doesn't think like you do."

She squinted. "Hey, are you worried he'll come after you?"

"You're damn right. He's a crack shot, and if he's acquitted, I'll be looking over my shoulder."

"Well, he's guilty, so you should have nothing to worry about."

"I hope you're right. Have you heard back about the bone scan?"

"No, hopefully today. You're coming for dinner tonight at my parents' house. Right?"

"I'll drop by, but I'm not sure about dinner. I'm also expected at the Bradley's."

"Oh." She turned her back and pretended to read the bulletin board. "My family would be extremely disappointed if you don't eat with us."

"What time is dinner?"

"Six o'clock."

She poured herself a cup of coffee and leaned against the table. "Mom suggested we move brunch to your house—she would bring everything."

"Sure, fine. I stopped and bought Santa presents for the twins. You said you'd handle Luke's."

"Oh."

"What?"

"I bought some, too."

I scrunched up my face. "Why?"

"I wasn't sure you'd remember. I'll save some things back for their birthday."

"Whatever."

"How's the Donovan case going?"

Like old times, I shared my current theory on suspects and their motives. She listened, as she used to, and said she thought I might be on to something.

"What will you do now?" she asked.

"Find the evidence I need. Put the screws to Grady LaMere."

"Patrice said he's spending Christmas with her family."

"When did you talk to her?"

"Last night. She called to find out how I was doing. She also told me about David. I guess she assumed you'd told me. You used to tell me everything."

Zing.

"It's sensitive."

"Well, it didn't surprise me he was having an affair."

"Why not?"

"Do you remember the department picnic Patrice hosted at their lake house?"

"Of course. What happened?"

"He was too interested in the women."

"Wasn't he just being a good host?"

"Nah, he was seriously flirting."

"Huh. I didn't notice. Did Patrice say anything else?"

"Zabrina had a hard time at the memorial service and is super depressed. I don't know what she expects. The girl's life imploded."

"True."

I CONTACTED DETECTIVE RYAN to give him the lowdown, starting with the Shakopee interviews.

"What made you go to see his mother?"

"I took a long shot."

"Well, it may have paid off big time. Want me to pick up Quinlan?"

"I think we should talk to him."

"Okay, I'll be in touch."

I CALLED PATRICE to update her and ask if Grady was there.

"Cal, it's Christmas Eve, and as much as I need you to solve this case, you will not disrupt my family's celebrations. On December 26, he's fair game."

"All righty. So how did the kids take the news about Waldo?"

"I haven't told them. What do I say? Merry Christmas, your father is a man-whore."

I laughed.

"Speaking of which, can we possibly keep this out of the news?"

"If he didn't kill Sonya, I don't see why it would be newsworthy."

"Of course he didn't kill her. Look, I should go. My family's giving me the evil eye. Merry Christmas to you and your family."

"Same to you and yours."

God rest ye merry gentlemen, deck the halls, and all that ho-ho-ho shit.

DETECTIVE RYAN CALLED ME mid-afternoon to inform me they'd picked up Quinlan. He asked if I wanted to be in on the interrogation. I said, of course I did. I immediately texted Shannon to tell her I was on my way to Minneapolis for an interview.

She texted me back: "Merry fucking Christmas."

I replied, "I suppose I deserve that."

I texted Dallas the same message about heading to Minneapolis.

She replied, "I thought we were okay."

"We are. Love you."

27

THE MPD HOMICIDE DIVISION was quiet on Christmas Eve. Those who could be home with their families were—except for work-driven assholes like me.

"You gotta see the film of the apprehension before you question Quinlan," Martha Gill said.

"Was his mother home at the time?"

"No, he said she was at work. She's an aide in a nursing home," Ryan said. "He tried to slam the door in my face, but my steel-toed boot stopped it. Anyway, all I could see was the back of his shaved head as he bolted out his patio door. He has elaborate tattoos of medieval weapons covering his scalp.

"Anyway, he was five feet into the snow before he fell on all fours. I thought I had him, so I trounced through snowdrifts. Before I reached him, he got up and took off again. I tackled him about three yards later. He was facedown in the snow, in his stocking feet and no coat. I patted him down and found nothing but a snack-size plastic bag with remnants of weed in the pocket."

Gill said, "I asked him where he was going without shoes. He said he didn't know. Said he ran because he was scared."

"We got him for fleeing but couldn't get him to confess to murder, but you can give him a go," Ryan said.

"But you gotta watch the film first," Gill said.

I did and laughed along with Ryan and Gill as they reminisced the comical scene. Gill handed me a bottle of water.

"Give this to him. You can play the good cop."

QUINLAN JERKED HIS HEAD UP and off his arms when the door opened—his eyes were screwy like he'd been sleeping.

"Robert Quinlan?"

"Yes?" he said.

"I'm Detective Sheehan from Birch County. I have some questions for you."

He rubbed his neck as he moved his head in a circle. He smelled like weed and cheap aftershave. I set the bottle of water in front of him.

"Thank you," he said.

"You're welcome."

I watched as he opened the bottle and gulped it half down. I could be imagining it, but my thought was Grady looked like him around the eyes. Same narrow face.

"Do you go by Robert, Rob, or Bob?"

"Robert or Rob."

"Nice tats. Really great work. You have it done in the area?"

"Yeah, a place on Chicago in South Minneapolis. You inked?"

"No, I'm concerned the ink goes directly to the brain."

The muscles around his eyes twitched as he considered whether I was insulting him or joking.

"What do you do for employment, Mr. Quinlan?"

"I work at the airport."

"Doing what?"

"I clean johns . . . okay?"

I spread my hands. "Nothing wrong with honest work. So, how do you know Brenda LaMere?"

He blinked a few times. "We're old friends."

"Before she made Shakopee Correctional her residence?"

He nodded. "We go way back. I knew her old man first."

"How?"

"Orty and I went to high school together."

"And were partners in the drug business?"

His head bobbed back and forth. "Okay, yeah, way back when."

"Brenda calls you her *boyfriend*."

He studied his thumbs as he rubbed them together.

"You visit her regularly. Don't you?"

Quinlan hesitated. He took a breath and slowly released it through pursed lips. "I've gone to see her a few times. She's lonely."

"Who initiated contact?"

"She did."

"How 'bout your old pal Orty? You visit his lonely ass, too?"

He shook his head. "No."

"Tell me about Grady LaMere."

"What about him?"

"I understand you've helped support him."

"I do what I can."

Bingo. Grady had another source of income.

"Took him under your wing? Taught him all you know?"

He closed an eye and winced. "I just watch out for him like Brenda asked me to."

"He looks like you."

Lifting a hand, he made a swipe across his mouth, then his eyes slowly met mine.

"He's your kid, isn't he?"

"Most likely. Never had the tests done."

"Does Orton know?"

"I wouldn't know."

"What's gonna happen when Brenda gets out? Are you two gonna be together?"

"Hell, I don't know what's gonna happen tomorrow. You have to take life as it comes."

"You're a real philosopher."

He cracked a smile.

"Does Grady know you're his father?"

"Brenda told him when he turned sixteen."

"How often do you see him?"

"Maybe monthly."

"Have you met his girlfriend?"

"No, sir."

"But you know who she is?"

He took a breath and nodded.

"And you also know that her mother and grandmother have both been killed?"

"Yeah, Grady called to tell me. He was very upset."

"But it was all planned, wasn't it?"

"I know nothing about it." He rubbed the side of his nose, scratched his head, then cleared his throat. He was displaying classic signs of lying.

I purposefully remained silent for a time, then said, "That Brenda." I gave him a smile. "She has dollar signs in her eyes. She figured out a way to have it made in the shade when she gets out next summer."

The red started creeping up his neck. He began fidgeting with the water bottle, ripping off the paper wrap.

"I bet Brenda's pretty persuasive. Convincing you to off Grady's girlfriend's family, then abracadabra . . . the girlfriend is next in line for the inheritance."

He screwed up his nose. "That's absolutely crazy."

"Crazy, huh? So where were you on the night of December eleventh and morning of the twelfth?"

"I don't recall."

"Come on, it's not that long ago."

"I'm sure I was working."

"We'll soon have a search warrant issued on your employment records, which means work schedule, phone records, and your credit cards."

His left eye twitched. Twice. Three times.

"When was the last time you were in Dexter Lake?"

"I guess it was when I picked up my niece to take to her college interviews."

"You have family in Dexter Lake?"

"My sister, Adelinda, and you know what? It could have been December eleventh. Yeah, it was, because her interview and tours were on Friday the twelfth."

"What's your sister's last name?"

"Moore." *Wowzer.*

"Is she married to Marvin?"

"Yeah, you know him?"

"I do. He worked for Sonya Donovan. But you know that, don't you?"

"Actually, I have no idea who the man works for. I try not to talk to him. He's not a nice person."

"So you just happened to be in Dexter Lake when your son's girlfriend's grandmother was killed?"

"I was not aware I was."

"Have you been to Kenwood lately?"

"Kenwood?" He laughed. "Yeah, like that's my stomping grounds."

"You three have high hopes, don't you? Like the little ol' ants and the rubber tree plant. Mm-mm. That's quite a mansion Zabrina lives in. Isn't it?"

"If it's in Kenwood, it probably is."

"But you've never been there, so you don't know. Well, I have news for you that I'm sure you'll be disappointed to hear."

I could see in his eyes his interest was piqued.

"Zabrina won't inherit any of it until she's thirty-years-old . . . *thirty*. That's a long time. And I have a sneaking suspicion she'll see the light sometime before that."

His head dropped, a hand moved to his temple. They'd never considered she wouldn't have immediate access to her money.

"Okay, Rob, you can make it easier on yourself if you tell me how it all went down. Maybe with your history of cooperating with the law, you can get some kind of plea agreement."

"I . . . can't . . . because I didn't do anything."

"Did you get your sis and brother-in-law to help you?"

"No. I didn't have a thing to do with any murders. I had no idea Marv worked for that lady. A guy does a good deed and what does he get? Accused of murder."

I continued for several minutes hammering him with the same questions phrased differently, but he gave me the same bullshit, so I walked out to find Ryan.

"You got a lot more than we did," he said. "Gill contacted Robert's mother. She's home and has given us permission to search the apartment. Martha's doing the paperwork on the search warrant. So let's give our buddy a place in holding and go see what we can find."

"Hopefully, my partner's Smith & Wesson M&P, forty caliber."

QUINLAN'S APARTMENT SMELLED like baked cookies and not marijuana. Ryan informed Quinlan's mother we had a search warrant and asked her to have a seat on the couch, but she stayed standing in the middle of the living room, wringing her hands.

"Should I shut off the oven?" she said. "I'm baking Christmas cookies."

"That might be best," I said.

Sugar cookies were cooling on flattened brown paper bags on the kitchen table. Two cookie sheets were on top of the stove ready to go in.

Ryan asked if she could turn off the television, which was tuned to a game show. A cheap artificial Christmas tree stood in the corner—the kind with green metal limbs and little greenery. A few wrapped presents lay under it on a patchwork quilted tree skirt.

"Your daughter lives in Dexter Lake?"

"Yes."

"And your son went to get your granddaughter to take her to college tours?"

"Yes, she had two in Minneapolis. Moriah's such a smart girl."

She gave the same date as Robert.

Ryan suggested I search Robert's bedroom while he and Gill took other rooms. I snapped several photos of the room, which was organized and clean. Even the socks in his drawers were arranged by color. I hadn't thought fastidiousness was hereditary, but perhaps it is, and there is hope for my messy toddlers.

While searching the closest shelves, I found a half-pound bag of weed in a shoebox. I took photos of it and placed it on the bed.

Vents are poor hiding spots because the police always check them first. Robert's bedroom's cold-air return vent contained a nine millimeter handgun.

Gill stood in the doorway. "Is that your partner's firearm?"

"Unfortunately not—this is a Glock, not a Smith & Wesson."

"Well, since he's an ex-felon and guns are no-no's, we can arrest him on that. We'll check the rest of the vents in the other rooms."

While they did, I looked at the linen closet right outside of the bathroom. On the middle shelf of the neatly arranged linen closet were two fluffy, sage-green towels taking up as much space as six of the worn blue towels next to them.

"Ho-ho, here we go." I snapped photos before I disturbed them to look at the labels: the sage-green were Ralph Lauren and the thin blue were Fieldcrest.

"Did you find something?" Ryan asked as he walked out of the second bedroom.

"Come look at this."

"What?"

"Notice anything odd about the towels?"

"Not really."

"See those two sage-green towels?"

He nodded.

Gill came up behind us. "The missing towels?"

"Yep. They're Ralph Lauren just like those missing from Sonya's pool area."

Ryan said, "Oh, I get it. The rest are all different colors."

"And a quarter of the size," Gill said.

I pulled them off the shelf and placed them in two large paper evidence bags.

His mother said, "Why are you taking my towels?"

"Where did you get them?" Gill said.

"Robert gave them to me."

"When?"

"A couple weeks ago."

Gill looked at me and grinned. "They are evidence and will be taking a trip to Birch County."

"Why would my towels be evidence?" she asked.

"They connect your son to a murder that occurred the night he was in Dexter Lake," Gill said.

Mrs. Quinlan's hand went up to her mouth as she literally fell backwards onto the couch.

WHEN WE GOT BACK to the MPD downtown station, Quinlan was brought back up to the same interrogation room. Ryan sent me in alone.

"How are you doing, Robert?"

"I'm tired and hungry and want to go home."

"Isn't that a song? 'Show me the way to go home, I'm tired and I want to go to bed . . .' something like that, anyway."

"It's Christmas Eve, man."

"And your mother is baking Christmas cookies."

He grimaced.

"Robert, where did you get the two sage-green Ralph Lauren towels we found at your apartment?"

"At a store."

"Which store?"

"Walmart. They had a sale."

I highly doubted Walmart sold Ralph Lauren towels.

"When?"

"I don't know, maybe a year ago."

"Your mother said you gave them to her recently."

"She's mistaken."

"Is your father still alive, Robert?"

"No."

"How did he die?"

"Heart attack."

"Did they do an autopsy?"

"Nope."

"What about your grandparents?"

"All gone."

"Tell me about their deaths."

"They got old and they died."

"Did they do an autopsy on any of them?"

"I wouldn't know. Why the family history?"

"I have my reasons. You like things orderly. Don't you, Robert?"

"Yes."

"You know who else liked order? Sonya Donovan. In fact, she was obsessive about it. She liked her towels stacked just so . . . uniformly. We know two towels are missing, and they're identical to the two in your closet next to the other threadbare towels. What's your explanation as to how they wound up in your linen closet?"

"How do you know they're the same ones? There's a million of 'em sold."

"Ever hear of DNA?"

I was in my bullshitting mode now. I needed more than Sonya's towels to arrest him.

"When older people die in their sleep, most people think, 'why go through the expense of an autopsy?' Happens all the time. Only Mrs. Donovan was a friend of the sheriff of Birch County. She demanded to know why her healthy friend died. Turns out—get this—she drowned. Well, it doesn't take a rocket scientist to know she couldn't drown and then walk herself up to her bed. Someone had to carry her."

He sucked on the inside of his cheek. I kept waiting for him to ask for an attorney because he'd been in the system enough to know how these things worked.

Martha came in to get me. When we walked back to the desk area, she said, "Quinlan used a Visa card in Motley at the Bricks Travel Center on December twelfth at 5:05 a.m. Purchases totaled $45.37. And Walmart doesn't sell Ralph Lauren towels."

I went back in and stood in front of Quinlan.

"Robert, our county attorney looks favorably on cooperation. If you tell me the truth, things will go much easier for you. Did Grady drive up to Dexter Lake with you?"

No answer.

"The security camera footage at Bricks Travel Center will tell us who was with you besides Moriah."

He took a deep breath.

"Was the murder Brenda's idea or Grady's? Say, maybe you're the mastermind. You figured out a way to kill the girl's grandmother to make it look like natural causes, then staged a drive-by killing of the mother. But I do have a question: Was shooting the girl an accident or to make it look real?"

He didn't answer.

"You needed a security code to get in the Dexter Lake house. Only a few people knew it. Grady was one of them."

Quinlan sank in his chair. He slowly covered his face with his hands.

"Which brings me to my partner's assault. You probably needed the code for the Logan house, too. And I don't know too many people who are privy to that information. Again, Grady pops into my mind."

"I want a lawyer."

Thursday, December 25

RYAN'S BOSS RECOMMENDED Birch County deal with Robert Quinlan first. Patrice met us at in booking at Birch County Detention Center at one o'clock in the morning.

"Excellent," she said. "I can't tell you how grateful I am, Cal. You gave me the most wonderful Christmas present."

"We're not done yet. We need his accomplice, which could be Marvin Moore or Grady."

"Grady doesn't know we have Quinlan."

"Good."

She put her hand on my arm. "Thank-you, again," she said.

As she started to walk away, I asked, "You doing okay?"

"No, not really."

"It'll get better. First thing tomorrow morning, I'm running over to Motley to get the film from Brick's Travel Center."

"It's Christmas Day. They may not even be open. It can wait until Friday."

"You do know we need a confession from Quinlan. We don't have any physical evidence other than the towels and the Motley transaction. His good deed cover was brilliant: picking up and taking his niece to her college interviews. Oliver may not even charge him."

"Don't say that." She put her finger on my lips, and the familiarity caused me to step back.

"I need to get home and get some sleep."

IT WAS TWO O'CLOCK when I walked into my dark house. I flipped on the light and walked to the kitchen. On the counter was a note from Shannon. She picked up Bullet and the Santa presents. She was making a point—I was neglecting my duties as a pet owner and parent. Trouble is, I agreed with her.

I looked through the fridge for something to eat. I poured myself a glass of milk, made myself a peanut butter sandwich, then another, and pulled down the container of Christmas cookies and ate half a dozen.

When I walked by the living room on the way to the stairway, I glanced at the tree. The hall light shone on the few presents stacked under it. I grabbed my jacket and keys and drove over to Shannon's. I let myself in with the "emergency key" she had given me and lay down on the couch near the Christmas tree. I pulled the throw blanket over me and closed my eyes. Sometime later, Bullet crawled up on the couch by my feet.

28

OICES. SHUSHING. SCURRYINGS. Bullet jumped down. His claws clicked on the wood floor. Small hands on my face. I opened my eyes. Lucy leaned over and kissed me with an open mouth right on mine.

"Good morning, little one," I said, grabbing her up on my chest.

"Daddy," Henry said, and crawled up on my legs, narrowly missing my groin.

"Luke, hold on," Shannon said.

She turned on the overhead light, causing me to squint.

"What are you doing here?" she said.

"I wanted to be here for this," I said.

"Well, you startled me. I wasn't expecting you."

"Is it okay? I didn't want to wake you up."

"Um . . . yeah, sure," she said, unconvincingly.

"I could go. It was wrong of me to let myself in."

"Well, yes, it was, but under the circumstances, it's fine."

"Mom . . . Mom . . . Mom," Luke said.

"What, Luke?"

"Can I start?"

"Yes, sure. Open one, then the babies can each open one."

She plucked Henry off me, and I grabbed Lucy. The five of us sat on the floor by the tree. Shannon snapped photos as the ripping and tearing began. The twins were more interested in the wrapping and boxes than the gifts. We took a moment to show them how to operate each toy. Shannon helped Luke put batteries in the helicopter; he tried to operate it but crashed it into the wall.

I went over to give him some simple instructions, and he soon had it flying all over the lower level and up the stairs.

As we were shoving the mountain of paper into large black garbage bags Shannon asked, albeit sarcastically, "So what was so important in the Cities?"

"I arrested Robert Quinlan last night."

"All by yourself?"

"No, of course not. Every case is a group effort. Let's talk about this later."

"Want some coffee?"

"No, I'm fine. By the way, my mom's having dinner at her house tonight. A Mexican dinner. She expects me to bring the kids."

She heaved a sigh as she pushed her hair back with a hand. "That's the first I've heard of it."

"It slipped my mind."

"Cal, what's going on with you? It's not like you to forget things like that, or choose not to be with your family on Christmas Eve. You could have waited until Friday to question Quinlan."

"Minneapolis picked him up. If they had let him go, he may have split."

"You don't know that."

I counted to ten as I bit my lip. This was the real reason we divorced. We didn't see eye to eye on even simple things. She was always letting me know she was disappointed, or how wrong I was on everything, and I was weary of it. But with the kids right there, it was not the time to get into it.

I put my coat on and said, "See you later."

"You do remember the brunch is at your house?"

"Sure. What time is everyone coming?"

"Around ten. You don't have to go right away, do you? Have some coffee."

"Yeah, I'll see you later."

"Cal, I'm sorry."

I nodded, called for Bullet, and left.

I MANAGED TO GET ANOTHER three hours of sleep, then cleaned up and waited for the group to arrive: Shannon and the kids, her parents, her brothers' families, and her grandparents. While the family went into the living room by the tree, Donna, my ex-mother-in-law, came to help me pour Bloody Marys and Mimosas.

"We missed you last night."

"Thanks for saying that, but I had to work."

"With the divorce, I suppose things are bound to change. I should have included your family and girlfriend today."

"It's better this way, Donna, trust me."

"Shannon said you're going to having a traditional Mexican dinner tonight."

"Yep."

"I miss you." She moved in for a hug and said, "It's so wonderful of you to have Shannon here while she recovers. She'll be able to see the kids when she wants and will have Clara's help."

"Actually, it was Clara's idea, and whatever Shannon wants to do is fine with me. I'm here for her."

Donna made a sad face and said, "You're a good man, Cal. I still feel terrible that your marriage didn't work out."

"Yeah, me too. But, Donna, I think you'll see it was for the best."

"Really?"

"Yes, really. I think Shannon will be happier with someone else."

Donna shook her head in disagreement, but managed a smile.

Brunch was served, gifts were opened, and when the twins got crabby and everyone was getting ready to leave, I suggested the twins stay at my place to nap. Shannon disagreed. I didn't argue and said I'd pick them up at four o'clock. Luke wasn't interested in going to my family's for dinner, and it was useless to push anything with him because Shannon wouldn't support it anyway.

THE FIRST SIGHT OF THE GLOW coming upon Bobby's driveway took my breath away. Luminaries bordered the driveway around a curve and up to his house. I slowed and pointed out the pretty lights to the Twinks. I stopped and snapped photos of their beautiful, innocent faces filled with awe and wonder. I never thought I could love anything as much as I loved these two children.

My mother and Bobby rushed out to carry the twins in, and while I gathered the gifts to bring in, sounds of Mexican music drifted out the open doorway. Rosarita smiled up at me as she helped take the coats off the babies. Taking the twins by their hands, Mom and Bobby walked them over to the Christmas tree.

"Let's open gifts right away," Mom said, grabbing a package for each of the kids.

Bobby turned to me. "She's been looking forward to this for months."

"But I thought Shannon and Luke might come with you," Mom said.

"She's with her own family. I didn't think to ask her."

"I did. I called her after I spoke with you."

"Aren't the grandmas coming tonight?" I asked.

"Oh, Mom and George decided to take a last-minute cruise, and Sylvia flew to California to be with Patrick and Angel."

This was the first time we weren't together for some portion of the Christmas holiday. I was disappointed in both grandmas for choosing not to be with my kids for Christmas, but Grandma Sylvia's absence surprised me the most. She was my paternal grandmother. Her son, Patrick, was my biological father. All those years ago when the truth of Patrick and Grace's sordid affair was discovered, the family disowned them. They took off for California, where Patrick eventually built a successful nursery business. When Grace died, he tried to reunite with me. I wasn't quite so willing to forgive and forget he'd abandoned me. But Patrick was Grandma Sylvia's son, and she had already secretly reunited with him. Grandma Dee and her shack-up boyfriend, George, were keen on experiencing as much of life as possible, especially casinos, which concerned me some.

I shook off my disappointment and watching Bobby and Mom delight in watching the twins open their gifts helped get me into the Christmas spirit. Bobby had made beautiful riding toys out of wood. The little truck and car had steering wheels and rubber tires that functioned. He varnished the wood instead of painting it, and the result was quite something.

Rosarita had knitted the kids multicolored hats and mittens, and Mom had made a large teddy bear for Henry and a cloth doll for Lucy. I was touched that every gift had been handmade. I received a five-hundred-dollar Herberger's gift card from my mother.

With Bobby and Mom's help, Rosarita prepared a traditional Mexican dinner of *pazole* (a soup), tamales, Mexican rice, a fruit punch called *ponche*, and flan. The kids particularly loved the tasty fried cookies called *bunuelos*.

Bobby then led the twins to the four-season porch where he had a monkey piñata hanging from a ring screw in the ceiling.

Mother whispered to me, "I couldn't believe Bobby put a ring screw in the ceiling just for the piñata. He said I could put a plant on it, but in the middle of the room? You and Bobby would hit your heads on it for sure."

He made my mother happy, but I was still concerned his secretive life would blow back on my family. But for now, the room was filled with laughter and smiles as the Twinks swung away with plastic bats at the monkey. Finally, with adult help, the piñata was broken, and toys and lollypops spilled out all over the floor. Their little faces said it all. They were having a blast. I left my mother and Bobby with the children picking up the treats and placing them into plastic bags and found Rosarita in the kitchen cleaning up.

"Thank you for the wonderful meal, Rosarita."

"I had help. I'm glad you came to see me. I wanted to tell you something about the night of the murder. I don't know if it's important," she said with a heavy accent.

"What is it?"

"All the lights in the house went on before two in morning."

"All lights?"

"The downstairs first, then later, the upper floor. Is strange, no?"

"*Si*, it is strange. Did you happen to notice what time they went off?"

"Four o'clock I look again. They all off."

"Well, this is very helpful. Thank you."

Along with the Fitbit and Rosarita's account, the time of the murder could be pinned down to between 2:00 to 4:00 a.m. This was an important piece to the puzzle. And in my estimation, Grady could easily have checked in at the vet clinic, left, drove the two hours, and gotten back well before anyone arrived at 7:00 a.m.

I HAD THE TWINKS BACK at Shannon's by eight o'clock, as promised. After I deposited them in the kitchen, I made three trips in from the car with the gifts. Shannon watched from the door and opened it each time I approached. Her frown deepened with each trip.

"What's all this?"

"My mom and Bobby went all out. Their gifts are all handmade, they had real Mexican food, and broke open piñatas. The trinkets and suckers are in one of the bags. You can dole them out as desired."

"I hope they don't get diarrhea from the food."

I frowned in reaction to her negativity. "It was all fresh food and delicious. I can't see why there should be a problem."

Her chin lifted. "Because it was probably too rich for their little digestive systems."

"Okay . . . we'll see."

I could hear the sounds of a computer game coming from the living room. I peeked around the corner. Luke was sitting on the couch with a new iPad. I picked up the large wrapped package and walked over and set it on the floor next to him.

"Hi, Luke, this is from your Grandma Hope and Bobby. I think you'll like it."

The box contained an official soccer ball, a baseball bat, glove, and baseball. Luke completely ignored me. When Shannon didn't encourage him to stop playing on the tablet, I gave up and walked away. When I was a kid, a package this size would have gotten my full attention, and I would never have been allowed to ignore an adult. Oh, well.

When I kissed the babies goodbye, Henry started crying and his arms reached for me.

"He's just tired. Don't make it harder by picking him up."

"Really? Okay, then. I'm out of here."

I had had it with the negative attitude, and I was beginning to regret agreeing to have her stay at my house during her recovery. But because she was my kids' mother and because of what she was going through, I would do what was right.

But it didn't stop me from mumbling to myself as I got in my truck, "I didn't even mention the luminaries or how much the kids loved dancing to the Mexican music."

I wasn't a block before Bluetooth picked up a call.

"Cal, the toys are beautiful."

"Yeah, Bobby made them. And my mom and Rosarita handmade the other things."

"I'm sorry I was such a bitch. I'm sure the twins' stomachs will be just fine. You know I'm not myself lately."

"I know."

"When I think this could be my last Christmas with the kids . . ."

"Aw, Shannon, you can't think that way." And now all the negative bullshit made perfect sense. She thought she was going to die.

As I approached my street, I saw a car back out of my driveway. Worried it was Hawk, I slowed down. I let out my breath when I recognized Dallas's Subaru Outback.

She rolled down the window. "Hi."

"Hi, gorgeous. Would you like to come in for a drink?"

"I would," she said smiling.

I let Bullet out while she parked her car.

"I should walk Bullet. You up for it? You seem to be dressed adequately."

"Sure. I didn't think to bring Willie."

"Want to go get him?"

"No, I walked him just before I came over."

I grabbed the leash, put on my stocking cap and warmer boots and gloves, and we started down the street.

Just looking at her made me smile. "So how are you?" I asked.

"I'm good, and I understand why you're avoiding me."

"I'm not avoiding you. I've just been busy."

She shook her head. "Regardless, I came to tell you something."

"Yeah?"

"Vince came to my house today to give me a Christmas present."

"Shit."

"I wouldn't accept it."

Bullet stopped to pee on a bush, and I waited for her to finish her sentence. When she didn't, I said, "How did he react?"

"He cried."

I kept quiet because I didn't think she was finished with what she had to say. But she remained silent, and we'd started walking again.

She said, "He said he was changed and had made a lot of mistakes."

My stomach clenched. Was she considering going back to that asshole?

She stopped. Bullet was pooping in the middle of the sidewalk.

I turned to her. "What do you want me to say? You know I love you, and I hope you don't go back to him. But I'm not ready for remarriage, and I don't think you are either, but maybe someday if you can be—"

She pushed herself up on her tiptoes and kissed me. I took her in my arms and kissed her back. A horn sounded from the car driving by. We pulled apart to look. It was Matt Hauser on his way to Eleanor's.

"Patient," I said, finishing my sentence.

"I'm in total agreement. Do you have a poo bag?"

"Oh, I forgot to grab one."

She pulled out a pink bag and picked up the smelly deposit without hesitation.

I took the bag from her and said, "Let's go back to my house."

At my place, I threw the bag in the trash, then we went inside. After she removed her coat, she pulled out a small wrapped present from her pocket. I went to the tree, picked up the small box, and handed it to her.

"You first," I said.

She unwrapped the small blue Tiffany box and smiled. "It's beautiful. Thank you." She asked me to put it on. I kissed her neck after I secured the silver pendant with her initial on it.

"Now you."

I started working at the wrapping. "Geez, you put enough tape on it," I said, grinning.

Inside was a silver keychain. Attached was a silver disc containing a picture of Bullet and me on one of the hikes we'd taken with Dallas and Willie.

"I really like it, thank you." I gave her a short peck on the lips.

"Mom loved her generous gift card to the salon."

"She deserves it."

"Now, where's that drink you promised me?" she said.

I turned on the fireplace and we sat on the sofa, sipped wine, and stared into the flames, my arm around her, both of us happy and content in the moment.

"Last night, Jamie and Scott said they never liked Vince. Evidently at the wedding, Scott had told him to be good to me, and Vince responded by saying, 'What? You think she's some kind of special princess or something?' And Scott told him, Yeah, I was special, and if he didn't realize it, he should walk. Vince laughed and said, 'Now you tell me.' He pointed to his ring, then gave Scott the finger. I never knew that happened until last night."

"Was this tale shared before or after Vince showed up?"

"After."

"Yeah, it's amazing what people will hold back."

She put her hand on my thigh—a dangerous thing to do. "Right here and now, let's make a promise to always tell each other the truth no matter what."

I smiled and nodded. "Sounds like a plan. Here's a truth—I want to go upstairs for pie."

She laughed. "I really want to, but . . ." She looked at her watch. "Oh, my gosh, my family's waiting for me. We're having family movie night, and I'm supposed to be buying popcorn and soda from the Quick Stop."

"Oh."

"You could join us."

"Sure. Dallas, I'm worried Vince will continue pressuring you to come back."

"Don't worry about it. I'm a big girl."

Then Bullet and I followed her over to her house. On the drive, I was beginning to realize I really enjoyed being with Dallas and wanted to spend as much time with her as I could.

I spent the next few hours with Clara, Dallas, her two brothers, Scott and Jamie, and Jamie's wife, Jen, watching a violent cop movie, *End of Watch*. Jamie had picked it. When I said goodnight to Dallas, I asked her if she thought there was a message in the movie choice.

"Since he didn't know you were joining us, I think the message was for me. I'm sorry. I'll have a talk with him."

"No, don't. If it continues, I'll say something."

"He's just being protective."

"I know, and I get it. My job is a risky one."

Weird. I thought I'd look good compared to Vince. I guess not.

"Does Scott want you to break up with me, too?"

"Nope, Scott loves you—like Mom does."

29

Friday, December 26

FRIDAY MORNING I TOOK OFF for Brick's Travel Center in Motley, stopping for coffee and cinnamon rolls at the Sportsman for the trip. Tony threw two more in the bag than I paid for.

The Brick's night-duty clerk had gone home already, but the store manager, Carl Bjornstad, told me all of the film was backed up on "the cloud," so I sat with him in his office at his computer while he scanned the feed until we found the time ten minutes before Quinlan's purchase was made. The gas lanes were empty until a 2005 black Chevy Cavalier pulled up to the end pump.

"There's your car!" Carl said.

Quinlan exited the vehicle to pump the gas. I couldn't get a clear view of the passenger because of the glare off the windshield, but there was definitely someone in the front seat. Then the passenger door opened. I fully expected to see Grady LaMere step out, but it was a girl, the niece. She moved quickly to the building. A few minutes later, she came out with a plastic bag. Quinlan also disappeared inside, then with a quick step, got in the car and drove off. I didn't see another passenger. With the footage recorded on the thumb drive I'd brought, I began my drive back to Prairie Falls.

After parking in the department lot, I made my way across to the building. First, I dropped the Motley flash drive off for Samantha Polansky to see if she could pull some good stills from it. She said to give her an hour.

I then made my way down to Patrice's office, but the door was closed.

"She in?" I asked Georgia, her secretary, who had a desk in the outer office.

"Yes, but she doesn't want to be disturbed."

"Can you have her call me when she's willing to be disturbed?"

"Sure."

Georgia had just asked me how the twins liked Christmas when her phone rang. She listened and said, "He's right here." She gestured toward Patrice's office.

When I opened the door, she was at her desk with her hands folded, looking all business-like.

"How do you want to handle this Grady thing?" she asked.

"We should bring him in for questioning today."

"Will you pick him up, or what?"

"Sure, I can go out and get him. But, Patrice, the reason I came down was to tell you the Motley tape showed Quinlan had his niece with him. I couldn't see another passenger, but I'm having Samantha enlarge the stills in case she can pick out someone in the backseat."

"Shoot me copies."

"Sure. Bobby Lopez's housekeeper told me she saw lights on in the Donovan house between two to four in the morning on the twelfth."

"That fits the estimated time of death. Oh . . . and I should have told you this straightaway. Oliver said with the towels and proximity to the crime scene we had enough to charge Quinlan, so I called the press this morning and informed them."

Oliver and Patrice were both filing for reelection—they wanted the credit.

"Tell you what, I'll go with you to pick up Grady," Patrice continued. "I've got some things to do first, so let's shoot for right after lunch."

MEANWHILE, I WENT BACK to my desk and did more research in public records on Robert Quinlan and his family. He was the only child of Joseph and Harriet Quinlan, born in 1973. Harriet married Joseph Quinlan the same year Robert was born. Joseph Quinlan died in 1994. With a bit more digging, I found Harriet had previously been married to Arthur Van Pelt, and they had one girl, named Adelinda, though she went by Della. Arthur Van Pelt died in August of 1971. Robert and Adelinda Moore had different fathers.

Samantha walked into my office and handed me five photos and the thumb drive. She mentioned she'd also emailed copies of the stills to Patrice and me. The photos were a little grainy, but you could definitely make out the faces. She also pulled one of the car and license plate. The niece looked familiar to me, but I couldn't place where I'd seen her.

AFTER I DOCUMENTED my Motley trip, I stared at the photo of Quinlan's niece, trying to place her. I was having trouble concentrating. My mind flit from the case, to Dallas, to Shannon's surgery next Tuesday. A knot formed in my throat every time I thought about her cancer.

My cell phone rang. Martha Gill.

"We had a very interesting conversation with Quinlan's mother this morning," she said.

"What did you find out?"

"Harriet Quinlan doesn't like Della's husband one bit. Evidently, about ten years ago Marvin turned into an authoritarian nut job. He got them involved in a church that operated more like a cult. She said Della went to Augsburg College for three years, then the money ran out; she had to quit school to work for a year. She met Marvin during that year and never finished college. They were married within months, and he moved her up north when Moriah was an infant. They couldn't afford one child, but had five more."

"Yeah, they are struggling financially."

"Oh, and I asked Harriet more about those towels. She said they were wet when Moriah handed them to her."

"And she didn't think that was strange?"

"He told Moriah some cock-and-bull story about washing his car, which she passed on to Harriet."

"Good info, Martha. Thanks."

"There's more. One of the old-timers at the station knew all about Harriet's first husband, Arthur Van Pelt. He was killed during an armed robbery in progress at a neighborhood liquor store. The owner tripped the silent alarm, and the police rolled up shortly thereafter and shot the robber. Van Pelt was killed by a stray bullet from a Minneapolis police officer's firearm. She won a big lawsuit of an undisclosed amount against the city. Anyway, according to one of her former neighbors whom she's remained friends with, Joseph Quinlan ran a hole-in-the-wall jewelry store in the same strip mall as the liquor store where Arthur was shot. Joseph and Harriet got married about a year after her husband's death. After the settlement money came, Joseph moved his shop to downtown Minneapolis. Within a year the shop went bankrupt, and they moved to a small house in Burnsville, then he went to work at a chain store in the mall, and she went back to work as a nurse's aide."

"How did Joseph die?"

"Natural causes. He died in his sleep."

"Do you know what Van Pelt did for a living?"

"He was a librarian at Augsburg."

"And that's why Della went there. Has Robert always lived with his mother?"

"Off and on."

"Well, putting Robert in Dexter Lake the night of the murder was huge for me. Thanks for the information about the towels. Maybe you can trace him to the drive-by."

"That's the idea."

30

FTER I'D GIVEN PATRICE the scoop, she said, "So, does this new information clear Grady?"

"Not necessarily. I want to question him again, but I've decided to send a squad out to bring him in a bit later. It will speak to our seriousness."

"All right, but it could be he didn't know anything about it."

"Sounds like wishful thinking."

She knitted her brow. "Honestly, the more I'm around him, the better I like him. I'd say it's more likely one or both of the Moores were involved."

"Quinlan didn't break in, so someone allowed him entrance. I'm going to bring them back in for questioning."

I SECURED WARRANTS ON GRADY and Zabrina's cell phone records, then arranged for Crosby Green to videotape today's interviews. I sent two patrol units to pick up the Moores because I wanted Marvin separated from his wife and daughter during transport.

When Greg Woods arrived at the home, he texted me, "The daughter was one of the passengers in the Camaro that went in the ditch the night of the storm."

"That's why she looked familiar," I replied. "Don't mention the incident to the Moores."

I fully understood, given her family circumstances, why she'd give a false name. Now it was a bargaining chip—if I needed one.

I texted Woods again. "What was your impression?"

"House needs paint, clean inside. Furnishings sparse. Six kids too quiet."

"Like something's wrong there?"

"Yep."

I sent Woods a quick "Thanks." None of what he said was surprising. While I waited, I did some quick research on Moriah. She didn't have a driver's license or a presence on social media. I was thrilled she was eighteen and wouldn't need her parents in on the interview.

MORIAH'S EYES MET MINE when I entered the interview room. My smile wasn't returned. Her back straightened as I took the chair facing her. She sat forward in the chair, her hands in her lap. She resembled her mother and wore a plain, white blouse and navy slacks—something an old lady might choose.

"Moriah, I'm Deputy Sheehan. Do you remember me?"

"Yes, sir." Her cheeks brightened as she gave me tiny nods.

"Do they call you Morry?"

She nodded again.

"I have a few questions for you."

More nods.

As I gave the necessary information for the taped interview, her eyes darted about the room, her expression fearful. Once finished with the identification process, I said, "Robert Quinlan is your uncle."

"Yes, sir."

I showed her the photo I had of her in Motley.

"This photo was taken early morning in Motley on December twelfth. This is you?"

She glanced at the copy and said, "Yes, sir."

"You were with your uncle, Robert Quinlan."

Her shoulders dropped, but the muscles surrounding her eyes tightened, as if she was relieved this wasn't about the underaged drinking incident, but confused as to why she was there.

"Yes."

"Was there anyone else with you?"

"No, sir."

"Where were you going?"

"To the Cities for my college visits to Bethel and Augsburg."

"Why didn't your parents bring you down?"

"They had to work."

I nodded. "How did it come about that Robert drove you?"

She nodded. "I was going to take the bus, but he volunteered to come and get me."

"When did he arrive?"

"Around three o'clock on Thursday afternoon."

"And you left for the Cities when?"

"At 5:00 a.m., because I had a tour at Augsburg at eight o'clock."

"And Robert stayed at your house on Thursday night?"

"Yes."

"Did he go out at any point?"

"He went with my father on a call."

"A call?"

"Yes, Father works part time for a maintenance company. There was a water leak somewhere."

"So Robert went out on that call with your father?"

"Yes."

"What time was that?"

"I'm not sure. I was sleeping."

"Do you know what time they returned?"

"I heard them come in around four o'clock. Uncle Robert and I were leaving at five o'clock, so I got up and got ready."

"Did you notice anything out of the ordinary during the time he was at your home? Were your uncle and father acting differently?"

"No, sir."

"Was Motley your only stop on your drive down to the Cities?"

"Yes."

"Your grandmother is Harriet Quinlan?"

"Yes."

"She said you brought her two wet towels?"

"They were Robert's."

"Did he say why they were wet?"

"He said he wiped his car off with them after he washed it."

"Were you with him when he washed the car?"

"No."

"Awfully nice towels to wipe a car down with, don't you think?"

She shrugged.

"So, you stayed with your grandmother that weekend and went on your tours."

She nodded.

"How did they go?"

"They went well."

"Good. And how did you get back up to Dexter Lake?"

"I took the bus."

"Who is Grady LaMere?"

Her eyes narrowed as her forehead creased. "I don't know anyone by that name."

"Brenda LaMere?"

She shook her head.

"It appears your parents don't have any extra money to help you with college. Am I correct?"

She nodded.

"Times are hard for your family?"

"They always have been. My father allows me to work to earn my own money, if I give ten percent to the church, ten percent to him, and put the rest in my college fund."

"Where do you work?"

"I babysit."

I imagine she told her parents she was babysitting the night of the storm.

"Your grandmother seems to value education. Has she offered to help you with college?"

"She doesn't have the money. Mother says Grandma helped out too many people already, but Uncle Robert says he'll help as much as he can. Also, I hope to work at the college and take out student loans."

I asked more questions about her knowledge of Sonya Donovan and her residence. Convinced she had nothing to do with her demise or had any knowledge of the murders, I ended the interview and walked her down to the lobby. I was showing her where to wait for her parents when Spanky entered with Grady and Zabrina. Patrice must have taken it upon herself to send Spanky to fetch them. Zabrina and Moriah locked eyes. I caught a glimpse of Moriah's smile as she said hi to Zabrina. Zabrina greeted her but kept pace with Spanky to the check-in desk.

"Do you know them?" I asked.

"I met Zabrina last summer, but I don't know the boy."

"Did you meet her through Zach Whitman, by any chance?"

"Yes, how did . . ."

"Where were you headed the night you ended up in the ditch?"

She glanced around to see if anyone would hear her. "To Zach's. Adam thought he was home, but he wasn't. Are you going to tell my parents about that night?"

"No, but I am going to give you a piece of advice."

"Okay."

"Stay clear of Zach and the boys you were with that night. They're trouble." I handed her my card. "If you think of something you haven't told me, or if you ever need help, you can call me."

She took the card and looked at it. "Thank you."

I then tracked Spanky down and asked him to work on the cell phone records, giving him specifics of what I was looking for.

I chose to question Della Moore next.

"The first time I interviewed you, you did not give me your given name—Adelinda."

"Oh, I haven't used it since I was a child. My father always called me Della, and it stuck."

"You should use Adelinda for legal purposes."

"Oh. I apologize, sir."

I went through my list of questions, and she gave me the same answers her daughter had. Robert and Marvin had gone out on an emergency call.

"Who does Marvin work for?"

"Mulligan's Appliances. He does after-hours service calls for them part time."

"When did he leave on this emergency call?"

"I'm not sure. I was sleeping."

"You didn't hear the phone?"

"No."

"How do you know Robert went with him?"

"Marvin told me the next morning."

"And you have no idea what time he left or when he came back?"

"No, I sleep like a baby."

"My babies always wake up in the middle of the night."

She gave me a half-hearted smile.

"So, your brother drove all the way up to Dexter Lake and all the way back to the Cities to take Moriah to her college tours."

"Yes."

"Is he always so generous with his time?"

"Family means a lot to him."

"Does he get along with your husband?"

"They have their ups and downs."

"What seems to be the source of the downs?"

"My brother has said stuff to anger Marvin. There were a couple years we didn't see my family at all."

"Why?"

"Robert lent Marvin some money a few years ago, and he hasn't been able to pay him back."

"How much money?"

"Four thousand. We got behind on our bills."

"Any particular reason why?"

"There aren't that many people in town who have somebody mow for them, and everybody has a plow on their truck these days, and he only subs for Mulligan's."

"Has Robert pressured you for the money?"

She shook her head.

"Tell me about your children."

"I have two boys and four girls. Moriah is our oldest."

I waited for her to ask why Moriah was being questioned. Odd that she didn't.

"Do you feel safe at home?"

Her head dropped, and her eyes went to the table.

"If your husband is abusive, for your kids' sake, you should get them away from him. Your boys will emulate him, and your girls will think that's the way they should be treated."

She looked away. She opened her mouth; her tongue touched her top lip.

"There are organizations who could help you."

She nodded. The look on her face told me she wasn't ready to take the step.

"Do you know your brother is being held in the county jail?"

Her eyes widened. "What for?"

"In connection with Sonya Donovan's murder."

A look of alarm crossed her face. "But what would he have to do with it?"

"Do you know Brenda LaMere and her son, Grady?"

"I know Brenda and her husband were friends of Robert's when he was young."

"Have you ever met them?"

"A very long time ago."

I showed her a picture of Grady.

"Have you seen this young man around Dexter Lake?"

"Should I have?"

"He's the boyfriend of Sonya Donovan's granddaughter."

"Oh, well, I'm never there when they are."

"Does he look like anyone you know?"

"He kind of looks like Robert did when he was young."

"Yeah. Now, is there anything more you want to tell me?"

She blinked away the tears forming in her eyes. "No, sir."

I tended to believe she knew nothing about Grady, or Robert's connection with the Donovan case, but I was pretty sure she now suspected her husband helped Robert kill Sonya Donovan—maybe to forgive the debt. Now, to prove it.

I WAS LOOKING FORWARD to interrogating Marvin Moore. He came into the room with his head down, shoulders bent forward, not at all the chatty, grinning goofball he was the last time he sat in the same chair. I read the man his rights, so all his words would be admissible in court.

Then I stated, "We have Robert Quinlan in custody."

His cheeks mottled. He began picking at one of the calluses on his fingertip.

When he didn't respond, I was certain he knew why we had arrested Quinlan.

"We have Robert's side." *As much as he'd give us.* "I suggest you give me yours."

He covered his face with his hands and mumbled, "Dear God in heaven."

"Whose idea was it to drown Mrs. Donovan? Yours or your brother-in-law's?"

"Look, I had no idea he was going to do that."

"Tell me what happened."

He looked at his hands while he picked at another finger. "Robert wanted me to let him in the house. I thought he was only gonna rob her. When I found out she was found dead in her bed, I thought he frightened her to death. But then when I heard she was drowned, I called him, and he said he didn't have nothing to do with it. And I guess I wanted to believe him."

"When did he ask you to get him into the house?"

"The day he came up to get Moriah, and I didn't even know he was coming up. Della arranged it without my permission."

I scratched the back of my head. "So, you let him in the Donovan home with a house key you have."

"No, sir, I did not."

"You said earlier you had."

"Okay, okay, maybe I did, but I didn't stay. I had an emergency service call."

"So instead of going on an emergency call, you and Robert went to Mrs. Donovan's?"

"Yes, but I was told the leak wasn't that bad . . . just a small leak."

"Did Robert ride with you or drive his own car?"

"He followed me to Donovans', I let him in, then went on the call."

I questioned him for another twenty minutes, but he wouldn't admit he went into Sonya Donovan's home with Quinlan. When the interview was over, Patrice was waiting.

I ran my hand through my hair. "I don't believe him. I think he stayed, but I have to check with Mulligan's to see if he even had an emergency call. His neglecting to tell me this on the first interview is highly suspicious."

Patrice said, "Yes. Are you going to question Grady now?"

I nodded. "First, I want to talk to Mulligan."

JOHN MULLIGAN SAID THERE was a report of a water leak in the Cherry Street Apartments' laundry room, and since Marvin was on call that evening, he was sent over to check it out.

"Would you have any way of knowing if it had been a false report?" I asked.

"False? Well, Marvin charged me for two hours, so I assumed it was legit."

"Do you know who called it in?"

"No, the calls are directed to a service, the service calls our guy . . . Marvin on that particular night."

"May I have the answering service number?"

"Sure."

I spoke to someone named Janet, who told me the service handled maintenance calls for a three-county area, and the operators worked from home. When a call came in, the person on duty contacted the appropriate contractor's on-call technician. I asked her the apartment manager's number, but had to leave a message.

31

PATRICE MET ME OUTSIDE interview room four, where Grady was placed.

"Zabrina insisted on coming with," Patrice said. "She's waiting in my office."

"Bring her to number three. I do have additional questions for her."

GRADY MAINTAINED HE WAS working the night of Sonya's murder, and I had nothing to prove otherwise—yet.

I leaned forward in my chair and placed a hand on my chin. "Grady, I have a hard time with all your lies. For example, why not tell your girlfriends the truth about your parents?"

His cheeks flushed with crimson blotches. "I know you went to see my mother. Tell me, would you introduce her to Zabrina?"

I rubbed my chin. I couldn't argue that one. "How do you feel about Robert Quinlan being your father?"

"He embarrasses me. They both do."

"But yet you visit her and take his money?"

"I only have one mother and Robert owes me something for doing what he did."

"What did he do?"

"Got my mother pregnant and into drugs. She's in prison because of him. She says he wants to atone."

"By killing your girlfriend's family?"

"Robert would never kill anyone. That's preposterous."

I raised a finger. "The evidence is there."

He opened his mouth, then closed it. Then said, "Well, if it's true, I'm appalled."

"And your mother convinced you to get your rich girl pregnant, so you'd be on easy street—and thus, so would she."

He drummed his fingers on the table. That part was true.

"But the grand scheme to expedite the inheritance fell apart because Zabrina may not want to tie the knot after all."

He lifted his chin and looked to the ceiling. "I'm trying to do the right thing by her. I mean, I don't exactly want to get married right now, but I'm willing."

"Do you know what I think? The night of Sonya's murder, you checked in at the vet's office, quickly did your chores, then took off for Dexter Lake. You met up with Robert Quinlan and helped him kill Sonya Donovan, then you drove back, making it to the clinic a good hour before the morning crew arrived. A few days later, Robert shot Justine and Zabrina in the drive-by."

He glared at me as he made a scoffing sound. "Wow. You think you have it all worked out. Except how much sense would it make for Robert to shoot Zabrina?"

"How did he explain it? Did he accidentally wound her? Or maybe he's a crack shot and thought if he'd wing her it'd look more realistic. I don't know; you tell me."

"It must be a requirement for detectives to have a fantastic imagination because you made the entire scenario up."

I smiled. "I'd say we're good problem and puzzle solvers. We put together all the clues. Some are small and remote, but place them together and presto, it all comes together. For example, the only way Robert would know what time Justine and Zabrina would be arriving home is if someone told him the exact time they were rolling up to the Logan house. We have cell phone records. We know you and Zabrina spoke minutes before the shootings."

"She had gone out to eat with her mom and begged me to come over, but I said I had to study."

"How convenient."

Tears began to roll from his eyes. I had him. He was ready to break.

"Grady, it's a terrible burden to carry all this inside. You'll feel better if you get it off your chest."

His hands lifted, he opened his mouth, then shut it, then through his tears said, "Robert was going to help me through veterinary school. How's he gonna do that if he's in prison for murdering Zabrina's family? And how is Zabrina gonna love me if my biological father murdered her family?"

His head dropped; the tears turned to sobs. I hadn't expected that spin.

"Did you suspect he'd killed Sonya Donovan?"

"Yeah, he talked about it after I started dating Zabrina. I didn't think he'd ever be stupid enough to go through with it."

"Did he want you to participate?"

"He asked me to get him into the house, but I refused."

"When was this?"

"Last summer . . . maybe August."

"Why not tell me all this when I first questioned you?"

"I regret I didn't, but I didn't want to be associated with Robert. And I certainly never thought you'd find out he was my biological father."

"People had to have seen you two together."

"I chose out of the way places where we wouldn't run into anyone I knew, and now I know why he gave me an untraceable throw-away phone to use to call him."

"Which was why you weren't using your own cell phone?"

"Yes."

"You knew he killed Sonya Donovan."

"Not at first, but when it came out she'd been murdered, I got concerned."

"And when Zabrina's mom was killed, and she was shot?"

"I was super upset. He wouldn't answer my calls. So I drove down to Burnsville and waited in his parking lot for two hours. He got mad at me and said to get out of there and not contact him because the police couldn't find out about our relationship."

"So who was his accomplice?"

"I have no idea."

"Do you know Marvin Moore?"

"No. Who's he?"

"Explain why you initially dismissed the notion Robert killed Sonya Donovan, when he talked about it a few months earlier."

"I didn't think he was serious."

"Did your mother ever discuss this plan with you?"

"The only thing she ever said was if I got Zabrina pregnant, then I'd have to marry her, and I could afford anything I ever wanted. I thought she was joking."

"Getting some girl pregnant so she'll marry you, then killing off her family so she inherits. Does that sound funny to you?"

His hands pulled into fists, and his face contorted. "I didn't think either one of them was that stupid."

"But you did get your girl pregnant."

"Not on purpose. What do you think I am?"

"What matters is that you know who and what you are. Okay, sit tight, kid. I'll be back."

I left him where he was and went to speak to Patrice.

She was waiting for me, clearly shaken.

"That little shit. He knew all along, and Marvin Moore was Quinlan's accomplice, and that freaky bastard lied through his big, yellow teeth."

"Or Grady's an accomplished liar, which wouldn't be a stretch."

She touched her temples. "Damn it. Wait until I tell Zabrina. That ought to be enough for her to kick him to the curb."

"Don't say a word to her. We need to know how much she knew and what she suspected. I may have to be tough on Zabrina, so don't come storming in there to save her."

"I won't."

ZABRINA WAS IN INTERVIEW ROOM THREE, on the other side of the observation room. She had a real knack for looking small and pathetic. Her "pity me" face, the diminutive way she held her body; her arm in a sling added to the persona.

"Zabrina, do you have your own key to your grandmother's Dexter Lake house?"

Her mouth turned down into a frown. "Yes."

"Where do you keep it?"

"On my key ring, with my other keys."

"How many keys do you have on that ring?"

She'd lifted a finger for each key she counted. "The Logan house, the lake house, my dorm room, Grady's house, my car, the garage—that's six. Why?"

"What do you think your boyfriend told me?"

"I have no idea."

Her eyes were blinking like hummingbird wings. She crossed her legs and started bouncing her shoe against the table leg. I found it interesting that she was so fricking nervous.

"First, tell me what you know about Robert Quinlan."

She stopped kicking the table. "Um, well, he's Grady's biological father."

"When was the last time you saw him?" I actually had no idea if she'd ever seen the man.

She looked up to the right then left as if trying to remember—or deciding what to tell me.

"I saw him . . . once . . . shortly after I had started dating Grady. We ran into him when we were at a coffee shop in Uptown."

Holy shit. "When was this?"

"A Saturday afternoon in September."

"Was this meeting planned?"

"No."

"What makes you think so?"

"Grady was surprised to see him."

"Not upset?"

"Yes, maybe a little."

"What did you think of Robert Quinlan?"

"He was nice."

"Nice, huh. How did he look to you?"

"I remember thinking it odd he wore jeans and a suede jacket because it was a warm day."

Probably to hide the Glock. "I meant what was your impression of his financial status?"

"I don't think about how much money people have. He's a pilot for Delta, so he must do okay."

"A pilot? Did he talk about what routes he flew?"

"Minneapolis to Las Vegas. He said he could get Grady and me on a flight anytime we wanted."

I nodded as I squelched a smile.

"What did you three talk about?"

She sat up straighter, leaned in. "Well, I can't remember the specifics of a conversation that long ago."

"Take a minute to think about it."

She sat for a few seconds, then said, "I guess mostly about his travels."

"Did he ask you questions about your family?"

"I suppose. That's what people do when they meet for the first time."

"What did you tell him?"

"Well, he seemed interested in my grandmother's radio show. He said Grady told him about her house in Dexter Lake. He said he'd love to see it because he was looking for a vacation home like that."

"Uh-huh. And did he ever see it?"

"I'm sure not."

"Did you ever see Robert again?"

She rubbed her neck and blinked. "No."

"Did those tattoos on the back of his head strike you as pilot like?"

"What tattoos?"

"All over the back of his bald head—medieval swords and weapons. You could hardly miss them."

"I think he was wearing a baseball cap."

"So why did you get pregnant?"

She leaned back, arms crossed over her midsection. Big sigh showing me I was annoying.

"It was an accident." She enunciated those syllables like it was none of my business. Pleased to have penetrated her feisty side, I continued my line of questioning.

"You didn't use protection?"

"I'm not a moron."

"Then how did you get pregnant?"

"The condom must have broke or had a hole in it. Duh." Her upper lip curled in a snarl. Feisty turned snotty.

"Do you remember an occasion when it broke? Or a time he didn't put it on right away?"

"Oh, my God, why are you asking me these questions? Are you getting off on it?"

"So glad you asked. Most guys Grady's age just want to get laid. You know that, right? Getting married is the furthest thing from their minds."

She rolled her eyes.

"It's my belief that the death of your mother and grandmother are directly related to your pregnancy."

She screwed up her face. As far as she was concerned, my theory was stupid.

"And what tips Saint Grady's hand is that he's eager to marry you. Now, one might ask, why would a poor young man possibly want to impregnate and marry a rich young woman? See what I'm saying?"

Her chin began to quiver as her face began to contort. The girl was going to let loose, and I had to just sit back and let it happen. I only wished I had thought to bring earplugs.

"Why are you saying these mean things to me?"

"Because you need to start getting wise to your station in life and what happened. You, a young woman from a wealthy family, have been played. Your boyfriend's family plotted this whole thing. And Robert? Grady's biological sperm donor? He cleans toilets at the airport. Yeah, Grady's loser old man and old lady are counting on you and your bank account to fund their future. Wait here a second."

I stated for the tape that I was exiting the interview, then went to find Patrice.

"Should I go in?" she asked.

"Absolutely not. I need a laptop."

"I'll get mine. It's quicker," she said.

I watched Zabrina's tears quickly subside when she didn't have an audience. Patrice rushed back in, opened up her computer, typed in her code, then handed it to me. I found what I was looking for and then went back into the room with my ammunition. Zabrina sniffed, letting me know she was still upset. I pulled up Robert Quinlan and Brenda LaMere's mugshots and placed them side by side.

"This is your future mommy and daddy-in-law. Meet Brenda LaMere, the woman who plotted your grandmother's and mother's deaths, and Robert the toilet cleaner, who carried them out."

She studied the mugshots and looked up at me. The look of horror on her face proved I'd succeeded in my mission.

"Now, when I ask you questions, you need to tell me the exact truth, so we can keep her in prison, cement Robert Quinlan's conviction, and nail his accomplice. Someone had to have helped Robert get inside your grandmother's house. Someone with access to the security code and a key, like Grady. He could have easily lifted your key off your keychain."

She made tiny little nods with her head. *Holy Christ. I may be getting through to her.*

"Has Grady gone with you to the Dexter house when your family was there?"

"He came with me for Thanksgiving."

"Was that the only time he was there?"

"Yes."

"Would you have used the security code in front of him?"

"Yes, because we were the first ones there for Thanksgiving."

"If you've heard or seen anything, I need you to tell me now. For example, did Grady seemed interested in when your grandmother was going to be up at the lake?"

Her brows furrowed, the wheels turning. "He did ask when we could use the Dexter house for a weekend—just the two of us."

"And what did you tell him?"

"It might have to wait until after Christmas because my grandmother would be there before winter break." The wailing began with a single sniff. "Oh, my God, oh, my God. Did Grady kill my grandmother?"

I tried to calm her, but she was on the verge of hysteria. I stood and motioned for Patrice to enter. When she did, I left to go into the observation room to watch how she would act without me there. Crosby indicated the video camera was still on.

"Good, let's keep it rolling."

"Do you think her boyfriend was in on it?" Crosby asked.

"That's the question. He's a convincing kid."

He nodded.

Patrice embraced Zabrina and said, "Shh, shh. It's going to be okay."

"Did Grady kill Grandmother?"

"I don't know, sweetheart, but he knew it could happen, and he didn't tell anyone. Nor did he mention anything about Robert to us when we first questioned him."

"I want him out of your house!" she screamed.

"I'll see to it."

Patrice took Zabrina down to her office, so she wouldn't have to run into Grady on the way out, then came back to the observation room where I was watching Grady, still in room four.

"How's he acting?" she asked.

"He's had his face covered with his hands almost the whole time you were gone."

"Do we have enough to arrest him?" she asked.

"Not for murder."

Her phone chimed. She looked up at me. "Samantha pulled up some information on Robert Quinlan we should see. She sent us both emails."

I pulled it up, and what she'd found didn't surprise me in the least.

"And that's where Robert gets his money," I said.

Patrice asked, "Okay, what's your best guess as to how Sonya's murder went down?"

"I've been playing this over and over again in my mind. If Sonya heard someone enter the house in the middle of the night and didn't expect anyone, she would have been scared and called 911."

"I agree."

"And if they surprised her in bed, she would have fought back and there would be evidence like scratches, bumps, contusions. There was none of that."

"So what happened, then?"

"I think someone she knew came in and went to the pool and made a lot of noise. Yelling, splashing around in the water. She awakened, went to the window in her bedroom that overlooks the pool, and recognized the person or persons. So she walked down to the pool to give them hell."

"Okay."

"But they're ready for her. Someone pulls or pushes her in. She can't swim, so maybe it was all they needed to do."

"That's about the best explanation anyone could come up with," Patrice said. "It could have been Marvin who helped Robert."

"Certainly."

"Cal, you never suspected David, did you?"

"You mean Waldo?"

I told her about my dream—that she killed Sonya for control of her money.

"Do you have such a poor opinion of me?"

"No, of course not. But my brain messes with me a lot."

"Mine, too. The thought David did it crossed my mind—that maybe she threatened to tell me about the affair, and he shut her up."

"Do you have any doubt he left the house that night?"

"I'm positive he didn't."

"How is he?"

"I don't know. I'm not talking to him."

"You'll eventually have to."

"Not if we go through attorneys. Who did you use?"

"Iris Kellogg."

"Shannon speaks highly of her."

"She was easy to work with, but Shannon and I were in agreement on almost everything. Are you sure you want to divorce? You could get marriage counseling."

"I'm not doing anything until after this mess is settled. And now, if you don't mind, I'd like to talk to Grady."

"Go for it."

Patrice gave him another opportunity to talk. He said he didn't know anything more and proclaimed his innocence. In a calm, controlled voice, she told him if it turned out he was involved in any way and didn't speak up now, she'd come after him with everything she had. I had a feeling she was quite capable of vengeance. Poor Waldo.

"You're free to go, Grady. Don't leave the state."

He gave her a disheartened look but said nothing. Then in front of him she made a call and told whoever to pack up Grady's things and set them out on the step.

Since a squad car had picked up the kids, I volunteered to give Grady a ride out to Patrice's home on Island Lake. I had driven a block when I said, "Do you have your car back?"

"Yes."

"What was wrong with it?"

"Water pump."

"Who drove you to pick it up?"

"I took a cab."

"I heard Robert's car had some muffler work done, too."

"Yeah, it was going."

"Fixed now?"

"Yes."

I was guessing about Robert's muffler. The witness who saw the drive-by said the car was noisy. And the evidence continued to mount.

A mile or so out of town, I said, "Zabrina told me Robert showed up one day while you two were having coffee in Uptown. Had you invited him?"

His head whipped toward me. "No!" he shouted.

"Whoa there, partner. Take it easy."

He turned his head away from me and stared out the window.

"Why do you think he just happened to be at that coffee shop at that particular moment? To my way of thinking, a man who lives in Burnsville and works at the airport is unlikely to hang out in Uptown."

"He had to have been following me."

"Stalking you?"

He nodded.

"Did you tell him about your rich girlfriend?"

"No, but I'm sure my mother did. I told him it wasn't cool and not to do it again."

"Just curious. How much money has he given you?"

Grady took a deep breath. "He paid for this year's tuition."

"So where in a toilet cleaner's budget does he get that kind of money?"

"He buys and sells things."

"Yes, he buys stolen goods and sells them on the Internet."

His cheek muscles tightened as he worked his jaw back and forth. "I didn't know. I never asked where he got the money. Why would I?"

"Did he tell you he was a pilot like he told Zabrina?"

"I knew he was a janitor."

"But yet you didn't set Zabrina straight?"

"I wanted to impress her. Okay?"

"And what else do you know about him you haven't told me? You're not being recorded now."

His head lowered, his hand lifted to his temple. "In October, he took me out into the country to practice shooting—he said for hunting season, but he had a pistol and a shotgun. We shot at cans for a couple hours."

"Where did you go?"

"South on 169 a little past Jordan, then west near the Minnesota River."

"Did he have the guns with him?"

"He keeps them in a storage locker in Jordan."

"What's the name of the place?"

"I don't remember, but it was off Quaker."

"Why that spot for shooting?"

"He knew the guy who owned the property."

"Do you know the guy's name?"

"No."

"Is Robert a good shot?"

"Hits the bullseye every time."

"Grady, look, if you're involved in this shit, it would behoove you to tell the truth right now. Maybe you were coerced into participating or didn't know what you were getting into."

Tears streamed down his face. "I didn't have anything to do with it, but I'm sure Zabrina won't believe that."

"Well, to be honest, I have a hard time believing it myself."

His eyes shot up to mine. "You think I could kill the love of my life's family and hurt her like that?"

"At your age, how could you know who the love of your life is? I believe there are many people you could meet and fall in love with—it's in the timing."

He scowled, then went back to staring out the window as we turned into Cadillac Jack's, which shared a driveway with the residences to the left of the restaurant/bar. Why did I bother trying to tell a kid about love?

When I dropped him off at his car, he got out without a word, slammed the car door, then walked with purpose to grab his duffle bag off the front step. Without looking back, he got in his car and drove off.

As I drove by Cadillac Jack's parking lot, I decided to pull over and make some calls. First, I phoned Ryan and told him about the storage unit in Jordan. Then I called Dallas and asked her if she wanted to go out for dinner at Cadillac Jack's.

"Sure."

"Invite your family if you want."

"No, I think I'd like be alone with you. Then after maybe we can have, you know, pie for dessert."

"Excellent."

I WAS ALMOST HOME when Tamika called. Her voice was full of excitement as she told me she remembered arguing with Zabrina about leaving the Donovan house."

"You didn't give her permission to leave?"

"Hell, no. Patrice would've shot me."

"Was Grady there?"

"Yes. The doorbell rang, and he went to answer it—and that's the last thing I remember."

"Where were you when the doorbell rang?"

"In Zabrina's bedroom helping her dress."

"Did you help her bathe?"

"I did, and that's what I get for being nice."

"Ryan and Gill will want to hear about this."

"I'll call them. Anton thinks I should have hypnosis to help me remember everything."

"Worth a try. When are you coming back to work?"

"As soon as I can."

WHEN I RETURNED TO THE OFFICE, John Mulligan called to tell me he went over to Cherry Street Apartments and could not see any evidence work had been done in the laundry room.

"There was dust on the floor by the machines, which would have been cleaned up along with the water, and I could see no new parts on either washing machine. The service operator said a man had called at one thirty, reported the leak, then hung up before she could get his name."

"Can you find out the number he called from?"

"The operator said ordinarily she would have called him back to get his name, but it was a blocked number."

Mulligan was upset to have been cheated. Given how Marvin also cheated Sonya Donovan, it wasn't a shocker to me.

"I just wonder how much he's taken me for over the years," John said.

"I wouldn't know, but you can always have a talk with Chief Magliano to put it on record."

DALLAS AND I WERE EARLY for our eight o'clock dinner reservations. We checked in the dining room at Cadillac Jack's, located on the lower level, then headed upstairs to the bar. We slipped into the only available booth in the back corner, and a new waiter made his way over to get our drink orders. He introduced himself as Dominic. He was a small kid with a friendly smile.

I preferred facing the center of the room: I wanted to see if anyone was coming at me. Zach Whitman was behind the bar, which didn't surprise me. He'd helped out his dad and grandpa, who owned the place before he was legally allowed to. When a heavy-set guy got up from the far end of the bar, his absence exposed Zabrina Bennett. She was smiling up at Zach.

"What are you looking at?" Dallas said, as she leaned out to have a look.

"Tell me what you think about the dark-haired girl at the end of the bar and the bartender."

"If I bend over much farther, I'll fall out of the booth."

"Come sit by me."

She slid in beside me, and I no longer had a view. It took Dallas only a few seconds to say, "I'd say they're into each other."

"That's Zabrina Bennett. The bartender she's flirting with is her boyfriend's roommate, Zach Whitman."

"Jack Whitman's grandson?"

"Yep."

"Hmm. I think her boyfriend has something to worry about."

"Her boyfriend is history, anyway. But my question is, is this a new thing, or has it been going on, maybe behind Grady's back?"

"Beats me, but they're kissing."

I leaned into Dallas; she leaned out farther. "Interesting," I said.

"Their names both start with Z. She'll think that's cute."

"Young love is fickle."

"It is."

"I wonder if he knows she's with child."

"Maybe it's his."

"Jesus."

My name was called over the speaker, and as we exited the bar, I waved at the two Zs, who didn't seem to be thrilled to see me. Zabrina's Miata was still in the parking lot when we left.

LATER THAT EVENING, as Dallas lay sleeping in my arms, I pondered the two Zs' relationship. Moriah Moore said she met Zabrina last summer. Did Zabrina know Zach before she met Grady? Did they hang out together when they were both up in Dexter Lake when Grady wasn't around? I wasn't sure it mattered.

Dallas and I spent the weekend at my house, and I rested up for what was sure to be one hell of a week.

32

Monday, December 29

FIRST THING MONDAY MORNING I called Ed Lindgren in Robbinsdale to see if he was back from vacation. His secretary, Susan Knoll, was going to see what she could find out about the footage from the security cameras around the vet's office where Grady worked. She said Ed extended his vacation until January 2, and she hadn't had time to check on it. This was the frustrating part of investigations—waiting on others, especially civilians living their private lives without concern about my investigative needs.

I erased Waldo David and Patrice from my suspect board and added Robert Quinlan and Marvin Moore. I also wrote Grady LaMere's name, followed by a question mark. Then I met with Spanky and Crosby and assigned them tasks for the next two days, because tomorrow was Shannon's surgery day.

WHEN DALLAS CALLED AROUND NOON, I invited her to come to my place for dinner. She declined.

"Isn't Shannon staying overnight because she has to be at the hospital at 6:00 a.m., and you're the one driving her?"

"Yes. Does that bother you?"

"Not at all."

"How about I pick up some takeout and head over?"

"I'm really beat tonight. Besides, you should focus on Shannon—she needs support and encouragement this evening."

"I have the Twinks for the foreseeable future while Shannon recovers, so you may have to be brave and come to my place."

"I'm not afraid to come, but it's uncomfortable for all of us."

"Shannon has to accept the idea I've moved on, like Vince will. Has he bothered you lately?"

"No, thank God."

"I'm relieved to hear it."

After I hung up, I had the distinct feeling Dallas didn't like how involved I was in my ex-wife's life.

Tuesday, December 30

I HADN'T CAUGHT THE WEATHER and news, so the new half inch of snow on the ground caught me by surprise. I left a note on the counter asking Clara to have Luke shovel the sidewalk.

Shannon's lumpectomy was scheduled for one o'clock, but she was to have an ultrasound first to insert a lead wire to the tumor site, then radioactive dye would be injected. The dye would follow the path the cancer would take to the nodes and direct the surgeon to which nodes to remove first for pathology. We'd have hours to wait for the dye to work.

We left at 6:00 a.m. After checking in, Shannon was taken back to prepare for surgery. I would be called when she was situated in a pre-op room. I took the opportunity to text Dallas good morning. She didn't answer, so I assumed she was in the shower or getting ready for work.

Within twenty minutes, I was called back to wait with Shannon. She had changed into a gown and had an IV line hooked up. We made small talk until her parents arrived at 8:45. Shortly after, Clara called. "Have you spoken with Dallas this morning? The clinic called and said she didn't show up for work, and she's not answering our home phone or her cell. I'm worried."

"I'll go check on her right now."

"Thank you. Then call me."

When I disconnected, I noticed Shannon and her parents had been eavesdropping on my conversation.

"What's wrong?" Shannon asked.

"It's something I need to take care of."

She nodded, her brown eyes revealing disappointment, which made me feel like an ass. I touched her hand. "I'll be back as soon as I can."

Adrenaline rushed through my body, my heart thumping as I made record time getting to the Bradley house.

There were no tire tracks in the driveway, indicating she hadn't driven her car out, nor did anyone drive in. However, there was a set of footprints to and from the street to the front door. I parked behind Dallas's Subaru, then entered the back porch. I knocked on the door leading into the kitchen. Willie was barking like crazy, but Dallas didn't come to the door. I tried the knob and found it unlocked.

As I stepped inside, Willie continued barking but didn't run to greet me as usual. I made my way through the kitchen and dining room calling out to Dallas. I shouted her name again and heard nothing but Willie barking. It sounded like he was in the guest bedroom, located off the living room. When I opened the door, a growling mass of black and white fur tore out. He followed his nose, sniffing about the room, then ran toward the sun room off the living room and veered left.

I found Dallas on the floor curled into the fetal position. Willie lay by her side. She had an arm around him. The light filtering in from the row of windows cast light on her face, which was swollen, bruised, and bleeding. *What the hell?*

I crouched down beside her and kissed her forehead. Tears streamed from her eyes. Her hands were shaking and her skin was cool to the touch. As I gave the details to 911, I yanked a crocheted afghan from the chair nearby and gently covered her. She was fully clothed for work: jeans, turtleneck, smock with paw prints on it.

I knelt by her side. "Where do you hurt?"

She pointed to her rib cage.

"Was it Vince?" I asked.

She nodded. "He wore . . . black face mask . . . but I saw . . . his eyes." Her voice was a whisper full of pain.

"I hope you scratched him."

"I tried . . . maybe I got his hand."

"Good. We'll do a nail scraping. How did he hurt you?"

"Pushed me down . . . punched and kicked me . . . over and over."

"I'm sorry, baby, to keep asking you questions, but what time did this happen?"

"I was . . . ready to leave . . . for work." She winced and uttered a halted sigh.

Willie whined and leaned forward to lick Dallas's hand. She patted his back. She lifted her head. "He kicked . . . Willie, too. Can you . . . take him . . . to Doc Foster?"

Vince, you asshole, you are dead. "Of course. Lie still now. We'll finish talking about this later."

I told her I was going to photograph her for the report. I snapped five before she asked me to stop. I stroked her hair and said, "They'll take more at the hospital to document your injuries."

"Okay."

I had to preserve the footprints to and from the front door. When I heard the first siren, I went outdoors and directed the first responder, Deputy Greg Woods, up the drive and to the back door. The ambulance was right behind. When the EMTs exited, I motioned for the techs to also enter though the back door. Billy Henderson and Erica Baker, my neighbor Iris's girlfriend, pulled out the ambulance cot. She handed Woods a bag, and all three entered the Bradley home without uttering a word and followed me. The ambulance cot rattled as they wheeled it across the wood floor.

As we approached, Willie stood and wagged his tail; his heavy panting was a clear sign of distress. Not only was his master hurt, but he also was most likely injured because Vince, the asshole, had kicked him. When dogs had pain they didn't show it like humans.

Woods crouched down to pet the dog. "He's a handsome boy," he said.

"He's such . . . a good dog," Dallas said as she squeezed her words through her pain.

"He was a rescue dog," I said. "They're both lucky to have each other."

Erica began questioning Dallas as to where she was feeling pain while she took her blood pressure and pulse. They asked her if she could roll onto her back onto the stretcher, which they had collapsed to just inches off the ground.

Dallas winced as they moved her with gentle efficiency onto the ambulance cot. Billy called to alert the hospital to an "incoming" on his walkie. Woods and I supervised her transfer into the ambulance. Erica was with her in the back, and before Billy shut the door I said, "Because this was an assault, make sure they bag her clothes, and do a nail scraping."

"We got it covered, Cal. Betty from the crime lab is meeting us at the hospital to gather the evidence."

"Thanks."

I then called Clara and told them Dallas had been hurt and taken to the hospital. I told her I'd come home and stay with the kids, so she could go to the hospital.

WOODS AND I STOOD TOGETHER and watched the ambulance pull out, our breath forming clouds of vapor, a second later another filling its space. When they were out of sight, Woods studied my face. I guess he was watching the unexpected tears roll down my cheeks. I wiped them off with my coat sleeve.

He put his hand on my shoulder. "I've seen enough of these things to know she's gonna be okay."

"Yeah, it's just hard to see someone you care about hurt."

"For sure." He gave me a single pat on the back. "Look, I should probably take off," he said. "You want me out of the crime scene, anyway. Right?"

I smiled and gave him a half-hearted shrug.

"Do you have any idea who did this to her?" he asked.

"Yep."

"Well, I hope you nail the bastard."

"I plan to."

I called Patrice. She listened to what I had to say about Dallas's assault. I included why I suspected her estranged husband.

"Well, maybe it is him, but Clara should make sure nothing is missing. Regardless, you can't investigate your girlfriend's assault. Austin will take the case. You can be in the background guiding him, but officially it'll be his. I'll call him right now."

"Thank you."

I waited a few minutes before I called Spanky. I told him about the footprints to make sure our lab techs brought Sirchie Snow Impression Wax, an insulating medium between the heat-generating casting material and the surrounding snow. He needed to take the impressions before the sun melted the prints.

Next, I called Prairie Veterinary Clinic and told them what had occurred. I was told to bring Willie in through the back employee entrance.

I didn't want Willie to have to jump up into my truck, and as I lifted him to the passenger seat, he yelped. I petted his head and said, "I'm sorry that asshole hurt you, little buddy. Doc Foster will take good care of you."

Dallas always brought him to work with her. He'd be comfortable there. Doc Foster met me at my truck with a cart. He said I was to assure Dallas she should take all the time she needed, and that they'd take care of Willie as long as needed.

WHEN I WALKED IN MY back door, Clara was just inside. She had the terrified look of a mother of an injured child.

"Dallas was assaulted. I found her on the sunroom floor."

She gasped.

I put a hand up. "She'll be okay, but she's hurting. Go to the hospital now, and I'll stay with the kids until I find someone else to watch them."

As Clara rushed out of the house, I noticed Luke sprawled on the sofa attached to his iPad as if it was an appendage. With all that had gone on this morning, I'd temporarily forgotten he was there. Last night was the first night he slept in his old room since Shannon moved them back to their old house. They would be staying with me until Shannon was well enough to go back to her place, however long that would be. Henry's crib was temporarily back in Lucy's room.

"They're getting your mom ready for her surgery now. I'll let you know as soon as I hear anything."

"Grandma Donna's going to call me. Where's Clara going?"

"To the hospital. Her daughter's been hurt. That's why I'm home—so I can find someone to watch you and the Twinks. Then I can go back to the hospital to be with your mom." *And Dallas.*

"Why don't you call Brittany? Mom and I saw her at the coffee shop. She's home from college."

"You are a genius, Luke."

He shrugged and tried not to smile, but the twitch of his lips gave him away. He liked being smarter than his "adoptive" dad, which was how I over-heard him referring to me to a friend.

"By the way, Luke, I noticed you shoveled the sidewalk. Nice job."

Another mouth twitch. I pulled out a ten-dollar bill out of my wallet and put it on the coffee table. No, I don't think parents should pay children to do chores around the house, but Luke was a different kind of kid—the ten bucks was behavior modification, and also I was trying to get him to like me again, as pathetic as that sounded. I should have started a tally chart with how many mistakes I was making with this kid.

Brittany Hackett had been our nanny before Clara. She worked for us for the two years she attended the community college in town. One quick phone call and Brit was packing a bag and on her way over. Because she made it a point to stop by when in town, the twins knew her. She was a lovely, smart young woman, who came from a dysfunctional family. Her mother was a nice lady, but weak and had horrible taste in men. Her main squeeze, Kent Silva, was in and out of corrections, and her sons were trying to live up to their daddy's criminal accomplishments. Brit managed to rise above shitty parenting to shine on her own accord. But then again, she had a different biological father than her brothers.

Twenty minutes later, Brit deposited her small bag by the door, and I said she should take her old efficiency third-floor apartment.

"Doesn't Clara use it?"

I lowered my voice. "Nope, she took . . . Colby's old room."

"Oh." She got that sad look everyone did when his name was mentioned. "Anyway, I don't have to be back at school until the end of January, so I can be here until then if need be."

"That's the best news I've heard all day."

Brit was a sunshiny soul. Her blond ponytail bounced as she danced across the room to sit next to Luke. Smiling, she rubbed the top of his head, mussing his hair. He grinned up at her.

"Hi," he said.

"Hi. It's so good to see you," she said, and hugged him. He hugged her back. I felt a stab of jealousy at how easy it was for him to relate to Brit. I understood his keeping me at a distance was a control issue, but it still hurt.

"Well, I should get back to the hospital."

"Okay," Brit said. "Don't worry about a thing here at home. We'll be great. Right, Luke?"

"Right." They did a fist bump.

"Hey, Luke, will you take care of Bullet?" I asked.

He nodded without giving me eye contact. The Twinks were down for their naps. I snuck a peek at their beautiful sleeping faces before I went back to the hospital.

33

C LARA WAS IN THE ER WAITING ROOM, her face a window to her worry. I sat beside her and patted her hand gripped onto the arm of the chair.

"How's our girl?" I asked.

"I'm waiting out here while she's having tests." She looked at me, her blue eyes welling with tears. "She looks awful."

"I know, but she'll be okay." When I put my arm around her, she started to weep. Within a few minutes, Nurse Shelly Newcomb came out and sat in the chair adjacent to Clara.

"How are you holding up?" she asked.

Clara bobbled her head. "I'm okay. How's Dallas?"

"She has four broken ribs, and she's in line for an MRI to rule out other internal injuries."

"Will she have to have surgery?" Clara asked.

"The MRI will tell us that," the nurse said.

When alone again, Clara stared straight ahead and said, "She said it was Vince."

"What time does your mail come?"

With a look of puzzlement, she answered, "In the afternoon. Why?"

"There were no tire tracks in your driveway before I drove in, so whoever hurt her walked in and left footprints in the snow."

She knitted her brows. "That's good, right?"

"Right. He must have parked down the block and walked up to the house."

"So his car wouldn't be spotted in our driveway."

"Exactly. He was wearing a mask, so we need to eliminate the possibility it was a home invasion or robbery. I'll drive you and bring you back right away."

"I can't leave now."

"The crime lab needs to get in. It'd be helpful if we knew if anything was missing from the house."

She sighed deeply and went to find Shelly to tell her she'd be gone for a short while.

CLARA AND I DID A WALKTHROUGH of her house. She looked in all the places where their valuables were kept, including the small safe tucked in the back of a basement cabinet. She declared nothing missing and clicked it shut.

"You should move your good jewelry down here to the safe," I said. "Bureau drawers are the first places burglars look."

"I want to go back to the hospital. Now."

When Spanky pulled up onto the Bradleys' driveway, Clara was already sitting in the car, so I spoke with him only briefly before heading back to the hospital. We'd traveled an entire block before Clara said, "Deputy Spanney is awfully young. Is he going to be able to handle this?"

"Definitely. Because Dallas is my girlfriend, he'll have to officially lead the case, but I'll assist him from the sidelines."

"I'm glad you'll be involved. How long will your people be in there?"

"Shouldn't take more than a few hours."

"Is your mother watching the kids?"

"No, Brittany Hackett. She can stay through January if needed."

"Oh, bless her heart."

"I hope Dallas is better long before then."

I WAS SURPRISED TO SEE Iris Kellogg sitting next to Richard and Donna in the waiting room. She was my backyard neighbor and the attorney who had handled our divorce. It was two o'clock, and I had anticipated Shannon would be out of surgery by now.

"Hi," Iris said with a smile.

"Are you visiting someone in the hospital?" I asked.

"Shannon."

Huh.

"She's still in surgery," Donna said with a note of frustration.

I sat down and shared where I'd been and why. The faces stared back at me with concern.

"That's awful, Cal." Iris said, "I'm sorry to hear that. You two are great together."

Donna and Richard locked eyes. Shannon's mom still held hope that we'd reconcile. Richard gave her a face I interpreted as, "Whatcha gonna do?"

"Do you have a suspect?" Iris asked.

"Her ex."

"Always the first person to look at." Iris turned to Richard and Donna.

"I could use some coffee," I said.

"I'll go with you. You two want some?" Iris said.

"Decafs, black," Donna said.

I followed her to the elevator. When the door closed behind us, I said, "I wasn't aware you and Shannon were close friends."

"You weren't?"

"Nope. Neither of you have mentioned it."

"It's not a secret."

"Your girlfriend was one of the EMTs who treated Dallas. She's good."

"Yes, Erica loves her job."

"Are you two still together?"

She smiled. "Yes, why?"

"Just curious."

WE BOUGHT FOUR COFFEES, sandwiches, and four oversized cookies, then made our way back up to the waiting room. We sipped and ate in silence, all of us glancing up every time there was movement outside the door. I was surprised when my mother and Bobby Lopez entered the room.

"Mom, what are you doing here?"

She used her explaining voice, slow and syncopated. "Clara called. She said you needed someone to stay with the children, so we drove right over, but Brittany was already there."

"Yes, she's covering for Clara while Dallas recovers."

She pursed her lips and looked at Bobby, who hiked his brows.

"Shannon's not out of surgery yet?" she asked.

"No, and I don't know why it's taking so dang long," Donna said.

"Sometimes they do more tests on the lymph nodes just to be safe," Mom said.

She turned back to me, "You know I'd be free labor, but I suppose a college student can use the money. Anyway, we stopped by Dallas's room to see how she was doing. My goodness, she's pretty beat up. Clara said they want to keep her overnight."

"Only one night?" I said.

"You know how they push people out of the hospital these days."

"I'm gonna run down and see her. What's her room number?"

"She's in 112."

As I stood to leave, the doctor entered. He crossed his arms across his chest as he delivered us the news. The lumpectomy was successful with clear margins, but the sentinel node biopsy was positive, so he proceeded with the removal of nine additional lymph nodes under her arm. That's what took time.

"Has the cancer spread to her lymph nodes?" Donna asked.

"We removed them only as a precaution."

"When can she go home?" Donna asked.

"Tomorrow morning. With the additional surgery she'll be in recovery for a while, so we're going to keep her overnight."

"When will she start chemo?" I asked.

"Oncology will set that up after she heals . . . probably in a month. She needs to take it easy for a few days, but she can resume most activities in five days."

When the nurse walked in, she took a gander at all of us and said there was a limit of two family members in recovery. I suggested Richard and Donna go in. After they left, I told Iris I was going to check on Dallas.

"Of course. Shannon will understand."

Right.

Mom and Bobby followed me out. "We're going to Cadillac Jack's for ribs tonight. You and the kids want to join us?"

"No."

"Why not?" Mom said.

"Mom, my time today will be split between the two women in the hospital and my two active investigations."

"Oh."

Bobby put his arm around Mom and said, "We understand, Cal."

I hugged Mom goodbye, shook Bobby's hand, then they walked off. Sometimes I didn't get my mother at all.

WHEN I WALKED INTO Dallas's room, she was sound asleep. Her brother Jamie and Clara were huddled, visiting quietly.

"How is she?" I asked.

"Besides being beat to shit?" Jamie said.

Clara put her hand on his arm. "Shh. The doctor said she's going to be okay and won't need surgery, but she'll need time to heal. If all goes well tonight, she can go home tomorrow."

Jamie glared at me. "Why aren't you out looking for Vince?"

"I can't because of . . . our closeness. My partner has the case. I'll call him to see what's up."

I went out into the hall. Spanky answered on the first ring.

"Woods and I are on the way down to the Cities to pick up Vince Palmer. Edina PD is going to be there to support us."

"Did you swab doorknobs and the fridge door at the Bradleys' for DNA?"

"Of course. Hey, guess what the vanity plate on Palmer's black Corvette says."

"No guess."

"'VNC BA.' What do you suppose BA stands for? Badass?"

"Big asshole?"

He chuckled.

"Check him for scratches. Dallas thinks she got him."

"Will do. I'd like to interview her tomorrow. Will she be up for it?"

"She's supposed to be released in the morning."

While still in the hall, I sent a quick text to Donna to ask her to contact me when Shannon was back in her room.

"How long will Vince be in prison?" Jamie asked.

"First, we have to prove it was him."

"It was him," Clara said, then set her jaw tightly.

"He was wearing a ski mask and she only saw his eyes. A prosecutor will need more proof to file charges. Hopefully she got his DNA under her fingernails when she scratched him."

"You mean without DNA evidence you may not be able to prove it was him?" Jamie said.

"Cal will do everything he can," Clara said.

"He better hope so," Jamie said, giving me a hard stare.

What did I ever do to this dick?

At seven, Donna called to tell me Shannon was in her room but very sleepy. They were going home and would pick her up tomorrow morning from the hospital. They'd stay the day at my house with her, which worked for me. I wanted to see for myself how she was doing, so I said I'd be right back and made my way to her room.

Shannon was awake. Iris stood at her bedside, her back to me. I moved to the opposite side and took Shannon's hand. She didn't pull it away.

"How are you feeling?" I asked.

"Pretty good."

"Any pain?"

"Not much."

Iris proceeded to tell Shannon about Dallas's assault, which I had not intended to do at the time.

"Oh, Cal, I'm so sorry. You should be with her," Shannon said.

Iris nodded.

Shannon said, "I'm fine. Go."

In a way I resented being dismissed. And why the hell was Iris still there?

CLARA PAGED THROUGH A MAGAZINE and Jamie played games on his phone while I watched Dallas sleep and plotted a strategy to nail Vince. Out of the blue, Zabrina and Zach's kiss popped into my head. How long had that relationship been going on? She threw Grady away like he was a piece of meat fallen on the floor, and that evening was kissing it up with Zach Whitman. I realize some people—young and old alike—change relationships like underwear, but those two must have been attracted to each other way before now. To an inexperienced young woman, Zach Whitman must have seemed like a real catch—handsome, confident. But the kid hung out with the local doper losers. Then again, maybe Zach and Zabrina were made for each other—shallow, narcissistic. I'd have to mention it to Patrice—and have another talk with Zach.

About nine o'clock I couldn't stop yawning, so I said goodnight to Clara and Jamie. As I kissed the sleeping Dallas's cheek, I noticed a strangely shaped bruise on her cheekbone. An impression of an object?

I thought I'd head up to Shannon's room one more time before I went home. Iris put her phone down when she saw me.

"How is she doing?" I whispered.

"Good, she's just sleepy."

"I'm on my way home."

"Me too—in a few minutes."

"Iris . . ."

"Yes?"

"Never mind."

CONCERNED WHY SPANKY HADN'T apprised me of Vince's apprehension, I phoned him on my way to my car. He and Woods were back in town—without Vince.

"He didn't show up for work, and he wasn't at his condo or his parents' house," Spanky told me. "One of his neighbors saw him driving out of the parking garage, before six o'clock this morning. He said he waved, but Vince looked straight ahead. He thought Vince looked angry. We watched his place for hours, then Woods said we should give it up."

"At least you have a witness seeing him leave about the right time. Dallas has a weird bruise on her cheek. Check it out."

"Will do."

I turned around and walked back to Dallas's room. I asked Clara and Jamie if they had any idea where Vince might hide.

"His family has a cabin next door to some friends of ours on Island Lake. That's how they met," Jamie said.

"Can you give me directions?"

I handed him my small notebook. As he sketched a crude map, he gave me verbal directions. I called Spanky back, but he didn't pick up. I left a message, headed home to change into my uniform and to grab my firearm, stopped back at the department, left another message for Spanky, logged in, signed out a vehicle, and when I still hadn't heard back from Spanky, I found Deputy Jenny Deitz and asked her to follow me out to Island Lake.

With the help of Jamie's map, I easily located the Palmer cabin. Jenny and I parked at the end of the driveway where we'd be hidden from the view of anyone in the cabin, and also, to block the exit in case Vince tried to make a getaway. The driveway hadn't been plowed since the half inch of snow overnight, and there were tire tracks.

"Let's walk on the edge in case we need to document the vehicle tracks," I said.

The reflective light from the waxing moon allowed us to walk in without using our flashlights. Our heavy boots crunched on the snow as we walked in time toward the cabin, approximately one hundred yards in.

A great horned owl's syncopated *hoo hoo hoo* sounded; I stopped and looked up to see if I could spot it, and Jenny smacked right into me. She giggled.

"Shh."

"Well, don't just stop," she whispered.

We approached the three buildings—all dark. The A-frame cabin sat between a garage to the left and another large shed to the right. Using my flashlight, I checked the inside of the garage through a side-door window.

"No vehicle. I doubt anyone's here," I said.

Jenny shined her light across the snow toward the large shed. "There are no footprints to the other building. It's probably where they keep their boy toys."

"But there are tire tracks and footprints to and from the cabin, so someone's been here today."

We walked around the exterior of the cabin and shined our flashlights through the windows. It didn't appear to be occupied. I knocked at the door, and as expected, no one answered.

"He may be out—or he left, which is what he should have done if he had a brain. Well, you may as well go back on patrol, Jenny."

"Golly, my heart was pumping thinking we were going to make an apprehension tonight."

"Not this time."

As we hurriedly made our way back to our vehicles, Jenny said, "I suppose he could have been out for a beer and burger, driven back, saw our vehicles and drove on by. Maybe we should have hidden our vehicles."

"Maybe."

"Thinking about burgers makes me hungry. I'm ready for break two hours early."

"Stop at Cadillac Jack's," I suggested.

"Eat with me?"

"No, I'm going home, but I'll check out the parking lot for a black Corvette."

Jenny followed me to the restaurant—no Corvette—so I waved at her as she exited her squad. Tomorrow was another day.

When I got home, the Twinks were in bed, but Luke was still up watching *Jimmy Neutron* with Brit. She had ordered pizza for dinner, so I microwaved a couple slices and joined them. When Luke fell asleep before the movie was over, I carried him up to bed. He woke as I laid him on his bed. He let me help him change into his pajamas, then I tucked him in. I brazenly kissed him on the forehead and told him I loved him. As I headed out the door, he called my name.

"Yes?"

"Is my mom going to die?"

I knelt by his bed and touched his arm. "No, buddy, they got all the cancer."

"Why didn't she come here like she said she would?"

"The operating rooms sometimes get backed up. Her surgery ended later than they thought, so the doctor wanted her to stay overnight. She's going to be just fine."

"Okay."

"Goodnight."

"Goodnight."

Wow. Progress. I hope I didn't lie to him just then.

34

Wednesday, December 31

I GOT UP EARLY, DRESSED IN street clothes, and went directly to my garage. I was on a stepladder pulling down a box from a shelf when someone called out my name, startling me. I wobbled. As I grabbed the shelf in order to steady myself, hands gripped the ladder. Bobby's hands.

"Jesus, Bobby. You scared the shit out of me." I climbed down toting the box.

"Sorry. I thought you'd heard my car."

"I was deep in thought."

"I guess so."

"What are you doing here?"

"I had to come to Home Depot and thought I'd stop by to ask if you were aware lights were on in the Donovan house the last two nights."

"They're putting it up for sale, so maybe they've been out there getting it ready."

"Figured they'd try to sell it. I imagine a property that pricey may sit for a while. If they want to unload it for a reasonable price, I may buy it for your mother."

"What's wrong with the house you have?"

"Nothing, but if I could get the Donovan place you could bring your kids out for a swim any time of year."

"You have too much money."

"Think so?"

"The question is, how do you earn your money?"

"You don't want to know." He laughed, as he always did when the subject of what he did came up. Part of me thought he was jerking my chain, part of me believed him.

I brought the box down and dug through it until I found what I was looking for, then shoved the box back up in its place.

"You know I have to reinvest in real estate soon. What's the baseball bat for?" he asked.

"You don't want to know."

"That's my line."

"So I've noticed."

He pointed at the bat. "Look, kid, what you're planning is a very bad idea."

"What am I planning?"

"You intend on delivering some comeuppance to Vincent Palmer for hurting your pretty lady."

I shrugged.

"You do know you'd be the first person they'd look at."

"I have a ski mask, just like the one he used when he assaulted her."

"Aw, shit, Cal. You go through with this and you can bet you'd be the one to end up in prison—and that's one place a cop does not want to be. You know I'm right."

"That piece of shit is not going to get by with this."

"He won't."

"I suppose you know where he is."

"My guess is that he's at his girlfriend's."

I shook my head. "Jesus Christ. Which is where?"

"You need to let your greenhorn investigator find him."

"What a dick."

"Me or Palmer?"

I considered. "Palmer."

He nodded. "He is."

As I made a move to go around him, he blocked my way.

"Okay, you'll have to move."

"Not until you put the bat back. Go to work and encourage your rookie partner to look up Palmer's cell phone records. He'll find out he's been communicating with this woman regularly." He punched me on the arm and said, "Put the fucking bat away."

"Don't you do anything." As I said it, I wasn't sure I meant it.

"Is that what you want?"

"What I want is the pleasure of kicking the shit out of him."

"Understandable."

I rested the bat on my boot. "But you're right—they'd come after me."

"I've done some checking into this guy. I don't like what I see."

"Like what?"

"I'll tell you when I know more."

"Bobby, just stay out of it."

"Why? What are you afraid of?"

"That you'll kill him."

"What do you take me for?" he scoffed, and walked toward his Escalade parked on the street.

"An assassin," I whispered.

SPANKY ARRIVED AT THE OFFICE about 7:00 a.m. "Sorry I didn't get your messages until this morning. My bad. Anything go down?"

I told him about the Palmer cabin.

"I'm waiting for the judge to sign the search warrants this morning."

"There may be something on his cellphone records that can help."

"Yeah, I'm hoping."

Spanky started his paperwork, and I had a visit from Patrice.

"Zabrina didn't come home last night and isn't answering her phone. I called Sarah, and she said Zabrina wasn't in Minneapolis. She must be at the lake house."

"You're probably right," I said. "Bobby said there were lights on out there for the last two nights."

"Two? Well, I don't like that. Do you suppose it's Grady?"

"You could send a patrol out to check," I said.

"No, I don't want it written up. I'll go myself, but I'd feel better if you came with me."

I sighed and rolled my eyes. "Let's go."

"You're not wearing your uniform."

"Want me to go home and change? I hadn't planned on coming in today."

"Fine."

PATRICE WAS QUIET for a few blocks before she said, "I thought we'd have Vincent Palmer in custody by now."

"Yeah, me too. Deputy Deitz and I checked out the family cabin on Island Lake last night. Looked like someone had been there earlier. He's probably back in the Cities. Spanky has search warrants and is going back down today."

"Why do you persist in calling him 'Spanky' instead of Austin? I think it's awful and unprofessional."

"Because he likes it."

She shook her head. "Do you think Vince Palmer took off for parts unknown?"

"Would be the smart choice."

"You have a look I've never seen—like you want to rip his limbs off."

"That would be accurate, but I won't. I know the consequences."

Bobby was right. If I took my Louisville Slugger to Palmer, I'd be the one to land in jail and would likely lose everything. Part of me wanted Bobby to kill Vince, or at least maim him. I was afraid with the right lawyer Palmer would land probation because assaulting Dallas was his first offense. And what had Bobby found out about him that he didn't like?

Patrice began to sing along with Brad Paisley as he sang "Whiskey Lullaby." She had a terrible voice. Somewhere between Prairie Falls and Bittern, she said, "David blames my job for the break up of our marriage."

"Do you agree?"

"He was in on the decision for me to run for sheriff. He knew how time consuming the job would be, and is that an excuse to have an affair with my friend's mother, for God's sake?"

"No, but sometimes people can't know how difficult a lifestyle will be until they experience it."

"I guess that's true. So I'm curious, will you support me or Matt?" she asked.

"Patrice, don't draw the line."

I glanced at her as she looked out the window. "You just answered my question . . . and if you, one of my friends, support Matt, then I'll have to rely on the civilian vote."

She considers me a friend? Huh.

THERE WERE THREE CARS in the Donovan yard: Zabrina's Miata, Grady's Mazda, and a white Nissan.

"Recognize the Nissan?" I asked.

"No."

"I'll run the plates."

Within a short time, we had the answer. "It's Zach Whitman's. I'm not sure this is a good situation, with the kiss I saw." I said.

"What kiss?"

"Zach and Zabrina at Cadillac Jack's."

"Oh, shit, that could mean trouble."

We got out and approached the door. Patrice had a key and let us in. The kids were not in the great room, which was littered with empty wine bottles and pizza boxes.

"Party time," I said.

She picked up a wine bottle. "They're drinking her good stuff. So where are they?"

"In bed . . . or in the pool."

"Good lord, I hope it's the pool."

We walked through to the back of the house. Patrice pushed open the heavy door to the pool. I stayed close behind. The heavy chlorine odor hung in the humid air. This was no pool party. Grady stood midway along the side of the pool. Zabrina was standing down by the shallow end. Zach, fully clothed, was treading water in the middle of the pool.

"This is screwy," I said.

Patrice and I simultaneously unsnapped the straps on our holsters and placed our hands on our weapons. We made no sudden moves as we moved in closer to assess the situation. Zabrina let out a sob, then wiped her eyes with her sleeve. Zach pointed to Grady.

"What's going on here?" I said, as I walked around Patrice.

"They lied to me," Grady screamed.

"No, Grady," Zabrina said.

"Grady, let's sit down and discuss this calmly."

He ignored me. The hair stood up on the back of my neck.

"Grady, kneel down and put your hands behind your head," I said firmly, calmly.

He ignored my request. I said it louder.

"This is ridiculous," Patrice said from behind me. She brushed past me.

Then, *boom!* Patrice's firearm came up and she fired. Zabrina screamed. Grady lifted an arm and fired several rounds at Zach. Zach dove into the water. Patrice pulled off a cluster of rounds.

By the time I had my weapon trained on Grady, he'd fallen to his knees and toppled over. His gun skittered across the tile and landed near the wall. Two seconds, max, it was over—and I hadn't taken a single shot.

As I called 911, I looked for blood in the water. Couldn't see any.

"Are you hit?" I asked Zach.

"No."

What with the ringing in my ears, I could hardly hear his answer.

Good thing water slows bullets. And good thing Grady was as bad a shot as Patrice was. If I'd seen the gun, I would have taken a head shot since he'd been standing sideways to us.

I holstered my firearm and knelt over Grady. I checked his pockets for additional weapons, then as I spoke to the 911 operator, I assessed his injuries.

"We have a nineteen-year-old male, gunshot wounds to his upper arm and thigh."

Lorraine said she'd dispatch the ambulance from Dexter Lake ASAP. They'd take him to St. Joseph's Hospital in Brainerd, as it was closer than Birch County Hospital in Prairie Falls.

Patrice was standing frozen in her tracks.

"Patrice!" I yelled.

She looked up.

"Put on gloves, pick up the gun, bag it and lock it in the Explorer. While you're out there, get the first-aid kit."

Without saying a word, she pulled gloves out of her pocket and picked up the gun. She moved zombie-like toward the door.

"You okay?" I asked.

"Yeah," she said.

ZACH HAD CLIMBED OUT of the pool and sat next to Zabrina on a bench near the changing room wall. She pulled her knees up, put her face between them and covered her head with her hands.

"Zach! I need some help here."

He looked at me.

"Get some towels out of the pool room."

Grady moaned.

"You're gonna live, kid," I said.

"It hurts."

Zach handed me the towels. "Now go back to Zabrina."

I wrapped the towels around the affected limbs. "Whose gun was that?" I asked Grady.

"You know."

"My partner's?"

"Yeah."

"Where was it?"

"Storage unit . . . in Jordan."

He must have retrieved it before Minneapolis police secured the search warrant.

When Patrice returned with the kit, I tied a tourniquet around Grady's upper arm and leg to decrease the bleeding. Patrice crouched nearby and held her head. She lifted a hand to show me it was trembling. "I'm a wreck."

"It's the adrenaline. I have to call Bemidji in with an officer-involved shooting."

"Shit."

LATER, AS WE WATCHED the ambulance pull away, I said, "This could have been a lot worse. I didn't see the gun in his left hand."

Her brows furrowed as she snuffled. "I knew something was up when I saw the fear in Zabrina's and Zach's faces. The media will have a heyday with this one."

"When's the last time you were at the range?"

"I don't go often enough. Why?"

"Why? You were shooting all over the place. Did you look at the back wall?"

She took a deep breath. "Shit."

PATRICE FOUND ZACH A LARGE terrycloth robe to wear and while his wet things were in the clothes dryer, Zabrina went upstairs to change clothing. I asked Patrice to go up and get Zabrina's side of the story. I would get Zach's.

I put on my iPad to record his initial statement. His hands shook as he pushed back his hair, still wet. Red blotches filled his cheeks, and he'd acquired a nervous tic near his eye.

"So what happened?"

"Zabrina and I were just hanging out when Grady showed up. I told her not to let him in, but she said it would be fine. Well, it wasn't. He started screaming at us like a lunatic."

"You were with his girl."

"Former girl. They broke up."

"Like five minutes ago."

He lifted his eyebrows and took a breath.

"How long have you and Zabrina had a thing?"

He closed his eyes for a few seconds. "I knew her before I knew him."

"Define 'knew'?"

"We met up here a couple summers ago, hooked up a couple times. Then she started dating my new roommate."

"What a coincidence. So . . . by hooked up you mean sexual activity?"

He nodded.

"What about lately?"

"During Thanksgiving vacation I saw her at a party up here. She told me Grady was already getting serious, and she didn't feel the same way. She was thinking of breaking it off. Well, then her grandmother died . . . and her mother, and, well, things got crazy."

"So you had sex at the party?"

"Yeah."

"So why were you all in the pool room?"

"Grady pulled out a gun and forced us back there. He was talking crazy— said Zabrina was going to get to feel what it was like for him to watch her grandmother drown."

"He admitted he saw her drown?"

"Yeah."

"What else did he say?"

"Just crazy shit like that. It was like he was high or something. On the way into the pool I whispered to Zabrina to tell him what he wanted to hear, so she told him they would run away to Las Vegas to get married like they planned. I think she had him believing it . . . then you guys came."

"If we hadn't, you might be dead. By the way, you do know she's pregnant."

He looked up at me. "What?"

"Yep, the baby was Grady's little gravy train."

"Well, now everything makes more sense."

"But . . . maybe you're the father."

"Nah," he said, but his cheeks bloomed pink as watermelon flesh.

PATRICE MADE COFFEE, and we all waited for BRO. Zach and Zabrina sat in stony silence side by side on the couch, while Patrice and I quietly compared their versions of the incident. They were remarkably similar.

Forty minutes later, while Zach was changing back into his dry clothing, car lights shone through the expansive window announcing Leslie Rouch and her two crime lab technicians' arrival. We gave them a brief rundown before they commenced to the pool area to do their thing.

"To save time, I'm going to show them where the stray bullets and bullet holes are. You stay here with these two," Patrice said.

When Patrice was gone, Zach appeared out of the downstairs and joined Zabrina on the couch again. The kids were staring straight ahead, both appearing shellshocked.

"Had you two considered Grady would be upset by the breakup?" I asked.

They ignored my question.

"Not in a talking mood? Okay, we can wait until we get back to the department to get your statements."

Patrice came back. "I have a headache," she said. "I need to find some Advil."

I admit I was relieved she was the shooter. If I had been, Grady would be dead, and I'd be on the hot seat. The BRO would justify the shooting, but good old Brenda LaMere would surely capitalize on the current public opinion of the excessive use of police force and encourage her son to sue.

I asked for a unit to transport Zach back to our department. When Deputy John Odell showed up, they took off. Patrice rode in my backseat with Zabrina. They didn't speak for the forty-five minutes it took us to get back to Prairie Falls. When Leslie arrived, she questioned the kids individually. Since we were not allowed to observe, Patrice and I went to our separate offices.

I called Silas Hill, Zach and Grady's roommate.

"Did you ever see anything going on between Zach and Zabrina?"

"Um . . . yeah."

"What?"

"They sleep together when Grady isn't around. I think Grady was starting to suspect them."

"What makes you think so?"

"Because he asked me if I thought Zach had a thing for Zabrina."

"What did you tell him?"

"I told him I didn't think so."

"Why?"

"Because Zach's my friend."

"You never bonded with Grady?"

"Not really. At first he seemed really nice, but he's got a side to him I don't trust."

"What do you mean?"

"He says creepy things out of the blue. One day we were talking about what pets we had as kids, and he said he wished useless old people could be euthanized, like dogs."

Wow. Like his grandparents? "Anything else?"

"Well, last fall, maybe September, a few of us were having a few beers. We were talking about how cool Cadillac Jack's was. Anyway, Grady started asking Zach questions about whether he'd inherit the business after his grandfather and dad died. Zach said he didn't think about it much, and it'd be a while. Then Grady brought up how rich Zabrina would be when her mother died. Zach said her mom was still in her forties, and her grandmother was in really good shape for an old lady. Grady got this weird grin on his face and said people got sick and died—or there were accidents, and that Zach and Zabrina could be rich before they knew it. I just thought it super weird."

"Did Zabrina hear that?"

"No."

"Did Zach know Zabrina's family?"

"Yeah. One weekend last summer when I went home with him, we were at CJ's—that's what he calls Cadillac Jack's. Anyway, Zabrina and her family came there to eat. That's when I met her."

"Did you think he had a thing for her back then?"

"Zach has a lot of girlfriends. I didn't think much about it."

"Silas, you'll probably hear about it on the news tomorrow. Grady pulled a gun on Zach and was shot by someone in our department."

"No shit. Did he shoot Zach?"

"No. Grady was the only one injured. He'll be okay."

"Man, that's like . . . totally shocking. What happened?"

"I can't discuss the details."

"Will Grady go to jail?"

"Oh, yeah."

IT WAS EXACTLY THREE HOURS before I was called down to give my statement. Leslie questioned me for an hour. She said Grady was in surgery, and would be held in the hospital until he was ready to be released to the Birch County Jail. She would interview him as early as tonight or tomorrow morning. She said Patrice put herself on administrative leave, but my leave would be delayed until after the holiday.

I then went to my office to start the paperwork on the incident. Spanky was there working at his desk.

"Did you trace Palmer's credit card transactions and his phone records?" I asked.

"That's what I'm doing now. We'll find him, Cal."

I began to write up my report; I wanted to finish before my administrative leave started. I had no problem taking two weeks off.

Spanky said, "I think I have something. Palmer has called this same number several times over the last few months. It belongs to a Cassandra Foley."

"Don't call. If he's there, it'll alert him, and he'll take off. Get the address and go on down."

"Now?"

"Yes, now. I'll go with you."

"No, Patrice told me you can't go near him. Don't worry about it. I'll find someone."

He grabbed his jacket and left. After he took off, I watched the clock, a useless habit. It would be a couple hours before he'd be at this woman's house.

When my phone rang, I grabbed for it so fast I almost dropped it. It wasn't Spanky, but Shannon. She called to ask me to pick up a crisp white wine. Iris was preparing a special New Year's Eve meal: lobster mac and cheese, salad, and baguette.

"I thought Iris's idea of cooking was opening containers of take-out."

She laughed. "She knows how to make a few specialty items, like you do."

"Huh."

I grabbed my jacket, stopped for flowers, then drove to see Dallas. She was propped up on the sofa, her face swollen and bruised. I set the roses on the coffee table.

"Pretty," she said.

When I hugged her, she started crying.

"I love you," I said.

"I love you, too."

I told her we were still looking for Vince and asked if she knew of any friends he might turn to. She gave me a few names, said she was sleepy, then nodded off.

Clara motioned me to the kitchen. She handed me a Budweiser. I sat at the table and watched as she cut the ends of the white roses I'd brought Dallas and placed them in a vase.

"She's so sleepy because of the medication," she said.

"I know. Where's Jamie?" I asked.

"He went home. Are they close to arresting Vince?" she asked.

"I think so. I can try calling Deputy Spanney."

"Please."

He answered after the first ring. "I was just going to call you. How's Dallas doing?"

"She's home, hurting, but we're thankful it wasn't worse. What's the skinny on the asshole?"

"We talked to the girlfriend. He's been staying with her, but she hasn't seen him since this morning. She didn't know he was ever married."

"Figures. Did she notice any scratches or anything?"

"Yeah, a fairly large scratch on his hand. He said he got it while hiking on vacation."

"I hope you're not parked in front of her place."

"No, down the street. We have an unmarked, anyway."

I gave him the two names Dallas gave me, then told him to stay in touch. I finished my beer, kissed the sleeping Dallas on the forehead, and went home to my ex, her friend, and my children.

WHEN I ARRIVED HOME with wine in hand, Shannon was on the couch and Iris was setting the dining room table. I managed to ignore the mess in the kitchen and poured wine. Over cheese and crackers and wine, Shannon mentioned she felt so good she would stay no more than a few days. Once the mac and cheese came out of the oven, we took our places around the table. Although the kids devoured the mac and cheese, I thought it marginal. Iris shouldn't cook.

That evening after the kids were bathed and in bed and Brit disappeared up to her quarters, Iris and Shannon found some chick flick on television. And because I could stand it no longer, I cleaned up Iris's cooking mess on the counter and stovetop and then scrubbed the sticky pots and pans, while she sat on my couch. After leaving the kitchen in pristine shape, I wished them a happy New Year, then excused myself and went up to bed.

I gave Spanky a call—no sign of Palmer. They were staking out the girl-friend's, and before they left for home they would run by the condo and his parents' house.

35

Thursday, January 1, 2015

A T 4:00 A.M. HENRY CRAWLED in bed with me. We both dozed off until six, when he stuck his finger up my nose.

I grabbed a diaper out of the twins' room then changed Henry on my bed. As I carried him down the hall, Bullet meandered out of Henry's room where Luke was sleeping. Dogs were better at reading humans than humans were. He's always seemed to sense Luke needed him. Or maybe he just liked him better than he liked me.

Bullet followed us downstairs. I let him out and set Henry near the box in the corner containing his toy vehicles. He immediately pulled out his favorite big rig. I smiled at Henry's growling as he rolled his truck back and forth over the wood flooring.

I glanced around the room. I headed for the glasses and four bowls piled on the coffee table before Henry got to them. Two had been used for popcorn, but the other two contained a disgusting layer of melted chocolate ice cream. As I passed the counter, I noticed the empty microwave popcorn bag lying on the counter, spots of grease and popcorn kernels dribbled across the granite surface. I filled a sippy cup of milk for Henry, put cartoons on, and after letting Bullet back in the house, I began to clean up the new mess Iris and Shannon had left me.

"Slobs."

"What?" Brit asked as she entered the room with Lucy in her arms.

"Oh. Just talking to myself. Hey, Lucy girl," I said and kissed her on the cheek.

"Down," she said, and she ran over to Henry to take his truck. He acquiesced to her frequently. He simply pulled another truck out.

"When I peeked in to see if she was awake, she was standing in her crib."

"Henry crawls out of his now. She'll soon be following suit."

She placed her hands on her hips. "Well, that little bugger. Should I start breakfast? I could make French toast."

"Perfect. And I'll clean up Iris and Shannon's mess."

"Oops. They aren't abiding by the house rules."

"Am I unreasonable to expect people to at least put their dishes in the sink?"

"Not by my standards."

Luke wandered in asking for a cinnamon roll.

"Cinnamon rolls?" I asked.

"Eleanor Kohler brought them over yesterday," Brit said.

"I wasn't made aware."

"That could have been on purpose," she said with a smile.

"It's a stinking conspiracy."

She laughed.

Spanky called to tell me Vince hadn't returned to the girlfriend's or his condo, and his credit cards hadn't been used for forty-eight hours.

"So he's not staying in a hotel."

Shit. Was he in hiding or dead? Damn. I hoped Bobby hadn't kill him. Really.

SHANNON GOT UP AT NINE O'CLOCK, still clad in her pajamas. I brewed her a cup of coffee and placed a cinnamon roll on a plate for her. While she was eating at the counter, there was a knock at the back door. Iris. I let her in, and Brit and I shared a look.

"Want a cinnamon roll?" Shannon asked her.

"Yum," she said and threw her coat over a chair and sat down next to Shannon. "I had to hide them from Cal, so there'd be some left for today."

I narrowed my eyes and said, "What else are you hiding?"

She scrunched her face and said, "Nothing."

When they'd finished eating, they left their dishes and went to the couch. Iris picked up the remote and changed cartoons to the news.

Luke sat up and said, "Hey, I was watching that."

Shannon said, "Go up to your dad's room to watch your shows."

He stomped off. Brit and I exchanged another look, then she cleaned up their dishes.

Iris left after lunch, and while Shannon and the Twinks napped, I watched football. Luke disappeared upstairs. I was sure he was on his iPod. Brit made a turkey dinner, and it was nice. Just the six of us—without Iris. After the babes were in bed that night, Luke, Brit, Shannon and I watched a Star Wars movie, and then we all went to bed early.

36

Friday, January 2

BEFORE I WENT TO WORK, I stopped by the Bradleys' to spend a few minutes with Dallas.

"Are you in a lot of pain?"

"The pills help, but then they put me to sleep."

"Well, Vince is nowhere to be found. Do you have any idea where he might go to hide?"

"No, and I don't think he'd dare to come back here."

"I could stay here tonight," I offered.

"No, Mom has her shotgun upstairs with us."

"Oh, great. Clara . . ."

"Yes?" She poked her head around the corner.

"Do you know how to shoot a shotgun?"

"Yes, I do. I used to go grouse hunting with Dan all the time."

"Dad always said she was the better shot," Dallas said.

"This concerns me. If he shows up, you dial 911."

"Okay, Cal, sure." She winked at Dallas.

Dallas was cracking a smile. "We'll be fine."

"You look like you feel better."

"I do."

I stayed with her long enough for a cup of coffee, then left for the hospital to speak with Grady LaMere.

One of our deputies close to retirement was standing guard outside his room.

"Hey, Ray, how's it going?"

"Gotta love this duty. Kid's not going anywhere. He's handcuffed to his hospital bed."

Ray opened the door for me and closed it behind me.

Grady looked up. "I thought you might be my grandparents."

"Are they coming up to see you?"

"Yes," he said.

"You're in a spot of trouble."

"I know. I've had my rights read to me."

"What did you tell Detective Rouch?"

"She didn't tell you?"

"I want to hear it from you personally."

"What? That I killed Zabrina's grandmother? Well, it wasn't me who pushed her in the water."

"Start from the beginning," I said as I turned on my iPad.

THE REST OF THE DAY I did paperwork, made phone calls, and organized my evidence in the Sonya Donovan case. I had almost everything in line to present to the county attorney to bring all the players down.

At five o'clock, I was headed home. I dreaded having to deal with Shannon and Iris. I liked Iris, I just didn't like her around all the time—nor did I appreciate the mess they left in their wake.

The house was unusually quiet. Brit was reading to the twins on the sofa when I walked in. The twins crawled off the couch and came for their bear hugs.

"Where's Shannon?" I asked as I held a twin in each arm.

"Home. She left a note for you on the counter."

> *Cal,*
>
> *Thanks for letting us stay with you. I should have realized I wouldn't need that much care, especially if I didn't have to take care of the twins. Mom and Iris will help if I need anything. Luke was disappointed when I told him we were going back home. I think that's huge, don't you?*
>
> *Thanks for offering to have me stay. I need to talk to you about something—so call when you have time.*
>
> *Shannon*

I set the twins down, grabbed a beer, and called her.

"What's on your mind?" I asked.

"Well, first of all, thank you for letting us stay at your house."

"No problem."

"I'm not sure that's true, but anyway, I'm rewriting my will. I hope you will agree that my parents get custody of Luke if something should happen to me."

"Not me?"

"He asked me if I was going to die. It broke my heart. I told him it was highly unlikely, but if it did happen, you'd take care of him. He objected. He said he'd rather live with my parents."

I didn't know what to say. My heart was heavy. An awkward silence ensued.

"He's at their house until they head back for Florida."

"Whatever."

"You sound mad," she said.

"He always gets his way, Shannon. What are you going to do when he's sixteen?"

"That will be my problem, now, won't it?"

"And it will be a big one. By the way, it seems strange to me you never mentioned Iris was an old friend when we hired her as our divorce attorney."

"What? You don't think you got a fair deal?"

"That's not the point. It's like you were hiding you knew her."

"Don't be silly. Anyway, she loves you and says I'm lucky you're the father of my children. And now I should go lay down. I'm tired."

"You might want to be careful you don't get Erica pissed off for taking all Iris's time."

"Erica's in New York with her family this week."

"When she gets back, then. Just sayin'. Be careful. Erica's a tough girl."

I heard a sigh before the line went silent.

THAT NIGHT AFTER THE KIDS were in bed, Brit and I found *House Hunters: Caribbean Life* on HGTV.

"I could live there," she said.

"I fantasize lying in a hammock under palm trees."

"Maybe you should take a vacation in St. Thomas."

My cellphone rang—Spanky.

"I have news," he said. "I'm on my way to North Memorial Hospital. We had an anonymous tip saying Vince Palmer was staying at a mom-and-pop hotel in Brooklyn Park. HCSO agreed to send a unit over to check it out. The owner cooperated, opened the door, and lucky for Palmer they did. He was passed out on the floor, an empty bottle of vodka in his hand. He was using his dad's credit card."

"I hope he doesn't wake up and escape."

"They're keeping an eye on him until I get there."

"Great. Thanks."

I told Brit I was leaving and drove to the Bradleys' to deliver the news.

Clara answered the door in her pajamas and robe.

"Sorry to come so late, but I have some news I wanted to deliver in person," I told her.

"About Vince?"

"Yes."

"Come in. Dallas and I are watching a movie."

Dallas was stretched out on the couch, pillows behind her. When she first saw me she smiled, then, studying the look on my face, she dropped it.

"What's wrong?" she asked.

I told her what I knew.

"Cal, I knew he was drinking again. On the day he assaulted me, the alcohol was coming out his pores."

"Has Spanky interviewed you yet?"

"Yes, yesterday."

Clara said. "Speaking of which, I think I need a celebratory shot of bourbon. Anyone else?"

"Not with pain meds, Mom," Dallas said.

"None for me either, thanks," I said. "I can't stay."

A few minutes later, I kissed Dallas goodnight and said, "We got him. You're safe now."

"Thank you."

"I didn't do anything."

"You love me. That's everything."

"I wanted to beat him to shit."

"I know. It's better this way."

37

Monday, January 12

I WAS ALLOWED TO RETURN to work from administrative leave after only one week. Patrice would be out until they ruled it a good shooting, which they would. My meeting with Spanky was first on my agenda. He outlined what he had on Vince Palmer: his DNA was under Dallas's fingernails and on the doorknob and Billie's collar, prints in the snow up to the Bradley house matched his boots found at the Palmers' lake cabin, the weird bruise on Dallas's cheek matched Vince's college ring, and neighbors reported seeing a black Corvette with the license plate "VNC BA" parked one block from the Bradley house the morning of her assault.

"You've done an excellent job, Spanky."

"*We've* done an excellent job."

"Shh."

It was about ten o'clock in the morning when Sydney Dirkson, Hawk's cousin, called me.

"Did you hear the news?" she said.

"No. What's up?"

"Mike was just handed a guilty verdict—voluntary manslaughter."

"I'm shocked. I thought he'd get off."

"Us too, especially after Nevada Wynn, a.k.a. Snake, testified Paul knew Norman Kramer intended to shoot Mike after the annuity check was cashed."

"But Snake's an iffy witness."

"Yeah, that cobra tattoo wrapping around his head and body is not exactly Boy Scout stuff. I heard it ends at his penis."

"What I heard, too."

"Anyway, Mike's attorney feels the judge was sympathetic because of the extenuating circumstances—Mike being held captive for three weeks and Paul doing nothing to help him. He has high hopes for a departure from the sentencing guidelines."

"How's Barb taking it?"

"Not well. She and Tom are at odds. I drove them to the courthouse and on the way home, she was going on and on about how it was your fault for not letting Mike speak to his attorney before turning himself in. Tom shouted at her to stop blaming you because you did what you had to do, and if the police bent the law for friends and relatives, what a mess this world would be in."

"Wow."

"Yes, wow. I was proud of him. Oh, and did you get my email on the information you asked for?"

"No. Did you include the bill?"

"I did. Cal, if you ever get tired of that side of the law, let us know. Pete says we could bring you in as a partner, expand the business."

"Oh . . . I'm not looking elsewhere at this point, but I like having options. You never know where life will take you."

I read the email, had what I needed, and made my way out to Patrice's house on Island Lake. But when I drove by Cadillac Jack's, I saw Zabrina's Miata in the parking lot. I called Patrice to let her know what was going to occur and why.

The bar was quiet at three in the afternoon. Zach Whitman's elbows were resting on the bar; he was smiling at Zabrina, who sat on the stool across from him. I took the seat next to her, which halted her adoring gaze at Zach. They appeared shaken by my presence. His hand smoothly swiped Zabrina's glass of beer away and replaced it with a clear soda.

"I'll have one of those," I said.

"Sierra Mist?"

"Yes."

He poured the soda from the tap and set it in front of me. "It's on the house."

"Thanks." I took a sip.

His eyes darted back and forth between Zabrina and me. She squirmed on the barstool as if she were sitting on a cactus.

"Grady was well enough to be moved to the jail today," I said.

Both kids stared at me mutely, active concern in their eyes. Zabrina nodded as a delayed reaction.

Zach finally said something to fill my purposeful silence. "How is he?"

"He'll know he was shot for quite some time, maybe forever, but he should be grateful he's alive. You too, Zach."

He nodded.

I cocked my head and looked at Zabrina. "Detective Ryan from Minneapolis PD, County Attorney Oliver Bakken, and I met with Grady today. He was offered and accepted a plea deal in exchange for information."

She squinted and licked her lips.

"He gave us the co-conspirators and accessories to the two murders and my partner's assault."

Zabrina's eyelashes batted a mile a minute. *God, I love this part of the job.*

"What does that mean for him?" Zach asked.

"For him? Mmm . . . he'll certainly serve less time than if he were convicted by a jury, and he would be convicted with all he's confessed to."

Zabrina straightened her back. "Thank you for coming to tell me this. I'm relieved the truth will come out. And I should be going. Patrice is expecting me to help with dinner."

I put my hand on her shoulder. "First, explain something to me."

"Okay," she said tentatively, sitting back on the stool.

"Why did you agree to marry Grady, then suddenly change your mind?"

She titled her head and looked me in the eye, as if a rehearsed move.

"Wait. Let me read you your rights first."

Her cheeks brightened with color as I pulled out the card in my pocket and read it verbatim.

"There. Now that we got that over with, why did you change your mind?"

"It was the pictures you showed me of his creepy parents."

"But you had met Robert before. Or was it the day Robert came to pick you and Grady up at the Logan house to take you to the airport? My partner refused to let you go, and Robert hit her with a fry pan from the kitchen."

"Yes. Maybe it was then."

"Why didn't you report the assault to us?"

"I was afraid Robert would hurt me."

"Zabrina, did you realize you didn't ask me who killed your grandmother and mother?"

"What? Well, be . . . because I assumed it was Robert and Grady—that's why they were arrested. Right?"

"Right. Grady thought by marrying you he'd become a rich man."

Her lip curled in a snarl. "God, I hate him. I hate them all."

I smiled. "Grady hadn't realize he'd been manipulated until you dumped him for Zach. Then it dawned on him—you were the catalyst for both murders."

Zach's mouth dropped open. He closed it, swallowed, and made his way down the bar and scrubbed the surface in wide circles.

Zabrina followed his movements with a panicked stare. Abandoned, she fixed her eyes on me, gathered herself, and said, "I broke up with Grady because I didn't love him anymore, and that's the truth." She'd sputtered her words, tears building in her eyes. "Whatever he said about me was to hurt me for breaking up with him. You do know that, right?"

"Let me tell you what I know. Your friends said you were tired of your grandmother's control. You wanted to go to UCLA, but she threatened to cut you off if you didn't go to Hamline. She even chose your activities in high school to assure your acceptance to her alma mater. Oh, on a positive note for you, Grady swore neither of you knew Robert was going to shoot you and your mom. I believe him. That was a big surprise for both of you." I pointed a finger at her. "Maybe that's when you actually changed your mind."

"You have to be intelligent enough to know Grady is trying to get back at me for choosing Zach over him."

"Maybe so, but I've got more. On the night your grandmother was killed, Grady used your car to go to work. Security cameras near Hawley's captured him arriving in the Miata. However, just before midnight, he left and didn't return until 6:00 a.m. That's some dinner break. Now here's the part I especially like. One of Zach and Grady's neighbors saw him pick you up after midnight."

"That's not true. It must have been someone else."

"You rode up to Dexter Lake in the Miata with Grady. You let him, Robert Quinlan, and Marvin Moore into your grandmother's house. You and Grady went directly into the pool and started making a ruckus." I pointed at her. "And that was your idea, little lady."

She started to rise. "I'm not listening to this garbage."

"Sit back down," came a voice from behind us. Patrice.

Zabrina complied.

"Your grandmother woke up when she heard the noise," I continued. "She saw you and your boyfriend out her bedroom window overlooking the pool, and she came down. But Robert and Marvin were waiting just inside the door to sweep her up and throw her in the pool. You were out the door before she even hit the water—so you wouldn't have to watch her die. Robert's brilliant contribution was to convince you and Grady it had to look like natural causes. He wanted to poison her—he even looked up untraceable poisons on his computer—but it was your idea to drown her. She was a non-swimmer and only a few people knew that."

"Lies, all lies. I loved my grandmother. Tell him, Auntie Patrice." Her face began to contort.

Patrice rolled her eyes and crossed her arms.

"Don't even think about bawling. It doesn't work with me," I said.

Her mouth turned upside down, her eyes fiery with rage.

"According to Grady, his mother started this whole thing in motion when she suggested he knock you up."

"Oh, please," Zabrina said as she rolled her eyes, still not understanding the gravity of her situation.

"Poking a hole in the condom worked. The problem was the murder plan—which grew from your hatred of your grandmother." I lifted a finger. "Don't deny that."

"Who said that? Sarah? She never did like me."

"Not Sarah. Your friends," Patrice said.

"Back to your plan. It wasn't well thought out—too many players, too much evidence left for us to find. For example, your roommate, Amber, found a damp Josie Natori silk nightgown in a plastic bag in the wastebasket in your dorm room. She kept it because she thought it was pretty and expensive. She was right—it retails for $495.00."

Zabrina was watching me in the mirror behind the bar now.

"Amber never told you because she thought you'd make fun of her. Erica packed a Josie Natori nightgown for Sonya when she went to the Dexter house. And, by the way, Granny was wearing a Fitbit watch. After the watch reset at midnight, Granny walked sixty-four steps, which is about the distance from her bedroom to just inside the pool door. I tested it. Grady says he took it off of her and put it in her drawer, which is where I found it. It's these little details which make my job interesting."

Zabrina pulled lips into a tight pout. Tears began streaming down her cheeks, but she didn't wail.

"Did you really think Grady would take the rap for you?" Patrice asked.

"He said he would . . ." *sniff,* "because of the baby. He said he'd love me forever."

"Forever, huh? Well, maybe you can write each other love letters in prison. And by the way, my guess is Zach, who's managed to already distance himself from you, was only in it for the banging. Now, let's have you put your hands behind your back."

PATRICE FOUND ME IN my office after Zabrina was booked. She sat down in Tamika's chair, waiting for me to say something, I waiting for her. Tears were streaming down her face.

"Zabrina's one angry little girl. She's on suicide watch because she threatened to kill herself. She has no idea how much she's screwed up."

"How does that happen? How does a kid of privilege not understand what she had going for herself? She never saw the flip side of life?"

"She was sheltered from unpleasantness, but I must say she wasn't one bit of trouble until she graduated from high school. She started partying, staying out all night. I suspected she was breaking free of the chain."

"The chain?"

"Sonya was tough on Justine, therefore, Justine was soft with Zabrina, who was fairly easy to raise: sweet, compliant like her mother. But Sonya was always controlling from the sidelines. Her meddling certainly backfired."

"I don't like blaming the victim. Something's wrong inside of someone who can kill their grandmother, I don't care how tough they are."

"Yes, I suppose so. Oliver says he's going to ask for no bail—he's afraid she'll flee or hurt herself. I'm glad I don't have to deal with her."

I nodded.

"I never thanked you for keeping David's affair out of the news."

"Only because you gave Waldo an alibi. Truthfully, I had considered you'd lie for him."

"I'd never lie about something so serious. I didn't advertise his DUI, but I wouldn't lie about it if asked."

"And I know that."

"He's accepted a position with 3M and is moving to St. Paul."

"That was quick."

She nodded. "I'm on leave for at least another three weeks. I'm using it to get Sonya's and Justine's affairs in order."

THAT EVENING WHEN I WAS finally able to return home, I relished the faces of my beautiful children. Their cheeks were the color of cotton candy; their perfect innocence washed away the face of evil and filled me with a sense of all that was good.

38

Sunday, January 18

INVITED MY FAMILY OVER for Sunday brunch, which Brit and I put together. I served Eleanor's cinnamon rolls, an egg dish, and a fruit plate.

Grandma Dee and her live-in boyfriend, George, were the first to arrive. They let me know they were headed to the casino right after they ate. Bobby and Mom arrived shortly after. He carried in two pies, and Mom gave me a large, thick envelope.

"What's this?" I asked.

"My memoir manuscript."

I frowned and put my hands in my pockets. I didn't even want to touch it.

"You might want to read it, Cal," Bobby said. "It's quite entertaining."

"Yeah, I don't think so."

My mother pushed the envelope into my stomach. I lifted my hands in the air.

"Are you letting Grandma Dee read it?"

"Might as well—in case it gets published. I titled it *My Wild and Crazy Life*," Mom said.

Grandma Dee said, "Will I have to move out of the state?"

"You might," Mom said, grinning.

"Then I better see what she wrote about me," Grandma said, grabbing the envelope.

During the meal, Bobby and I kept eyeing each other. I had questions, but I needed our conversation to be private. The opportunity didn't arrive until after Grandma Dee and George left to throw their money at the casino and Mom was reading the kids stories before their naps. I asked Bobby to come along on Bullet's walk.

We didn't get ten steps before he said, "You want to know if I had anything to do with Palmer's apprehension?"

"Yes."

"I followed him when he left his girlfriend's place. He went to the liquor store. He came out, I gave him a long-time-no-see hug and whispered in his ear to get in the car. We drove to a vacant parking lot a few blocks away."

"A little strong-arming?"

"You can call it strong-arming, I call it getting him to listen to reason. Anyway, we had a long chat. I laid out what we needed from him—to immediately sign over to your sweetie the condo and half the assets. He's going to lose everything anyway."

"Why is he losing everything?"

"The FBI has been investigating him for months for his involvement in a loan fraud. He and another cohort have been writing loans to fictitious individuals, then keeping the money for themselves. They make a few payments here and there to keep from foreclosing."

"Good God."

"The feds should be swooping in any day."

"Well, at least you didn't kill him."

"Kill him? You have a vivid imagination, Calvin."

I shrugged. "You're very secretive; my imagination fills in details. I suspected you offed Sonya Donovan so you could buy her house."

Bobby gave out a raucous laugh. "Speaking of which, I put in an offer; it was accepted yesterday. It's a Valentine's surprise for your mother, so don't tell her. We move in on February fifteenth. Back to Palmer. I told him if he ever showed his face in Prairie Falls again it would be the last thing he did."

"Were you our anonymous tipster?"

"I followed him to a hotel. He checked in and wasn't coming out, and I wanted to go home."

We walked in silence for a block before I said, "You have too much money to be a government worker."

"I told you, I made a killing in real estate."

"Interesting choice of words."

He grinned. I'd feel better believing he was government. At least he'd be controlled.

39

Saturday, August 8

DALLAS AND I ATTENDED Spanky and Sadie's outdoor wedding, held in Nuremberg Park. We were staying at the Sheraton West near Ridgedale Center, as were most of the deputies, and we were to meet Tamika and Anton Frank in the hotel lobby while we waited for the limo.

As we took the elevator down, I kissed Dallas and said, "You look fantastic. Your pretty dress matches your aquamarine eyes."

"I don't look fat in this?"

"Are you kidding me? You look amazing."

Shannon had told me she wasn't coming, so when I saw her standing with the Franks, I knew there'd be a problem. Dallas lost a step when she spotted them. She tended to avoid functions where the three of us would be present together. And to top it off, Shannon was wearing the same dress Dallas wore, and I'm pretty sure women are mortified when that happens.

"Hey, you changed your mind," I said to Shannon after we joined the circle congregated near the front door.

"I'm in between treatments. I felt good, and I thought, what the hell—I'm going."

"Well, great," I said as I squeezed Dallas's hand.

Shannon was wearing her wig tonight. It looked like her own hair: thick, strawberry blond. Since she'd lost her hair, she wore a deputy baseball cap to work, but outside of the department she also used scarves and other decorative caps.

Shannon turned to Dallas. "I see we not only have the same taste in men, but in dresses, too."

An uncomfortable few seconds of silence elapsed before Shannon filled the gap with: "I think the dress looks better on you, Dallas."

"Don't be silly. You look great."

"You both look fantastic," I said lamely. I forced a smile.

Dallas was understandably quiet from the hotel to Nuremberg Park, and then at the park she selected chairs two rows behind Shannon and the Franks.

I leaned in and said, "You are beautiful."

"The same dress? Really?"

I patted her knee. Luckily the violin music began, averting uneasy conversation.

On the limo ride to the reception at the Lafayette Club on Lake Minnetonka, the only words Dallas uttered for the entire fifteen-minute drive occurred when we pulled up to the front door of the stately white clubhouse. She said, "Well, this is quite something."

"Yes, and so are you," I said and kissed her on the cheek. One side of her mouth lifted, and her eyes rolled. I needed to stop pandering.

Cocktails and champagne were served in a reception room to the right of a fountain. I excused myself to find the men's room, and after, I got waylaid by a couple deputies who asked me where Sheriff Clinton was. I was also curious as to why she hadn't shown up. Then they started talking about the union vote to support Matt Hauser for sheriff. The election was going to be ugly.

When I finally shook loose, I found Dallas talking with Crosby's wife, Trish. Dallas must have thrown down a few glasses of the bubbly because she was all smiles.

"Feeling better?" I asked.

"Oh, yeah," she said. She pulled me aside. "Shannon is in a lesbian relationship with Iris."

"Huh?"

"You heard me."

"Who told you that?"

"Tamika, in the ladies' room just now. She asked me what was wrong, and I told her I was uncomfortable being around Shannon, and she said why would I feel that way because Shannon was in a lesbian relationship with Iris Kellogg. Iris was going to come to the wedding for their coming-out debut, but Iris's grandmother broke her hip."

I caught Shannon's eye from across the room. She smiled and finger waved at me. I guess I knew she and Iris were more than friends, but it was a little shocking to hear it said aloud. I had disregarded my gut-level feelings for months, and now I felt like a fool.

"Excuse me for a minute."

I made my way to Shannon.

"Can we speak privately for a moment?" I asked.

"Sure."

I led her out on the lawn down by the water. I repeated what Tamika told Dallas.

"Oh, Cal, I've tried to tell you several times, but I couldn't find the right words."

"You found the words when you told Tamika and God knows how many other people."

"I knew you'd be hurt."

"I'm hurt because you didn't think enough of me to tell me before someone else did."

She looked at the ground. "I'm sorry. You know I love you. It's just that I feel so much more with Iris."

I put my hand up to stop where that comment was going.

"Cal, I can't deny my true self anymore."

"When did this start?"

"When we were nineteen, the summer we met."

"Wow."

"We went back to school that fall, and I felt ashamed of what we did. I was raised to believe being gay was wrong. I wrote to her and told her I'd met someone else—Chad. I pretended my way through a courtship, engagement, wedding, and marriage. When he died, I was conflicted. Sure, I was grieving, but I also felt a terrible guilt. I wasn't the best wife to him . . . or you."

I screwed up my nose. "You told me Chad was the love of your life."

"Um, no. I said I already had the love of my life."

"You were referring to Iris?"

"Yeah." She glanced out on the water.

The sun glinted off Lake Minnetonka's blue water as the cruiser yachts paraded by. Some of the passengers on a smaller boat waved to us. Shannon waved back.

"Did you cheat on me with her while we were married?"

"No."

"Do your parents know?"

"Yes. Mother asked why Iris was always at my house."

"How did she take it?"

"Much better than I thought."

"Okay, I'm piecing some things together here. The night of the party when Hawk got drunk and told me he'd shot Paul, I thought you were mad because Iris kissed me hello. But it wasn't her kiss that set you off, it was because she was with Erica."

"Exactly."

I hit my head with a fist. "Damn, I'm a fool."

"How would you have known? And you must know I didn't pretend my feelings for you—you were my best friend. I wanted it to work because I love you."

"And we have such beautiful babies. I was good for something, right? Being the sperm donor?"

"Don't be that way."

"What way? Blindsided? Lied to?"

"I'm sorry. I didn't choose this life. I wanted to be who my parents expected me to be. I didn't want to be the stereotypical dyke cop."

"Jesus Christ. Stop degrading yourself." I cleared my throat. "Shannon, look, we're good. You have a right to love who you love and be happy, and I like Iris."

"Thank you. She adores you, too." She leaned up to kiss me on the cheek.

"Does Luke know?"

"Do you think he's old enough?"

"It's your call, but I'd tell him before he hears it on the bus or playground."

"Oh."

"I hope our agreement still applies. No sleepovers with lovers when it's our week with the kids."

"Absolutely."

"Good. I gotta get back to Dallas."

"She may be more comfortable being around me now."

"I think you're right."

And the rest of the evening was comfortable and quite enjoyable. We dined on steak and salmon, danced to the band, and drank too much. The five of us left the wedding close to one o'clock and sang along to the Red Hot Chili Peppers all the way back to the hotel. We made drunk plans to go on a beach vacation together. Hungover the next morning, we had breakfast with the crew of deputies, then left in a caravan for Prairie Falls.

THAT EVENING, PATRICE CALLED to tell me Zabrina had given birth to a baby girl the day before. That's why she hadn't made it to the wedding.

"How's she doing?"

"She had a hard time of it, but the baby's healthy and beautiful. Zabrina didn't want to even hold her. She'll spend a couple days in the hospital before she goes back to the jail. I bring little Evelyn Justine home tomorrow."

"So you're going through with the adoption?"

"Yes, it's what Justine would have wanted."

"Then, congratulations."

"Thanks . . . I guess. So, how was the wedding?"

"Fun. You missed a tasty meal of steak and salmon."

"I bet. Okay, I'll see you soon. I'm taking a couple weeks off, then will work part time for a few months. Carol Knight will be filling in for me."

Maybe Carol Knight should be running for sheriff, I thought.

ZABRINA HAD PLED GUILTY and would serve only about ten years. By the time she was released, she'd be one year shy of having access to her mother's inheritance. For her safety, arrangements were made for Zabrina to be housed in the Wright County Jail, rather than in Shakopee with Brenda LaMere, who was sentenced to an additional sixteen years for conspiracy to commit murder. Rumor had it, Brenda and Grady LaMere planned to file a civil lawsuit against Patrice and Birch County.

Many lives were ruined in the name of greed, but one good thing that came out of Sonya's death was the Sonya Donovan Memorial Scholarship Fund Patrice set up. The first recipient was Moriah Moore. She received enough to pay her tuition at Augsburg College.

Della Moore moved her family down to the Cities to live with her mother, Harriet Quinlan. Harriet and Della bought a house in Burnsville and started their own house-cleaning service. An anonymous benefactor made it possible. I had my suspicions it was either Patrice or Bobby Lopez.

As soon as I hung up from Patrice's call, Mom called to tell me she signed a contract with an agent for her memoir. Bloody hell. I supposed I better read it now. She mentioned her current project was a crime novel—the story of how her son solved the Sonya Donovan murder. Over my dead body.

Acknowledgements

When writing my novels, I frequently call upon the expertise of those who know far more than I on many topics, and I continue to draw from the knowledge they freely shared with me at one point along the way. Special thanks to Hennepin County prosecutor Debbie Russell, Attorney Marc Berris, Maple Grove Police Officer Ryan Modeen, Dr. Tom Combs, Hennepin County CSI Sarah Buck, Orono Police Chief Corey Farniok, Officer Steve Sterm, and all the speakers who've shared their expertise and time with the Twin Cities Sisters in Crime. A shout-out to Lee Lofland and his informative blog geared for crime writers.

Special thanks to Char Squire for allowing me to draw from her personal breast-cancer fight to use in this novel. Thanks to Darrell Maloney for editing my manuscript and to Timya Owen and Rhonda Gilliand for beta reading *Love 'Em or Leave 'Em Dead*. Your help was invaluable. Also thanks to the talented Amy Jauman for crafting the snappy teaser ad! Thank you to the Twin Cities Sisters in Crime, with whom I can freely talk crime writing without receiving a raised eye. Your friendships have come to mean so much to me. Also, thanks to the wonderful Women of Words (WOW) west and north, for their valued friendship, support, and encouragement.

Once again, thanks to my incredible husband, Tim, my go-to man for questions on several topics; my "favorite" children—Stacy and Shawn, and their loves: Drew, Kristen, Emma, Hudson, TJ, and Nolan. Also, to my cherished extended family and friends (old and new) for their continued support. Thank you to my readers for showing up at my signing events, inviting me to your book clubs, and buying my books. Your encouragement and smiling faces spur me onward to continue to fabricate more stories.

And finally, thanks to the fantastic folks at North Star Press of St. Cloud: Corinne, Curtis, and Anne, for believing in and publishing my work. Your patience and hard work are much appreciated.

CPSIA information can be obtained
at www.ICGtesting.com
Printed in the USA
LVOW10s1605060317
526275LV00001B/1/P